LOVE TRIAL

B. C. GOODWIN

BALBOA.
PRESS

A DIVISION OF HAY HOUSE

Balboa Press books may be ordered through booksellers or by contacting:

Balboa Press
A Division of Hay House
1663 Liberty Drive
Bloomington, IN 47403
www.balboapress.com
1 (877) 407-4847

Because of the dynamic nature of the Internet, any web addresses or links contained in this book may have changed since publication and may no longer be valid. The views expressed in this work are solely those of the author and do not necessarily reflect the views of the publisher, and the publisher hereby disclaims any responsibility for them.

The author of this book does not dispense medical advice or prescribe the use of any technique as a form of treatment for physical, emotional, or medical problems without the advice of a physician, either directly or indirectly. The intent of the author is only to offer information of a general nature to help you in your quest for emotional and spiritual well-being. In the event you use any of the information in this book for yourself, which is your constitutional right, the author and the publisher assume no responsibility for your actions.

Any people depicted in stock imagery provided by Thinkstock are models, and such images are being used for illustrative purposes only.
Certain stock imagery © Thinkstock.

Print information available on the last page.

ISBN: 978-1-5043-0961-5 (sc)
ISBN: 978-1-5043-0962-2 (e)

Balboa Press rev. date: 09/04/2017

ABOUT THE AUTHOR

B. C. Goodwin was born in Melbourne Australia. He now lives in Brisbane with his fiancé and two kids. Mr Goodwin has been a storytelling enthusiast his entire life, loving all its aspects from movies to books, from ancient myths, to history. That love of storytelling was where he found his passion for writing.

Now with his hobby turned adventure, he would like to give back some of what other story tellers have given him. This is his first novel, but it won't be his last.

Hope you enjoy the book.

PROLOGUE

Death is but a result of life. The end of a journey we all must take.

Sometimes we never get to finish our journey the way we planned, the way our dreams wished. David's journey still goes on, cruel in its fortunes. His path didn't end with his beloved Isabella, and his beautiful four-year old son Ian. David's family's journey was cut prematurely, stolen and ripped away from him through blood and mayhem.

That was why he was here seeking vengeance. David didn't plan on taking action tonight, but the unstoppable force of payback drew him in too close for him to resist. Acting now could result in his death, but he didn't care. Why would he? He had already lost everything. He had lost the beating heart of love. Love was but a memory now, vanishing alongside his wife and child.

David watched the source of his desire for revenge. David wanted to see if the person responsible for his love-loss had any remorse for what he did. If he even had a soul under his black devil's heart, because only the devil's evil influence could make a man do what he did.

John Black was the name of the man that put a pillow over his four-year-old son's face until he breathed no more. And it was John Black that had raped his wife and slit her throat, all because he lost on a bet. It was a lot of money riding on the bet, but still just money. Money was nothing compared to a human life, at least that was David's opinion.

David knew it was John Black who did the deed, because his fingerprints were found at his house. He was caught on a security camera outside his home and his semen was found in his wife. You would think with all that evidence the man would be behind bars, right?

Wrong.

All the evidence that tied John to the case magically disappeared before his trial, ultimately making him a free man. A rapist, a murderer free on the streets because of the corruption plaguing our justice system. Money would have been the weapon used to free a killer, supplied by the club no doubt. John Black was a member of the Creatures of Chaos bikie club. He wasn't anywhere near the top of the ranks, but the club looked after its own.

John Black sat around a campfire in his backyard drinking piss with two other guys. They were laughing and having a good time. They were all laughing after getting away with a double murder. No guilt drove John mad. No sorrow took hold of him. He was happy, rejoicing in his freedom.

To say rage ravaged David at the sight in front of him would be an understatement. The rage that took hold of him could only come from where love had once been. Love turned to hate was the deadliest weapon known to man. It turned men crazy, dangerous. It turned men into beasts.

David didn't intend engaging them that night, but seeing them laughing and enjoying themselves was too much. The final push came when an opening for violence called out to him. The offer was just too tempting to pass up.

One of the three men got up from his place by the burning fire and went to the bushes to drain the beer from his gut. David saw this and a dark violent inner beast saw the window of opportunity. It willed his legs to move silently, to creep up behind the man and wrap his arms around his neck and squeeze.

The man struggled as hard as he could, but his inferior strength was no match for David's. David held on until the body went limp. He watched the body drop like a sack of shit to the ground falling in its own urine.

This guy wasn't the man he was after, he wanted John Black.

John was still sitting in front of the fire drinking beer and laughing, having a good time, but it wasn't going to last if David had anything to do with it. The two remaining men had their backs to David. They sat transfixed by the sparking dancing flames.

The two men would be drunk or half drunk at least. That was good. Drunken people had slower reaction time, they were unsteady on their feet, and overall drunken people became stupid. David made his way over to the men. He didn't rush like his rage wanted him to. He walked up to the men casually watching carefully in case they turned and he had to rush forward. The sound of David's footsteps were casual. David didn't try to hide his stalking of his prey. His footsteps were of the man lying unconscious in his own piss.

John, the one he wanted, didn't notice it wasn't his mate returning from the bushes until it was too late. David walked right up to John's other mate and drove his knuckles into the side of his face. David heard the jaw break under the strain. The guy slumped down on his chair and he wasn't going to wake up for some time.

"What the fuck?" John squealed fumbling for his gun, too stunned to move quickly, and it cost him.

David bounced on John landing a punch in the middle of his chest knocking the breath out of him and making him double over on the ground. David quickly seized the gun and tossed it to the side.

"Remember me?" David yelled, eyes flaring up with white-hot fury. The man still couldn't breathe properly, only sucking in half breaths but was able to say, "Fuck you, David."

David smiled a pained smile that came from the demon inside knowing blood was coming. Not holding back, getting straight to the point David asked, "Why did you have to kill them? Why didn't you just kill me?"

John spat on the ground, drool still hanging from his teeth as he said, "What would be the fun in that? I wanted you to suffer. You can't suffer if you're dead. Killing your family, the people you loved would be worse than death for you." He was right about that. What John did was worse than killing him. It had ripped out his heart and squashed it, fracturing his soul. Living on without them was hell.

"You didn't have to kill them," David said, his voice breaking whilst grabbing John by his shirt and shaking violently.

"Yes I did. You made me suffer. I bet all the money I owned on you to lose that boxing match. I told you to throw the fight or there would be consequences," John spat out, "I just didn't think you were stupid enough to ignore a request from me and the club."

"I told you and the club to fuck off. You're the stupid one for betting against me," David roared back.

John thought he had an opening to get free and tried to throw a punch at David's face. The fist missed by a mile, but David's elbow didn't miss John's nose. The crack of snapping cartilage was followed by a yelp of pain and blood gushing down his face.

"I told you, you had to lose the fight or I would fuck you up. If you just lost the fight your family would still be alive," John screamed back nasally, anger filling him with unmatched hatred. "I had to teach you a lesson. One you can't learn if you're dead. I didn't want to kill you David, just like you won't kill me. You're a good fighter in the ring, but you're a soft-cock out of it, you're not a killer like me. You're weak. Just look at you. What I did, killing your son and fucking your wife like she had never been fucked before has already broken you, just like I knew it would."

David hands tightened around John's shirt. The rage filled the beast inside him. He said, "You were wrong about one thing."

"What? That you're soft-cock?" John suggested with a smile, thinking he was witty.

"No, that I'm not going to kill you," David said quietly, almost in a whisper but laced with daggers. John saw then he had pushed too far. He saw his fate in David's eyes as he was lifted up and his head thrust into the fire. David's hand was on the back of his neck holding him in place as he thrashed in agony.

John's hair caught fire first before David could hear his skin start to sizzle. David pulled him out of the flames right before the fire claimed his life. John rolled on the ground yelling in torment. His face melted like wax.

David's life was of a living ghost. John's life was now of pain.

The beast inside David roared again wanting more, needing more. So David gave it more. David caught the man rolling on the ground, holding him still as his fist smashed into John's face. Once, twice, three times. And again, and again until John's nose was touching the back of his skull and his brains were splattered all over ground.

Once his raging wrath had subsided David peered down at his trembling hands painted in blood, reality coming back around at the sight. David stared down at what he had done and was disgusted with himself. He was a monster. He let his inner beast takeover and this was the result. He had become a creature coming out from the darkness to slaughter the living.

What would his wife and son think of him now after seeing what he had done? They would be horrified; even they would think he was a monster if they had seen what he had done. He couldn't save them when they were alive, and he had dishonoured them by becoming the same monster that had killed them.

David looked down at the blood on his hands, and knew he would never be able to wash the blood off.

CHAPTER 1

The gears changed on my bike, simulating a hill climb. The increase in resistance made my legs push harder, making me exert what little energy I had left. The beats were to some techno song I had never heard before. It wasn't my Katy Perry or Taylor Swift, but it was good workout music. Each beat filled the room like waves crashing down on me. Each bass thumping pulse vibrated through my entire body.

The instructor yelled into the microphone that was attached to his head. The microphone was wrapped around his head so the little foam bit ended up in front of his mouth. The trainer's voice travelled through the speakers overpowering the music for only the length of the words. His chatter was that of encouragement, which I ignored to concentrate on the movement of my legs. All I could do was will my legs to keep pedalling, and try to drown out the pain that the lactic acid was responsible for.

I looked to my left to see my best friend in the world, Tara O'Neil, struggling with the same artificial hill climb as me. Sweat was beading off her face. Tara's bright-red complexion had overthrown her sun-bronzed face.

A little smile crept across my face with the insight that she was in as much pain as I was. The ten-inch display in front of me indicated that the class had reached the top of the hill of death; a little nickname I liked to call it sometimes when I was about to cry. Reaching the top of the hill, the pressure on the pedals decreased making my legs feel much happier. I looked up to see everyone in the room, which

1

comprised of about twenty-five people, all take a sigh of relief. It was like a tonne of bricks had just been lifted from upon our backs.

Tara, panting through laboured breaths asked, "How do you talk me into these classes every week? Last week was a pump class, the week before it was tae-bo. I must be insane listening to you."

"I just tell you your ass is looking a bit big, and then you come running," I joked. A frown appeared on her beautifully featured face, and then the smile seeped through, along with a right-handed fist into my shoulder.

"If I came here every day like you, I would kick your ass at these classes," Tara smiled.

"You wish jellyfish, but I'm happy if you want to come with me every day," I invited.

"I think I'm good. I'd rather get my exercise in other ways," she said with a lustful wink. I just smiled back at her sex reference, not having the energy at the moment to laugh.

Tara was taller, slimmer, and had bigger curves than me, but I was stronger and fitter, and she never let me forget it. Tara only went to gym when I dragged her here, but I loved it. I came here every day to sweat my ass off. It was good fun.

The fitness instructor at the front of the stage yelled out the cool-down instruction. There was no laboured breathing in his voice, while the rest of the room was struggling for air. Asshole, I thought to myself.

Once the class of cycling torture had finished, I stood at the water dispenser behind a large girl filling her water bottle. It was always pleasing to see large people at the gym. They were the people who looked in the mirror, didn't like what they saw, and wanted to change their reflection.

Those people wished to improve their way of life. They were sick of accepting things the way they were, and wanted to improve their lives and themselves. My hat went off to them.

Myself, I had never had a weight problem – luckily. I liked the feeling that only being fit, and eating good foods brings. I had to admit I was a sucker for cheeseburgers though, and I couldn't forget chocolate.

The endorphins flooding through your body as you workout are a natural high I loved. I even liked the next day when you couldn't move because all your muscles were sore, slowly repairing themselves, making you stronger. It was like a very sore reward for a good workout. There was no gain without pain.

Taking care of my body and not taking it for granted was my high; a healthy lifestyle was my drug. But put a cheeseburger and a salad under my nose and I would pick the cheeseburger every time.

The large girl in front of me moved to the side, and then emptied half the bottle of water down her throat, replenishing the liquids that now soaked her clothes. She choked on the water. It must have gone down the wrong hole. The girl let out a cough that sounded like a dog's bark. Yes, her cough sounded like a dog's bark, I wasn't calling her a dog. I just needed to clarify.

I started to fill my own bottle when Tara came up behind me, leant over my shoulder, only because she can, being a good six-inches taller than me, and asked, "So what have you got planned for the rest of the night?"

Tara worked most nights at a club, so when she got a night off she always wanted to do something. I once suggested going to the club where she worked and she just told me I wouldn't like it. I asked if it was a gothic club or something, because I would hate that. If it was not today's pop music then I didn't want to know. She just nodded and told me something like that. All I knew is she gets paid very well. Tara always had mountains of cash lying around in her room, so there must be some guys giving some good tips with their drinks. I mean one look at Tara's face and I could understand why.

I looked up into those big blue eyes, "I'll probably just go home, and watch a movie," I lied. I already had plans, but I was not telling anyone, especially Tara. If I told Tara, it would inevitably ruin the surprise I had in store for my beloved.

The surprise is for my boyfriend, the only man I had ever loved. This love had been in my heart ever since I first meet Sam at high school five years ago. His love was all I want in the world. As long as I had Sam, I had everything.

I didn't tell Tara, because, like the big mouth she is, Tara would tell Jane, Jane would tell Greg, and Greg would tell Sam. The vicious cycle of old high school buddies.

Tara talking in her lovey-dovey voice, and fluttering her eyelashes at me commented, "I just thought you might be meeting up with Sam?"

I turned my back to her and returned to filling my bottle so she didn't see the lie in my eyes as I replied, "No, just having a quiet one at home with Mum tonight." Tara knew I had movie nights with Mum all the time, so it was a good cover.

I then changed the direction of the conversation, steering it away from my lie and turning it around to Tara's favourite topic, Tara.

"What about you?" I said. "Got any big events on this evening? Maybe like a date with a big muscled man?"

Tara laughed out saying, "No plans as of yet with any sexy boys."

I noticed that she turned away from me as she responded, just like I did a moment ago when I lied. Tara must have some guy on a string I thought to myself, and then dismissed the idea when she added, "But I would take up an offer from that extremely hot instructor over there." A smile crept up on my lips. That was my best friend Tara.

Tara could have just about any man she wanted. With her perfect body, big boobs, tight ass, long blonde hair, a face of a goddess that could enchant any man. But somehow she always seemed to enchant the bad boys; the hot guys that just wanted the trophy of banging the hottest girl in the club. When I entered a room with Tara all the eyes in the room locked on her. I was invisible next to her. Myself, being a short brunette girl with nothing extra extravagant about me; I was a plain Jane in contrast.

I was not ugly by any means, but a girl like me had no hope competing with a woman built like a supermodel. Tara was what all supermodels wanted to look like. I was just a shadow on the wall next to her.

That's okay though, because I had something she didn't. The thing everyone wants. The thing you go your whole life searching for, and only finding it if you're lucky. What I had was love. The love of a good man, the love of my beloved Sam. As long as I had him, I didn't need anything else.

Tara could easily find a guy, but finding the right guy was the challenge. Maybe that instructor would be the next on Tara's love list, who knows?

"I bet if you gave him your sexy, come-and-get-me look, you would have him crawling up to you on his hands and knees begging for a date," I said.

Tara whipped her hair over her shoulder, gave me her sexy face and then talking in her hot seductive voice said, "Do you mean this stunning facial expression?"

"That's the one, but I think your lips need to be a bit more pursed," I said, fine-tuning her move.

"But, seriously, do you have plans tonight," I said with a sincere tone, not wanting her sitting at home bored.

"Was thinking of having a girls night out with you and Jane, but if you have a date with your Mum and a movie, then I guess my plans are shot," Tara replied trying to make me feel guilty.

"Maybe tomorrow then if you're free. I'll call you tomorrow to see if you're working," I said, getting ready to leave.

I would call her tomorrow. I'd tell her all about what I planned to do next. Tara would understand why I had to skip on the girls' night. I didn't like neglecting my bestest buddy, but a girl's got to do what a girl's got to do.

"Fine," she huffed, "but you better not blow me off again, or I'll kidnap you and force feed you vodka until you are more agreeable to my suggestions."

"Deal," I agreed.

I said my goodbyes to Tara and then headed straight to the change rooms with a skip in my step and a whistle in my heart to get ready to launch my impending surprise on my unknowing boyfriend.

$\mathcal{I}$ turned off the headlights in my Renault Koleos. The engine came to a stop after I pressed the start/stop button on the dash; no twisting keys in my car. I didn't want to ruin the surprise by Sam noticing my car from his window so parked behind a big Ford F-350 truck. The car park was basically empty except for about five cars. On a busy day it holds about a hundred vehicles, so basically empty summed it up pretty well.

I turned on the interior light to check myself over, making sure everything was perfect. My hair styled after two hours of straightening and curling it, check.

My makeup looked great after making sure I had the right consistency between not looking like a drag queen, and looking like I had no makeup on at all, check.

Eyelashes curled, check.

I had a light shade of pink lipstick on my full natural lips, not to brag. The lipstick was traced perfectly on my lips for now; I did plan on leaving traces of it all over Sam's delicious body though, check.

Sexy lingerie, black with red lace that was almost see-through. Boobs pushed up giving the impression of big full tits. Panties pulled up exploiting my well-toned squatter's ass, check.

Black high heels to make my legs look longer, which helped a lot when you're only five foot three. The extra few inches the heels made me the ideal height for Sam to have his way with me from behind too. So win, win. Besides high heels just look fabulous, check.

To finish off the masterpiece I put on a long black trench coat that came down past my knees. What was a surprise without wrapping paper? And who didn't like unwrapping a present, check.

Called Mum to tell her not to wait up for me.

"Hello," Mum answered.

"Hey Mum, it's me."

"I know darling, I saw your number come up. I'm not that old you know?"

"It did take you a while to get used to the new phone, so I was just making sure," I poked.

"Yer, well, technology has changed a lot since my day," Mum admitted.

"When was that again, cavemen days?" I teased.

"Ha ha, very funny, my witty girl, so what's up?" she queried.

"I have plans with Sam tonight, so don't wait up," I said. I was twenty-two years old, and I still had to let my mother know where I'd be. I suppose it was a good thing she still worried about me; it showed she cared.

"Okay, hun. Have fun, and be safe," she said.

"I will Mum. Love you."

"Love you too, bye for now."

"Bye," I said as I hung up.

Mum, phone call done, placed phone in centre console so I didn't have any interruptions, check.

Now, with the checklist ticked off, I had to get into Sam's office without him spotting me.

I wanted to walk into his office, see his eyes open wide with surprise, and his jaw hit the floor when my coat fell off my shoulders.

Sam worked at a window manufacture company. He was the son of the CEO of the company, and had been groomed his entire life to take over the business once daddy dearest stepped down. The company was doing really well at the moment. They just landed a huge contract from a private builder with a very rich investor. A fifty-level sky-rise construction, so you could imagine there were going to be just a few windows needed for the job.

The factory where Sam worked was closed, it being 8:30pm. The employees all finished up about 5:00pm, maybe 6:00pm if something was urgent for the following day.

The doors would be locked, but I knew where they keep a spare key – to the left of the front door in a lockbox. The lockbox opened with a number combination, and I knew the combination.

The five cars left in the parking lot must have been the cleaners', plus Sam's car, of course. I just had to dodge the people inside, staying hidden in the shadows. I felt like a sexy secret agent preparing for a mission. I had to get to a designated position to achieve my objective.

I scoped out the area, no one in sight. I made my way to the lockbox, retrieved the key, opened the door and sneaked inside. Once the door closed behind me I stood still, looked around and listened for anyone that might be close by.

Not spotting anyone I used my ears to try to locate anyone in the building. I had to use my ears because unfortunately I cannot see through walls. I wish I could see through walls like Supergirl, but us mere mortals have to use what God gave us, and somehow noise can magically penetrate through walls where my vision can't.

With my eardrums not picking up any sound I decided to proceed. I opened the door to the stairwell to make my way to the second floor and Sam's office. I barely got through the door when I ran straight into a dirty smelling cleaner with a vacuum strapped to his back. So much for me being a secret agent, and then I thought maybe I need my ears checked.

The filthy man jumped in surprise, and my heart just about leapt out of my chest. The man regained his composure.

"Who are you? And what are you doing here?" Not giving me enough time to respond he continued, still breathing hard, "You almost gave me a heart attack."

I lost my voice due to the shock of someone being in the stairwell. I thought I had been so careful; I had nearly given myself a heart attack. My face must have displayed my dismay because the man's eyebrows narrowed and his lips formed a straight line. His posture conveyed a man ready to pounce on an intruder.

After what seemed like ten minutes but was properly only about five seconds I stuttered out the words, "I'm Sa... Sa... Sam's girlfriend."

The man responded with an edgy tone, "Sam who?" My first thought was, how could this dirty man not know who Sam was? Then the realisation dawned on me, he was testing me.

"Samuel Rushton, his name is printed in big bold letters on the side of the building. *RUSHTON WINDOWS* it reads," I responded a bit smugly. "You could find him on the second level at the end of the hall. I'm guessing he would be the only one left still working."

"Girlfriend you say," he declared. Then added a "huh," at the end.

"Yes, a matter of fact, I am. Sam asked me to pick him up because his car is in the workshop being repaired. So if you want the boss's son pissed off with the likes of you for harassing his much-beloved girlfriend go right ahead lose your job right here, right now," I said in a hurry not knowing how I had thought up all those lies so quickly.

The man's demeanour changed after my outburst. His shoulders dropped, eyes relaxed and surprisingly a hint of a smirk flashed across his face. If I'd blinked I'd have missed the flash of smugness, but it was there.

The man's hands flew up as he said, "Alright calm down, I just had to ask. You don't have to threaten me. They don't pay me enough to be the security guard as well." Then that smirk repeated itself like a bad déjà vu moment as he said, "Good luck with your beloved Sam."

With that he pushed past me leaving the smell of his body odour lingering behind. I held my breath as I walked up the stairs so the stench of BO didn't get lodged up my nose. I just hoped it didn't stick to my clothes. Walking up the stairs I figured that I would suck at being a secret agent. Maybe if I had all those 007 gadgets I would have got to Sam's office unseen, then again probably not. In hindsight though I was the boss's son's girlfriend so that awarded me some perks.

Even though I hadn't got to Sam's office without being detected my plan was still a go. Sam still didn't know I was here, and I still looked great.

I had called Sam earlier. He explained to me that he had a mountain of paper work to finish before tomorrow. He told me he would most likely be working until about 10-ish, so I thought I could give him a well-deserved break. I was going to give him something to help him relax, something like a full body massage. I was quite certain that that would sustain him until he finished his work. And when I say full body massage, I meant that there wouldn't be any part of his body that wasn't satisfied by the end.

Sam had been working so hard lately, the poor thing. That's why I planned to do some work on him, and I was very good at my job – if you know what I mean. A girl would never admit this to anyone, besides maybe her girlfriends, but I was so horny at the moment.

Sam and I never seemed to have time for each other anymore. We normally only saw each other three times a week as it was. We both still lived at home. Sam said he didn't want to rent, and with me studying and only working part-time, a bank wouldn't give us a loan. Besides living at home for free, getting your washing done, food cooked, bills paid wasn't a bad way to live while you're still young and liked to dance.

The thing was though, even when we did spend time together Sam was so exhausted he just went straight to sleep. We never got to hop on the good foot and do the wild thing anymore, and I missed our wild thing moments. It was not all about sex though for me, it played a part of course, but it's the closeness that I missed more than anything. I missed the naked snuggles afterwards, the soul-searching conversations lasting until the sun came up. It felt like we were drifting apart at the moment, so I was hoping that this would put the gasoline on our spark and turn our love back into an inferno.

Sam had been very distant lately as well. Everything seemed to be an effort. His work was always getting in the way. He said he's working hard to secure a future for us, but all work and no play makes Sarah a very horny girl.

That brings us back to the present. The plan was to change all that with what I had in store for tonight. I was going to rock his socks off, or more importantly his underwear.

The office floor was dark, the street lights glimmered through the large tinted windows letting in only enough light so that I could make my way through the maze of walls and desks without tripping over.

The office at the end of the hall was my target. The room had horizontal window shutters covering every window. The light from the room seeped through the edges letting me know that Sam was inside. The square-framed light acted as a beacon for me to follow, like a sailor at sea, seeing the lighthouse in the distance drawing him back home to his loved ones.

When I got closer to Sam's office I started to hear noises, like someone was in pain.

It sounded like a woman in pain.

No.

The sound became unmistakable as I ventured nearer; the noises were that of people making babies. Sam must be watching porn. That had to be it, porn. Then that smirk from that smelly cleaner popped in my mind's eye, he knew.

My heart was bounding now, afraid that he might be...

I didn't even want to think of any possibilities other than he was watching very loud porn.

I had to know though, I had to be sure. With the shutters blocking each window my vision into the room was obscured. How was I going to secretly find out what was going on inside?

I guess I could have just walked in, catching him with his pants down in front of the computer screen, and then finish what he started. But if I found another scenario in that room, then I just didn't know what I would do.

Then, as if the Devil had left me a peephole to look in to the fiery burning depths of hell, I spotted a gap in the blinds. The shutters at the very right of the room had got caught on something, leaving just enough space for me to look through. I stood outside the peephole, building up the courage to look through. My hands were shaking, my pulse was racing, and I felt a little light-headed. I took a few long deep breaths to calm myself.

He is only watching porn I uttered to myself. Did I really need to know what Sam was doing inside there? I could go home right now.

I could just tell myself he was watching porn and jerking himself off, and then that would be that, no harm, no foul.

I could stay with Sam in ignorant bliss. This was the man I had loved since high school, my first love, my first lover, my first everything. This was the man I was meant to marry one day. I was going to spend the rest of my life with this person. I exhaled the last deep breath then took a step backwards, thinking I just couldn't do it.

I looked down at myself opening my coat; I had done all this for him. If I left now I would always wonder what happened in that room. I would be living a fantasy of my own choosing; believing what I chose to believe. Then without hesitation I took two steps forward and looked inside.

CHAPTER 3

My heart sank to the floor like a ship's anchor dropping to the bottom of the ocean, or maybe it was more like my heart bursting out of my chest and then exploding on impact as it fell on a landmine.

Everything I am, everything I love, evaporated in that instant.

My mind will never be able to erase that sight. That sight will be forever seared on the back of my eyelids to torture me for the rest of my life. I felt like a failure as a woman. I was so stupid to have loved him so deeply. The feeling of worthlessness rolled over me like a bowling ball. It made me question everything.

Where did I go wrong?

How long had this been going on?

Had our whole relationship been a lie?

How many lies had he told me?

Did our sex life get boring?

Did I get boring?

Was I a starfish in bed?

Why wasn't I good enough for him to stay loyal?

I am who I am from all my experiences, and now all my experiences had been a lie. It was like I had been erased in that moment, I had lost my identity, I was left blank, empty, my inner being swept away by a raging gale.

In that room of betrayal, Sam stood slightly angled with his back to me. His pants were around his ankles, and he had a pair of long legs wrapped around his waist. I could see his ass tensing with every thrust into her. It made me want to hurl.

The woman lay with her back on his desk, her face hidden from my sight. All I could see was her large breasts shaking up and down with every impact of Sam's hips slamming into hers. Her moans were so loud it almost came out like a scream. Then I noticed a tattoo on her ankle, a tattoo of a dove.

I knew that tattoo.

The woman's arms reached up, hands lacing around Sam's neck. She pulled herself up so they were in an infidelity embrace. Her head sat on Sam's broad shoulder as he kept moving in and out of her. I could see her face as clearly as the moon on a clear night sky. I had seen that face for most of my life. I knew that face nearly as well as I knew my own.

Tara, that bitch.

In my disbelief I accidently rocked forward, my hand came up and slapped on the windowpane to stop my head from colliding. I locked eyes with Tara; she had looked straight to where the noise came from, straight into my wide eyes.

Tara stopped mid moan. The look of terror took over the look of pleasure. The gap left open by the blinds wasn't huge, but Tara knew my face as well as I knew hers. She knew it was me. I could see in her frightened expression that she knew. Tara knew she had just lost her best friend forever. There was no coming back from this.

Tara's mouth opened to say something, but before the words came out I stumbled back. It was like I copped a punch to the face, the knuckles being the force of seeing my best friend shagging my boyfriend. I almost fell over a chair as I scrambled backwards. Luckily I was able to grab hold of a desk and regain my balance. This was the last place I wanted to be right now after seeing that unseeable sight. I had to leave – so leave I did.

All women that have worn high heels knows that they are not the best shoes to run in, so I didn't feel totally humiliated to say I only took four steps before I tripped over my own feet and landed on my hands and knees.

I was sure it would have hurt more if I wasn't freaking out so much, but with all the emotions raining havoc through my body, all the fall did was slow me down. I kicked off my three hundred dollar shoes and ran like hell. My favourite pair of high heels was just left behind like Cinderella's glass slipper.

What I should have done was storm into that office and thrown them at their heads. Then at least I would have got my money's worth.

At first, when I got outside I ran straight towards my car needing to get as far away as possible, but then, once I reached my Koleos, I was disgusted by it. I saw Sam and Tara's faces through the windscreen. They had driven with me in that car more than once. I had made love to Sam in that car. That car was tainted by forgery. The forgery of fake intimacy through friendship and relationship; both being betrayal of the heart.

The memories that car held were too unbearable for me to handle, I couldn't even look at it. It repulsed me to a state that made me sick, like vomit sick. Before I could think of what to do I was off running on bare feet again, in God knows what direction. Not the smartest thing I had ever done, but I wasn't quite in my right mind at that point in time.

I didn't want to stick around and take the chance that Sam and Tara would follow me outside. I couldn't handle that confrontation right now. I don't know how I would react. I would either turn into a blubbering mess or grab the first solid object and start swinging it at their heads.

I ran as fast as I could for as long as I could. I had no idea where I was going, I was just running. I couldn't see anything with all the tears streaming down my face. It was like running with fogged up swimming goggles on. The lights were all hazy and I could only make out the blurry outline of objects such as cars and buildings.

I couldn't tell you about anything I ran past, because I wasn't able to distinguish anything in great clarity. Everything I saw was that blinding sight of Sam pounding Tara on his desk. I must have run for at least thirty minutes in bare feet before I had to stop. The skin on my feet was not very tough to begin with so thirty minutes of running on gravel and concrete tore the soles of my feet to ribbons.

Every step ground another layer of skin away until there was nothing left but raw flesh and blood.

The pain in my knees and wrists was starting to kick in too, due to that fall in my three-hundred dollar six-inch heels.

I came across a park bench that was just off the footpath alongside the tar road. I sat down put my head in my hands, then cried uncontrollably until I had a splitting headache. I had not cried that hard for a long time. I spent all of my tears until they had dried up like a gamblers wallet at Las Vegas.

Just as my wailing had turned to low sobs a stranger's voice came out of the darkness like a lightning strike jump-starting me back to reality, breaking me out of my internal nightmare of sorrow.

"What's the matter good lookin?" the sly greeting said, coming through as a rough raspy voice, like a pack-a-day smoker.

I wiped my eyes scraping away the fog that coated my eyeballs, so I could focus clearly once again.

I saw three large men in leather jackets; each cowhide had a symbol of a beastly motorbike on it.

The logo of the bike was one with a monstrous face where the headlight should be, and with two massive horns as handlebars.

There were words that curved over the top of the horns, written in capital letters spelling, *CREATURES OF CHAOS mc.*

One minute earlier I would have said to myself, how could my day get any worse? How wrong I would have been.

With the arrival of three gorilla bikies, I suddenly became aware of how little clothing I had on. I was basically naked under my trench coat.

I looked down to make sure I was all covered up, and thankfully I was.

I pulled my coat that little bit tighter against my nearly bare skin underneath, hoping it might act as an invisibility cloak.

By the time I looked up again the largest of the three men had sat right next to me placing one arm behind me along the bench.

This guy was the largest man I had ever seen. If I was in a fantasy land I would think he was a giant. He wasn't huge like a man that had

had too many pizzas, but a man that had taken steroids for breakfast, lunch and dinner, and lived in a gym for the past ten years.

He towered over me like I was a five-year-old girl. He must have been roughly seven foot. I really would have looked like a child next to this man.

As he slid up closer, the massive man smelt like a *Lynx* deodorant ad with an underlying smell of cigarette smoke, petrol fumes and burnt rubber. The man had a *ZZ Top* beard that shone a blonde, red colour.

I didn't know the man's name and I didn't particularly want to find out, he was as scary as he was humongous. In the end I just came up with nicknames for him and his two mates, who were as equally intimidating in their own way with their tattoos and leather.

The guy that sat next to me I nicknamed, Mr Big Bikie.

The guy that stood to my left I nicknamed Mr Druggy. He was nearly as tall as Mr Big Bikie, but probably half the weight. His build was more like a beanpole with skinny arms and legs.

The guy's skinniness was most likely the result of too many drugs and not enough food. His face was gaunt with black bags under his eyes, probably from a lack of sleep.

Drugs like ice or speed can keep you up for days, so I've heard. He had long shaggy hair that came down to his shoulders and a rough unshaven five pm shadow.

The man to the right I called Mr Shaved Head. He was much shorter than the other two. He looked about Tara's height at five foot nine, but he had the body of a bulldog, short and stocky. Also, hence the nickname, he was clean-shaven, with a shaved head.

He wore a leather vest exposing his arms that were so cut up with muscle that they gave the impression that they were about to explode, with the bulging veins for detonating cord. All you would have to do is light one up then, BOOM.

The tight skin that covered his muscles upon muscles was coated in tribal black tattoos; they actually looked quite impressive in a scary way.

I gathered my courage to peer over at Mr Big Bikie next to me. He had very distinctive tattoos. On the left side of his face a tattoo curled around the outside of his eyebrow that spelt the words, *RIDE OR DIE*. On the right side of his face four tattooed teardrops dripped under his eye.

I didn't respond to Mr Big Bikies question, because I was scared out of my wits. I was probably so frightened due to the fact that I had no idea where I was, my phone was in my car, and I just realised my keys must have fallen out of my pocket when I fell over outside Sam's office. Oh yes, don't forget there were three very terrifying men surrounding me, and not looking very friendly.

Mr Big Bikie continued, "Had a bad date or something?"

I responded in a low quiet voice, not able to muster anything above a whisper, "Something like that."

"You do know that no dates are permitted here without our say so, don't you?" he expressed, running a single finger down my neck, making me flinch. Now I was confused as well as frightened. What was me having a date any of their business.

"Who do you work for?" Mr Big Bikie followed on.

In my confused state I didn't know what to say.

"Is it the Insurgents?" Mr Big Bikie continued. Still my lips wouldn't open, still trying to make sense of it all. "I know you don't work for us, so who do you work for?" Mr Big Bikie said, growing more impatient with every non-response.

"I don't know what you mean, I don't work for anyone. I'm a student finishing my diploma," I replied in the same quiet tone.

"Are you really that stupid to come out here, work in our neighbourhood and then feed us that horseshit," Mr Shaved Head said, cutting in.

What is going on here, I thought to myself. Unless, when he referred to a date, he didn't mean a date in the conventional sense, but what a date would mean for a prostitute.

"I'm not a prostitute," I blurted out when the realisation set in.

"Sure you're not, little one," Mr Big Bikie replied. "Tell you what; show me what you have on under that coat, and if it's not a hooker's uniform I'll believe you."

Great, of all nights to ask me to prove I wasn't a call girl. I realised if I don't open my coat I was proving my guilt, and if I did open it I would look the part. So I was damned if I did, and damned if I didn't.

Whichever way I tried to swing this, I wasn't going to be able to convince them I wasn't a street worker. I would have to come at this from a different angle. That is, lie my ass off and be over-apologetic.

"I'm so sorry. I didn't mean to end up in your neck of the woods. You were right, I am that stupid," I said pleading for sympathy, trying to sound as ditsy as possible.

The three men just looked at each other, speaking unspoken words. Their facial sign language conversation gave me enough time to come up with some more bullshit.

"I got into a car with a complete nut case. When we found a private place to start our date, he pulled out a knife then tried to get a freebie or kill me. Who knows?" I claimed, still trying to appeal to their sympathies. "I was able to fight him off, and then run away. But he had stopped in an area unfamiliar to me, and that's how I ended up here, wherever here is?" I said, hoping my fiction would be enough.

Mr Big Bikie stared at me sceptically, "So, you're saying you're a victim of your own negligence and stupidity for going out with no pimp to oversee your activities."

"My pimp is a drunk, and couldn't protect cheese from a mouse," I whispered, not meeting his eyes, staring down at my bloody feet, acting ashamed.

Mr Shaved Head said impatiently, "Let's just teach her a lesson for working on our turf, and go back to the clubhouse, I'm hungry."

What was the lesson? I was afraid to wonder. Whatever it was, it didn't sound pleasant, and I wasn't about to ask to find out. I had a few guesses of what that lesson might be, and I'd do my best not to find out.

Mr Big Bikie turned his head to Mr Druggy, "What you think?"

"I think she could be profitable. That pretty little face would look good with come squirted all over it," Mr Druggy answered, his eyes giving away his envisioning of the scenario. "I say we pump her full of enough drugs so she forgets her own name, and make her work in our brothel."

A shiver ran down my spine from that proposal. I think I would rather die than be exposed to that treatment. I couldn't think of anything worse than being someone's sex slave. To me, getting raped every day and night would make death a sweet relief.

Mr Big Bikie looked back to me, "Well," he said with a sigh, and then placed a massive hand on my shoulder. I flinched under his touch again. These guys were as bad as the villains in movies. I thought people like this only existed in films and novels.

"My friend over here," Mr Big Bikie said, making me face Mr Shaved Head by turning my head with his large hand, "wants to beat you so bad that your own mother wouldn't be able to recognize you."

Then he turned my head to Mr Druggy with the same engulfing hand and said, "He wants to put a needle in your arm then make you work for us."

He then turned my head to face him. His breath smelt like cigarette smoke mixed with beer, "And I think lessons need to be given to people that don't follow the rules." Mr Big Bikie caressed my head like he was petting a dog, "I think you could be a good little money maker for us if you swapped sides, but I don't need any fallout from whoever owns your little ass. So I'll give you a way out of this."

Thank God I thought, a way out of this dilemma that doesn't end in me getting beaten, kidnapped or used as a sex-toy.

"All you have to do is what your kind do best. Just show me and my mates a good time with that pretty little ass of yours and we will give you a free pass," Mr Big Bikie went on to say, crushing my hopes of letting me off easy. I was stunned and terrified from the proposition of blackmailed rape. I didn't know how to reply. I didn't want to reply. He didn't leave me with very many options; well, any good options anyway.

How would I get out of this situation unscathed or even escape with my life if I didn't agree to his terms? I could feel my heart rate beat to a new high, it made my hands start to shake. I had to ball them into fists to hide my anxiety. My non-response gave Mr Big Bikie a time slot to tell me the meaning of his facial tattoos.

"The 'RIDE OR DIE' tattoo over my eye doesn't mean riding a

motorbike and die by the sword. It stands for: ride my cock or I will strangle the life out of you."

He paused to study my reaction, to let the fear sink in deeper. I didn't seem to disappoint. I felt the blood drain from my face. I must have gone a ghostly white colour.

Then Mr Big Bikie added, "The tear drops under my other eye are a reminder of all the girls that have said no to me." He pointed a finger to the side of his face just under where the teardrop tattoos were, "I have a spot right here for you if you want?" he offered.

He spoke about strangling the life out of me, with a voice so calm and collected. He spoke in such a nonchalant way that it seemed he didn't care if I said yes or no. Either way he was going to get his jollies. I could see in his eyes and feel it in my bones that he would have no problem murdering me right here, right now. All the options I could think of to survive this encounter ran through my mind. I didn't come up with many options, and none really had a high probability of succeeding.

I thought I could make a run for it, but not knowing where I was, was nearly as bad as running into a dead end. There was also the issue of my now throbbing bloody feet. When I scanned the area for anything I might be able to recognise, like a landmark, shops, or familiar street signs I just came up blank. All I could see around me was what looked like the continuation of the industrial area where Sam's company was. There were factory buildings that had concrete walls, with Colorbond steel roller doors large enough for a three story house to fit through. Every roller door had a different number above it, and all had different product names, all with large display signs that were all no help to me.

The factory directly in front of me had a sign reading, "Foam Supplies" in giant big bold lettering with an underlining catch phrase that read "Cutting and fitting all your foaming needs."

I remember thinking sarcastically what a great help that shop would be in my predicament. I could make them a nice comfy couch to sit on, and then maybe they would fall asleep so I could sneak away.

All the other buildings around me were too dark to read any of the signs. None of them were open. There was no one inside that could help me. Even if they were full of people, it would take a special someone to stand up and frighten off these three. Trying to make my way to a nearby building for help was out of the question. I came back to running away, but I don't think I could manufacture enough adrenaline to overpower the pain that would course through my feet with every thud on the pavement.

I thought I might be able to steal a phone off one of them, but all phones were coded these days so I decided against that. Another thought was to fight my way out. But my Tao Bo fitness training I learnt at the gym was no match against three grown men, one of whom had a build like Arnold Schwarzenegger in his *Conan the Barbarian* days.

Calling out for help and someone actually hearing me was doubtful at best. Someone hearing me and then coming to rescue me was even more doubtful. The same thing could be said if I tried to wait it out for a car to drive past. Even if I was able to wait it out for a car, no one would stop anyway. I had three big scary bikies shadowing me to shoo them away, besides no cars had driven past since I had been here anyway. So, that circumstance was just as unlikely to save my neck from the chopping block as any of the others. The option that scared me the most was giving them what they wanted. Letting them do whatever they wanted to do to me. Just going with it, have some fun, make it a payback for what Sam did to me. Sam was shagging Tara so why couldn't I bang a few bikies. Why take the chance of getting beaten, raped or murdered.

But I wasn't that kind of girl. As mad as I was at Sam, I could never stoop to his level. To me, lovemaking was exactly that, making love. I didn't like any of my options, the latter being the only one that would see me through intact, but there was still no guarantee that they would let me go afterwards. After the story of Mr Big Bikie's tattoos I'm guessing he would assume I would subdue, and be their little plaything for the night. So that's exactly what I wanted them to think I had become – their little sex puppet.

"Okay," I said. "I don't really want to be remembered as a tear drop under your eye, so I think I'll start off with a little strip tease to get in the mood." I tried to keep my voice even and without any signs of fear, but I'm pretty sure my voice quivered a bit. "If that's alright with you?" I added, wanting confirmation to begin. Mr Druggy let out a hoot of excitement, and then sat on the opposite side of me on the bench. I was now sandwiched between the two large men.

"Alright, little lady, give us a show to raise our cocks," Mr Big Bikie said slyly, relaxing back on the seat. Mr Shaved Head looked totally uninterested, like he had seen it all before. He looked like he would have much rather splattered my brain matter all over the tarred road than see me dance around naked.

That's two out of three distracted then. I got up off the park bench, almost falling from the pain shooting up my legs from my raw feet. My body quivered from nervousness as I started, but I thought I covered it up quite well with a wiggle of my hips. I had only performed one lap dance in my life. I didn't think I was very good, but I still got my desired result, a mesmerised man with a hard member. In this instance my aim wasn't to allure, but to distract. I needed all the blood from their heads to go down to their one-eyed snake.

I started doing the sexiest dance I could imagine; trying to imitate all the music videos I had ever seen with girls shaking their booty. Then slowly I unbuttoned my coat, letting it drop to the ground revealing my almost naked body. Then I bent over to pick it up, giving them a perfect view of my ass. My red lacy black G-string panties didn't disappoint. Mr Druggy couldn't help himself and smacked my ass. The slap hurt and I'm pretty sure it left a handprint, but I ignored it and kept dancing. Turning back around with my trench coat in my hands, spread out wide so it was covering my breasts all the while dancing to the sound of *She Bangs* by Ricky Martin playing in my head.

Mr Druggy grabbed at his crotch to straighten something out. Mr Big Bikie was leaning back on the bench with a grin from ear to ear, and Mr Shaved Head stood with his arms crossed, his posture yelling hurry up and get on with it. I decided this was as good a time as I was going to get, so I made my move.

I flung the coat over the two bikies sitting on the park bench, and then started running as hard as I could in the opposite direction to Mr

Shaved Head. All I had to do was outrun Mr Shaved Head. Surely the guy did all weight training and no cardio. Hopefully he smoked ten packs of cancer sticks a day, too. I hoped that he would start coughing up a lung after twenty metres so I could get away. But with the soles of my feet so badly worn down, I didn't like my chances of outrunning the man with the shaved head; he had aerodynamics on his side.

I had to try, though. I wasn't just going to be their play-toy. I would rather die fighting, than play slave on my knees. I got to about the twenty-five metre mark before I was reefed back by my hair. I could feel my scalp part from my skull; luckily it stayed attached. The little guy was fast, much faster than I would have predicted, then I did predict. I knew it was futile, but I screamed at the top of my lungs. It was a long torturous cry, a scream that would have rumbled the mountain of Olympus. Mr Shaved Head still had hold of my hair as I was thrown to the ground. I fought back as best I could. Striking wildly, like a snake that got caught by its tail. I was able to land one nail-scratching blow across his face. I could feel my middle and ring fingers nails rip through his flesh.

That short-lived triumph was soon squashed by a landing fist to my face, catching me on the cheek, right under my left eye socket. Everything went white. You would think everything would go black, but I found out after that punch, when you get hit in the head and you don't get knocked out everything goes white, not black. It leaves you in a shocked daze. If that punch was any harder my lights would have gone out for sure.

The first thing to come back through the pain was my awareness of my surroundings. Then I felt myself being dragged back to the bench by my hair. I was limp, but still conscious. I was lifted up, and then dropped over the backrest of the seat head first, so I was fully bent over with my butt facing the moon. I was just able to catch my head before it slammed down onto the seat. I recovered enough of my senses to push myself back up, but found I was held down by Mr Big Bikie. Mr Shaved Head had moved aside for the hulk of a man to stand directly behind me. I felt my panties being ripped off exposing all my womanly parts. I felt his cock rubbing up against my leg. I thrashed, kicking and screaming, trying to get free from his grip. I began crying through the wailing, knowing I was about to be violated, knowing I couldn't do anything to stop it.

"Let me go," was all I remember saying through my tears. Mr Big Bikie didn't let go. The only guy I had ever been with sexually was Sam, and his little feller was like a tooth pick compared to Mr Big Bikie's tree trunk. I can say this for all the girls out there that forcing something big into a small hole doesn't feel good. If it did, giving birth to a baby would be orgasmic.

He leant over and whispered into my ear, "You should have finished your dance, and then fucked me like it was your first time. I love seeing the pain register on girls' faces from my oversized cock. You would have loved it by the end." Mr Big Bikie stood back up straight, his voice moving away as he said, "But now, because you tried to run away, I'm not going to be gentle. I'm going to rape you and it won't feel good by the end. Then I'm going to watch as my boys rape you. Then once they're done, I'm going to kill you, and add another tear drop to my eye."

"Fuck you," I shouted out at the top of my voice, in one last stand of defiance.

"No," Mr Big Bikie replied, "I'm going to fuck you."

I felt his cock slide up the rest of my leg, getting ready to penetrate me and most likely tear me open. Time seemed to stand still in that instant. It was like falling off a cliff, seeing your impending doom approaching, and knowing you have no wings to save yourself. It seems a bit of a cliché but your life does flash in front of your eyes in moments of distress.

My experience was not so much as my whole life springing forth through my mind, but of my overall actions that led me here. All the choices I had made. The people I had befriended. The people I tried to impress so they would like me. The things that influenced my actions such as my parents, the music I listen to, movies, TV shows, TV commercials, sporting figures, politicians. It all helped shape the life I had led, and it led me to this. It made me ponder, was I really happy with my life before today? Did I really like the friends I had?

Were my choices my own? For instance, did I watch that movie with Sam because I thought it would be good? Or because someone told me it would be good? Did I make that choice myself? Or did they make it for me? All of these things blazed through my consciousness within a second. It felt like my whole life had been lived by someone else. It felt like I was a character in a computer game where I was being controlled by an outside force, and now a digital sign popped up over my head that read *Game Over.*

Then somehow someone pressed *continue*, and I got another chance to play this game we call life.

A man's voice came out from the darkness. I didn't understand what was said, but I knew it wasn't one of the bikes; the voice came from too far away. After the night I've had I figured it had to be the Grim Reaper himself coming to get me. I expected to see a black silhouette of a man carrying a scythe in one hand, and skeleton fingers that possessed the touch of death in the other. Perhaps I was already dead, and this was my own personal hell.

I raised my head to greet this new arrival. I could only see out of one eye due to the other being swollen shut from that face shattering blow from Mr Shaved Head. Once my head had stopped spinning and I focused my one eye, I saw a man wearing a black hoody step out of the shadows.

"Let her go."

CHAPTER 4

To my surprise it wasn't the Grim Reaper with his scythe coming to cut me down. It was a lone man who seemed to have as much chance as I did of taking down these three muscle-bound bikies. His tone of voice held no hint of fear when he said, "I don't think the lady likes that very much, so let her go."

"Get out of here before we do the same to you," Mr Shaved Head threatened.

"Do you mean rape me?" the newcomer countered. "Sorry mate, but you're not my type."

Mr Shaved Head glared at the guy wearing the hoody with intent to destroy, as if he wanted to squash him like a bug. When the realisation struck Mr Big Bikie that the hooded man was not just about to leave, he zipped himself back up. A sigh of relief came out of me. I dared to hope. That was until Mr Big Bikie bent back down and whispered in my ear, "Don't go anywhere I'll be right back to finish what I started." Mr Big Bikie then gestured to Mr Druggy to hold me in place.

The man in the hoody stared directly at me ignoring the two steroid loving psycho bikies closing in on him and asked me, "Do you want me to get you out of here?"

"Yes. Please help m…," my response was cut prematurely. I could have sworn I heard my ribs crack from the force of Mr Druggy's knee hitting me. All the air was sucked out of me from Mr Druggy's knee colliding with my ribs. I had trouble breathing after the blow. I had never had the wind knocked out of me before tonight. The only sport

I played was netball and that was a non-contact sport. So, being winded was pretty unnerving the first time. The feeling of never being able to take in another breath was overwhelming right up until something gives, and your lungs start to function again.

Between laboured breaths I was able to look back up. Mr Shaved Head got to the man first. He stood about three or four inches shorter than the guy wearing the hoody, but that didn't seem to deter the bikie in the slightest. He walked straight up to the guy and then threw a fist directly at his face.

The bikie was fairly quick for such a thick man, but the guy wearing the hoody was faster. He dodged the incoming blow, and then countering with an elbow to the jaw, knocking the bikie out cold in one strike. Mr Shaved Head fell back hard, his head hitting the concrete on impact. The sound was sickening, like a walnut being cracked open by a hammer. I remember his arms were still outstretched towards the stars as he lay there twitching on the ground. Mr Big Bikie hesitated at the sight of his mate lying unconscious on the pavement, and then he began to laugh ecstatically.

What the hell was wrong with these people? I thought after seeing Mr Big Bikie laughing insanely at his KO'd friend.

"Didn't see that one coming, he is going to be pissed when he wakes up," Mr Druggy expressed from behind me, still with a non-concerned attitude. I did feel his feet shift when his mate fell though, if that was any indication of anything.

"So you can handle yourself, good for you," Mr Big Bikie said through his finishing chuckle. "My friend there is a little bull-headed. He rushes in before thinking, even before me and that is saying something. I've never seen him go down quite so hard before though, especially from only one hit," Mr Big Bikie continued with real admiration. "So, good for you I say, but you will find that I will not be so easy to knock out." Mr Big Bikie put one hand inside his jacket to reveal a knife that Rambo would be envious of.

"My friend here hasn't come out to play in a while," Mr Big Bikie articulated, gesturing towards the blade. "I'm sorry about this mate, but now I'm going to gut you like a pig."

"You're fucked now," Mr Druggy said with excitement in his voice.

The hooded man was silent, probably because of the blood-curdling knife Mr Big Bikie held in his hand but, to my dismay, he didn't take a backward step. I felt sorry for the hooded man, risking his life to save me. He didn't even know me; I was a complete stranger to him, and now he was going to pay the ultimate price for trying to do a good deed. They always say *nice guys always finish last*. That's because bad guys cheat.

Who said chivalry was dead? This guy was going to die proving everyone wrong, or right if they were talking about the dead part.

This man was my knight in shining armour, and now he was about to get slayed by the dragon. If only he knew the dragon could breathe fire. I should have just said no when he asked me if I needed help. Now there were going to be two dead bodies lying in a ditch. I really didn't want this man's death on my conscience. No ordinary man would risk his life this way; this man was a special breed, or just plain crazy.

I made up my mind; I couldn't let this happen. My fate was sealed, but his didn't have to be. He could still run away. Maybe, if I'm lucky he could call the cops, and they could come save me. At least they had guns to take down this monster.

I only got out, "Get out of here," before a fist smashed into my kidneys. The pain was excruciating. Before tonight I had never been punched either; now, twice in one night, lucky me. The pain was awful, but it wasn't going to stop me from looking up to see what happened next.

Mr Big Bikie lunged forward with his knife, thrusting his arm out towards his opponent. I thought he had pierced the hooded man's chest. I was expecting to see him stumble backwards clutching his breast with blood spraying out everywhere. After I blinked a few times to be sure what I saw was actually what I saw. I was left speechless when I made sense of the performance in front of me. I wasn't the only one seeing it and trying to make sense of it. Mr Druggy choked on his own tongue when he figured it out.

The hooded man must have caught the thrust while stepping backwards. From my perspective it looked like Mr Big Bikie stuck the knife through the chest of the hooded man. The bikie had, however, overdone the lunge with the knife, convinced he wouldn't miss his target. In doing so, he lost his stable footing putting himself off balance slightly. Then with the hooded man's backwards momentum, along with the forward momentum of the bikie, it made it possible for the hooded man to grab the larger man's wrist with one hand. Then, using his other hand to hit down on the bikie's elbow, bending his arm back on itself along with the pointy end of the blade that finished up in Mr Big Bikie's neck.

It all happened so quick, the hooded man moved so fast I nearly missed it. The next thing I heard was a gurgling sound coming from Mr Big Bikie, followed by him turning around to face Mr Druggy. A shocked expression was etched onto his face. You could even have said his face was covered with fear. An emotion I don't think this huge man had ever experienced before. Mr Big Bikie then pulled out the protruding blade from his neck and a fountain of blood shot out going everywhere. The knife must have hit a major artery in his neck. A spray of blood hit Mr Druggy in the face. As the blood splatter hit him he recoiled taking me along with him. Some of the blood landed on me too, I wasn't expecting it to feel so warm. Then before I knew it I was hurtled forward again over the seat. Mr Druggy had taken hold of the back of my head and forced it back down with tremendous force and speed. The last thing I remember seeing was the base of the seat advancing towards my face.

CHAPTER 5

$\mathscr{L}$ouis Cole lay in bed alone, dreaming of being king of a vast empire with servant and sluts all around. Louis always slept alone. He didn't like sleeping next to a woman. He hated giving up half the bed or being woken up unannounced by the loss of bed sheets, or even a sleepy woman's arm hitting him in the middle of the night. Louis loved fucking woman, seeing the pleasure and pain on their faces as he forced himself inside was entertaining to watch especially when pain was the response. But sleeping next to one was annoying. The last time a woman slept next to him he kicked her off the bed. Not figuratively but literally. It was a bit much killing someone for pissing him off while he slept but he had done it before. Better to sleep alone, cleaning up the messy dead body in the morning was always a downer.

Louis Cole ruled this city. He had all the right people in his pocket and he had his Creatures of Chaos brothers as his army. He was untouchable. Louis's brother Jordan was out running things while he slept. Jordan was his younger brother, big and terrifying to most. Jordan loved the club but he was content, he didn't have Louis's ambitions.

Louis wanted to rule the world while Jordan just wanted to fuck, fight and do drugs. That was why Louis was Captain of the ship, and Jordan was first mate. The system worked and that was what made them unbeatable. The brothers Cole were the reason that the Creatures of Chaos Melbourne chapter had reached new heights, unimaginable heights.

Jordan was out with Ben and Neil tonight overseeing things. Ben was only a little guy but was good backup for Jordan, not that his monster of a brother needed any. Ben could scrap with the best of them though, so he was still handy to have around. Neil was tall and looked scary, but not worth a shit in a fight. The guy never sleeps due to all the drugs he takes, so he would tag along with anyone that was still up running around. Neil wasn't the sharpest tool in the shed but he knew his drugs, so he still played a key role in their business. Louis couldn't see Neil living more than another five years with all the drugs he was taking. It was a shame. He would have to start looking for a possible replacement soon.

Louis was still dreaming of being king, passing down judgment to the people who wouldn't follow his orders, when a banging rattled the front door and disturbed his sleep. Louis woke up with a start, going straight for his sawed-off shotgun next to the nightstand.

People knew not to mess with the Cole brothers, but there were some stupid people out there. Louis suspected he always had an enemy out there somewhere. In the past Louis and his brother had killed a lot of people to get to where they were today. Killing that many people created lingering enemies with guns in the shadows, it was just Louis who always saw the bullets coming and ricocheted the bullets back at the shooter.

Louis put on some shorts and headed for the front door where all the noise was coming from. He took in a deep breath readying himself to shoot this crazy person in the face. He flung open the door, and jammed a twin barrel shotgun in the man's face. Louis was one blink away from pulling the trigger when he realised that the face that was about to be pumped full of lead belonged to one of his jacket brothers, Neil. Neil jumped back, not expecting to be looking into the eyes of a weapon. Louis didn't know what Neil expected, warm fuzzy hugs after thumping on his door in the middle of the night. Whatever it was, it wasn't nearly getting his head blown off.

"You fucking idiot, I almost blew your head off," Louis said lowering the gun.

Louis's eyes then narrowed, sharpening on Neil. Louis's face twisted in disgust at his Chaos brother, and then Louis's alarm clock started to peep inside his head. Louis could tell Neil was wired. Neil always looked that way with wide eyes that were all pupils with black bags underneath, sweating, and not able to stand still. But this was something in itself.

Neil was even more wired than normal. Something bad had happened and it wouldn't be good for him or the club Louis suspected. Louis looked Neil up and down before he asked, "Whose blood is that, Neil? And where are Jordan and Ben?"

Neil started spraying out words, none of which Louis could make any sense of. Neil sounded like an auctioneer on crack. All of his words were mashed together coming out as one long stream of noise.

"Shut up, you moron. Your jabbering will wake up the whole street," Louis barked. He took one step outside grabbed Neil's blood splattered shirt, and then dragged him inside. He walked Neil into the lounge room then tossed him on the black leather sofa. Louis then walked out the room needing to get some medicine for Neil. He made his way to where he kept his weed, filled as much green as he could into the cone of his titty bong and brought it back for Neil with a bottle of water.

Louis had to mellow him out. Neil's head looked like it was about to explode from whatever happened. Neil's speech sounded as dry as a desert, and he was sweating like a fat bitch in a disco. Hopefully the water will allow him to talk and the weed would slow down his words to an understandable level.

A moment later, Louis walked back in the room holding a bottle of water, and a pair of boobs. Neil was transfixed on the boob bong. He rubbed his eyes and looked again. Realisation slowly kicking in that the boobs Louis was carrying was in fact a bong and not a sex toy.

The bong had a steel stem protruding from between the breasts, with a cone sitting upon it that overflowed with greenie goodness that Neil was even more mesmerised with when he found out what it actually was. He ignored the water, and snatched the pair of bong boobs out of Louis's hand, but he was careful enough not to drop one flake from Mary Jane's breasts. It was a skill that took an experienced hand. The smoke filled his lungs as the flame from the lighter followed the weed down the pipe. The exhale of smoke looked like clouds as it filled the room. The smoke then hovered in the air above Neil's head like speech bubbles out of a comic book. Now Louis just had to fill them with words he could read.

Neil now in a daze was snapped back to attention when Louis clapped his hands together in front of his face, nearly making him spill bong water all over himself. Louis snatched the bong back and gave Neil the water.

"Drink it," Louis demanded while sitting the bong down on the coffee table in front of Neil. "What happened?" Louis bellowed.

Neil then started to run Louis through the night's episode in actual English. Neil started with running into that whore of a witch that was working on their turf. He began squealing about what she looked like; telling him about her tight little frame and how he wanted to use her in the brothel, but Jordan had a better idea of teaching her a lesson by giving them a free shagging. Then he told Louis how the bitch started with a strip tease and then tried to run away halfway through.

Neil kept going telling Louis how Ben caught her by her hair, dragged her back, and punched her in the face, but not before the witch screamed out some summoning spell, bringing forth some hooded creature that ended up knocking Ben out with one elbow to the head.

Neil then hesitated after that, choking up. He was scared to say what happened next. Louis could see that, a frog could see that. Neil hadn't mentioned Jordan. Louis knew Jordan wouldn't have stood back and just let Ben get KO'd without stepping in. If Neil was afraid, then Jordan must have been knocked out too, or maybe taken in by the cops for killing the guy. Neil looked up, not even realising that he had been talking to the pair of bong knockers on the table the whole time. Louis stood over Neil with an unreadable persona. Control was one of Louis's key elements.

"Then what happened?" Louis urged him on. Knowing Neil needed a push to finish his story. Neil shuddered.

"The demon stabbed your brother in the neck with his own knife," he said.

Louis ran through a number of scenarios in his head but that wasn't one of them. His brother was a tank on human legs. Neil must be trippin'. Then Louis looked down at the blood on Neil's shirt again. Louis roared internally seeing the truth in it. The truth was in the blood and the reason why Neil was so frightened to tell him. Louis's brother was dead.

Louis didn't move as realisation set in. He didn't show any emotion, he just asked more calmly than any man should be capable of asking right after finding out his brother was just killed.

"How did you get away?" When Neil didn't answer straight away, Louis added, "Did you not stay and help your brothers?"

Louis's voice sounded cold, like there was ice underlining his tone. But still Louis didn't move. If a stranger walked in the room they would have thought everything was okay, but Neil knew better.

With the chronic levelling Neil out, calming his senses Louis could see Neil knew he had to tread carefully here. Neil then said softly, "I rammed that witches head into the seat. I think I killed her because she went all limp afterwards. I would have made sure I killed her but then that demon came for me." Neil looked down in shame, not even able to make eye contact with the titty bong.

"I had to flee. If I hadn't, I would be lying dead on the pavement next to Ben and Jordan. If that guy went through Ben and your brother so easily I wouldn't have stood a chance," Neil said defensively.

Louis just stood there not saying anything, just staring down at Neil. The only sign Louis gave that there was rising conflict in him was his right eye that twitched every few seconds.

"I know I had to tell you first so we could go back out there in numbers, and bleed that demon out," Neil finished saying, stopping suddenly as Louis moved forward closing the distance between them.

Louis moved far too quick for Neil's liking because he flinched back spilling some of the bottled water on himself. The rage that escaped Louis's body was gone as fast as it came. Louis's face took on one with a settled arrangement of outcomes, all the moves he had to take step by step now programmed in his head. Louis took in a deep breath, releasing his clenched fists, and then leered down at Neil. Then he sat right next to Neil and placed an arm around his shoulders.

"It's alright, Neil. I'll get those demons don't you worry. And then how did you put it, bleed them out," Louis said, playing along with Neil's storytelling of the supernatural. Neil relaxed under Louis's reassurance. Louis could see he was thinking that everything would be okay and everything was forgiven. Neil focused his gaze up, relief now washing over him.

"I'm sorry, Louis," Neil whimpered.

"Sorry for what?" Louis replied, fangs starting to reveal themselves purposefully.

Neil's gaze became blank, not knowing how to answer. Thinking the answer was obvious, even to him. He looked confused. He thought he had been forgiven, that he had done the right thing in the end. Louis didn't break his stare on Neil. He just waited patiently for a response.

"I'm sorry that Jordan is dead and I ran away," Neil said shakily, not knowing if that was the answer Louis was looking for. Louis's arm tightened around Neil.

"Oh. You're sorry that you were a coward and ran away leaving Ben unconscious, and my baby brother bleeding out on the sidewalk," Louis answered, pausing for the theatrical effect before he added, "Oh, sorry for that."

Neil became very still and rigid under the weight of Louis's heavy arm. Louis's arm started tapping Neil's shoulder, like he was pounding on drums as soldiers marched into battle.

"Do you know what they used to do to a deserter back in the old days?" Louis asked. Neil shook his head, not able to form words.

"They used to cut off the deserter's head," Louis said, answering his own question because Neil couldn't. "Lucky for you we aren't in the old days anymore." Neil didn't move, not that he could have anyway with Louis holding him down. Louis wasn't as big as his brother but not by much, and he could possibly be just as strong.

"You know Neil, if that was me watching one of my Chaos brothers being stabbed in the neck; you know what I would have done?" Louis verbalized, each word holding the venom of a deadly scorpion. Neil, too frightened to answer, just shook his head again.

"If I was in your position I would have snapped that slut's neck making sure this hero's rescue was pointless. You properly just put her to sleep. Then I would have taken hold of my brothers pig sticker and then rammed it in his heart, killing him quickly, rather than letting him die slow and alone like you did." Louis's grip became even tighter around Neil's shoulders as he mentioned the way he would have killed his own brother to put him out of his misery.

"Then with the instrument of my brother's salvation and destruction, I would have gone in swinging, no matter the outcome," Louis said, with an unwavering glare on Neil. Neil's eyes were locked back on to the ceramic tits, too fearful to move, too terrified to make eye contact with Louis.

"I'm sorry," Neil muttered again nearly inaudible to Louis's ears. Neil bit down on his lip, gathering his willpower to look up into Louis's big brown eyes. He couldn't see through the mask that hid the rage on his bikie brother's face and that was the way Louis wanted it for what he was about to do. Louis's grip became like a vice, locking Neil into place then a glint of silver sparkled across the room.

Neil screamed out in agony as his nerves registered what had just happened. He looked down at his stomach to see a dagger sliding from one side to the other, crossing the length of his lower abdomen, spilling his intestines all over the floor. Louis got up slowly with the bloody blade in hand, peering down at his club brother. He watched as Neil tried to put himself back together again and failing at it miserably.

Louis's favourite way to kill was by strangulation but knives and daggers were a close second. Strangulation was better suited to killing women anyway. He almost wished he had killed Neil with his hands, using the fingertips of God to kill just as the man himself does. It was just, even with all Louis's control he needed it over quickly. Louis still had his limits in self-control. Louis's brother was dead, and now he was going to have to kill a lot more people to satisfy his need for blood.

The game had begun.

Right before the light left Neil's eyes and his soul went down to the abyss Louis said coldly, "I forgive you brother."

CHAPTER 6

My world has turned into softness, like I am aloft a white fluffy cloud in the skies of heaven. All my thoughts have gone. There is nothing but a feeling of tranquillity. The clouds then begin to turn grey, growing forever darker until they are almost black. There is only enough light to see the outline of the clouds now. Then I hear the sound of thunder. I find it strange because thunder always follows lightning, and I haven't seen any sparks of light dancing through the sky.

My world becomes still, everything freezes into place except the rolling waves of thunder. The noise echoes, bouncing back at me. Then I see it. The lightning flashes, and with it comes memories. The memories of my last awaken state. The images all shine brightly inside my head, lighting up my mind's eye. They flow like a film reel in reverse. The park bench moving away from my face, a mysterious hooded man, three bikie men, running, Tara, Sam, together, my life, pain.

I open my eyes – sorry, eye. I touch my closed eye that I am unable to open, heat is radiating out of it, and it is tender to the touch. I am lying flat on my back upon an extremely comfortable bed. The sheets feel like satin, smooth and silky. The doona is thick and warm.

The feeling of total pandemonium sets in. Where am I? Am I safe? Or am I still in danger? For all I know Mr Druggy pulled out a gun and shot the hooded man. It wouldn't surprise me if the guy could dodge bullets though, since I witnessed how fast he could move, but in reality nobody is faster than a speeding bullet. Then after shooting the hooded man, Mr Druggy might have dragged me to his brothel, never to see the light of day again.

The bed starts to move like an earthquake rumbling. I am not alone. There is someone in the bed with me. Fear engulfs me, I am still in danger, and my nightmare isn't over.

I rolled over to face my assailant, my ribs felt like a Mack truck had driven over them when I moved. I pushed through the pain to end up staring into the most gorgeous jade coloured eyes.

A beautiful little girl stares back at me. The little girl was lying on the bed right next to me watching me intently. She couldn't be any older than five, I thought. The little girl wore a yellow sundress, with a red ribbon that held up her mousey brown hair.

Before I could open my mouth to say something the little girl blurted out, "Hi, my name is Claire. My uncle told me not to wake you, but you woke up on your own. So now I can talk to you."

Claire could not contain the excitement in her voice as she asked, "What's your name?" Then added in the same breath, "And did you win your fight?"

I was flabbergasted. Expecting to be assaulted, then to find a tiny person asking me questions, I was struck dumb. All the fear and anxiety left my body at one look of this little girl's smile. I couldn't help but smile back. Claire's questions fully went in one ear and out the other though.

"Sorry, what?" I said dumbly, with a dry rough tone.

"What's your name?" Claire asked again.

"Sarah."

"I like that name. I have a friend at school with the same name and she's nice," Claire blurted out again. She didn't even pause to take a breath before adding, "So, did you win your fight?"

The scenes of last night came flooding back again, but this time I was able to push them back to the darkest corners of my mind before I went mute.

"No," I replied.

"I thought so. You do look pretty banged up. She must have got you good. But don't worry I'm sure you'll win your next boxing fight," the girl said, with all the innocence of her age. Through her smile I could see that she was just trying to cheer me up. Clare must have thought I had been in a boxing match, and that was the reason why I was all mangled up. Better that, than knowing the truth I suppose.

I sat up in the bed, moving slowly to minimise the pain. I then surveyed my surroundings. I was in what looked like a man's bedroom. The room definitely didn't have the touch of a woman. The bed even smelt like a man. The walls were all bare except for one black and white picture of a man wearing boxing gloves with a name at the bottom that read, *Sugar Ray Robinson. The best pound for pound fighter of all time.* The room had a set of wooden drawers with a small TV on top, a bedside table and that was it. There was no colour, no style, all plain and unfurnished, definitely not a woman's room.

"So, Claire do you know where we are?" I asked, hoping for a name of a town or city, anything to figure out where I was. What I got was Claire's smile growing even wider, if that was possible, and her telling me with love in her voice, "We are at my uncle's house."

She seemed to look off into empty space before she added, "My uncle is the best. He is so much fun, and he always has chocolates and movies and so many fun games to play." I cut her speech short because she gave me the impression that she could go on about her uncle all day. I didn't know this little girl, I didn't know this uncle, I didn't even know where I was, all I knew was I needed to go home.

"Where is your uncle now?" I said with a little too much interest.

The high interest level I gave off was to hopefully avoid this uncle character, and then hopefully to escape, but Claire misread my reaction for enthusiasm to meet her uncle. She bounced up off the bed like a hopping kangaroo and yelled, "I'll get him for you; I'll be right back."

"No," I almost screamed out after her, but caught my voice at the very last second. My cry out was all for nought though, because the girl was out of the bedroom in a flash. She was fast for such a small kid I thought; I was impressed and terrified at the same time. I was just able to make out Claire's voice from outside the room a moment later.

"Uncle David, Sarah's awake."

I shouldn't have given her my real name I thought as I heard it come out of her mouth. Everything else I heard after that was just muffled noises, nothing clearly audible, but it did sound like a man and woman arguing.

I heard footsteps coming down the hall. What do I do? What can I do? Who was I going to encounter? Would it be some psycho that saved me only to kidnap me, and keep me as a slave? Or could I still be held captive by the Creatures of Chaos gang? My mind automatically went straight to the worst possible outcome. Maybe because of the night I just had. I was told once, plan for the worst, hope for the best.

A man walked into the room holding a glass of water with Claire hot on his tail. The man looked down at Claire.

"Go back to the kitchen please. I'll be there in a minute." Claire turned around reluctantly, but not before shooting me a big smile and yelling, "Bye, Sarah."

The man turned back to me, and said in a deep calm smooth voice, "Your name is Sarah." What he said was meant to be more of a statement, than a question so I said nothing.

"Well, hello Sarah, my name is David." David waited for a response, and when it was clear he wasn't going to get one he continued, "Would you like a glass of water?"

Before my brain even had time to process the offer, I blurted out, "Is it drugged," David looked honestly taken aback.

"No," he sighed, "I would never," but halted, knowing my apprehension. I was afraid to meet his eyes; I was frightened of what I might see there. The eyes are the windows to the soul, and I found it the best way to read people's emotions and desires. I just wish I'd read Sam's and Tara's eyes better so I wouldn't have got myself in this mess. Last night, those bikies had icy killer mischief in their eyes. I didn't want to see that coldness in David's eyes too.

David didn't say anything, and then when the silences became uncomfortable I mustered up my courage to lift my eyes. What I saw wasn't a man made of rage and wrath. He didn't have a murderous glint in his eyes. There wasn't even any lustful desire to take advantage of me.

What I saw was sorrow, compassion, and protectiveness. A longing to right the wrongs of other people, but at the same time there was a side of this man that was dark and hidden, sad almost. He was what I thought Batman would look like if he was real. A man of good deeds, but had to use violence to achieve them. I knew by the way he looked a little hurt when I asked if the water was drugged that this was the man who saved me, and wasn't part of the gang that was going to kill me.

"Are you the man that saved me last night?" I asked to make sure. David nodded.

"Will you let me go home?"

"You are in no danger here. No one is going to hurt you, but I can't let you leave just yet. We have to talk about a few things first," David responded, leaving no room to object. He walked over to the drawers, opened the middle one and pulled out a pair of tracksuit pants, and then placed them at the end of the bed.

I was still under the covers; instinctively I pulled the doona up to act as a barrier between me and everybody else. Realising what I was wearing last night or the lack of what I was wearing last night, made me wonder what I had on now. I looked down to see a man's blue t-shirt and a pair of cotton boxers. It felt like I had socks on too, but the compression was much tighter. I couldn't see that far under the covers to find out for sure, and I wasn't about to take my focus off David.

"Did you dress me?" David's face flushed, he looked away for an instant to regain his composure.

"I wrapped you up in your coat first, after…" I could see he was recalling the events in his mind. Then sidestepping the question he said, "When we got back I had someone take a look at your injuries. I'm sorry I didn't take you to the hospital, but the guy I used to treat your wounds, and check your concussion is just as good as any doctor you would have gotten at a hospital. I would have taken you to the hospital if any of your injuries were life threatening."

Knowing he still skipped my question I repeated, "Did you dress me?" His red face gave me his answer anyway. The fact he did blush, said something about the man.

"Yes, I dressed you in some of my clothes," he admitted. "I hope you don't mind? But I didn't have anything else and I thought it would be better than you waking up naked."

He had seen me naked, and had dressed me, but he had a point. I was pretty much naked to begin with anyway. Now it was my turn to go a bit red faced. I'm sure the bruising on my face covered most of it up, though.

"This doctor of yours, what did he do to me?" I asked, not bothering to comment on the naked factor anymore.

"You had to get five stitches on your forehead from where that bikie slammed your head into the park bench," he said. "Don't worry about taking them out, the stitches are dissolvable after a while." I touched my forehead feeling every stitch as he continued.

"Your feet where pretty torn up so he bandaged them. He checked out your abdominal region, and suspects you got a couple broken ribs, but no internal bleeding. Your eye is swollen shut but nothing seems to be fractured or broken," David said, talking like an expert nurse would have done. "The swelling will go down with time, ice will help with that. All in all, you will physically recover completely." I didn't miss the physically comment.

David walked to the side of the bed, took a sip of the water to prove it wasn't drugged, and then placed the glass on the bedside table. I instinctively leaned in the opposite direction creating more space between us. David noticed this, his stare captioning my trepidation.

"You have nothing to fear from me, Sarah," David said, "The water is drug free. I can get you some pain relief if you are in pain, but I understand if you refuse."

"No, I'm good. I've never been a big fan of aspirin anyway," I said, hoping his understanding was genuine.

"Get dressed, and then meet me down the hall. We need to talk," David commanded in a non-threatening way.

Then he left me alone to get dressed.

CHAPTER 7

I stood outside the door at the end of the hall. I was building up my nerve to enter the room where I could hear David talking to some lady. The girl really didn't sound too happy. Every step I took to get there caned the soles of my feet, even through the bandages. But the pain I could handle, what came next in that room was something that was out of my hands.

David didn't come across as a bad guy, but why wouldn't he let me leave straight away? Why didn't he take me to a hospital? What did he have to talk to me about?

I had no idea what we needed to talk about. I thought everything was done and dusted. The only thing we had to talk about was what happened last night, and I didn't really feel like revisiting that topic.

I mean David did his job and he saved me. Patched me up while I was naked and unconscious, which I still found a little unsettling. Even if David was honourable, he still would have seen me naked. I was still exposed and helpless in front of him. That was enough to make any girl uneasy around a guy. There was only one way I would find out what he wanted to talk about though. I might as well take the bull by the horns, and lead the charge.

I walked through the door gingerly. I walked into a kitchen that smelled like bacon and eggs. David sat at a round dining table, while Claire sat next to him totally mesmerized by an iPad and ignoring the food on her plate. Claire wore big black Sony headphones that enveloped her tiny head. The noise cancelling headphones would

44

fully block out the outside world. I guessed that was the point while David and this woman talked. The woman was leaning up against the kitchen counter, giving me the biggest greasy as I walked in.

"Sarah, please sit down," David said, gesturing to a chair on the opposite side of the table as he saw me walk in. "You have already met Claire," he said looking over to the little girl who was none the wiser. "She has total tunnel vision when she is on that thing," David added patting Claire's head.

"This is my sister, Georgia," he said, waving a hand in the grumpy woman's direction.

"Hello," I said sheepishly. Georgia ignored my greeting. Her scowl growing even more defined.

"Why are you being so nice to this prostitute, haven't you done enough for her," Georgia spat the words out like venom. Then she turned on me.

"Do you even know what you have gotten yourself into? If my brother winds up dead or hurt because of you, no person on this earth will be able to protect you from me."

I wish I could have shrunk down into my chair to get away from this woman's wrath; Georgia was a scary woman. I thought I was meant to be the angry one, being kept against my will and all. But this woman's anger squashed mine like a bug.

The worst part about what she had said was that she thought I was a hooker. I know the worst part should have been the death threat or even the fact that she thinks David would still be endangered, but the hooker comment stung more. If Georgia thought I was a prostitute, then it was safe to assume David thought I was one as well.

David sat there calmly waiting for Georgia to cool down. When Georgia's fingers loosened up, and her face lost its shade of red, David said, "Sis, I love you, but maybe I should talk to Sarah alone."

"Fine," Georgia grumbled. Then, looking directly at me, added, "You take heed to what I just said, little lady."

Georgia walked over to David and gave him a hug, then whispered something I couldn't hear into his ear. I thought I saw a tear roll down her cheek, but I couldn't be sure. Georgia then picked up Claire with the iPad attached, like an extra limb. Then she left the room.

"Sorry for that. She worries about me, but that's still no excuse for being rude," David said.

"That's okay," I said not wanting to be rude myself.

Silence then cast its shadow over the room. I sat patiently. I didn't want to say the first word. I couldn't, I didn't even know where to begin.

"Sarah, what do you remember about last night?" David asked with a sympathetic tone of voice.

I really didn't want to dig up those memories. They were still so fresh and sore. But I didn't think I had much of a choice. I didn't think I had a chance to get out of here until I had talked this through with him. They do say talking helps you get through hard times, letting bad emotions build up and fester can destroy you. I didn't want to end up with depression. I didn't want to survive those bikie bastards only for my own mind to kill me later.

I still had my guard up around David, but the guy had a trustworthiness that only came from a kind-hearted soul. I knew the man wouldn't judge me. I mean, the man thinks I'm a hooker and still he treats me with respect. I did however start my recollection of what happened at the park bench. David didn't need to know about Sam and Tara, or anything about my life. It was probably best he just thought I was a call girl. I proceeded to tell him everything I could recall. How the bikies wanted me to seduce them. Then, trying to escape; then nearly getting raped, and then seeing him appear out of the darkness.

I told him how I saw him take down the bikies. I kept that last part brief, though. I didn't mention the knife and where it ended up. David leaned on the table, elbows spaced apart, his fist grasped by his other hand. It wasn't a threatening posture, but more of a thoughtful one.

"What do you remember about, as you put it, *me taking down the bikies*," David probed. That must be what he wanted to know. That had to be what this talk was about.

"I saw a knife," I said. Then going for the conclusion I asked, "Is the man dead?" David looked down at his hands, lost in thought, considering how to proceed, and then sidestepping my question he went on to say, "You were good enough to tell me your side of the story without trying to mislead me. I would have known if you were lying," David clarified with such conviction. "You don't want to tell me about how you ended up there. That's fine. But I need to know if there is anyone going to come looking for you, like a pimp or a rival bikie gang."

David stared intently at my face, looking for a sign or something. Maybe he could read faces or body language. Maybe he was like that guy from that TV show, *Lie to me*. I loved that show. For instance, when you asked somebody a question, and then they moved their eyes up and to the left, that indicated that they were using the part of the brain for visually constructed images. That meant they're making something up, that meant they're lying.

Body language signs were just as easy to read for someone who knew what to look for, too. If someone was lying they most often avoided eye contact. They might touch their face, throat or mouth; they were all signals of a liar. Perhaps I should have paid more attention when I talked to Sam and Tara. It was normally the people closest to you that could deceive you the best. I think it worked that way because they had your trust and you were not looking for disloyalty. Trust was a fine edged sword that could stab you in the back, I have come to learn.

"No bikies or pimps will come searching for me. But I live with my parents, and they will come looking for me if I don't contact them before long," I said, staring back into his unflinching eyes, kicking myself for exposing my personal life. I just couldn't help it. His eyes made it fall out of me.

Gazing into his eyes I noticed for the first time, that he was beautiful. His eyes were a deep ocean blue. He had short cropped hair, a square unshaven jaw line that wasn't overpowering or out of proportion to the rest of his face. His nose was ever so slightly bent, maybe from a break. He was not beautiful like a man model was beautiful. He didn't have the clean-shaven perfect skin, and a face like an angel. His handsomeness was that of a man. David had that look that derived from strength, fortitude, power and leadership. Some people were just meant to be leaders of men, and David just gave off that vibe. David had the persona of a man's man. He reminded me of a Sean Connery or Tom Selleck, but in their mid to late twenties. David sighed, drawing up the courage for something, I guessed.

"I made a promise to myself years ago that I would never use violence again. Violence seems to always lead to more violence. But I know saving you was the right thing to do. No matter what you did to get yourself in that position, no woman should be treated like that," David said, peering down at his hands. "I still see blood on my hands whenever I look down."

The way David explained about seeing the blood on his hands seemed to go deeper than just last night. But I sat in silence not wanting to interrupt by saying something moronic.

"I go for a run every night. I don't live that far from where I found you. I was running home from the gym that I go to in that industrial estate. That's why I was there, that's why I heard you scream. Your cry called to me. I couldn't just turn a blind eye. I couldn't just keep on running," He said. I could see the turmoil, fighting its way up.

"When I saw what those men had done to you, and what they intended to do, I had to intervene," David paused. I knew now, he was building towards my question. I could see he was almost there. I could see he was struggling to say what he wanted to tell me. "I killed that man while saving you. Beside running away I didn't have a choice, and I was not going to leave you to be tortured."

David's words came out like a confession. Like what he did wasn't in self-defence that, because he had had the fortitude to act, it was wrong somehow. That, when others would have shied away, he was brave and heroic. That, because he killed someone while saving someone, made him a killer. He was punishing himself as he thought he must. He was weighing up whether his actions were noble, or just destructive and sinful.

I had seen people getting murdered, tortured and all kinds of horrific profanity in movies, but never in reality. I guessed it blunted the blade for me. Yes, I cringed as I watched last night. Yes, I was in shock, but I wasn't overwhelmed by it. I wasn't so devastated by the sight that I was like a mouse trapped in a corner by a cat, trying to hide with nowhere to go.

Those bikies were going to rape me at the least. Those men gave the human species a bad name. I didn't feel pity when I saw Mr Big Bikie dying; I felt relief. I had never entertained the idea of posing myself as the killer. I always put myself in the victim's shoes when I watched that type of movie, but now I wondered what David would be going through.

To save a life, he must end one. How would I feel, if I took a life?

Would it be like blowing out the flame that burns within, leaving only darkness? I had no bloody idea how I would feel. I think a person's imagination can only stretch so far. What lies beneath the surface of our being, in our beliefs is unknown. Until that thin fabric is torn open to reveal the horrors below, I didn't think anyone could truly have any idea how they would feel about killing someone, self-defence or not.

"I would most likely be dead, or I would want to be dead if you didn't save me. So thank you," I said with sincerity.

David ignored my words of appreciation. His face went hard, his eyes narrowing, "Do you know who it was that I killed?"

"Some Creatures of Chaos woman bashing, rapist, murdering asshole," I snorted out. Then a second later I added, "Besides that, I have no clue."

"He was all of those things, but he was also the brother of the head of the Creatures of Chaos bikie gang. His name was Jordan Cole," David said, to enlighten me.

"Is that supposed to frighten me? Do you think I care?" I said with conviction and no fear in my speech. David gazed deep into my eyes, like he was probing for my soul.

"Most people are not afraid of a stranger. It's not until you know them and what they're capable of that you learn to be afraid," David said putting me in the most people category, like a common sheep.

"You said that you live with your parent's, right?" David asked.

I nod. Not sure where he was going with the question.

"What if they find where you live? Then break into your house hunting for you, but instead of finding you they come across your mum and dad," David pushed.

What an outrageous scenario, I thought. Like that would ever happen. But David wasn't finished.

"Then they torture your folks for information about you. Then, once they get what they want from them, they execute them because they can't leave any witnesses. But not before raping your mum right in front of your father."

The mental image of my mother being raped made me shudder. I was only moments away from getting raped myself. I knew the helplessness you felt, I wouldn't wish what happened to me on my worst enemy, and I was only sexually assaulted, not raped.

"Do you think you would care then?" David said, his voice wavering as he delivered the last word.

I just sat there staring at him, not needing to answer. I was right before. This went deep for him. It wasn't killing the bikie that hurt him the most. There was something violent in his past, a wound that hadn't quite healed.

"Trust me, Sarah. I know what this gang is capable of and something like that can happen," he choked out.

David stood up, turning his back to me. David seemed like a man that didn't display emotions openly, or lose control of them easily. I had only just met the man, but I had the feeling this was uncommon for him. I reckoned David had suffered big time in the past. I can tell you that sort of pain only came from loving something more than you love yourself, and then having that something stolen away from you.

My pain knew his pain.

I thought of Sam in that moment. I loved him with everything. He was the man I was meant to marry one day. I had planned to have a family with him, and grow old together. Sam was one thing I had that was special. I felt like I had a hole in me now. I was broken without him, but I'd rather be broken than live a lie. And I saw that loss in David.

"You're right," I admit quietly, finding my voice and needing to speak, "I don't really care about what happens to me," I declared, only half believing my own words, "but I do care what happens to my parents."

My parents were all I had left now. I was twenty-two years old and the only friends I kept in contact with were from my old high school days. Jane, Greg, Tara and Sam, were the sum total of my massive close friends list. I lost touch with everyone else I was close to in school.

That's the way of the world; sometimes you just drifted apart like a current in the ocean towing you away, leaving your friends on the shore. Jane and Greg had been a couple for as long as Sam and I had. They had always been the duo we went to for a double date, or talk relationship problems with. Tara of course was my BFF of all time. Well, that was until I found her bonking my boyfriend, and I was not stupid enough to think that was the first time either, Sam and I had been having problems for months now.

No, Tara could go jump off a bridge for all I cared, hopefully face first so she would smash that pretty little face of hers. Then there was Sam. The lying, cheating, sleazy love of my life that was now dead to me. With us splitting up, I was pretty sure Sam would get Greg and Jane. He could take Tara too. Sam and Greg were always closer than I was with Jane, so that meant they were gone from my life. I would have bet Greg knew about Sam's affair with Tara as well, and if Greg knew then Jane knew and that meant all my closest friends had been lying to me.

I realised through that thought process that all my best friends had been betraying me this whole time, and that I had never had any true friends. I had been alone all along. That left me with no one but Mummy and Daddy.

I worked at Target three days a week, and there was no one there I would call a close friend. I studied online now, finishing my Accounting Diploma. I submitted everything via internet access so no classroom full of people to buddy up with. I was alone. I only had myself to hold on to in the dark of night.

David turned back to face me. Stared at me for a long moment, seeing my exterior wall crumble.

"There is hope for you yet, Sarah," he declared. David's full composure had returned, with no sign of his earlier fervent display.

"Do you care what happens to my sister, my niece, and me," David queried.

I pondered this for a tick, wondering what his sister and niece had to do with anything.

"I wouldn't want any of you getting hurt," I said, "If that is what you are getting at?"

"That is exactly what I am getting at," David said, "because, depending on what you decide to do next, will set in motion a course of events that we will have to take." There was such seriousness to his voice, that it overshadowed everything that had come before. This guy took paranoia to a whole new level.

"I am not going to hold you prisoner, or force you to do anything you don't want to do. After we talk you are free to go," David remarked, his protectiveness nature showing through. "The only reason I didn't take you to a hospital was because of what you might say, and who you might say it to could put yourself and my family in danger. I didn't save you last night so you could kill yourself today and I will not let anything happen to my family again. So I have to make sure you know what you're in for."

I believed him that danger could still be afoot. There was so much raw emotion flooding out of him that it would be impossible not to believe him. You couldn't fake that. I suspected it had something to do with that word 'again' he'd mentioned.

He portrayed trust and honesty, but people were what their actions make them, not their words. Just another thing I had come to learn in the past ten minutes as a result of my dishonourable friends. I would just have to wait and see if David was a man of his word.

"The Creatures of Chaos will be after both of us now. If they find us they will slit our throats without a second thought," he said, making me stiffen in my chair from his frankness. I just realised that I had been clenching my fists so hard that my nails had left indentations on my palms.

"Surely they couldn't find us, they don't know our names or where we live," I said shakily.

"The Creatures of Chaos run the drugs and girls in this city, which brings in a lot of money. That much cash buys power, and that power buys reach. That reach extends to finding someone with nothing else but a description," he explained. "That tall skinny bikie on drugs saw both of us clearly before he ran away, and if that stocky guy remembers anything when he comes to, it will be our faces."

"I thought only the police could find someone with just a face," I challenged. David smiled a worrying smile.

"The cops have the help of the public. It's more difficult without the public's help but not impossible. Plus the bikies have the police bought and paid for, and can buy a great computer hacker. However, if you want to make it easy for them, file a police report or go to a hospital, because that will be the first place they will look."

I thought my nightmare was over. Hearing that just confirmed that I was still asleep, dreaming unable to wake. I was waiting to see Freddy Krueger next. I must have looked lost in thought, because David continued, "If you go to the cops, I won't stop you, but you will never know if that officer you're talking to works for the bikies or not. And then, when they find you, and they will find you, because even if you talk to one of the good ones, your report will be logged into their database, where any good hacker can get to it," David paused, letting it all sink in, "and if they find you, they will find me. So you see why we needed to have this chat." I nodded. I still thought David was over-paranoid, but I got it.

"So what I need to know from you is what are you planning to do from here?" David requested.

"I don't know," I said honestly. After a moment of deliberation, I decided to just say what was on my mind. Probably a bad move, but it was an authentic one.

"I really haven't given it any thought. It all just happened so fast. I haven't even had time to think," I said. Working backwards I went on, "My first thought when I woke up was to get home. Get somewhere safe and familiar. And if you are a man of your word, then I don't have anything to worry about when it comes to that."

I sighed, really hoping David was who he appeared to be. I didn't want to continue, but I pushed through anyway before I lost my nerve. If I couldn't talk to the man who saved me, then I couldn't talk to anyone.

"Then, last night with the bikies all I could think of was escape." I paused, "You must be wondering how I came to be in the middle of nowhere," I said, gearing up to get through it. "The answer is because I found my boyfriend having sex with my best friend. So I ran and kept running until my feet wouldn't let me take another step." I looked at him. "So now do you get it?" I snapped. "I'm not some hooker that knows about all this crap; I don't know what I have stumbled into. I am just an average girl that works at Target until I finish my accounting diploma," I said, tears tracking down my face. I had finally lost it, I thought. I saw David's face soften though.

"So, forgive me if I haven't had much time to ponder the idea of going to the police, and telling them I was bashed and almost raped by a gang of bikies," I squeaked out, my throat closing up from the raining tears.

"So, you had a pretty bad night then," David replied with the biggest understatement of a lifetime.

Laughter took over, my tears didn't stop, but my sobs turned to chuckles. When I could breathe properly I retorted, "I suppose you could say that."

It was good of David to break the tension with some humour, even with a joke as bad as that. I expected him to say something else but he didn't. I looked up to see David just sitting there staring at me not whispering a sound, he was just sitting there as silent as a picture hanging on the wall. He was still after an answer. I was not leaving here until he had one, I suspected.

He was waiting for my emotions to straighten out, he was giving me time to decide. He wasn't telling me to hurry up, or even pointing out that I hadn't answered his question yet. The man was waiting patiently until I figured out what I wanted to do. He was not trying to persuade me to do what he wanted, but waiting for me to do what I wanted.

I don't know why I spilled my guts about my relationship troubles. I wasn't planning to earlier. It wasn't something I would normally share with a stranger. There was just something about this man. I didn't know when it changed; in a moment of self-reflection and contemplation I came to the realisation that I trusted this man.

Even though he saved my life, he was still just a stranger to me. David just didn't feel like a stranger though. In a matter of minutes I felt like we had become friends. We were on the same side now. It felt like the time I joined my netball team outside of school. I didn't know any of the other girls, but we had instantly become team mates.

The way I perceived it was going through the same traumatic experience that tied us together. The feeling was something unrecognisable to put into words, it tethered us together like our future paths were going down the same yellow brick road. If I believed him about how dangerous the bikies were, my life or our lives would be in terrible danger. If I went to the cops it would only shorten my life span. If I didn't go to the cops then we'd still be looking over our shoulders, but there was a higher chance that they would never find us.

"I won't go to the police but I can't guarantee that I won't see a doctor," I stated, making up my mind. I waited for him to object but he didn't. "What do you suggest we do from here, then?"

"Go home and take care of yourself. Heal up until your wounds are better and unnoticeable, and then go back to your normal everyday life," David suggested. "Try to use this night of misfortune as a building block to grow stronger, don't wallow in self-pity and get depressed by it. Try to live by the words, *whatever doesn't kill me, makes me stronger.*" David reached into his pocket and pulled out a business card then handed it to me.

"If last night's circumstances ever get too hard for you to bear, and you need someone to talk to, please don't hesitate to call me. You don't have to go through this alone. You can ring me whenever you need, anytime, anywhere."

The card was for a personal trainer in fitness and health, martial arts and meditation teachings. It also had his name, David Powers, and his mobile number.

"Thank you, David, for everything," I said.

"Let's get you home, Sarah."

CHAPTER 8

*D*avid and I drove into my Springwater estate. Compared to where David lived, my estate must have looked very upper class. If you broke the world into three categories rich, poor and middle class, my street would probably be somewhere between rich and middle class, whereas David's residence would probably be more like middle to poor class.

David had a nice car though, one that didn't really fit in his neighbourhood. He had a black Holden ute SS Storm series with a 6.0 litre V8 engine, that pushed out 270kW at 5600rpm, which makes the horsepower just over 360 horses. So that basically meant it goes fast. That's all I understood out of all that when David told me. He said that he needed a nice looking car to give the impression that he was successful. No one was going to take a personal trainer seriously if they rocked up in an old rust bucket of a car to a boot camp session. The ute was always good for carrying around all the equipment too, he added.

David parked at the end of my driveway, trying to get as close to the front door as possible, knowing too well I was going to have trouble walking. My driveway was about thirty metres from the road. Our house sat on about three quarters of an acre. Our two storey house was modern looking, brick veneer with two square pillars out the front covered in a white sparkling stack stone. The house had five bedrooms, with five bathrooms, and a three-car garage – more than big enough for Mum, Dad and me.

Being an only child I got a little spoilt having four bedrooms to choose from. My bedroom faced west, so I got the afternoon sun.

The balcony that's joined to my room was a good place to sunbake in the summer. The idea of getting a tan now, seemed ridiculous; just a waste of precious time. I was trying to look good for a guy that didn't appreciate me, or even want me. Let alone I was increasing my chances of skin cancer.

All the things I did to please him like putting on makeup, wearing nice clothes, doing my hair, painting my nails – I could go on but I won't. It all seemed so wasteful. I mean it hadn't made Sam stick around anyway did it? If a man wanted me for all of those things, he was not really getting the real me. Sam had been getting a fake impersonation of me I realised. It was what I thought he wanted. It was amazing the insight you got once you'd been betrayed by the one you loved. A man should like me for who I was inside, he should want to have sex with me for what I looked like naturally, without all the fundamental extras, and if not, he could go fuck himself.

David turned to me in the driver's seat, then asked, "So you know what to tell your folks?"

"Yes," I replied. "I remember."

On the drive over David had told me to tell everyone that I had been involved in a hit and run car accident. It was the best excuse that fit all my injuries, except for my feet, which I would just tell the truth. I was running away from my cheating boyfriend.

If my parents made me go to the hospital to get checked out, which I was betting they would, it would be the best way to disguise my injuries. If I said to the hospital it was a car accident their records would show that. If anyone came searching they would be looking for assault victims so hopefully I'd get overlooked as a car incident.

David got out of the car first to help me to my feet, which still hurt like a mother. My feet seemed to be sorer now than when I woke up. Maybe that fright to flight instinct had worn off.

David placed my arm around his shoulder, which felt more like a rock than a man's shoulder. David's body fat percentage would have to be about five percent or under. The guy was nothing but muscle underneath his shirt. He then put his hand around my back to my hip, careful of my bruised ribs. I didn't get five steps past the car to the front door before it opened, and my father came out, looking furious.

I'm sure he started to say, where have you been young lady. Just like he did when I was fifteen, but all he got out was, "Where have..." then stopped in his tracks. He nearly choked on the oxygen in his lungs when he saw my face. Half my face was swollen, I had a stitched up gash on my forehead, my makeup streaked all down my face, my hair like a wild woman, and a strange man basically carrying me to the front door. I must have looked like I just survived a war zone. He couldn't even see the fist and knee size bruises on my sides or my raw feet.

Dad rushed over to me taking my opposite arm to the one David had around his shoulder.

"What happened?" Dad asked.

"Car accident," David responded for me.

"Who is this?" my father demanded, glaring at David ignoring his response. Then turning back to me, "I'm calling an ambulance," he stated, not asking but telling.

My father went straight for his iPhone in his back pocket. He was acting totally frantic, his handsome face distorting and flushing red with distress. I had seen him like this but once, when I broke my arm after falling out of a tree. He ran around not knowing what to do, or how to help so he tried to do everything at once.

"Dad, please, let's just go inside and I'll explain everything," I pleaded, just wanting to sit back down, and get off my feet.

Dad's response was, "Okay, okay, let's get you inside first." He then slid the phone back into his pocket, taking a deep calming breath to gain back some normalcy.

David through all this stayed quiet, not overstepping his bounds, after that pointed glare from my Dad. I would have shut-up too. I had been on the end of a few of those piercing stares myself. It was easy to know when to close your mouth. My old man could look quite menacing when he wanted to, plus saying something like calm down, would probably just make things worse.

Dad and David walked me into the living room, sitting me down on the couch. Dad was a little more composed now. He was just pacing back and forth instead of running around in circles.

"What happened?" Dad asked again, not slowing in his pacing.

I ran through our half fake story. Telling him I had a fight with Sam, ran off bare foot and was hit by a car. David had witnessed the incident, then took me to a hospital, and stayed with me, then drove me home.

"Well that at least explains all the phone calls from Sam," my father said.

Dad seemed to believe my lies. I had never lied to my father like that before. I had told a few little white lies in my time but nothing of this magnitude. I prided myself on being an honest daughter to my parents. I'm not sure my Dad would understand why I would want to stay tight-lipped about being a victim in a bashing by bikies, and a witness to a self-defence killing. Also I didn't really want to find out how he would react to the news either, more people might get killed.

I'm pretty sure the only reason David stuck around was to make sure I told the car crash fiction to my parents, and so didn't implicate him in a manslaughter incident.

Dad walked over to David with a stern look upon his face, my heart rate speeding up as he did. I didn't know what my dad was going to do. I had had enough drama in one day to last me a life-time, so I didn't really feel like any more at the moment. My mind came up with multiple scenarios. Was he going to punch David in the face for not contacting him sooner, hug him for bringing me home, or just throw David out on his ear? Dad lifted his hand in greeting.

"My name is Conner Smith. Thank you for bringing my daughter home." David didn't hesitate. He took my father's hand shaking it.

"David Powers, sir," David responded, "And I just did what any good man would do."

"There are not too many good men left in the world," Dad replied, "Sarah was lucky to have you look out for her." More than you will ever know Dad, I thought.

My Father stood toe to toe with David, staring straight into his eyes. Dad wasn't trying to threaten or intimidate David, but testing the man's character. I saw him do this to Sam the first time they met and Sam buckled under my father's stare, but David just held that stare with unnerving ease.

Dad then asked, "Were you able to make out the car that hit my Sarah?"

David standing straight and proud replied, "Sorry, sir, I just heard the impact then came running."

David had answered straight away, with no hint of a lie in his demeanour. He must have rehearsed this in his head a million times for it to come out so authentic. Dad, satisfied with David's bravado, turned back to pacing the room before saying, "Pity you didn't catch him, I would love to get my hands on the guy driving." My father balled his fists into weapons, wishing he could use them on the man who did this to his little girl. Releasing his frustrations he loosened up his hands, and then ran them through his salt and pepper hair.

"David, I hope you don't mind but I think this is a family matter now," Dad asserted with authority. Not to undermine David, but to make sure he was obeyed. It was his polite way of telling David to leave.

"Yes, sir. It was nice to meet you, Conner," David replied, daring to use Dad's first name.

"Likewise, I'm sure," Dad said.

David came up to me as he was leaving placing a hand on mine, and then squeezed it slightly as a way of saying goodbye. David was between Dad and me, and facing me. So Dad couldn't see David's face when he winked at me through a crooked smile that took the hardness out of his features, and letting out a gentler side. The wink was for the trust I just proved to him, but that smile had something behind. Maybe he felt a responsibility for me now after saving me, or maybe the smile was from somewhere deeper, closer to the heart.

"Take care, Sarah," David uttered, then walked out, not looking back.

That was the first time I remember seeing him smile, and it was directed at me. I felt my face flush and I couldn't look at him. I was sure that Dad didn't notice my shyness; my face being in a state of disarray and all. I didn't think the red flush could have burned through the purple bruising anyway. The reaction took me by surprise. I hadn't acted like that in front of a boy since Sam first spoke to me. I found David attractive, well very attractive actually, but I hadn't even broken up with Sam properly yet. I also looked a mess, I just went through the worst night of my life and now I was acting like a schoolgirl with a crush after he winked at me.

I was seriously messed up. I must have lost some brain cells in that concussion. I did however want David to trust me, and with that wink I thought he just might.

I could hear the rumbling of the V8 as it left the driveway, as I asked Dad, "Where is mum?"

"She's out grocery shopping," Dad answered. Not wanting to get off topic, Dad stopped his pacing to face me, "Why didn't you call us as soon as you got to the hospital? We have been worrying about you all night after you told Mum you would be with Sam, and then an hour later Sam called looking for you." I was kind of ready for this one so the answer came out fairly smooth.

"Well for one I was unconscious, and two I didn't call because I left my phone in my car, and I don't know your mobile numbers off by heart," I said, playing defensive. It was good we got rid of the home phone or that excuse wouldn't have worked.

"I'm just glad you're home now. This is what I have always been terrified of. You coming home all battered and bruised," Dad said, genuine fear in his tone. Dad was just like Mum with all the over-parenting; he worried because he loved me so much. I always found it endearing, playing along because it made my life so much easier to be treated like a kid. But seeing with open eyes for the first time in my life, I realised I had just been lazy.

"I'm sorry, I didn't mean to worry you guys."

"Darling, you don't have anything to be sorry for," Dad told me, stopping his pacing once more. "I know I get a little worked up sometimes, but can you blame me? This time I was right to worry." I just looked at him, my one working eye doing the talking for me.

"I mean look at you, you're a disaster," he joked with the truth, a smile spreading across his face.

"Thanks for stating the obvious, Dad" I replied, with a smile growing from my lips.

"What did you and Sam fight about? Do I have to strangle him?" he asked in a voice that I couldn't make out if he was joking or not. I figured he was going to find out one way or another, so I just blurted out the truth.

"You just might have to strangle him." Dad's eyebrows narrowed awaiting the bad news. "I found him cheating on me with Tara," I said, not being able to meet his gaze now. I felt a little ashamed to have befriended such a backstabber bitch and for getting romantically involved with such a wandering dick. I wanted Dad to be proud of me; not to think I was a loser who couldn't keep her man.

"Wow," Dad groaned, "That would of hurt," he added understanding the agony in my heart.

"It's their loss, sweetheart. You are an amazing, kind, warm person that is too good to be hanging around the likes of them," he said.

With tears starting to build up in my eyes, I said, "It's over for good this time."

This wasn't the first fight we had ever had. We had nearly broken up a few times. Every other time it was over small petty things, like Sam getting too drunk at a party and acting like a complete ass in front of his friends. This time, however, was neither small nor petty. This was something unforgiveable; this was a one-way road to break-up town.

Dad sat next to me on the couch placing a comforting arm around my shoulders. I flinched back not meaning to. I got lost in a memory of Sam. I was reliving last night's Sam and Tara spectacle. I had forgotten where I was for a second, and when Dad touched me I jumped instinctively, thinking it was Sam.

If Dad noticed the movement, he didn't show it. He stuck firm giving me the reassurance I needed. I was home, among family, safe and loved. I hadn't flinched when David touched my hand, or when he helped me out of the car. You would think being touched by a strange man I had only known for a couple of hours would repulse me after what I had just been through. Did that mean anything because I wasn't repulsed by another man's touch? Maybe I was thinking too deeply about it. It was just David had a presence about him. Being around him straightened me out somewhat, made me more level-headed. I felt focused, because I had to be. He made me want to endure, no matter the cost, or else what he did for me would be for nothing.

Now David's gone, I was home safe and sound. Now I would have time to think and ponder. Now I could drift back into the scenes of last night's torment and get lost there if I was not careful. I started to fall down into that bottomless pit of memories right then and there. I began reliving last night in slow mode dragging out the nightmare, until Dad snapped me out of it with a loving hug. I was so lost in thought I hadn't even noticed I was still crying.

"Sorry kiddo. I know you loved him, and for Tara to do that to you makes it twice as bad," he said. "You must have run for quite a while for your feet to get so sore."

I nodded my head because the words wouldn't come out through my blocked throat. I leaned into my father's chest fully sobbing uncontrollably now, tears leaving a wet patch on his shirt.

I stayed there hanging on to my father for God knows how long. Time lost all meaning, even meaning lost all meaning. I was home in my father's arms, and that was all I needed at the moment. I think I just needed to know that some things never change. That my Dad would always love me and be there for me, and he didn't disappoint.

"Hey kiddo," Dad began, "I better call your Mum, and tell her to come home. Then we can figure out what to do next."

CHAPTER 9

*A*fter my mother came home, she gave me a hug that seemed to go on for an hour, crushing my tender ribs the whole time. I just didn't have the heart to tell her. Instead I just suffered through the loving gesture.

When my mother finally let me go she had calmed down enough to talk. We discussed or more correctly Mum and Dad discussed my imminent future.

First they took me to the emergency ward at the hospital as I predicted, and despite my protest. After waiting for two and a half hours I finally saw a Dr Lee. He announced that the doctor that treated me before did a great job bandaging me up, but he still wanted to run a few MRI scans.

The results on my brain came up fine, no swelling or life threatening brain trauma after being knocked unconscious. There was no fracturing of the eye socket, just a lot of swelling that would go down with time. My ribs were badly bruised but not broken, and the raw skin on my feet was nothing to worry about as long as I kept them clean.

Overall I had no majorly serious injuries, just some cuts and bruises that should all heal up nicely. Doctor Lee even said that the gash on my forehead might not even leave a scar, because the doctor that did the stiches did a wonderful job. I wished I knew the doctor that David used, I still didn't know whether I wanted to shake that doctor's hand or slap him across the face.

My parents wanted me to go to the police and report the incident, but I had talked them out of that one luckily. I was pretty sure you could get into a bit of trouble by giving a false police report, plus not telling them about the bikie getting a knife in his gullet probably wouldn't go down too well either, if they ever found out. Not that I would live long enough for them to find out, according to David.

Mum and Dad weren't very happy about my decision, especially Dad. I think he wanted to punch the guy that did this to me. I'm glad I didn't tell him the truth now; he might have walked straight into the Creatures of Chaos clubhouse and started swinging fists towards people's chins. Fortunately they had listened to reason, once I said there was no point giving a statement seeing I was knocked out cold, and couldn't remember anything. And David wouldn't be any help because he hadn't seen the car, so there was nothing for the cops to go on anyway.

Dad had countered saying, "What if the person feels guilty and turns himself in, and with no incident report the culprits would go unpunished."

"If the person feels guilty for driving off and leaving me for dead he would just have to live with that feeling for the rest of his life, and I will just have to hope the guilt would be punishment enough," I answered.

Somehow I think the driver or, in retrospect, the bikies wouldn't have the slightest hint of guilt from what they did to me. In fact I reckoned they would have done a lot worse if they hadn't been interrupted. And I reckoned they still plan on doing worse.

After going through all this rubbish with the bikies, the impact of it, along with the Sam and Tara fiasco, had changed me. For the first time being treated like a kid was really starting to bug me. I knew my parents only wanted what was best for me, but being told what to do was really starting to drive me nuts. My parents always think they know what is best for me, and up to now I really hadn't fought them on that front. I always gave in, taking heed of their wisdom. But sometimes I thought we needed to make our own mistakes, to learn from them, to grow the wisdom inside ourselves. If we always followed the words of others, even our parents, we would never trust our own judgment.

I would always be their little girl, I knew that. But I wished they saw me for the woman I was becoming. To be honest I hadn't really given them much of a reason to look at me any other way. I suppose because their little princess still lived at home, still didn't have a full time job, still got her meals cooked for her, her clothes washed, bills paid. It would be easy for them to still see me as a child needing to be taken care of. I thought it was time for me to grow up. Maybe after I could walk, though.

After last night, I realised that life was short. I had to get myself out amongst it. I had to start really living my life, taking charge and start taking responsibility for my life. Stop living idle, be the master of my destiny. For instance, dating a two-timing loser; that had to go.

Not realising I was dating a two-timing loser I had to become more aware. I had to learn to stand up for myself. For instance, running away from Sam and Tara screwing right in front of me instead of confronting them, I should have thrown my shoes at their heads. That had to happen.

I decided that I would never run away again, fear be damned. I wouldn't be that weak ever again. I had cheated death; I had been given a second chance. I dared not squander it, I would embrace life, I would not be afraid of it anymore. I would make life my playground. I would wipe the slate clean with my bloody clothes, and then leave everything behind to burn and rot into the soil. My life started here. I was going to make this day my new beginning. Yes, that definitely sounded like a plan. I really intended to follow through with all that, but for the moment I was exhausted.

On the drive home from the hospital it felt like I had dumbbells attached to my eyelids. I fell asleep in the car ride home, unable to keep my eyes open. I only woke up after the sound of the engine had come to a stop, and my mother kissed my good cheek, and then whispered, "We're home darling."

I didn't know how I got upstairs with my sore feet, and my brain still half asleep, but when I stood outside my bedroom, with my hand on the handle I wasn't able to open it. I wasn't afraid. I was too tired to analyse my emotions, so I just went to one of the spare rooms. Lay down on the bed then drifted off to sleep.

CHAPTER 10

I found myself alone in the dark. There was no light, but somehow my body was illuminated. It was like my body was glowing with an inner light, and it wanted out. I looked around and there was nothing but blackness. I was in the darkest depths of space, and all the stars in the galaxy were gone. A voice then came from the darkness; it was David's voice.

My heart leaped, my pulse quickened. Then that light from within me shot out of my chest shooting a beam of sparkling bright white light that cast upon David so that he stood like a god bathed in heavenly light. David stood about fifty feet away, not moving, not making his way towards me. It felt reassuring just having him there in my vicinity.

A smile spread on my face, I was happy, I felt safe with him there nearby. Then a giant hand cut across the beam of light plunging David back into darkness. A man stood in front of the light that sprang from my breast. The man was forcing the light back inside me. I could feel my light dwindling. The man moved closer. The closer he got the more of his features I could make out.

The man was Sam.

It was Sam that had a force like a black hole, compressing everything around it, making it small, controlling it, and then owning it. Sam never wanted me to be what I could be, he wanted to change me into his own making; a tiny little compressed black speck amongst the stars. Sam was now pushing with both hands against my light, taking one step at a time, getting closer and closer to me.

Sam was trying to keep me in the dark. I cried out to David, "Help me," but my voice rebounded back to me. Sam was close enough now for me to see his shadowy features perfectly. His demeanour looked sad, his mouth moved but no sound came out. By the movement of his lips, I understood by lip reading his words, "I love you, Sarah." Sam was still walking towards me, still extinguishing my light with every step.

I cried out again, "Help me David."

A voice washed over me, it wasn't like sound waves that travel through you into your ears, but like that voice inside your own head. But this voice wasn't mine, it was David's.

"This is a battle you must fight on your own," David's voice had said.

How could he leave me to have my light put out? Wasn't he my saviour, my protector, my knight in shining armour? Why wouldn't he save me? Then the voice came back, not David's this time but my own, "You must be your own saviour, you have the strength within you. You must unleash the force that has been pushed down for so long. Only you have the power to bring forth your inner light."

Sam's hands were on my chest now. No light escaped my chest. The glow of my body was beginning to fade too. My hands and feet were getting swallowed up by the darkness. I was terrified. I couldn't go back to the darkness after experiencing the light. It would be the end of me. A determination then flooded my body giving me strength. An unknown strength I had never felt before. Strength I never knew I had.

I tensed my muscles creating a hard shell over my entire body. Sam's hands were forced back a bit. It was just enough for my light to encompass my limbs again. Sam pushed back down with all his might, but he couldn't break through my barrier. Sam then mouthed the words, "But I love you, Sarah." My hard shell cracked, his hands pushing back down on my chest again.

"No," I said quietly, having to make an effort just to get that single word out. Nothing happened. Sam's pressure was still forcing me into nothingness once more.

"No," I screamed again. This time I was willing my entire being behind the scream. All my pain and hurt, all my love and desire, every little bit of strength I had went into that scream. My light exploded out of me like I was a nuclear bomb. The blast evaporated Sam, and all the darkness along with it. My surrounding turned to pure white, there was no darkness, no shadows to get lost in, just white bathing light.

I was breathing hard from the effort I used up fighting Sam's darkness. I looked up to see David still standing there where he was before, but now he was bowing towards me, a sign of respect.

"I knew you could do it," he spoke in my mind.

I awoke after that. My body still in pain, but now I was enlightened. I remembered the dream and the wisdom it gave me. I spoke the words out loud so I would remember in the morning.

"I have the power to create my own destiny."

$\mathcal{I}$can stand on my own two feet again; one small step for me, one giant leap for feet everywhere. I still couldn't see properly out of one eye, but I'll take the good with the bad. The next day the pain in my feet along with the rest of my body was still there, but I found the pain bearable, like I had grown accustomed to the discomfort. It was like I had always had it, it was like it was a part of me now.

The physical pain was a good cover for the emotional misery too, which I found even more torturous to deal with. That dream last night had given me another outlook on life, just one more new revelation I had uncovered. That dream had given me hope for a brighter future without Sam. It gave me an inner strength that only came from getting knocked down and then forcing your way back up.

Now I was actually up and awake I had such a craving for coffee. My head pounded for it. I just realised that I hadn't had a drop since my old life went down the toilet. I headed straight downstairs to the kitchen. The house was silent except for the creaks in the staircase. The house was almost creepy when you were the only one up walking around. It always made me move that little bit faster.

I always had the feeling of being watched, like someone was spying on me from around the corner and was waiting to pounce on me. I needed noise to fight the silence away. Once I reached the kitchen the first thing I did was to go for the TV remote. My mother liked to watch TV while she cooked. She loved all those cooking shows. It got her motivated to get her own hands messy with food, which was great for Dad and me. I thought I might start getting her to teach me a few things in the kitchen now I'm changing my life from a negative to a positive.

The TV came alive and I started to flick through the channels. There wasn't really anything worth watching, so I just left it on the channel nine news. I wasn't even paying attention to what was on, I just needed some background noise; something to scare the bogieman away.

I turned to the half-full kettle pressing the button down. The glass kettle glowed blue with little LED lights around the base as it started to boil the water for my coffee. I made my coffee a double shot so that the caffeine gave me more of a kick. Once my coffee was done I went to sit down at the dining table to enjoy my cup of Joe.

As I placed my cup on the table I noticed in the middle of the table was my phone, car keys and my three-hundred dollar pair of high heels. I just stared at them stupidly for a moment before walking up to the inanimate objects. I had to touch them to be certain they were real, and it wasn't my mind playing tricks on me. I had been hit in the head, you know. To my relief, my eyes were not playing tricks; the keys, shoes and phone were definitely real. Now I was left with the question, how did they get there?

I picked up my phone punching in the four digit combination to gain access to the phone's criteria. There were one-hundred and fifty-four missed calls. I clicked into the call history. All the calls were from only three people. Mum made up thirty-seven of the calls. I got one from Tara, and the other one-hundred and sixteen were from Sam. Sam was persistent if nothing else. I hope he felt as bad as I looked, which was pretty bad at the moment. I hoped the guilt of what he did burns away at him, and he couldn't live with himself so then he felt the need to cut off his little pecker.

I checked my messages next. There were nearly as many messages as there were missed calls, all from the same three people. I didn't want to read any of them. I didn't want to drive down that road at the moment so I deleted all the messages straight off the bat, along with Sam's and Tara's numbers. I then decided to get rid of Jane and Greg too, because, when I look back, I am sure they knew about it. Sam had been distant for a while now, that was why I went to surprise him with the booty call in the first place. I remembered talking to Jane about it and she just kept blowing it off, always trying to avoid the topic. Saying things like, "Don't worry, it's just men, they're always hot and cold," or, "Don't be silly, Sam loves you." Now I highly suspect she was just dodging the subject because she didn't want to get caught in a lie.

Once I cleaned up my contacts I deleted my call history. Then I attacked my photos, deleting all I could find of the foursome. I wanted to completely erase them off my phone and from my life. I then moved onto social media. I only really used Facebook. So, to make things easy I just deleted my whole account rather than trying to sort through hundreds of photos of the group. I wanted to start anew; I was leaving my whole life behind. I was not curious whatsoever about those messages that Sam left. I didn't want to hear one word that man had to say.

Amongst Sam the toad's messages were my mother's of course, who I will always love. I didn't need to read any of her messages because she said everything she needed to say yesterday, when I came home.

I saw a single message from my former best friend, Tara, too. Being honest with myself I was close to reading hers, but decided against it at the last second. Tara and I had been friends ever since I could remember. I had always lived in her shadow, always one step behind. I was always silver to her gold. I had never cared before about running second place, because I had loved her like a sister, and I knew she loved me back. In that I thought we were equals, but I guess I came out second best again. I did want to know why she betrayed me like that though. In a way her betrayal hurt even more then Sam's did. Sisters were supposed to have each other's backs; sisters before misters or chicks before dicks, was what we used to say. We always thought boys were like aliens. We never ended up having a full understanding of their kind. We always knew boys were a dangerous commodity, but your girlfriend was supposed to be your safety net, so for your best friend to stab you in the back like that was unthinkable, and unforgivable.

I was tempted to read her message, but that temptation wasn't strong enough to override my disgust I now felt for her. My thought process was: why should I have to listen to what they have to say? Why should I have to listen to them try to justify their actions, to try and manipulate me into forgiving? It was pathetic; I wouldn't have a bar of it. I wasn't going to put myself through that. Today was a new day, my new beginning. I had been reborn from the darkness, through pain and suffering and now I would come out a whole new person. I still wondered how my stuff got to be on the table though. They should have been still at Sam's work. As if my mother had read my mind or just saw me staring at them, she blurted out from behind me, making me jump in surprise.

"Your father went and picked up your car yesterday after Sam dropped off your keys and shoes."

"Oh, that makes sense" I responded. Then, after changing my thought patterns to what she just said, from the empty void it just came from, I quizzed, "Sam came here?" and then added straight after, "What did he want?"

"Sam just wanted to talk to you about last night, but I told him you were sleeping, and you would speak to him when you got up," Mum answered.

"Oh," I uttered, giving me time to think. "Did you tell him what happened to me?"

"No, my darling, it wasn't my place to tell him anything," my mother said. She went to the cupboard to grab a mug for her coffee. Mum loves her coffee just as much as I do, daughter like mother in that regard. "Your father told me that it was over between you two. Is that true?" she said.

I realised with that question that Dad hadn't told her what happened between us. I was relieved and disappointed at the same time. I knew I would have to bite the bullet sooner or later about telling her. With Tara gone that moved Mum up to best friend status. It was pretty sad, but my Mum was awesome so I didn't care.

"It's really over this time," I replied, knowing Mum's follow up question would be, "What happened?"

"I went to surprise Sam at work and found him with Tara," I revealed to her a little shyly. Mum winced a bit at the news. She knew the damage that would have on me, the heartache attached. Mum had never taken to Sam. I never knew why she didn't warm to him. She was always pleasant and nice to him for my sake, but I could see she never thought of him as part of the family as he was intended to be. I guess she always saw through his façade that I was blinded by.

"I always knew Sam had a wandering eye, but I could tell he loved you deeply. I thought that would have been enough," she said. She looked as shocked as I was. I don't think the surprise was about Sam though.

I found I was right when she added, "But, Tara. I always thought she was a good girl, a bit wild, but a true friend."

"That's what I thought too," I concurred. "Who knew she was a knife in your back type of girl," I added, barely able to get out the last word. The thought of how much I loved her and all the good times we had spent together started to flood in.

Mum looked at me with sorrow. My pain was her pain. I could see she felt it too. Tara basically lived here as a kid. Mum was like a second mother to her. Mum came around and sat next to me, her coffee placed on the table, steam lifting from the hot liquid.

"It will get easier," she said.

"I know," I replied, not really knowing. All I knew at the moment was that the ache in my heart still burned and the only thing that seemed to seal the wound was hate.

"Have you spoken to either of them yet?" she asked.

"No, and I don't want to," I said bitterly. I spoke with more emotion behind it than I meant to, and with more of the hidden hatred I now felt for them. I turn to face my mother. Her brown hair had a few grey strands flowing through it these days. Her hair was all tied up in a ponytail. She had no makeup on and she was wearing a dressing-gown and even now I thought she was still a stunningly attractive woman. I just hoped I still looked half as good at her age.

Mum's beautiful face had such sadness to it at the moment. I swear she felt my pain, and I was not talking about the cuts and bruises. I still felt so ashamed like I did with Dad, like I let them down, like somehow it was my fault. Which I know it wasn't, but the feeling was still there, and I couldn't shake it. No words would form in my brain and come out my mouth. I didn't want to lie anymore, and I didn't want to tell the truth. I wished I could tell her what really happened after I found Tara and Sam together, but I knew it was for the best if I didn't. After a moment's hesitation Mum placed a hand on mine rubbing it slightly. When she thought it was safe to talk again she asked, "Does Sam know it is over?"

I thought about this for a minute. We hadn't spoken since I caught him with his pants down, literally. So maybe he thought our relationship was still salvageable. I don't know why he would want to salvage anything. He was the one who went astray. He was the one who didn't want me; he wanted my best friend instead. But who knew what that toad would come up with, in his tiny brain between his legs.

"Not in so many words, but I think he'll get the point eventually when I don't talk to him for the rest of my life," I said looking out into empty space still trapped inside my own head.

"I think you owe it to yourself to get some closure. It might help with the healing process," Mum pronounced with full understanding of my situation, and only having my best intentions in mind.

"Maybe you're right," I said, "I'll think about it."

When does that shift happen, from when your mother went from being a Mum to a friend, and then just as quickly transformed back again, when she got up from the table and asked, "Do you want me to make you some pancakes with ice cream?" That sounded like some good break up food.

"Yes, please" I said, "But you have to show me how you do it?" Mum looked back at me confused. I could see the words in her brain saying, that's new.

"Alright, honey, but you just watch for now and finish your coffee."

"I can do that," I confirmed giving the task at hand my full attention.

Mum walked to the fridge to gather the ingredients before asking, "Do you think you want to speak to Tara again?"

It was like she had said the Devil's name because just then my phone rang. I had deleted Tara's number, but I knew the last three digits of her number and the numbers that now flashed on my phone matched Tara's. I looked at my Mum asking with my wide eyes, what do I do?.

"Do you want me to answer it for you?" she offered.

I thoroughly thought about taking her up on her offer. I could ignore the call but today was the day to get rid of all my trash, so I picked up my phone and answered.

"Hello, who is this?" I asked knowing full well who it was. The reply took a while to come. She must have expected her info to come up on my phone, and for me to know who I was talking to. Maybe she was thinking of hanging back up.

"It's Tara," she finally said very carefully.

"What do you want?" I snapped back quickly, wanting to get this over with.

"I wanted to say sorry," she said shakily. I had never heard her like this before. There was already loss in her tone of voice.

"Sorry, not accepted. Anything else?" I snapped again.

"I really am sorry, Sarah," she protested.

"I really don't care," I declared, "But what did you expect? You can go shag my boyfriend behind my back, and we can still be best of friends when I find out?"

"I know I stuffed up, but I don't want to lose you. You are my best friend."

"Well you should have thought of that before you slept with my boyfriend," I bark back.

"I know, and I'm sorry Sarah," she replied, her voice starting to crack, the loss growing louder.

"You broke my heart, Tara. We were supposed to have each other's backs," I choked out getting emotional as well.

"I know," she said again.

"Just tell me one thing," I demanded, "Why would you throw away a lifetime of friendship for a root?"

Tara had been tame and apologetic so far, but with that question something snapped, and the real Tara came out. It was a side of Tara I had never seen before. Her tongue must have started to fill up with the anger she had hidden over a lifetime of friendship with me.

"I was jealous of you and Sam. Okay?" she sneered. "Did you ever wonder why I strutted around all the time? Why I always walked in front of you in clubs?"

I didn't answer her. I was taken aback by the change in her attitude, and the fact that I might have never known the real Tara. She went on after my silence answering her own question, "It's because you're little miss perfect; with the perfect parents, the perfect boyfriend. You're the girl next door. You're the girl all the boys want to take home to mummy."

I heard the tears in her eyes as she went on, "I just wanted to take some of that perfect for myself. I'm not like you, Sarah. I'm just the pretty poster on the wall that gets replaced next calendar month by another pretty girl."

Tara's sobs came out harder now. All this built up hidden envy flowing free was overwhelming her.

"If you are trying to make me feel sorry for you it won't work," I said.

A new wave of strength came over me, stopping me from breaking down. I never knew she bottled up all those feelings towards me. I always thought I was in her shadow, but it seemed she thought I was the brighter star in the sky.

"I'm just saying I hated you for being so perfect all the time," she admitted.

"Then why be my friend at all if you hated me so much?" I asked, finding it harder and harder to keep myself level.

"Because you were the girl next door for me too. I loved you as much as I envied you," Tara wailed.

"You know there is no coming back from this don't you?" I said, forcing the words out.

As much as I wanted to hate Tara, I couldn't. I tried to hate her. Hating her dulled the blade she left in my back, but her blade missed my heart and I just couldn't hate her.

I was pissed off at her for sure, and I could never stand to see her face again, but hate was a strong word. I didn't want to see her dead or anything. There was too much sisterly love for that to vanish overnight. She really was like a sister to me, but I was right with what I said however; there is no coming back from this. That sisterly bond broke with her betrayal.

"I know," she said, the sound of tears falling echoed through her voice.

"Have a nice life, Tara," I said, and with that I hung up, not bothering to hear her goodbyes. My mother was pretending not to eavesdrop as she cooked, but it was all undone when she put down the bowl, and came around and gave me a lasting hug.

"At least you will always have me."

"I love you too, Mum," I said.

After a long moment of hugging I said, "I was really looking forwards to those pancakes and ice-cream."

"I totally forgot," Mum responded. "The coffee hasn't turned on all the switches in my brain yet."

I turned to the TV wiping my face getting any tears that had dropped unknowingly. Then I realised my bad luck runs in twos when I noticed a news reporter pop up on the TV screen holding a microphone to her mouth. She was standing in an industrial area, just outside a strip of white and blue barrier tape. Police were scurrying around everywhere, and a body lying on the ground covered with a plastic tarp.

CHAPTER 12

My blood ran cold, my hands started to go clammy. I didn't think I even blinked, my eyes not wanting to miss one millisecond. My focus was undivided. All that was left in the world was me, and the reporter on TV.

The news reporter spoke, *"Last night at approximately nine pm Jordan Cole, aged 32 was involved in a fatal stabbing. Jordan Cole was one of the Creatures of Chaos motorcycle club's leading members. Mr Cole was allegedly a prime suspect in the trafficking of drugs, such as cocaine, heroin and ice. Mr Cole was also famous for his prostitution connections."*

A picture of Jordan Cole, aka Mr Big Bikie appeared on the screen. That was him alright. I would never forget that tattooed face. The words "Ride or Die," were tattooed over his eyebrow, making it undeniable that that was the man that wanted to rape, and murder me.

A cold shiver ran up my spine. My hands were clutching my coffee cup so hard that I was afraid that it might shatter in my hands. The whispering sound came across my consciousness as the memory of Mr Big Bikie said, "I'm going to fuck you." The feeling of his sex organ running up my leg came with it. I crossed my legs in reaction.

A police officer appeared on the screen next, the name at the bottom of the screen read Sergeant Daniel Spade.

"What can you tell us about the case?" The reporter asked.

"The deceased name is Jordan Cole and it appears he suffered a knife wound to the neck. We recovered a set of prints off the weapon but we won't know the results until a later date," Sergeant Spade said.

"Do you have any idea who is responsible?" The reporter asked next.

"No we do not. We can only speculate at this stage," The sergeant answered.

"Do you think it could be a rival bikie club? The Creatures of Chaos club has been at war with the Insurgents for years," the reporter said.

"We don't have any evidence to suggest their involvement, but we are not ruling them out either. Thank you, that will be all." Sergeant Spade turned away.

The reporter's face appeared back on the TV set as he started saying, *"Jordan Cole is the younger brother of Louis Cole, who is said to be a key member of the Creatures of Chaos bikie gang also."*

A picture of Louis Cole flashed up on the TV. Louis looked much like his brother but without the tattoos on his face. Louis and Jordan had the same hard edge look to them. Had the same short cropped hair and piercing eyes, but Louis had more of a businessman look rather than an outlaw. I didn't know why, but the sight of Louis scared me more than Mr Big Bikie. Perhaps it was because I knew he was still out there, searching for me, and wanting to kill me.

The reporter continued, *"Experts say that this could lead to another bikie war that will leave a trail of dead bodies in its wake."*

I had almost forgotten where I was, and who was there with me. My mother's voice came into focus once the news report finished, "Sarah, are you ok?"

I turned to look at my mother. I didn't respond. The inescapable feeling of being trapped flooded my psyche, like there was nowhere I could go to get away from those people. Somehow those bikies had even followed me home. I could tell my eyes had grown wide with fright. I felt dizzy. My chest hurt, and I found it hard to breathe. I think I'm having a panic attack I thought, either that or a heart attack.

"Is everything alright Hun? It looked like you were in some sort of a trance, and now you have gone as white as a ghost." Mum walked around the kitchen bench towards me.

Before I knew it I blurted out, "I'm fine Mum. I just need to lie down for a minute."

"That sounds like a good idea, darling."

I got up and speed-walked to my room, not able to get there fast enough. I even forgot about all the bad memories that the room contained. I just ran straight to my room out of habit. I closed the door behind me, falling to the ground grasping my chest, trying to get control of my breathing. I had such a deep sensation that I was about to die. That this was going to be the end for me. I had lived through the terrors of the previous night, only to come undone by a news broadcast.

After what seemed like forever, but was most likely only about ten minutes give or take, my breathing started to return to normal with long even inhales and exhales. The pain in my chest had receded to a dull ache, and the dizziness in my head had diminished. Still lying on the carpet on my bedroom floor, I made the effort to try and sit up slowly, trying to regain my equilibrium.

What just happened to me? I wondered.

The fear that washed over me was intoxicating. Seeing Mr Big Bikie knocked my feet out from under me and then seeing his brother Louis nearly dug my grave. Louis was still out there; the whole Creatures of Chaos brotherhood was still out there searching for David and me.

I told myself I would be strong, that I would triumph over fear, and that I would come out victorious to its onslaught of impacts. I was not going to let fear dictate my life, I was meant to be the dictator. I had underestimated the effects of fear. Wishing to be rid of fear and actually ridding yourself of it was a lot harder than I first thought. Fear had rendered me mute, numbed my senses to happiness. It then left behind pain and a sickness that nearly swallowed me up. My world had turned into a sunless, endless night, where I was exposed to all of the world's conflicts and its miseries.

Baby steps, I told myself, before I hit the bottom of the bottomless pit. I got up off the floor. I stood up straight, took in a long empowering breath, and shook my hands like they were wet, trying to shake off that episode.

Step one. Take back what was mine starting with this room. I pulled off the bed covers, and threw them next to the door. I went to my chest of drawers, gathered up all Sam's clothes that he left behind for when he slept over. I then pulled out any of my clothes that reminded me of him or Tara and tossed them with the rest at the door. I went through the entire room collecting anything that was Sam's or Tara's or reminded me of them. It took me six trips of going up and down the stairs, bumping in to walls with my new found depth perception, and my feet starting to throb, to drag all of the now radioactive remains outside to the backyard.

These belongings had to be eliminated. I found myself in the garage sorting through my father's junk until I found what I was looking for. An old jerry-can that was full of unleaded petrol for the lawn mower. I dragged the jerry-can out to the pile of clothes, books, diaries, jewellery, pictures and everything else that was part of my past that I wished to incinerate.

The last thing I added was my three-hundred dollar shoes Sam dropped off. The shoes I left behind that fateful night. I placed them neatly on top thinking they are totally worthless to me now. I emptied the jerry-can onto the stack of possessions, only leaving enough fuel for a line leading back from the awaiting fire ball.

I lit a match, watched the flame ignite into existence. I watched it move with the wind, like it was dancing. Like it was trying to speak to me; saying I am yours, give me food and I will do your bidding. The match left my hand flying through the air until it came upon its delicious meal I prepared for it. The flame didn't disappoint. It ran the length to the pile of memories, then engulfing them in a destructive force of heat with ferocity to consume and destroy.

Eventually all matter was transformed into a black melted crumbling pile of char and ash. All that was left at the end was a pile of burnt remnants, just as my feelings had become for Sam and Tara. They were gone with the ash in the wind, leaving nothing but a blackened stain on the earth.

I returned back to my room finding it practically empty. I had converted my room into a blank canvas. The room was now full of endless possibilities, a place to create new hopes and dreams.

CHAPTER 13

Two weeks had passed like a blur; day after day, hour by hour, and minute after minute all rolling into one long stream of a fuzzy fog of time. On the plus side I could now cook pancakes, and did my own laundry; baby steps remember.

No one from the Creatures of Chaos gang had come after me, so I was starting to feel safe in my own home again. I was still going to follow David's advice though, just in case. I hadn't returned to work yet. My work was pretty understanding after I told them I had been hit by a car. If only it was the truth.

My aches and pains were healing up nicely, which was a plus. I could see out of two eyes now, so that was a positive. I still had some leftover bruising though. It had gone that yellowy sick colour now, but Dad said that was a good thing; I didn't know if I agreed. I could walk now without that needle like acupuncture agony on the soles of my feet, so that was a win. I hadn't had another panic attack thankfully, no more news reports for me.

I was starting to feel like I was getting control of myself again. I thought I was becoming the master of my own universe, but little did I know that I had a long way to go before I held that title. The looming black hole left in my solar system was the light sucking, matter comprising, Samuel Rushton. When I deleted Sam off my phone I also blocked his number so he could no longer call me. I didn't even answer any unknown numbers just in case it was him. That still didn't stop Sam from trying to contact me through other sources, though. Sam called Mum trying to get through to me. She told him that she wasn't going to be the middle woman between us, and I would talk to him when or if I ever wanted to.

I don't think he got the point, because he kept calling Mum until she got me to block his number from her phone as well. Sam must have thought my mother was more persuadable to his charms. How wrong he was. She was the one that saw through his disguise from the start. She only played nice for my sake, and because she was a too nice of a person to be rude.

He never tried calling my Dad, however.

Now I think about it, I don't think my Dad ever liked him much either. Maybe Sam picked up on that fact and kept his distance, or it wouldn't surprise me if my Dad frightened him, somewhat. Dad always tolerated him, shook his hand and talked the small talk, but the more I think back there was no joy in it for Dad, it was just empty conversation.

I thought I understood the meaning behind the saying *Love is blind*, now. I wish my parents had said something, but then again if they had, I wouldn't have believed them, hence the saying. I had thought about what Mum had suggested about ending it properly. She thought I should have that face-to-face breakup. That I should say all the things I've wanted to say, find out all the stuff I've been scratching my head about, to have that closure a five-year relationship deserves.

I came to the conclusion that Mum knows best. I did need to have a talk with Sam. I needed to get my message across that we had broken up, and for him to leave me the hell alone. I needed to put this whole mess behind me, and move on with my life. But I couldn't do that with Sam lingering behind the bushes. I didn't even understand it. I thought by the fact that he was sexing someone else that he didn't want me any longer. I told you men were like aliens from another planet; totally impossible to understand.

I was psyching myself up for the Sam encounter. As much as I denied my true feeling, I still felt something for Sam. Much like Tara after five years of loving someone, that love didn't just disappear after one night, much as you wanted it to.

The feelings I felt for Sam had morphed into something else though. My love for him had darkened, the passion was the same but it had turned to hate. With Tara I was more disappointed and disgusted rather than hateful. I might even pity her a little now after that phone call, but when I thought of Sam rage was starting to fill my vision.

I said before, that hate was a strong word, but in this case with Samuel Rushton the meaning was living up to its full potential. I blamed him for everything; my broken heart, losing my best friend, getting bashed and almost raped. It was entirely his fault.

On the flip side, the longer I waited to build up my nerve, the longer Sam would have to stew in his pot, boiling up to a point of insufferable suffering. The thought made me smile.

That moment when you thought you were in control of the situation. That you thought you were playing the game by your set of rules. It was then you could misread the layout, and realise that there were no rules in the game of love. I realised this by a knock on the door.

The knock on the door came to me as an echoing sound rattling around in my head, like someone consistently trying to bang in a nail that won't budge. At the same time I became nervous. I can't see through solid objects, I still wasn't Supergirl. I hadn't had the slightest clue who was knocking at the front door. It could have been anyone; a sales person, Mum's friend Jill, or kids selling cookies for charity. My heart started to beat a bit faster. I got butterflies in my stomach when I heard that continuous pounding on the door. There was no way I could have known that it was going to be my sly ex-boyfriend at the door. But somehow my gut knew it was Sam.

My body was sending me signals the only way it knew how. It was speaking to me through an accelerated heart rate, and butterflies flying around in my stomach. It was trying to warn me of an upcoming confrontation I wasn't looking forward to, that I had been putting off.

My father answered the door. I was in the front lounge on the sofa too frightened to move, too scared that I might be right about who was at the door. I was close enough to be able to hear my father say, "She doesn't want to see you right now. Don't come back again unless invited, or else I'll call the cops and that's only if I don't feel like chasing you down with my five iron."

I could hear the anxiety in Sam's voice that was mixed with frustration and urgency when he replied, "Please, Mr Smith, I have to talk to her. I'm going crazy here."

"I can see that, Sam. But that doesn't change the fact that she doesn't want to see you right now. So jump back into your shiny red car and get off my property," Dad demanded. I could hear Sam stutter something unintelligible before I heard the squeak of the door hinges as Dad started to close it on Sam's face.

I don't know why I got up, but I did. Maybe I just wanted to get this confrontation over and done with. Whatever possessed me to take the leap through the flames I'll never know. What I did know, was that Sam wasn't going to go away without some sort of closure. I would have bet a thousand bucks that he would have camped outside on the nature strip if I didn't go outside to talk to him.

The guy sounded desperate, and desperate people do desperate things. I caught the door mid-swing with one hand, and my other hand landing on my father's shoulder. Dad looked at me giving me his, are-you-sure face, before letting go of the door, and stepping back so I could pass. But that was only after I shot back my, I-got-this face. Dad and I had always had an unspoken language, like sign language but with face expressions. I opened the door, then stepped outside, closing the door behind me. I stood in front of an unshowered, unshaven, sleep deprived, and very distressed version of Sam. His demeanour changed when he saw the bruising on my face. Sam's expression went from a guilty anxiety to one of showing genuine concern.

"What happen to you? Are you ok?" Sam asked, with anguish in his voice. He took a step towards me arms outstretched reaching for mine forgetting the turmoil between us. He was put back in his place when I instinctively took a step back banging my head on the door. I masked the pain that shot down my spine as the contact was made. I had got good at hiding pain in the last two weeks.

Sam's face dropped, remembering the reason why I took a step back rather than a jump into his embrace for comfort. I had forgotten that Sam didn't know about what happened to me. Sam and I were once like one. There wasn't one thing that other didn't know. We talked about everything. Our deepest darkest secrets all exposed on the floor for the other's mercy. Now I questioned everything, had I ever really known this guy?

"I was hit by a car, but I'm fine now. No thanks to you," I said, trying to rub as much salt in the wound as possible.

"You look terrible Sarah, when did this happened? Did they catch the guy?" The questions would have kept rolling off Sam's tongue, like a throat full of spew if I hadn't cut him off.

"It happened the night I found you banging my best friend," I spat out, anger rising up at the sight of him. Sam went to say something but was silenced with an uplifted hand sign that told him to stop and listen.

"I know you didn't just come here to insult the way I look, so what do you want?" my words came out sounding more tired than I wanted them to.

"I didn't mean to insul…," Sam said before being cut off by the stopping hand again.

"What do you want?" I repeated, more forcefully. Then I answered my own question by adding, "You obviously don't want me, why don't you just go and harass Tara?" I snorted out, the anger growing stronger inside me. Sam hesitated, wanting to choose his words carefully before speaking.

"It wasn't like that with Tara, it was just sex. There were no feelings involved. I don't love her, I love you. I can't live without you. Sarah, can't you see that?"

"It was just sex, huh?" I huffed.

"Yes," Sam responded, signs of hope in his eyes. The hope I could understand his actions. The hope I could sympathise. The hope I could forgive.

"So tell me Sam. Is the sex with me that bad you had to fuck someone else to get your rocks off, and the closest pussy around will do?" I said shattering any hope in his eyes.

"No, you're not bad in bed, it's just…," Sam declared before pausing, realising the word slip. I noticed the word slip too, so I pushed the issue.

"It's just what, Sam? The grass is greener on the other side, is that it? Do you want your cake and eat it too. Or maybe you want to sleep with Tara, and keep me on a leash like a well-trained dog?" I growled.

No response came, so I pushed again. "It's just what, Sam?" I repeated with a menacing tone that sounded a bit like my father's voice when he got angry.

"A guy just wants variety in his sex life. You know people are not supposed to be monogamous, it's a proven fact," he said, with a straight face.

"Bullshit. Don't use that excuse on me. People are what they choose to be. I stayed monogamous for you. That is just a cop out and you know it."

The fury inside me was about to explode, the fire burning behind my eyes had coals searing hot. Now I was on a roll, so I asked, "Did Jane and Greg know?"

Sam looked down at his feet as he replied sheepishly, "Yes." Just as I thought. Now I was getting answers, I asked another one, "How long have you and Tara been having an affair?"

This one looked harder for Sam to answer, it took longer anyway before he said, "Just a few months."

"Just. I am beginning to hate that word," I declared, "So all the times you were too tired to be with me, or working late, you were with her?" Sam looked down again, obvious shame breathing through him as he responded, "Yes."

"Just tell me one last thing, Sam. Why Tara? Why my best friend of all people?" I questioned.

"It was Tara that hit on me," Sam said, trying to pass the buck. As mad as I was at Tara, Sam could still have said no. He could have been faithful to me, even if he was telling the truth.

"So it was all Tara's fault then," I hissed back.

"No, not all her fault, but mostly," Sam said, with a look of pure honesty spread across his face.

"You are unbelievable. At least if you had owned up to your actions I would have respected you that little bit more, but you are as low as a man can go. I don't know how I ever loved you for as long as I did," I said, getting fully frustrated and fed up.

I had had enough of this conversation. I had only got madder and madder since I walked through the door. If I thought I had any feelings left for Sam, they had vanished now. Mum was definitely right, I did need this closure. All I wanted was to get rid of this man from my life, starting now.

"If you didn't get the hint before by my ignoring you, then let me make this clear. We are over. Don't try and contact me anymore, you are a stain on my existence. You are a misspelled word on my essay that I want to rub out. I hope you and Tara have a wonderful life together. Bye Samuel I never want to see you again," I told him. Then turned to go back inside, not wanting to look at his sorrowing face any longer, or hear any more of his bullshit.

I felt a hand grasp my arm, then the words, "I love you, Sarah, I'm sorry." I shook his hand off not looking back, my patience wearing thin. Sam's words came first, "I made a mistake. Please take me back." Then the hand landed on my arm again. The grip was more solid. I wouldn't have been able to merely shake it off this time.

When he grabbed me I remembered feeling hopeless when those bikies had me over that park bench. I remembered feeling exposed, feeling like a toy about to be passed around from person to person. I made a promise to myself that I would never be that hopeless again. Then, some primal instinct took over. All my rage and fury erupted into one moment of wrath. I spun back on Sam as quick as a snake striking its prey, but my prey was Sam's nose.

The closest thing I had ever done to throwing a punch was the fresh air punches we did in Tae-bo, but that all changed when my fist connected with impressive force on Sam's nose. The sound of a twig snapping came from the impact. Sam was taken by surprise, stumbling about three spaces back, his hands covering his nose, blood already leaking through his fingers. Now, moving gracefully like a cat stalking its prey, I covered the three steps before Sam even looked up.

My leg swung hard up between his legs, sending his balls straight through to his eye sockets. The blow made Sam hunch over and drop to the floor, curling up like a frightened mouse. I stared down at Sam, stunned at what I had done. It was like I was just a bystander watching myself from afar. I stood over Sam with my heart pounding, hands shaking and feeling totally exhilarated. The feeling of power and dominance washed over me. I was no longer the victim but the aggressor. The feeling was almost evil in nature, but enlivening and thrilling, like I was God passing down a punishment to the wicked and sinful.

Awareness then shot through me, like I just had woken from a dream. The feeling of euphoria washing away, like a raindrop rolling down my naked skin until it hit the ground being absorbed back into the earth. I ran back inside, and slammed the door behind me. I leaned my forehead on the door, breathing hard in amazement of what just happened. My breathing eventually slowed, and my heart rate returned to a natural rhythmic beat.

"Are you okay? Darling," the voice was my mother's I realised after a moment. It didn't change the fact that the question startled me. Both my parents were staring at me with worried expressions on their faces. My mother's words took a while to reach the part of my brain that would come up with a response.

"Sorry, what did you say?" I replied, needing more time to think.

"I said 'Are you okay?'" my mother repeated. This time I understood her question.

"I really don't know," I finally replied truthfully.

I really didn't know why it felt so good to do something so bad.

CHAPTER 14

"*Such* is life."

A phrase said by the infamous Australian, Ned Kelly. His final words, if I remember correctly. It rang true for so many people in bad situations, but only those that accepted their fate found the full understanding from this quote. "Such is life" meant an acceptance of the unpredictable fortunes of existence.

I didn't know if there was a divine power that set in motion the events that lead us down the path to cause and effect. As if the sisters of fate from the old Greek pagan gods were real. As if Lahkesis, Atropos and Clotho determined the destiny for every man woman and child. It would be as if everything was predestined, and not coincidence or the luck of the draw.

But what I did know was that most people were ignorant to the plain and simple fact that, life could be cruel. People could be cruel, and all actions had consequences, good or bad. Ned Kelly's course of action led him to the noose. Mine led me to where I was today, sitting in my bedroom, living with my mum and dad with nothing left to lose. I had hit rock bottom, I had hit the ass end of that bottomless pit. Now all there was left to do was start to climb back up.

Luckily for me my story did not end there. I had the good fortune to be able to analyse my past, manage my present and coordinate my future. Live by my own ideals, reassess my life and shape it the way I saw fit. The philosophy I was choosing to live by now was, *Life is what you make it*, and I would make it mine. Screw the sisters of fate, I would spit in their faces and tell them I would determine my own destiny and you would never make me a victim ever again.

What I did to Sam was not the right course of action, I knew that. But it was the one that happened. I couldn't change the past even if I wanted to, which I didn't. The thoughts of what I did keep creeping back to me. The brutality that was thrust through me, it unleashed something. I knew what I did to Sam was wrong, but a beast inside me rose up and kicked some ass. And I loved it. With a clear mind that wasn't corrupted by my brain's amygdala, the part of the brain that dealt with my emotions; the part that was being flooded by my brain's neurotransmitters and the hormones, adrenaline and noradrenaline, that caused that moment of pure fury. I knew the science behind my outburst, after a Google search, of course. But what came out of me was something translucent, something that felt alive that took over my body.

I wouldn't wish that savagery on my worst enemy, and then there I go inflicting that sort of severity on Sam in a fit of rage. The man I once loved. Had my morals changed that much? Or was there just a part of me that needed to be released, something bottled up until it was shaken and the cork popped. Like a demon locked in a cage, and then given the keys to come out and play. Something David said to me came to mind while sitting on my bed scrutinising every word, every movement, every feeling, and every action I did while confronting Sam.

"Violence should never be the answer. It always leads to more violence." David's words were left ringing in my ears, never quite fading away, always sounding back up again.

Going over the whole encounter with Sam again and again in my head I always returned back to the violence. I kept remembering the feeling of ecstasy. The satisfaction I felt inflicting physical pain on him. I had never felt anything like it, it was exhilarating. I had never felt more alive. David's words repeat in my mind again, "Violence is never the answer." It made me wonder, was this how serial killers thought? I knew what I did was terrible, but it felt so good. This must be the inner turmoil that plagues the minds of the insane. Or was it insane to squash these savage impulses because we were led to believe that it was wrong from the law of the land.

What if the laws were wrong? What was wrong or right anyway? Who was the judge of good and evil? Everyone had their own interpretation of these notions, and it made you wonder who really had the right to judge anybody. Was it wrong to steal a loaf of bread to feed a starving family? Either way you looked at it, it was my opinions that count to me. It was my notion of right and wrong that mattered, nobody else's. I had always thought violence was never the answer. I never should have done what I did, no matter how good it made me feel. Fighting should only be used in self-defence or to protect loved-ones from harm.

David's business card caught the corner of my vision, like a clue to a puzzle I had to solve. The answer to my ultimatum was under my nose the whole time. I picked it up, reading the words again to make sure I had read it right the first time.

David Powers
Phone 0423 568 985
Personal trainer in fitness and health
Martial arts teachings
Meditation teachings

The answer was right in front of me the whole time. I didn't need to go native in the wild searching for blood. I needed to learn how to control my built up anger. I needed to learn how to release my frustration calmly, and govern my wrath with self-diligence.

I would get David to teach me how to fight, how to protect myself with self-defence, how to use what I learned wisely, and not to lash out in violence unnecessarily. Violence was never the answer; I hoped I could put those words into action.

CHAPTER 15

I heard the purr of David's V8 Holden before I saw the black beauty turn the corner. I had called David the previous night, telling him everything. The panic attack I had after watching the news report of Jordan Cole's death. The fight I had with Sam, and how I kicked the crap out of him. I told him I wanted to start anew, and put my old life behind me.

I didn't think David was going to take me up on my request to learn martial arts. I was surprised when he agreed, and even more so when he said we could start the next day. I was thinking maybe he would want to keep his distance since half the country was out hunting us down. But for some reason he jumped at the chance after I told him what I did to Sam. Maybe David just needed the money, who knows? I was getting what I wanted, so I'd be singing Kumbaya by the campfire tonight.

I hadn't gone back to gym since the incident. For one, I still had that purple yellowing bruising my face and the gash on my forehead that could be recognised, and David told me not to go out until I was fully healed. And, two, I really didn't want to have to punch Tara in her perfect nose if I ran into her there.

My body had healed up enough to go back. My feet were back to normal, the cut on my head wasn't going to stop me, and my ribs weren't so tender to the touch now. When I previously went to gym I normally went in the mornings, unless I did a fitness class with Tara in the afternoons, and that wouldn't be happening any more. I found that I had the most energy to burn after the sun had just risen. I was fresh and vibrant in the mornings, ready to start the day off with a bang – after a coffee, of course.

I had always been a morning gym goer, so I asked David if we could do a morning session. David complied. He made the session start at six in the morning. A bit early for my liking, but David said he had other appointments to go to after, so I took what I could get. The time was now 5.57am. I was hoping he was going to be late, but three minutes early would have to do. At least I was ready on time. It might not have gone down too well if I was still in bed, and Mum or Dad had to answer the door. At least I got down a cup of coffee before he arrived, otherwise it was a no go.

The sky was still black; stars still littered the horizon encircling the moon. The sun wouldn't come up this time of year until about 7.30am. Standing outside my house illuminated by the front outside light, I watched as David rolled up the driveway. David insisted on picking me up. He told me it would just be easier than giving me directions. He was good enough to fit me in on such late notice, so I wasn't about to start complaining.

I hopped through the passenger side door, flopping down ungracefully on the bucket seat. The car smelt like a lavender air freshener, that I saw hanging off the reversing mirror. The interior was immaculate, not a speck of dust could be seen. The cab was warm, a pleasant change from the cool morning air.

"Good morning, David," I said, a little bit more chirpy than I felt. All things aside it was still only six in the morning, maybe the excitement of what was to come was giving my unconscious mind an upbeat attitude.

David stared at me with a ferocious intensity. I swear he was burning a hole down to my soul with his eyes. I began to feel a bit awkward, shifting in my seat uneasily. Did I have something on my face, was my hair out of whack, was I wearing the wrong clothes. I was about to ask what was wrong, when he grumbled, "Morning, Sarah. Buckle up." Then he thrust the gear stick into reverse and backed out of the driveway.

"So where are we off to?" I asked, trying to make things less uncomfortable.

"You'll see. It'll take about twenty minutes to get there," he muttered.

"Alrighty then," I replied flatly, not knowing what else to add after his short sharp reply. The rest of the drive was in silence. After about ten minutes driving the houses started to disappear. There were no streetlights overhanging the road anymore. Instead they were replaced by gumtrees, tree ferns and shrubbery.

Even in the dark, with only the car's headlight to expose the scenery, the green was so vibrant, the landscape so lush and full of life. In a matter of ten minutes we went from suburbia to bush, from concrete to dirt. How did I not know that we lived so close to the wilderness? I guess I had never wanted to know. If there wasn't a McDonalds around, then it was too country for me.

The road started to climb. I was used to flat straight roads, these were near vertical and beyond curvy. I would have been scared to drive them, but David seemed to have no troubles at all, taking each turn with ease. Either it was David's great driving, or it was the car, but we were gliding around the coiled path with barely any noticeable g-force. I could see now why David insisted on driving.

A scary thought swam into my head as I looked around at the non-existence of human beings. What if he was taking me into the bush to kill me? He could push me off a cliff or something. He could just say I fell. For that matter he could just drive off, leaving me splattered on the rocks. It was dark, and no one knew where I was or who I was with. I only told Mum I was going training, I didn't tell her I was training with David. She probably just thought I was going to the gym.

What if David thought I had become too much of a liability, the risk of keeping me alive outweighed the risk of killing me. A dead person couldn't give away your secrets, but a live one could. Maybe that was why David was acting so cold towards me. I mean, how well did I really know the man? A couple hours' worth, it definitely wasn't long enough to know he wouldn't kill me; I had seen him kill before, after all. David was still basically a stranger. All the good notions I had about him could have just been really bad personality judgment on my part.

How David disposed of those bikies was a frightening thought. When it came to thinking what he could do to me, I wouldn't stand a chance. David was a man who could wipe you off the face of existence with one touch. So, getting rid of me would be child's play for him.

The two parts of my brain were in constant battle at this point, one side saying: he is taking you up to the mountains in the middle of the bush to do away with you. The other side was saying: don't be ridiculous, he wouldn't save you just to kill you later.

The anticipation was becoming unbearable. The sun wasn't even up yet, darkness still coated the earth. I was in unfamiliar territory, and I was with a man I barely knew. The same man that had stuck a knife in a man's throat. It was in self-defence, but still David was a man you didn't want to get on the wrong side of.

I was two minutes away from exploding with a barrage of questions, and insinuations when David turned off the road into a gravel car park. The car park was naked, except for one lone shining streetlight at the foot of a concrete staircase. There was a sign under the light casting a shadow like a crucifix, with writing too small for me to read. David switched the car off then turned to face me.

"Before we go any further, I need to know a few things," he demanded.

"Okay," I said, "but I need to know something as well."

"What do you want to know?" he said, letting me go first.

"Did you bring me up here to kill me?" I asked, staring at him so intently, gauging his response, waiting for any sudden threatening movements before making a run for it. David grinned, a sad crooked grin. It was a grin of sympathy not judgment at my accusation.

"No, Sarah, I would never hurt you," David answered strongly, and then quickly added, "You never have to fear me, alright?" I looked into his unflinching eyes and saw the truth in them. I also saw a protector, not a villain. It was then I knew that the man who saved me that night was the same man in the car with me now. It was then, in that moment, I knew I would never doubt him again.

I nodded, and squeaked out, "Alright."

I didn't realise I was holding my breath until I exhaled, and then needed to replenish my air supply. I was so over-paranoid after what happened to me. This was the first time away from home without my folks. My parents had become my protective security blanket that I had been clinging on tightly to. I had lost faith in this dark dangerous world, and thought everybody was out to get me.

David gave me the moment I needed to calm down before he spoke, "What do you plan on doing with the skills of the deadly arts?" I was not sure how to reply; I had never heard martial arts referred to as the deadly arts before. Then again, after seeing what David could do with the art form, deadly was the right call.

"I don't know," I said. "Maybe never get the stuffing kicked out of me again." David didn't find my words amusing, just kept his eyes fixed on me.

"I ask you this because if you plan on hurting any more people, I'll take you back home, and I'll never see you again," David said with no hesitation of chucking this car in reverse and taking off.

"No, I would never hurt anybody needlessly or on purpose. What I did to Sam was just an instinct reaction," I answered honestly, "I don't know how better to explain it. I just lost it for a second, and when I regained control he was on the ground bleeding." David stared at me weighing up my response. Perhaps he was doing that *Lie to me,* thing.

"I believe you. It is easy to react out of anger and lose control. It happens to the best of us," he said. It was a general term, but I think that statement was directed more inward. I thought I saw guilt splash on his face, but I could be stretching the thin line. "I also believe you wanted to hurt your ex, like he hurt you. Am I right?" David continued, needing to confirm what he already knew.

"Yes," I admitted, not even thinking about lying, "But I didn't know I wanted to hurt him till after I punched him in the face. The feeling I got afterwards was thrilling, and terrifying at the same time. I unleashed something inside myself that I need help to control. That is why I called you."

"I thought as much, or we wouldn't be sitting here right now," he said. "Tell me again why you want to learn the deadly arts."

The question, I thought, was a given, I had already answered this in some degree. He knew what happened to me. He should have known that I never wanted to be put in that situation again.

"So I won't ever feel so helpless like I did that night when you rescued me."

"That's only part of it," he said, "That was the first time you hit someone," a statement not a question, "You enjoyed it too. I can see it in your eyes. I heard it over the phone. There is a fire behind your eyes that wasn't there before, a flame that burns for more. Your heart is good, but you had a taste of a drug and you want more. Am I right?" I looked away.

"Yes," not able to look at his angelic face.

I am ashamed of myself, and I am astonished that he was able to read me so well, and with such ease. Then it dawned on me, he knew. David knew that feeling of the thrilling power as you hurt someone. He knew that dark side of being a human, and how good it felt to embrace it. It was that animal instinct that came out, and took over when you overshadowed a person you had just knocked down. That feeling that uplifted you to massive heights and you didn't know whether you would keep soaring the skies or crash back down to earth.

David had experienced the lust for blood, and he had mastered the beast within. He knew. I bottled that one away for another day.

"Ok then, I will teach you how to control your rage. You will have to learn how to control your whole being, mind, body and soul," David said, "All are equally as important as each other when learning self-control."

"Are you going to teach me meditation, like on your business card?"

"I will teach you control in all areas, and yes, meditation will be part of it." David paused, looked down at his wristwatch then went on, "One last thing I need to know. How much do you want to learn? And how dedicated are you going to be in learning what I need to teach you?"

Without even thinking, and looking soulfully into his eyes, I said unwavering "I want to learn everything." Our gaze held, until he blinked it away.

"It won't be easy, and you will get frustrated at times. I won't be teaching you self-defence until I think you're ready," he said.

"I'll do whatever it takes."

"Okay then, let's get started."

I knew David could tell from my attitude that I was dedicated to the cause. That I would live and breathe his instructions, that this was now the single most important thing in my life. I had nothing else to look forward to but this.

"Okay," I echoed, after a long moment.

"Before we start you have to promise me something," David said.

"Alright, if I can," I responded.

"You can, and you will, if you want me to teach you," David said authoritatively. "I only have one rule, and you must never break it or we are done."

"What is it then, Mr Cryptic?" I said, trying to lighten the mood unsuccessfully.

"Never, and I mean never use what I teach you on anyone, unless your life depends on it," David declared.

"I promise," not needing to say anymore. The look in my eyes exposing the truth in my promise.

Outside the car the air was much colder, probably more noticeable after jumping out of a warm car. David spotted me wrapping my arms around my body, and then rubbing my arms trying to keep warm.

"The air is thinner up here, makes it colder. But don't worry though; you will be warm enough, soon enough," David told me.

I hoped he was right because I was freezing. David walked over to the concrete staircase throwing a backpack over his shoulder. He put one foot on the first step, then said, "This is the thousand step Kokoda memorial walk. It takes an average person an hour to reach the top; I want you to do it in less."

Hang on, I thought. Then expressing my thoughts in words I

asked, "I thought you were going to teach me how to control my emotions. How does this help?"

"You will see the wisdom in the climb by the time you reach the top," David said with the first smile on his face since I got into the car.

"If you say so, Sensei," I replied unenthusiastically.

"Up we go," David urged with equal enthusiasm.

There were no lights clearing the path for the track, so David had given me a flashlight so I could navigate the steps safely.

Half way up David started to tell me about the battle fought at Papua New Guinea over sixty years ago. Saying that it was arguably the most significant battle the Australian's faced in World War Two. If the Japanese had pushed Australia out of the region they would have been open to attack Queensland.

"Many more lives could have been lost if they had reached Australian shores. The men that took the fight to the Japanese were cast as heroes. They saved many lives at the cost of their own. Over six-hundred men died, and over one thousand were wounded in the battle. This challenge is just a minuscule taste of what those men went through. Those men didn't walk on concrete steps, but instead trudged through mud and slop for days with heavy packs half my weight. This is a way to show them tribute."

David was a deeper man than his biceps suggested. There was so much to this man – unlike anyone I had ever met. He surprised me at every turn. David said that this track was just a splash in the ocean compared to what those brave Aussies and the Fuzzy Wuzzy angels went through in the war.

I had to hand it to those diggers; they must have been some tough men. These steps were hard enough, let alone if they were made of mud. The whole time through the story David's breath stayed even, no rapid breathing or loss of breath, the man must be super fit. I bet he could go for hours without breaking a sweat.

I was struggling big time, my legs burned, I thought a few time that I was about to pass out from lack of oxygen to the brain; or vomit all over my shoes. David's pace up the stairs was unattainable for me, but I did my best to keep up. I wanted to prove to him I was no slacker.

By the time we reached the end of the stairs I was covered in sweat, my face must have been flushed red, my legs felt like jelly, and my lungs were about to fall out my mouth I was breathing so hard. But I made it without hurling on my feet, so win, win. I was bending over, my hands on my knees when David passed me a bottle of water.

"Well done Sarah, you did a lot better than I thought you were going to do," he praised.

"Thanks," was all I was able to get out.

I took the bottle undoing the lid about to scull the entire thing when David said, "Don't drink too much or you will throw it back up."

Once I caught my breath, I asked, "Are we going back down now?"

"Not just yet. You haven't seen why I dragged you up here at this ungodly hour. And we made it just in time too. Follow me," he said. I was curious to see what I had to travel a thousand steps to look at, so I followed David as he started to walk towards a clearing.

At the edge of the clearing was a lookout point. David told me to turn off the flashlight plunging us into darkness, or so I thought. I was so overwhelmed by reaching the last step, and trying to recover my composure that I had missed the sun starting to break through the black of night. It was starting to creep up over the mountains, painting a spectacular reddish orange on the clouds.

Along the path the foliage was so dense that no light passed through, and I was so focused on putting one foot in front of the other that I forgot the sun was coming up.

The colours reflecting off the clouds were becoming fuller and richer with every passing second. I could say with certainty that I had never sat down and watched a sunrise before. Up here with David, in the ambience of nature, waiting for the sun to peek its nose over the hill I realised there was tranquillity to the world I had never noticed before. With all the ugly things the world had to offer, there was as much beauty to match it. You just needed to know where to look.

The sun then stuck its head from upon the mountainside bathing us in its light. The view was magical.

CHAPTER 16

That night after the stairway to Kokoda, I slept like a baby; a baby with a full belly of milk, that is. I don't know if it was from the exertion of powering up those stairs, or from the realisation that there was still beauty left in the world that made me sleep so soundly. Either way I was grateful. It was the best night's sleep I had had since that life-changing night and, God, it felt good. It was good to learn that life hadn't turned into a shade of grey, where everything was just black and white and everything in between.

Seeing that sunset was a reminder that life can be full of colour too. That life can be full of unexplored adventures, that there are new experiences, and new sensations to be had. I had been shown that life was still worth living, and we must prove ourselves worthy of it. That life was a gift, and through persistence, courage and determination life could be great, and you could overcome any adversity. Above all, my first assumption of David was right. I never should have doubted him. He showed me kindness when others showed me malevolence. He showed me beauty when others showed me ugliness.

I lay in bed, the morning sun through my window casting shadows, and I thought to myself, I had another lesson with David today. I was grateful it wasn't quite so early this time.

How was a man like David still unattached? He hadn't told me anything to the contrary, but by the look of his house and only getting introduced to his sister and niece, I was sure he didn't have a girlfriend.

How could it be that no woman had snatched him up? There had to be a reason, just another layer that was David, I suppose.

The confusion that was settling in on my brain was insufferable. I had so many conflicting emotions at the moment. Love could be a fickle thing. Not that I loved David, but if I was ever going to love again, the notion of David being that man was not unappealing. I had loved Sam for so long, and so deeply that the idea of loving another man at the moment was absurd to me. There was only Sam in my world, love was Sam, and Sam was love. Now he was gone, my heart was shattered, and now the thought of letting anyone else back in terrified me to the core of my bones.

David probably was just taking pity on me, maybe he was just trying to clean me up, straighten me out and then set me free back on the world. Just as a park ranger did with an injured animal. My wing was broken and he was just nursing me back to health so I could fly again. David wouldn't like me in that romantic way anyway, and I didn't have those feelings for him.

Well, being truthful to myself I didn't know what feelings I had towards him, but there was something rustling around in my heart for him. I didn't know if it was just some sort of kinship, friendship or what. What I did know was that he was the closest thing I had to a friend outside family, even if I was paying him to spend time with me. Whatever the case, I was happy for the first time, in a long time. The strange thing was I think I was happier now than when I was with Sam. I felt free and only now after feeling free did I realise that I had been caged.

I saw hope, when before all I saw was pessimism, and nothing but a fruitless existence. I went to sleep that night with David on my mind, and I was sure a smile was painted on my face all night.

I couldn't believe I ever thought he could have hurt me, the notion seemed silly now. Could the man of your dreams ever be real, or could there only ever have been a shadow of a man that could never live up to your highest expectations? Was that man always out of reach, or was he just like a whisper in the wind?

I thought Sam was that man; that man that would fill my life with love until the end of days. But I was obviously wrong, I couldn't have been more wrong. If I was wrong about Sam, how could I ever know if I was right about someone? How could I trust my own heart now, if my heart had already led me down the wrong path? It could do it again.

If there was a path of love laid out for me, how could I walk it without falling off again? The fear of falling was so extreme now after Sam. I would be forever walking with my eyes closed, and the path would gradually become narrower and narrower making it easier to slip and fall, and then I would burn on the lava rocks of lonesomeness. I'd end up alone with a million cats, and then I'd be known as the crazy cat lady, Meow.

I think love should be when you look into the eyes of your lover and tears start to fall, because you couldn't imagine a life without them. Love was holding on to someone, and never wanting to let them go. To be able to feel their heart beat as your own, and breathe as one.

I loved Sam wholeheartedly, but I never had that earth-shattering love I had heard about all my life. Perhaps that kind of love wasn't on the cards for me, maybe that love didn't exist at all and it was only fictional made up words in a book. I couldn't see how I could ever trust love again after Sam. The saying, "Better to have loved and lost, than never to have loved at all," was lost on me. I failed to see the wisdom in it. But I lived in the hope that one day I would.

CHAPTER 17

Louis slid the blood-drenched brass knucklebusters off his hands, dropping them on the wooden table. Louis didn't see the point in risking breaking his knuckle on some Insurgent guy's face. He had once punched a guy in the mouth without his busters on and one of the man's teeth got lodged in his bone under his skin between his knuckles. The brass busters were just a tool of the trade, occupational health and safety would be proud. To Louis the busters were more a practicality than an instrument for extra destructive damage. Doing this sort of work Louis normally had to hold back his punches anyway even without enhancing his fists with metal. He didn't want to concuss the Insurgent bikie member. Louis couldn't get information out of a person that was forcefully put to asleep.

Louis picked up a cloth to wipe his hands clean of blood, sweat and spit. He watched Ben as he struck his own Insurgent pimp in the face over and over again. A few more hits of Ben's fists and the pimp might die, Louis surmised. Ben did get a little carried away sometimes when the smell of blood was in the air. It was part of his charm that Louis liked.

"That's enough Ben," Louis barked. "I don't want to kill them just yet."

Ben sighed, and relinquished his bombardment of fists. He flexed his hands, opening and closing them as he came over to sit next to Louis. Then he grabbed a rag to wipe the blood off his own hands. Louis looked down at Ben still flexing his hands testing to see if they were broken. Ben wouldn't have cared even if they were. He liked the feeling of flesh hitting flesh too much. It resulted in uncountable broken bones in his hands, but everyone to their own, Louis thought.

The two Insurgent men were tied to chairs, and now were sitting in a pool of their own piss and blood. The two beaten men continued to spit out mouthfuls of saliva and blood instead of choking on their own bodily fluids. Louis and Ben had been at this for an hour. They had been interrogating the rival bikie members, trying to get any information that might lead them to the persons responsible for Jordan's death. They had been totally unforthcoming so far. They hadn't given them any information on the hooker Neil had talked about, or the guy that had stepped in and killed his brother.

"These two either liked getting their heads caved in, or they don't know anything," Ben said, throwing the blood-stained rag back on the table.

"Yes, I figured as much," Louis agreed, looking thoughtful.

Louis had assumed that the girl was one of the Insurgents' call girls, but now he wasn't so sure. The two pimps that they had been beating the hell out of for the past hour ran all the girls linked with the Insurgents, and they knew nothing about the girl in question.

"Maybe the girl isn't a prostitute," Louis stated thoughtfully. "She could have just been in the wrong place at the wrong time."

"Sounds a bit unlikely," Ben coughed, "Who else would be out there at that time of night dressed in only their underwear?"

"A girl meeting up with her boyfriend for a booty call," Louis suggested.

"I guess it could be possible," Ben admitted, "Then what about the guy? The guy must have had some serious training to take down me and Jordan."

Louis tightly clenched his own blood-soaked rag at the sound of his brother's name. It was the only sign he gave that his blood had risen to a hotter degree.

"There is a boxing gym down the road from where they found my brother. Perhaps the guy was returning home from there."

"Maybe, but it seems a stretch," Ben replied.

"I have already told Aiden to check it out, I'm not leaving any stone unturned."

"Aiden, is that the want-a-be skinny kid I've seen at the club house?" Ben said, through a laugh. Then went on to ask, "You trust him with all this stuff?

"Say what you want about Aiden, but the kid has skills on the keyboard. Aiden's been doing a lot of work for me over the past few years and he has never left me disappointed," Louis replied.

"Well if the kid is dealing with all your secrets, and is still breathing then I guess he must have a few skills."

"Plus," Louis said, "he is the son of one of our lost bikie brothers so I know he'll be loyal."

"Seeing is believing," Ben said. "Who knows though, the kid might surprise me."

"Well, we are about to see something because Aiden's on his way over now," Louis announced.

Just then the door to their concrete walled room opened and Aiden Mathews walked in holding two orange A4-size envelopes.

"Good, you made it," Louis said, standing up.

Aiden slowed as he took in the sight of the two bleeding bashed men. Louis watched Aiden as he stared. Aiden was still young and spent most of his time behind a computer screen. He probably had never seen this kind of anarchy up close. It was one thing to watch the results of violence on a screen at home where you were safe, and another to see it up close and personal. It was a whole new experience, to smell the blood in the air, to taste it on your tongue and to feel the fear of the victims in the room.

"I... I think I found something," he stuttered not taking his eyes off the prisoners. Aiden was a virgin to all the blood, Louis knew that now. Louis might just have to pop his cherry and make the kid kill one of them. There was nothing more thrilling than your first kill.

"So what did you find?" Ben asked forcefully, eager to prove Aiden incompetent.

"I think I found the two people you are looking for," Aiden said.

One of the Insurgent men looked up, hope in his eyes. The battered man had the look that, if the kid was right, then it would stop the fists from flying. The hope twinkled in his bloodshot eyes.

Aiden pulled out two pictures from one of the folders, "Are these the two you are looking for?"

Ben snatched the photos out of Aiden's hand taking a closer look. Actual surprise flashed on Ben's face as he announced gleefully, "That's definitely the girl, and I'm pretty sure that's the guy. He did have half his face covered by his hood. Well done, Aiden."

Ben peered back down at the faces he had seen that night he lost his friend, "I got you fuckers now," Ben said to the picture, like the faces on paper had ears to listen. Louis just formed a smile knowing it wouldn't be long now before his revenge was breathing in front of him.

"How did you find them?" Louis asked Aiden. Aiden got all giddy at the question, forgetting the two tortured men behind him.

"Well, the girl was easy," Aiden said happily, "after you gave me her description and told me her injuries I checked all the local cop shops and hospitals. There was no police report made that fitted the criteria, so then I moved onto the hospitals. There wasn't any assault victims that matched but a hit and run victim that lined up perfectly. Her name is Sarah Smith. She's just an ordinary girl that studies online and works at Target." Aiden waved one of the orange envelopes in the air indicating Sarah's information.

"The guy was a little harder. I checked that local gym you told me about and one name popped out at me. David Powers," Aiden waved the other envelope. "Do you remember John Black getting arrested for the murder of a woman and child a few years back?"

"Yes," Louis answered.

Louis remembered alright. John Black was a low-ranked member that had cost Louis a small fortune getting his charges dropped, and then the stupid idiot winds up dead a few days later after getting attacked by the Insurgents.

"Pass me the picture of David."

Louis looked hard at the picture, trying to remember the face. Then it all came back. David was a fighter, a good one at that. They lost a lot of money on a fight David was supposed to lose and no one lost more than John Black. So John killed David's family as payment.

The whole betting on the boxing scene was more Jordan's area. Louis still loved to watch a good fight, but thought making money off betting was small fries compared to selling goods like drugs and pussy. Ben probably should have known though but, like he said, half his face was covered. Louis didn't think Ben was involved with the whole John Black thing anyway. Besides it was a few years ago and Ben had been hit in the head a lot in that time.

Aiden started back up again as he explained, "Well, I remember hacking the police files about the case, you know, just for fun. I remembered the woman had a husband, named David Powers. The same David Powers with the gym membership down the road. And now I'm guessing that John Black's death wasn't the work of the Insurgents like everyone thought. I reckon it was David."

"Good work, Aiden." Louis congratulated. "Did you get all their personal info?"

"I got all the girl's stuff no problems, but David doesn't have much that will be useful. I got David's bank details, driver's licence, all the stuff you need for a gym membership. But all his mail is sent to his old address that was released to new tenants not long after his family died. David's only family is a sister and niece, and they're off the grid too. David looks like a man with something to hide, and David's trail all went dark right after John Black's death."

David Powers, the man that killed his brother. Perhaps Louis should have looked closer into John Black's death, but Louis was just so pissed off with John and how he had cost him so much money that he was almost happy the guy got his face burnt off.

Aiden handed the envelopes to Louis, and then Louis passed them onto Ben. Ben grabbed them greedily, knowing what Louis was going to ask of him, "Go check this Sarah Smith chick out and bring her to me alive."

"Will do, boss," Ben said happily.

"And don't leave any witnesses. Sarah won't be going back home after I'm done with her." Louis then turned to Aiden and asked, "Can you put everything you found on my computer?"

"Yer, no problem," Aiden said. Louis then turned to the two tied up men, whimpering in their own filth.

"Well I guess we don't need these two anymore," Louis said, walking over to one of the helpless men, then paused. "Aiden, because you did such a great job did you want to kill one of them?" Louis asked like he was handing him a well-earned beer at the end of a hard day's work.

Aiden spluttered and gagged on his words eventually mumbling out, "That's alright."

"Nonsense, Aiden. Ben won't mind if you take his kill. I expect he will get to play his blood and games later when he runs into Sarah," Louis said, then added more formally asking Ben, "You don't mind do you, Ben?"

"Not at all mate, they were starting to bore me anyway," Ben confirmed, a smile on his lips as he watched Aiden squirm.

"He's all yours, Aiden," Ben said, with a slap on Aiden's back.

Louis walked back over to Aiden guiding him over to the two Insurgent men.

"The first time is the scariest, but what you feel now you will never be able to recreate no matter how many more people you kill," Louis uttered.

Both frightened men looked up at Louis. The full weight of Louis's implications sinking in, their fates were literally in Louis's hands. The same hands that wrapped around the closest man's throat and began to squeeze.

"I'll show you how it's done," said Louis, "Watch and learn Aiden. It's your turn next."

CHAPTER 18

*T*wo months later and my old life was still trapped in the abyss of the past. Sam and Tara were gone from my life never to return. I had not heard one word from either of them since I'd hung up on Tara and kicked Sam in the nuts. That was the way I liked it, that was the way it was going to stay. The past two months were focused on the future, and turning myself into an independent woman. I was doing everything for myself now. No more being lazy and letting my parents do everything for me. I even cooked Mum and Dad dinner one night. They said it was nice, but their faces told a different story. It's still the effort that counts, right?

The main focus in my life was David's training regimen. The program wasn't living up to what I had imagined. I was thinking punches and kicks, but what I got was nothing of the sort. He hadn't even taught me any meditation stuff either. The closest thing we'd done to meditation was when I was exercising he told me to concentrate on the particular muscle group I was working on at that moment.

I know David had told me I would get frustrated, but I wasn't expecting him to be so right. He did also say that he would teach me the punching and kicking stuff when he thought I was ready.

I felt ready. I just didn't know why David didn't think I was. I didn't know what I was missing either, or what I had to prove to him to make him see that I was ready. In the end, I did say I would stick it out, so stick it out I would. One thing I would say was that I thought I was already pretty fit, but David proved me wrong. After every session I was buggered.

My training mainly existed of stretching, muscle strengthening and endurance training. To build up my stamina, strength and flexibility David had said. We did break it up with some push-ups, dips and few other body weight exercises. There was lots of core training as well, such as sit-ups, blanking, leg raises just to name a few. But every session was mainly lots of running, squats, and lunges. We never went to a gym. We always went outdoors, either at a park or a walking track. If it was raining he just gave me a plastic poncho and we continued. I would have complained, saying this was all just a waste of my time. However, David was able to see me every day without fail, and that ended up being the highlight of my day.

Not learning how to kick someone in the butt was getting tedious, but seeing David every day was worth it. Just being around his high intensity, lifted my spirits. The session times changed around a little bit too, due to his other clients, and my return to work, but when David set a time he was never late, he was always on time.

I was hoping he had some sort of game plan for me; otherwise all I'd be good at was running away, and I was pretty sure I would be able to kick someone in the shins fairly well too. I had put everything else aside for this, all I could do was trust his judgement, and hope David knew what he was doing. I even quit my gym membership to train with David full time. I would have paid David properly, but David only asked for the same as what I was paying at my gym, which was only seventy bucks a month. I knew a personal trainer was at least fifty dollars an hour at my gym. I had used one a few times to show me the ropes when I first started, so I knew David was undercutting himself big time. Just another reason for me not to question David's training methods.

David had given me some insight to his method of madness though, saying the reason why he was training me this way was because my body needs to be able to handle all the movements and techniques he was planning to teach me. David told me I was quite fit already, but my body still needed some conditioning, a little fine-tuning, as he put it.

I still couldn't see the bigger picture. I did have my suspicions, however; he might be seeing how dedicated I was, seeing if I would do the boring stuff before I got to the fun stuff. I thought perhaps he might be worried about teaching me how to fight in case my beast side returned. My best guess was he was just sussing me out, wondering whether or not I would use what he taught me on some unlucky soul just to feel that rush of power again. To be brutally honest I still had my own doubts about being able to control myself. I just didn't know how David could see my ambiguity on the matter. I still just wanted to learn the punching and kicking stuff though.

As the days ticked over I grew closer to David. Every day I got a little bit more of an understanding about the kind of person he was. David was not always so cold and serious. Sometimes through our sessions together he actually seemed happy and to be enjoying himself. But the seriousness always returned before long. David's internal walls would always get bricked back up, blocking the real David from breaking through. That hard look he had, always found its way back. It was a look of neither happy, nor unhappy, always just that happy medium. It seemed every time his happiness shone through with me, and he looked at me with that amazing crooked smile, it shocked him back into his mundane ways.

One Monday morning as I got into his car, David said, "I've got something different planned for today. It's something I think you will benefit from." David always liked to leave a tiny bit of mystery.

"Is it skydiving naked?" I guessed. "Oh, oh, I know rock climbing upside down?"

"Close, I was thinking of a naked pole dancing workout, but I don't think it would be risky enough for your liking."

"I do like long poles," I teased.

David whipped his head around to face me. His face had a boyish stunned expression. The car veered a little onto the gravel before David brought it back onto the road. I loved getting underneath his skin like that. It showed his humanity, and it proved he was not always perfect; which he was most of the time. Besides I was single now, and a little honest flirting never hurt anyone.

"You are really going to get along with Joe, I think," David said, after cooling down and the redness left his face.

"Who's Joe?"

"You'll find out soon enough."

"I guess it is pointless asking you where we are actually going?" I said.

"You are correct, Miss Smith, but don't worry you won't have to wait long to find out."

"What about bungee jumping?" I asked, determined not to give up my guesswork.

"You won't guess it."

"You can't stop a girl from trying," I added.

"I wouldn't dare try."

"Is it dancing?" I suggested, hopefully.

Not knowing what David had in store for me, or where we were off to. The only thing I had noticed was that we were headed for the city, which was unusual for our normal day out. Every other day we went in the opposite direction, towards trees. Now we were going towards steel, concrete and skyscrapers. The change in routine baffled me. Thinking whatever I was about to do was going to be a lot different from what we normally did. With my excitement spiked, my intrigue fully loaded, I wiggled around in my seat unable to sit still, my anticipation making me fidget the whole car ride.

After a further fifteen minutes of battling traffic, and with me still trying to guess today's activity – coming up, lastly, with base-jumping off a building – we pulled up beside this old run-down building. Some of windows were boarded up, and the ones that weren't were caked in dust. The paint over the bricks, high enough not to be covered in graffiti, had almost entirely peeled off. The place looked two-hundred years old and the wind would blow it over at any moment.

We stopped just outside in an old parking lot. A half dozen cars littered the spaces. I stared at the building with bewilderment. Then I had to express my concern and asked, "Are we going inside there? It doesn't look very safe."

"The building is old, but it was built to last. Buildings were built strong in the old days, so don't worry, she'll stay upright for you," David assured me. It made me feel a little better, just a little.

David and I jumped out of the car, then walked towards an old red weathered door. A man stood next to the door, leaning up against the brickwork that was coated in tagged graffiti. He had a cigarette in one hand, and smoke came out of his nostrils as we approached. He was wearing old jeans and a green hoody. The man yelled out as he spotted us drawing closer.

"It's about time you got here. You're late David."

"I'm never late," David, responded.

"What do you mean, you're five minutes early that's late for you," the man said, butting out his ciggy.

David walked over, holding a hand outstretched for the man to shake. Mr Smoking man grabbed it, and then pulled David in for a hug, patting him on the back. The man spotted me over David's shoulder. Releasing him from the embrace, he said, "I didn't know you were bringing such good looking company, I would have dressed up a bit if you'd told me."

David stood between us, "Joe this is Sarah, Sarah this is Joe."

Joe turned to David, "Is this who I think it is?" David nodded.

Joe's eyes widened, surprise glancing over his face, "Well I didn't even recognise you with all your clothes on. You are looking much better."

Now it was my turn for shock to fall down on my face, "Sorry! Do I know you? And what do you mean, with my clothes on?"

Joe smiled, then folded his arms across his chest, "I suppose you wouldn't know me, but I know you."

He looked at me like I was a piece of art he had constructed; then he added, "Who do you think kept you looking so pretty?" I touched the fading scar on my forehead, realisation dawning on me.

"Yep, that was me. That cut has healed up nicely," he commented as I lowered my hand from my forehead. "I really do, do good work. I'm a little bit out of practise, but it just shows how awesome I am," Joe said, cocking his head up, and stood in a pose like a model would on a photo shoot. This was the man who patched me up that night.

He didn't look like a doctor, and he definitely didn't behave like one. Before I knew it, I voiced my opinion.

"So you're the famous doctor?"

"Famous only in certain circles, but I do have my groupies," he said.

Taking a longer look at the man, I added, "You don't look like a doctor?"

"That's because I'm not, sweet cheeks. But you should see me in scrubs. Sexy," he said in such a way I couldn't help but smile. Joe certainly had a way of lightening the tension, even though all my concerns were spiked, and knowing full well he just side-stepped the question with a joke.

Before I could ask if you're not a doctor, then what are you? David leaned down to face me. Making a point of directing his words to me, but saying them loud enough so Joe could still hear, "Joe might not look it, but he is more than capable."

"Thanks mate," Joe said slapping David on the back. "Don't worry I won't tell anyone you said that."

"He thinks he's funny too," David added not breaking eye contact with me.

Joe faked being insulted and said, "I am funny."

David was still close enough for a breath of wind to blow the smell of his cologne in my face. The sudden fragrance made my head spin, and I forgot Joe was even there. The smell was overpoweringly sensual. It was like he was the pied piper and luring me in closer. I found it so enticing I had to turn away, afraid that David might notice my attraction to his aroma. David must have thought I turned away in concern, because he went on to say, "I did mean it about Joe. Beside all the bad jokes he is much more capable than he appears."

I believed him about Joe; the proof was in how well he patched me up. I was just glad the one thing David wasn't accustomed to seeing was lustful flashes. If he had been attentive to my body's urges, seeing my face fill with red hot blood he didn't push it to eruption status by calling me out on it.

I had only been free from a five-year relationship for a couple of months, but I felt confusing feelings towards David. We played around flirting all the time, I caught him looking at me longer than normal on occasion, and he made me go red-faced sometimes, like now. It just felt too soon to be having these feelings. But that was the thing about feelings they told you what to do and it was up to you to act on them.

Joe's acting hurt pose changed to one of gratitude, "Ohhh, thanks mate. So you do love me after all." Then Joe's eyebrows narrowed, "Hang on a minute, was that a compliment or an insult?" David just gave Joe an over-exaggerated smile, and then walked inside the building, always keeping that level of mystery.

I went to follow David into the dilapidated building, feeling a little uneasy being left outside with Joe the not-so doctor. As I moved Joe moved with me got in front and put a hand out to shake. His joking tone was replaced with a serious one that I hadn't seen yet, "All jokes aside, it really is nice to be able to talk to you this time, and to see you doing so well."

I took his hand, shaking it, "Well, I guess I have you to thank for my speedy recovery."

"I guess you do," he said looking thoughtful, like he had to think hard about accepting the applause.

Before I could rethink it, I added, "Thank you for patching me up that night." All of Joe's arrogance returned after the praise.

"Any time, little lassie," Joe said, putting on a bad Irish accent, "I'm just glad I got to talk to the girl that David can't stop mentioning all the time. It was starting to get annoying only having a bloody image to go with the name." I was going to overlook it, but I wanted to investigate, I needed to know.

"Does David really talk about me all the time?" I asked, with my heart swelling for the response.

"Like you wouldn't believe."

Joe still had that cocky demeanour act, but act was the key word. If you looked past his flamboyant mask you could see an intelligent calculating man. He was only telling me this to gauge how I felt for David; just inquiring about him talking about me probably gave him his answer. But still, that didn't mean what he said about David was a lie. Could David really like me like that? I dared to question. No I shouldn't question, I decided. My heart was a lockbox. No man was going to wound me ever again. The only way I would get cut deep again was if I let someone in close. Besides David was no rebound guy, he was too grand for that. He was much too handsome, too sexy. Stop that, stop it, stop it, I shouted to myself.

Before I could change my mind about asking follow up questions, Joe added with a grin, "We really shouldn't leave David waiting, he might think you couldn't keep your hands off me, and we are making out or something." My mouth dropped, but before I could tell him how wrong he was, Joe was already through the door and out of sight. It took me a second to compose myself. Before I stepped inside I thought to myself, Joe was right about one thing, he was funny.

When I got inside it took a moment for my eyes to adjust to the darker surroundings. When my eyes did come into focus, I saw a mountain of food. There must have been at least fifty loaves of bread, with buns and rolls, enough to feed an army. But that wasn't all, there was a whole lot of fruit and vegetables, some packaged meat, all sorts of canned and boxed food, packs of pasta and rice, loads of milk and a whole lot more hidden behind the mountain of bread. I was standing in a huge kitchen, I realised. David was standing at a table sorting out the canned goods.

"David what is all of this?" I queried. Dumb question I know. It was food obviously, but it was the one that came out my mouth. David knew what I meant.

"This is a soup kitchen. All the food is for the homeless and needy. I get it donated from bakeries, supermarkets. Wherever they sell food I have probably asked for donations." I stared at him, unable to look away, transfixed by the man who stood in front of me. I thought a little noise like a squeak came out me, but I couldn't be sure.

"Most of the food is right on its use-by date, or one day off. It's still perfectly fine to eat. If I didn't grab it, it would have been thrown in the trash."

"That's horrible," I said. I looked around at everything on the bench, "that would be a lot of wasted food."

"I know, right. I was going for a late night jog, and saw a supermarket throwing out loaf after loaf of bread. That's when I decided to create this," David said, opening his arms up, gesturing to all that surrounded him. "We cook it all up, and then serve it to the people needing a good hot meal."

Our eyes locked, mine were unwilling to look away. Mine were unable to look away because I was totally mesmerised by this man. Sometimes I thought that David couldn't be real, he was just too good to be true. I couldn't not be bewildered by this man. The strange thing was, though, that he couldn't seem to look away either.

"Will you help us cook, and serve it up?" David asked breaking me out of my reverie of him.

"Of course I will," finding my voice in the nick of time, hoping my staring wasn't too obvious. "I'm not much of a cook, but I'm slowly getting better though. My Mum still does most of the cooking at home."

Joe's head peeked over my shoulder, "Sarah, I don't think it's going to work out between us. I need a woman that can cook. Sorry love." His head was to one side, his bottom lip pushed out to make a sad face.

"You're so funny for such a round guy," I said as I poked his round belly with my finger.

"Did you hear that David, the girl has her own bad jokes," Joe sounded genuinely impressed.

"It probably would have done you good to be with a girl that can't cook, but I think you're right. I think you would have trouble keeping up with me, if you know what I mean," I said, sending Joe a wink. Joe's mouth dropped in surprise from that one, so I finished him off by saying, "I really wouldn't want to drive you to a heart-attack with all that extra cholesterol," I paused for a beat, "Oh well, you will never know what you missed out on." I crinkled my forehead, and smiled as sweet and innocent as possible.

Joe moved to put an arm around David, before admitting his defeat, "This one is a little firecracker. She's all yours big fella; see if you can keep up with her." Joe walked over to a couple of other guys starting to prepare some vegetables.

"Not bad Sarah. Beat Joe at his own game. Well done," David praised. I couldn't help the grin on my face. It was spread from ear to ear as I started to help David sort the food.

CHAPTER 19

After sorting, cooking and preparing the food, the noise outside the kitchen in the main hall began to increase. The sound was similar to a football stadium before your team kicked a goal. The voices of men and women chattering to each other, people laughing, even the sound of children playing. All that cacophony of sounds mixed together creating one loud ruckus that made us more determined to get the food out.

David came through the doors, the sound intensifying as the doors opened, and then diminishing when the doors closed behind him. David looked around the kitchen, searched for something. That was until his gaze fell upon me; then he strode over to me, obviously finding what he was looking for – me.

"Do you mind helping Joe serve the meals out front? He needs a hand out there," David requested. "It's more busy than usual."

"Yes, sure," I said, willing to do anything to help.

"It does mean a lot of interaction with strangers," he said. He let his words sink in before asking, "You think you're up for it?"

"I think so," I answered, a little bit less sure this time. His question made me nervous all of a sudden; wondering why he had had to inquire about me interacting with others. Did he really think I would snap under such a low strain? Or did he think I would be afraid of meeting a lot of new faces after that crazy bikie introduction?

"You'll be fine. Joe will look after you," David said, reassuringly. I think he had asked just to see how I would react. I reckoned he would have convinced me to go out there even if I hadn't been willing.

"Having Joe there to help me is supposed to make me feel better, is it?" I joked, shaking off the nerves. It was like I was back in fourth grade about to go out on stage in front of an audience, and do a performance in a play.

"A friendly face is still a friendly face, even if it is layered over condescension," David said smiling at me.

"It's fine, I'll be fine," I reassured him.

David then headed for the swinging doors that led to the main room, with me walking on his heels. Rows of tables and chairs lined the room. The room was filled with an uncountable number of people. A long line had formed by two tables that were positioned at the front of the large hall, just outside the kitchen doors. The tables had all the prepared food in big pots or in wicker baskets. Joe stood at the table filling up bowl after bowl. He really did need the help. Every second the line seemed to get longer and longer. The quicker I got out there the better.

David's focus momentarily switched from me to a man at the back of the large room. The man wore an old Driza-Bone jacket, and a very worn cowboy hat that hid most of his face. The switch of David's focus was there for but an instant, but it was there. I think I noticed more than I should, when it came to David. David either didn't know I noticed, or didn't care that I did. If I had to guess I would have picked the latter. David put a hand on my shoulder, a finger grazing the skin on my neck ever so softly, but the touch was enough to send tingles through my nervous system.

"Joe will show you what to do, I'll be back soon." Without looking back, David headed off in the direction of Mr Cowboy hat. I took a mental note to ask David later what that was all about. At the moment however, I had hungry people to feed.

"So how can I help, good lookin'?" I asked Joe in a playful tone.

"Grab plastic bowls, and start loading them up, if you please," Joe's demeanour had taken a very businesslike approach. His entire playful attitude had disappeared. I could see now, the man he became while he was working, very focused and driven. He took his work very seriously. Time for fun and games later, we were here to do a job, no mucking around while working. If you were going to do a job, do it properly; that was the work ethic I got from Joe's workmanship. That was when I could see him sewing up my head like an artist with his paint brush; his paint brush being a needle and thread, and his canvas being my head. Probably not the best comparison, but I think it still works.

I followed Joe's work ethic, letting him lead by example, leaving the fun and games outside, giving a professional appearance while starting to load up bowl after bowl of what looked like a beef and vegetable stew. Looking around the room, not everybody looked homeless. There were the obvious people with uncombed hair, beards down to their navel, dirt on their faces and clothes, and the people who hadn't had a shower in months. The ones that surprised me were the normal folk; they just appeared to be like everyday, run of the mill people. If you saw them on the street, you would be none the wiser. There were entire families here that you would never have guessed were going hungry.

Then it hit home. You didn't have to be living on the streets to be in need of a meal. These people most likely had enough money to put a roof over their heads, clothes on their backs, basically just the bare essentials of living, and that was about it. I was assuming most of their home cooked meals were just rice and potatoes.

The hungry were not just the homeless, I found out. There were single mums, the unemployed, the elderly, street kids and they were all in need of a good meal. It really made my problems look minuscule compared to the need to eat. Wars had been waged from such things. Not being able to put food on your plate, and going hungry that was something to worry about. And here I was sometimes too full to eat all my dinner, so I threw the scraps in the bin. I didn't even think twice about wasting food. For me food was always plentiful. How lucky I felt now after seeing this.

There must be other people out there like me, wasting food while there were people starving. This was not happening on the other side of the world in Africa where all you could do here was donate a dollar to a charity, but it was happening to people just a short drive away.

I thought my country was better than that. You didn't hear about the hungry on the news, the homeless sleeping under bridges or the families struggling to feed their kids. What does that say about our society? Maybe if more people were aware more could be done to help. I mean, I didn't even know what atrocities were going on in my own neighbourhood. It made me concerned to think about what else I was blind to. I feared to imagine.

As I passed out bowl after bowl, every man, woman and child said thank you. Everyone was so grateful for their meal. At a restaurant or a fast food outlet, hardly anyone would have the manners to say thank you, but here, with the poorest social class of people, there was the highest class in decency, morals and overall manners.

I knew now why David had asked me to help serve on the front lines. Why he had said that this experience would benefit me. Just getting back out amongst it shone a light on the world, exposing hidden crevasses where things were not always what they seemed. Just interacting with these people had done so much to my ego, I was never the most social of butterflies, but just saying a friendly hello to a stranger was not that scary. It was a little confronting at first. At the start I was a little nervous; I didn't know what to expect, I wasn't sure if people were going to be rude, or disrespectful towards me.

Before this when I thought of a homeless person I thought dirty, angry, crazy person. Now my perception was changed forever; seeing everyone with smiling faces, happy positive energy flowing from them, the atmosphere that this place unleashed put me at ease within moments. My shoulders lost their tension, my hard straight-up stance softened, and once I passed through all my anxiety, I became happy.

Serving these people made me realise how introverted I was, thinking only of myself; my own wants, my own needs. I wasn't thinking that I was part of a community and I could make it better. Instead of being a lone wolf on the outskirts of town peering in to see what I wanted to take, I should have been the horse carrying the cart full of supplies for the community. When the line of hungry people had drawn to a close and all the people had knives and forks in their hands, and were filling their mouths eagerly, I seized the opportunity to strike up a conversation with Joe, asking a few of those questions I had earlier.

"How do you know David?"

"I was David's cut man when he boxed," Joe replied automatically. I was shocked. What was a cut man? Did he deliberately cut David? Why David would let Joe cut him was beyond me, the notion made my stomach feel a bit queasy.

"You cut David on purpose?" I asked suspiciously. Now I was wondering if Joe was the man I thought he was. That Rodney Rude, happy-go-lucky, hardworking nice guy might all have been a disguise. I was second-guessing my judgement again. Some part of me now, after getting bashed by bikies, always went straight to the worst-case scenario. I had thought Joe was a blood crazed loony.

Joe saw the distress on my face and smiled, "Only if it came to that," he said trying to, but failing to reassure me. My heart-beat began increasing when he admitted to cutting David. Before I added another thought into my paranoia Joe continued, "Sometimes in a boxing match your eye will swell up, so much so you can't even see out of it. It's my job to make a small incision letting some of the fluid out, so the boxer can continue the fight. Not that I had to do it to David though."

I relaxed inside, my organs untwisting and felt much relieved. I did know what it was like to have a swollen eye. Not worth a scar on my face to bring down the swelling though, I thought. Men and their games.

"Oh," was all I came up with as a response. How witty I am sometimes.

"Also when a boxer gets a cut in a fight, either from a glove, head clash or maybe an illegal elbow, whatever the case, if blood runs down into the eye limiting their sight, the fight will be stopped. The cuts have to be treated between rounds as quickly as possible, and as effectively as possible. So you see, Muffin Buns, a boxer needs a cut man, and I was the best in the business," Joe pointed a thumb at his chest. "I really am that awesome."

When I didn't react to his self-assessment, Joe went on, "Like I was saying, boxers needs someone to patch them up quickly and effectively so they can keep beating the snot out of each other. Also what I do, and most importantly, I assess their state of mind. I check to see if they have concussion or not, if they have the effects of dehydration. If there is any situation where there could be dire consequences if the fighter continues I stop the fight."

That put things into perspective for me, "That's how you were able to fix me up so well," I concluded.

"Yep, I have been around a few cuts and bruises in my time, a few unconscious people too," he said with a wink. "People are much easier to work on when they're out cold, they don't move as much, you see," Joe joked.

"I was starting to think you were some sort of seamstress. Just good with a needle and a thread," I teased

I thought if I told him the truth; that I thought he just loved to cut people, just so he could sew them back up again; it might not go down so gratifyingly. Joe barked a laugh, an uncontrollable laugh that was so infectious it got a chuckle out of me too.

"No, no, Sarah I do know what I am doing," Joe reported, wanting me to understand that he did have some background knowledge in the matter, and that he wasn't just a joking clown. "But, for your information, I am good with a needle and a thread. You should see me hem up a pair of pants."

Getting serious now I asked, "Did David tell you what happened to me?" As I asked Joe if he knew the details of that night, I straightened up, I wasn't sure I wanted to know the answer, but I had to find out. Joe looked at me, no doubt seeing the tension in my body.

"No, but I have a few ideas. I know it wasn't a car crash, for one." All the air in my lungs was sucked out of me by that last comment.

"Then what do you think happened?" I asked in my sheepish tone of voice, not really wanting Joe to guess, but unable not to ask.

"I have my theories, but that's all they are. I don't need to know what happened to help out a friend. David told me to keep a lid on it, so I will."

Joe stopped for a second clearing his throat then added, "David's like family to me, so you don't have to worry yourself about what I should or shouldn't know."

If David trusted Joe, then that was good enough for me. A sigh of relief exhaled from my mouth, the stress must have been visible on my face because as soon as it left my body the mood in the air changed.

"You know, Sarah, David was one of the best fighters I had ever seen. He was unbeaten. So quick no one could catch him, he had power behind every punch too. Incredible strength for his weight class, one clean hit to the jaw, and then out go their lights. David would have gone all the way to the big time, if that thing with his wife and child didn't happen," Joe's expression soured with the memory unfolding behind his eyes.

"What happened to David's wife and child?" I inquired, knowing it couldn't have been anything good. "I didn't even know he was married."

"Sorry, little lassie, not my story to tell. I thought you knew. I think I have already said too much" Joe said, while picking up some empty bowls. Changing subject, he said, "Looks like that's about it for today, we better start cleaning up."

I began picking up empty pots and cutlery, before saying, "You know I learnt more about David with you in the last five minutes, than I have the whole time I have known him."

Joe expression saddened, his posture slouching, "David doesn't like to talk about his past. I think he's afraid of being happy. I would warn you about opening up old wounds, but it might do him some good if he opened up to someone." Joe seemed to take a deeper look at me before continuing, "You know, you remind me of her."

What? The word screamed in my head. I reminded him of David's ex-wife. I didn't even know she existed until two seconds ago. If Joe thought I reminded him of David's wife, then David must have seen her in me too. My mind started yelling questions at me.

What happened to them? Where were they now? Did she leave him and take his kid? Was that the reason why David had done all of this for me because I reminded him of his ex-wife? Did he think I could replace her?

I placed my fingers on my temples. I rubbed in a circular motion, trying to clear my thoughts. The massage made this sudden headache subside slightly. It was all too much. What was I to think now, what was I to do? And where the hell was he anyway?

That was the last question my mind yelled at me before I was able to cease the bombardment, and it was the question that lasted, circling around. David had been good for ages.

Joe's voice broke through my reverie, "David needs a friend, it's been a long time since he's had a friend." A flicker of a smile flashed across his face, "Besides his best bud, me, of course." I rolled my eyes. "I'm getting sick of his mopey attitude, I need someone to help share the load," Joe said, only half-serious, I thought.

Joe took in a deep breath then started up again, "But seriously, it's good to see David with somebody besides his sister and niece. Just promise me one thing."

"No guarantees," I retorted not knowing what to make of it.

"Be gentle with him, hey," he requested.

I thought Joe was going to ask something a bit harder to do, but I think I could manage that, so I said, "That shouldn't be too hard. But no promises." With that, Joe walked back into the kitchen, leaving me with a lot to think about.

CHAPTER 20

$\mathcal{D}$avid had said he would be right back. So where the hell was he? Everybody had gone. All the people with smiles and full bellies gone with the food. The main hall was deserted. The tables were cleaned spotless, chairs on tables so we could clean the floor underneath, which now had a mirror finish. It took a lot of elbow grease to get it that way, but we did it. That was my workout for the day I concluded. The kitchen was now clean and tidy. The doors locked leaving Joe and me outside in the cold of night waiting for David's reappearance. At least it wasn't raining I thought, trying to put a positive spin on the boredom.

"Where do you think he is?" I asked Joe, growing ever impatient.

"Wherever he is, he must have a good reason for leaving us to do all the cleaning up. I mean my hands are still as wrinkled as a prune from all that soapy water," Joe grizzled.

I hated waiting around with nothing to do. At least when I was cleaning I could think of the task at hand, but waiting idle was brain popping insufferable. All the questions I was left with after my conversation with Joe just kept floating around up there like a broken record on repeat.

"Have you tried calling his mobile?" I asked. Joe looked at me dumbly.

"Go on, you try, I hadn't thought of that," he said sarcastically.

"All right, I will," I replied defiantly. I rang David's phone, the receiver on the other end rang, but I heard a dual noise, a ring tone, close.

I looked around franticly, searching for David, but that was until I noticed a flashing blue light coming from David's car. I peered through the passenger side window to see David's phone singing a come answer me tune.

"Damn. You could have just told me his phone was in there," I said.

"What would be the fun in that," Joe responded grinning.

The sound of thudding footstep hitting the pavement reached us before David turned the corner at a full sprint, only slowing to a walk when he got close. He was out of breath. I had never seen him out of breath before. He could climb a thousand stairs no problem without even breaking a sweat, but now he was out of breath. He could hardly utter a word he was that puffed out. He must have been running full sprint. What in the world would make him run to utter exhaustion? A sinking feeling washed over me, I let the fear of the unknown settle in.

"Sorry, I kept you waiting," David announced, still struggling to breathe.

"What's wrong?" Joe asked before I had the chance.

"Hopefully nothing, but we have to go. Please get in the car, Sarah, we have to go just in case," David ordered.

I did what I was told, the urgency in his tone made it clear that I should listen, and not stamp my foot down and demand an explanation. I had never seen David act like this, panicked and flustered. Saying a quick goodbye to Joe with a little wave of my hand, I jumped straight in the car. I heard David saying thanks to Joe, and then I saw him pat him on the shoulder, but he didn't stop as he made his way to the driver's seat.

David's car really did have some balls. David didn't hold anything back. I was thrown back into my seat by the g-force as we took off, tires squealing, and the smell of burnt rubber filled my nostrils as we left Joe in a cloud of white smoke.

"Where have you been?" I asked cautiously.

David's full attention was on the road, both hands gripping the steering wheel. He only took one hand off for a gear change that pulled me back into my seat with invisible hands. David turned to me then back to the road. Silence filled the air with tension. I was not going to ask again. I knew he'd heard me.

It seemed like an eternity before David answered, "I was with a man that knows his way around a computer. That's all you need to know about that, but what he found does involve you, and your folks."

"My folks?" I said, confused, and then redirecting my thought process, quickly added, "What did you find out?"

"The Creatures of Chaos have found you; they know where you live. They know where you work, who your friends are, they know about your ex-boyfriend, they know everything," David told me through gritted teeth, angry at himself for letting it get this far and being so unprepared. Our worst nightmare had come to fruition. If they found my details, his wouldn't be far behind.

"Fucking hell," I cried out. I tried not to swear too often, but I thought this occasion called for it, and somehow I thought I might be swearing a bit more than usual in the upcoming future. Then it happened again. I could feel pressure building in my chest; I was having trouble breathing. I was having another panic attack. Everything seemed to be crushing down on me.

"Focus on my voice," David called out, from what seemed like a distance even though he was right beside me. I couldn't say anything so I just nodded. David started to sing, and it was awful. Every note out of tune, just think of a dog trying to sing, David was worse. All my attention had shifted from the bikies knowing where I live, and knowing how to find me, and my parents being home, to David's half bark, half howl singing voice. My breathing became less erratic, enough for me to force out the words, "Please shut up, I think my ears are starting to bleed." David stopped his ungodly singing, becoming quiet to give me time to recover.

"Sarah we have to talk about this. I'll talk, you listen. If it becomes too much for you, we'll stop. Okay?"

"Okay," I replied.

"The Chaos brothers only found your whereabouts today, so hopefully they haven't made a move on you yet, but they will." David spoke smoothly, unlike his singing. I tried to stay calm, tried to not get over-excited. David continued, "First things first, we have to tell your parents the truth about what happened that night, and then all of you have to lay low for a while, get out of town, and stay off the grid. Try not to use credit cards, stick with cash. Stay somewhere that can't be traced back to you. Somewhere that's not connected to your family, like a friend's holiday house or something."

"How did they find us?" I asked weakly.

"From your hospital records," David answered. "They didn't know your name, but they did know what injuries to look for, car crash or not."

David picked up my phone passing it to me, "Call your parents. Tell them they are in danger, and they need to pack some clothes, and get ready to leave. We will be there in fifteen minutes."

I took hold of the phone like I was handling a grenade ready to explode. I clicked into Mum's number. The call rang out. I removed the phone from my ear.

"Mum didn't answer. I'll try Dad." I called Dad and got the same response. David pounded the steering wheel with one hand.

"Is there any chance they could have gone out for dinner or something and left their phones behind," he asked hopefully

"I don't think so," I responded, my throat almost getting choked up. I steadied my breathing, taking in long deep breaths. I wanted to scream. I wanted to punch something. I could feel the beast inside me rise. It was the creature inside me that was levelling me out.

David threw the car's gearstick into fifth making the engine scream out in excitement of being driven to its full potential. The force of the acceleration pinned me back to the seat once again. If the urgency wasn't there, if we didn't need to get back to my house as quick as possible, if I didn't need to get to my parents and get them out of there, the speed we were traveling would have scared the pants off me but, as it was, I found myself wishing for more speed. The thought crossed my mind like a wave toppling on top of me, if they had found me, had they found David and his family?

"Do they know it was you that… you know?" I was unable to finish the sentence, to find the right words to say: killed Jordan Cole.

"They know my name and history, but I live off the grid now so they don't know where I live. I moved my sister and niece somewhere safe. Just in case," his tone fell flat, like that was one problem taken care of. There was no time for unnecessary distractions like worrying about his family when they were already safe. We had to concentrate on the task at hand – getting my parents out of the firing line.

We arrived into my estate in record time, a time that would have made a race car driver jealous. David had slowed the car to a crawl.

"What are you doing? Come on, my parents could be in trouble," I said with the urgency of a loving daughter.

"There is no point rushing in there being careless and getting caught by the same people that might have your mum and dad. We have to think through this, be smart."

Put back in my place knowing he was right, I asked, "What do you think we should do then?"

"First, look out for a motorbike. They will be hidden in plain sight. Remember this could still be a false alarm," David replied, looking from one side of the street to the other. He drove around the estate close by my house. Close enough to walk easily and not far enough away that would make their escape a lengthy operation. Just when I let in the hope that it was all a false alarm, that Mum and Dad where just out for a dinner date, I saw the glint of shiny alloy, a chrome finish that broke through the darkness reflecting the moon's light. I knew what it was before we drew closer, before I saw the silhouette of a bike unfold. The outline of five motorbikes beamed back at me. The bikes looked more like Harley Davidsons than racing bikes. The high handlebars, was what made me think Harley; they were unmistakeable in the glow of the moon.

"There," I shouted, with a forefinger outstretched, pointing in the direction of the bikes. David brought the car to a stop by the side of the road. He unbuckled his seatbelt then opened the car door. Without turning back to see if I heard, David commanded, "Wait here, I'll be back in a second."

He just stood maybe two metres away from the car, still and silent. Scanning the area for bikie stragglers I guessed. Then once everything appeared clear he made his way across the road towards the bikes. I could see him place a hand over an engine; his hand just hovering over it for a moment before pulling and yanking at God knows what on the bike. The bikes were hidden in plain sight, just like David had said. The bikes were parked on someone's front nature strip. Anyone that looked would think the owners of the bikes were in the house behind them.

Once David was done doing whatever to the first bike he moved onto the next and out of sight. A few long minutes later David reappeared again, walking fast back to the car. The car door opened and David got in.

"What did you do?" I inquired.

"I disabled their bikes in case we have to get out of here in a hurry. I don't want them able to follow."

"So it is definitely them?" I asked, hoping to be told differently.

"Unfortunately, yes. I found a Creatures of Chaos vest on one of the bikes. The bikes were still warm so they can't have been here too long," he paused, "Your parents might still be alive."

My world rocked, all my walls came crashing down. All my hopes of this being a false alarm went straight out the window. The Creatures of Chaos had my parents.

CHAPTER 21

The implications of what David just told me were life-changing. "Your parents might still be alive," David had said. But there was a chance that they might not be. The entanglements of threads I had weaved had snared my parents. They had been tangled up in a spider-web, ready for the Creatures of Chaos to eat.

We knew there were at least five Chaos bikies here. It was likely they were already in my house holding my parents captive or, worse, they had already murdered them. This was entirely my fault. If something had happened to them I would never forgive myself. I thought that that notion would just set me into another panic attack, but the fear I had now was not for myself. The fear I had now was for the people that raised me, the people that loved me unconditionally. These were the people who looked after me when I was sick, put a Band-Aid on my knee when I fell over.

My parents were now the only people in the world that I loved without thought, without any conditions, without any provocation. The unconditional love was the tie that binds us as family. That love for my parents, and their impending doom awoke the sleeping beast that lived inside me. My own creature of chaos took away my fear and wanted payment in blood. I calmed myself, coping the only way I could. I fuelled myself with hatred, and unleashed my built up rage.

It came out slow and in all directions. I felt anger at Sam for lying to me, for dealing the deck of cards that laid out my future. Fury at Tara for betraying me after a lifetime of friendship but, most of all, the pointy end of the spear was directed towards the Creatures of Chaos. They had bashed the shit out of me, they almost raped me, they made me live in fear, they came here to try and kill me and my parents. They even made my own body attack itself in panic. I had felt like a dog cowering in the corner while being beaten by its master. But now I knew I could take the beatings and survive.

I was going to use this raging fuel as a weapon, because now I knew you could only beat a dog so much before that dog had nothing left to lose. If you beat a dog it would either be a broken shell with all the fight being whipped out of it or the dog would fight back against its master with no regard for its own life. I refused to be a broken shell. I would be the dog breaking its teeth on the steel cage bars to get in the fight. I would never run away again, I would stay and confront my fears and fight. I was just fed up with being scared, with being beaten, and with all the evil in the world. Sometimes it took a monster to kill a monster, so a monster I would become.

It was then, thinking of my parents dying and with the beast inside scratching at the door, that I realised, after just having one, that I would never have another panic attack. I would have to be a slave to the fear of death to have another panic attack and now my chains were broken. I didn't want to die, quite the opposite actually. But something inside me gave way and death didn't seem so scary when the only two people in the world I loved could be dead.

So that left me with an ultimatum right here and now. I could run like I did when I found Sam and Tara together; saving myself, still having to look over my shoulder and blaming myself for their deaths. My parents would want me to live regardless of what happened to them. They wouldn't want me to be controlled by emotion and risk my own life.

On the flip side, what did I want? I wanted to flay those bikie bastards alive with a rusty butter knife. I said before I wouldn't run and I meant it. I had done my running from battles. I was done running. I was going to fight back and risk losing my own life to save them. If I ran now I would live, but I would be dead inside. Better to fight and die under the sword, than to be ruled by it. And you never knew, maybe I wouldn't die; perhaps I would come out on top with the sword in my hand.

I sat in David's car that was parked on the opposite side of the circuit that goes round my house. We parked there to be closer to the exit of the estate for a fast getaway.

"We have to get my parents out of there. They are all I have left," I said, pleading with David, knowing he was my only chance of getting them out alive. With all my determination and anger I knew I couldn't take down five big bikies by myself with no weapons. I needed David, the sharpest weapon I knew.

"I'll save them, and bring them back here to you. But you have to stay here. I don't think it's a good idea for you to come with me." I started to interject, but David held up a hand, "I don't want you getting hurt again and, besides, your parents wouldn't want you in a dangerous situation."

"No way am I staying here. They are my parents, and my responsibility. I'm going with you and, besides, I know my house better then you. You will need me to navigate," I countered, throwing in something that I could contribute to the rescue. Also, by the way I said it, with such determination and intensity, he knew there was nothing that was going to stop me from going in there to rescue my parents.

I could see David knew this argument was only going to end one way, because he just retorted, "Is there any way I can get you to stay here without tying you to the steering wheel."

"Nope. I thought you would have put up more of a fight," I said, knowing I had gotten my own way, and I wasn't about to get hog tied.

"If it was my parents in there, God himself couldn't keep me from trying to save them," David replied, before jumping out of the car. As he got out of the car he pulled out a flashlight. No, not just a flashlight, it was a batten with a LED light on the end.

"There will most likely be five men with guns inside or around my house and you plan to take them out with a flashlight," I said, not cloaking the worry underlining my tone.

"That's all I need and, besides, in close proximity my flashlight is better than their guns. By the time they have lifted their guns and flicked the safety off, I have already cracked them over the head with my flashlight," David said putting sense to his tactic.

"At least do you have one for me," I asked not wanting to go in there naked.

"No," David said quickly, then added in a softer tone, "You don't know how to fight yet, and you will just get yourself killed."

"Well whose fault is that?" I said, glaring at him.

David's head dropped, either in frustration or in guilt for not teaching me how to fight earlier. His hand slid into his back pocket, and then he handed me a pocket knife.

"Push the catch at the bottom, and the blade will be released. Then you can flick the blade up." I did as instructed. The blade was only about three inches in length, but it was better than nothing. Besides it's not the size that counts, it was how you use it.

"Keep it hidden; you need to be very close to use it effectively. Only pull it out at the last second if you need to use it," David warned. I closed the knife then slipped it into my pocket.

David's demeanour hardened, eyes narrowing, skin around his mouth tightening, seriousness covered his voice as he said, "Just stay behind me, stay quiet, and stay out of my way. If you need to tell me something tap my person, then sign with your hands or whisper in my ear. I don't want you getting in harm's way." His last words came out with such concern, that I got the hint that David had started to care for me more than a normal personal trainer would care for his client.

My house was dark, like someone had cut the electricity at the power-box. The only lights came from the faint glow of the solar panel garden lights that were scattered around the gardens.

After scouting out around the house, we saw there was one man standing by the front door, and one standing by the back; both carrying hand guns at the ready. Both looking alert and focused; ready to shoot anything that moved.

We determined the best way to enter the house undetected was through the laundry door on the side of the house. The two men would be too hard to take down from a front-on attack. We wouldn't be able to get close enough before they could put a few unwanted holes in our bodies. Luckily they didn't station men on all four sides of the house, because if they had we wouldn't be able to enter undetected. However, that meant if two guys were outside at least three were inside. If there had been two bikies per bike, then there could be a max of eight men inside the house, tearing it apart, and abusing my folks.

The laundry door opened with a squeak. My heart was already pounding, like a boxer on a speedball. My nerves were on the edge of their seat too. All my senses were heightened, so that squeak seemed like a siren going off, alerting everyone to our presence. But in a matter of fact, the noise was probably not much louder then a mouse's squeak.

I was in way over my head. Last time I tried to sneak around trying to play James Bond, I ran straight into the night working cleaner within the first few minutes. Now I was sneaking into my own house, with at least three men inside who wanted to kill me, and two outside who wanted to do the same, and all of them would be on us in seconds if they spotted us. This time if I made a wrong move I was pretty sure I wouldn't be able to talk my way out; this time I would get a bullet sandwich.

If David was afraid he didn't show it. He was the only reason I had faith that we could all get out of here alive. What I saw that night when he saved me was remarkable, something out of a comic book. I was hoping David had some sort of plan and wasn't just winging it. I do know one thing, though. This wasn't the first time he had done something like this, he was acting too cool, too confident, too sure of his actions. Either that or the man could dodge bullets and I was not ruling that one out just yet.

I was to stay behind David as he took the lead, and I wasn't to make a sound. It wasn't hard to locate where they were holding my parents. I could hear them through the walls. They didn't have to stay that quiet, seeing that our closest neighbours were at least a hundred metres away.

I could hear my mother's muffled sobs. A man yelling commands, demanding answers, and the sounds of fists colliding with flesh. I had to bite my tongue, literally. It was the only thing I could do to stop from shouting out their names, and telling them I was coming to save them.

We made our way to the living room where my parents were being manhandled, keeping quiet, being careful not to run into anything that could make a noise. The house was trashed, and our possessions were littered all over the floor making it so easy to step on something in the dark.

It wasn't like in the movies, when the hero sneaks into a house with a flash light blazing. In real life there was no sneaking into a dark house with your flash light on, because you would stand out like dogs balls if you did. We were so close now; my parents were just in the next room. David held up a hand, I stopped instantly, shock ran through me like an electric current running through a wire cable.

He leant over and whispered in my ear so quietly that I could just make out the words, "Do you trust me to keep you safe." I nodded not wanting to make a sound.

"Hide somewhere in this room, and then count to one hundred. Then scream as loud as you can," David said, his voice as low as possible. I could feel my eyes grow wide, I latched on to David's arm shaking my head no, not wanting to let go. He was going to leave me there alone with nothing but a three-inch pocket knife.

"Have faith, Sarah, I will get you and your parents out of this," David said, his eyes so trusting, his mouth so close to mine, his breath warm against my lips. I could almost taste him, he was that close.

David cupped my face in his hands, his hands on the sides of my jaw, and half on my neck. He lifted my chin so I was looking straight into his eyes, "You can do this Sarah; I won't let anything happen to you. I need a misdirection to catch them by surprise."

I understood why I had to stay behind, but I didn't have to like it. I didn't want to play the bait on the lure. I wanted to play offence, not defence. But I would play my part this time; there was too much at stake and not enough time to argue. David's hands were still tenderly cradling my face, I let go of his arm believing in his confidence, but I didn't let go of his stare. Then he did something so unexpected, so fortuitous that I was left spinning.

He kissed me, so tenderly, so sensually I forgot where I was in that instant. I didn't know how it happened, but I lost myself in that kiss.

Time seemed to stand still, like that moment of time belonged to us. His slightest touch lingering on my skin, lasting a lifetime. My eyes closed, I didn't want to open them. I didn't want to wake up to the reality of our situation.

Then snapping me back to reality, and letting that moment slip away through my fingertips, David said, "I had to do that at least once." It wasn't a goodbye kiss I realised, it was a just in case kiss.

"Now hide, and start counting to one hundred," he directed.

I opened my eyes, feeling his touch leave me, willing my head to stop spinning so I could regain my composure. As things started to make sense again our moment was swept aside. And David had gone with it, vanishing into the darkness of the house.

I looked around the room for somewhere to hide. I had seen enough movies to know the first place a person looks, was under the table or in the closet. So they were out of the question.

There was, however, a display hutch along the far wall of the room that was not totally pushed up hard against the corner, it left just enough room for me to squeeze behind. The hutch was wide enough to conceal my body from all angles except if you stood flat up against the wall. It wasn't the best place to hide but it was the best I could do under the circumstances.

I started to count inside my head: one, two, three...

The total absence of surrounding sounds in the room I was in, made what was happening in the next room to Mum and Dad so much more surreal. I envisioned them tied up to our dining room chairs. I did notice two missing. My mother with a bloody lip, tears streaming down her face, clothes torn, and a man dressed in leather holding her down. My imagination could see my father's face swollen from multiple punches, a man in gloves asking questions, but not getting the answers he wanted so he kept hitting him over and over again. It was like I was in the room with them, in the corner, just watching. Letting all the events unfold, not moving to lift a finger to help, but I was here, and I was going to help, they just needed to hold on I bit longer.

Nine, ten, eleven...

I could hear one of the men's voices clearly as he asked with a demanding tone, like he was used to this way of speaking, "Where is she?"

"I don't know," my father said. It came out sloppy and slurred, like he was drunk. Thud – the sound of fist impacting on face – then a groan of pain. That was my father's face, my father's pain. My body tingled with rage.

Sixteen, seventeen...

"Don't make me ask you again, old man. My knuckles are starting to get sore," the demanding voice went on.

There was something familiar about that voice, then like a lightning bolt to the brain, the image of Mr Shaved head flashed across my eyes. I would never forget that night, even if I wished to; it was a picture super-glued to the wall of my brain. I had tried to push that night to the back of my mind, but that night was burned into my brain with perfect clarity.

Twenty-one, twenty-two...

"I don't know, and even if I did, I wouldn't tell you," my father replied, his voice coming out thick with agony.

I was waiting for the next thud, but it didn't come. Instead Mr Shaved head said, "Maybe we are going about this all wrong. Your wife here is a pretty little thing. I can see where your daughter gets her good looks."

Dad's voice roared out, "Don't touch her, you deal with me you twisted maniac."

"Conner, you are in no position to be demanding anything," Mr Shaved head said calmly. "Calling me a maniac, just gives me more incentive to punish your wife for your uncooperative behaviour." I almost saw the smirk cross his face, the enjoyment of inflicting pain and misery.

Twenty-eight, twenty-nine...

"I think the best way to make you talk is to have a little fun with your wife," Mr Shaved head suggested. "Don't you think?"

"No," my father cried out, almost pleading.

"Jay," Mr Shaved head said.

"Yer, Ben," said a new lower sounding voice that I assumed was Jay.

"Please put your cock inside Mrs Smith, and don't take it out until she stops resisting, or she asks for more," Mr Shaved head ordered sadistically and so casually that it sounded like he was asking him to go down the street to buy a bottle of milk.

My mother screamed, but it was muffled like she was gagged. I could hear shuffling, thrashing. I guessed it was my father trying to break free of his bonds.

"If you touch her, I'm going to kill the lot of you," my father yelled through pointed teeth.

Thirty-five, thirty-six...

"Just tell us what we want to know, and Jay here won't impregnate your wife," Mr Shaved head said with a casualness in his tone, as if this was just another day at the office. For him I guessed it was.

"Okay, I'll tell you where she is. Please just don't touch my wife," Dad uttered, his voice sounded defeated. It was broken like I had never heard it before.

"So it seems you love your wife more than your daughter. I was starting to think it was the other way around," Mr Shaved head's voice sounded a bit more chipper, like a man about to get everything he ever wanted.

My mother made more muffled noises, like she was trying to yell, "No."

"Shut her up, before I have to come over and do it myself, and if I have to come over there, Conner here, might not indulge us about his little princess's whereabouts," Mr Shaved head barked.

Forty-four, forty-five...

Then I heard more struggles, a noise like someone being roughly forced to sit down in a chair. I could hear the feet of a chair slide back on the floorboards. I assumed my mother was strong-armed onto the chair.

My father's voice followed, "Sarah has gone to the movies with her boyfriend, just down the road at the local plaza."

Silence followed. Mr Shaved head must have been weighing up the confession, mentally checking whether or not to believe him. Seeing that I broke up with my boyfriend a few months ago, Dad was indeed lying. Dad wasn't ratting me out. He was just making up a story to stop them from raping my mother. Now Mr Shaved head just had to believe his story.

Fifty-two, fifty-three...

"See, was that so hard?" Mr Shaved head said, "We will have to check it out first before we let you go." There was something off about his voice though, like there was some misleading involved. My optimism for my parents not to be murdered by the hands of these lunatics had risen. It was wishful thinking.

Then something dawned on me as my hopes were lifted. They had been using their names. They could have been using aliases but I didn't think they were. There was no hesitation before the names rolled off their tongues. The two men outside were not wearing masks, so I was guessing these guys weren't either. If they were not masking their faces, they were not planning on leaving witnesses. That meant they were not going to leave anyone alive that could ID them.

Sixty-six, sixty-seven...

Mr Shaved head or Ben, as that Jay character had called him, broke my train of thought as his voice echoed through the house, "Hang on a minute, according to our information Sarah broke up with her boyfriend. You wouldn't be lying to us now would you, Conner?"

How did they know this? I thought with confusion.

Dad was quick to reply maybe, too quick, "No, no, no, they are trying to work things out I think, kids never know what they want these days."

Seventy-nine, eighty...

"Oh, I see, but there is only one thing, Conner, I don't believe you, and because I think you just lied to me I am now going to shoot your wife in the stomach," Ben said with a menacing tone, one with no hesitation, one with no doubt that he would do what he stated he would do.

Eighty-six, eighty-seven...

My heart sank, disbelief flooded my judgement. This couldn't be happening. I was dreaming. Yes, that was it. I was in bed having a nightmare, all I had to do was wake up, wake up, wake up, wake up I thought over and over again, but something inside me kept counting, knowing I was just trying to detach myself from the situation.

Ninety, ninety-one...

"Please no, shoot me," my father hollered.

"Don't you see, Conner; you hurt me with your lies, so now I'm going to hurt you. And I can't think of anything that will hurt you more than watching your wife bleed out. Watching her die slowly, and in terrible pain on the cold floor," Ben said icily, and then added, "And there will be nothing you can do to save her."

"Please," my father pleaded.

I couldn't believe what I was hearing; it had to be a bluff. It had to be.

Ninety-five, ninety-six...

The sound of the gunshot reached my ears with a bang, making me flinch. Then I screamed uncontrollably, unable to stop.

CHAPTER 22

*O*nce I was out of breath, and my scream had faded with it, I heard footsteps heading in my direction. I didn't care anymore; if that bullet had been for my mother I wasn't about to stay hidden in the shadows any longer. I was at least going to let her know that I was here.

"Mum," I shouted.

Tears filling my eyes, snot dropping out of my nose, I must have looked a disaster but I didn't care.

I squeezed back out of my hidey-hole, to confront a man lifting a silver hand gun in my direction. There wasn't much light in the room, but there was enough for me to see down the barrel of the gun that held a bullet with my name on it. As my life was about to end, I wasn't afraid, a calm washed over me. If I was about to die, dying with my family was not the worst way to go out. Better than being raped and beaten to death in the middle of nowhere, all alone, and scared. That was what could have been my fate not too long ago. No, dying with loved ones around was not the worst way to go.

As I was expecting to meet my maker the other side of my brain clicked on, starting my inner debate. Dying this way was not the worst way to go for me, but it would be for my parents.

A sickening crack split the room in half. The man's head fell forward, then he collapsed on the ground, but not before the gun went off.

The spark from the muzzle of the gun almost blinded me through the darkness. The bullet must have missed me by millimetres; I could feel the wind shift close to my arm, making my skin grow goosebumps. When my eyes adapted back to the darkness, I saw David rushing over to me fast and quiet with the grace of a leopard.

"Are you okay? Have you been hit?" David asked whispering, fully panic-stricken.

"No, I'm okay" I replied in a dazed whisper.

"I got all of them except the man in the room with your parents."

Parent, I thought, correcting David in my mind, and soon to be parentless if we didn't get in there to help. I didn't know how David took down the other men, and I didn't care, all I cared about was saving my father and hopefully my mother.

"Call out to the bikie in the other room, keep his attention on you so I can flank him. Whatever you do, don't go in that room with him," David said, before vanishing once again.

"Ben is it? I took down your boy, Jay. That was his name right?" I said with that same strange calmness that I didn't know I possessed. It came with that eeriness feeling. That feeling of not being fully in control, like it was me but it wasn't. It was my beast. The creature I unleashed on Sam. It was not scared of death and it craved blood. I was a woman running out of things to lose. My mother was dead or dying, my father held prisoner by a crazy man, and that crazy man was acting as executioner. He was holding the rope to the guillotine, with my father's head now on the chopping block.

A chuckle came from the next room. It was a bit unexpected. I was expecting outrage, fury and what did I get? A chuckle. After his giggling amusement had passed, Ben spoke, "Well, well, well, you're full of surprises, Sarah. That is who I am talking to?" I didn't answer straight away, so he went on, "Why don't you come in here, and we can have a good face to face chin-wag."

"I don't think so, Ben," I said dragging out his name to signify that I didn't trust that that was indeed his real name.

"If you don't come in here so I can see your pretty little face, I'm going to leave you parentless," Ben said.

"No Sarah, get out of here," my father yelled at me.

Then an impact of flesh hitting flesh sounded. The smack filled the room, followed by gagging, and then choking. My dad had been hit in the throat. He was struggling to draw breath, the desired effect of silencing someone. I couldn't leave and I could not go in that room.

I knew if I didn't go in there Ben would murder my father. He didn't seem like a man that bluffed. I just had to keep him talking. Keep his interest spiked so he wouldn't shoot me straight away. I just needed to give David enough time to get in position. Just before I turned the corner, before facing the holocaust in the next room, I picked up the gun I was almost shot with moments earlier. I stuck the gun down the back of my pants, lifting my loose fitting shirt over it to hide the bulge.

The room was a mess. All of our stuff was spread over the floor. Paintings were ripped off the walls, with holes replacing them. The room was lit by some sort of battery-operated lantern, so I could see everything quite clearly. But the holes in the walls, and our meagre possessions lying broken on the floor weren't what caught my eye. That was all just seen through a haphazard glance before sighting my mother lying on the ground in an expanding pool of her own blood.

I wanted to run up to her, wrap her up in an embrace. To tell her I was sorry for leading them here, tell her it was all my fault, and most of all, I wanted to tell her I loved her. But I couldn't. Not yet, not before seeing this man standing in front of me bleeding in his own river of blood.

My mother's bleeding was good and bad. It meant her heart was still beating, and I could see her rib cage expanding then compressing. She was still alive, but she wouldn't be for long by the looks of the blood loss. I still remember from my physical education class from school that the average human body could hold approximately five litres of blood, and there seemed to be about half that spreading over the floor. She was going to need a blood transfusion to survive this, I predicted. She could have all the blood she wanted from me if I had any left at the end of this encounter.

My father was tied to a chair with black duct-tape, still breathing hard after that hit to his windpipe. His face was swollen and bloody; blood was all over his blue shirt.

He turned to me as I walked into the room, his eyes wide with fright. Not for himself, but for me. I could tell that he couldn't go through seeing me shot too. At the moment he still had hope that at least I would survive. It was his fear that communicated to me. It was his fear that gave him away.

It wasn't until I broke eye contact with my father that I noticed Ben standing behind Dad with a gun pressed against his head. I knew Ben wouldn't shoot me straight away. He loved seeing the suffering of others. He would want to see the pain he inflicted upon me first.

How did I know this? I knew this because I was afraid I was becoming the same creature he was, and that horrified me more than the bullets in that gun. It scared me because I wanted to see this man bleed through his eyeballs, to hear him cry out in agony. I wanted to see the light vanish behind his eyes. I wanted him dead, I wanted his whole gang dead, and that was what frightened me, because I didn't want to feel that way, but something inside me did.

"I remember you, Ben, but I named you Mr Shaved head," I said plainly. "I like that better so I think I will keep calling you that."

"I didn't know I was that memorable," he retorted with a smile, taking my words as a compliment.

"Well you did leave me with a good reminder," I said pointing to my once swollen eye, "If I remember correctly I left my own mark on you too?"

Mr Shaved head raised his hand to touch the faded fingernail imprint on his face, before saying with an odd respect, "That you did, Sarah. You are a woman after my own heart. Too bad I will have to cut out your heart before the night is through."

"That won't be a problem, I don't have a heart left for you to take," I said convincingly.

Mr Shaved head's smile widened across his face. This man was a real psycho. He loved that I admitted to being broken inside. Seeing and inflicting suffering must be this guy's hobby. I bet it got him off too. That was why he seemed less interested in raping me that night than his bikie buddies. He would have preferred to beat me bloody rather than stick his cock in me, or maybe he needed to beat me bloody before he could get it up to rape me; very serial killer of him.

I looked back to Dad, recognition worn on his face like a glove. The realisation that this attack wasn't just random, but calculated, planned then executed. He knew now that what happened to me that night was no car accident.

"You really are something, you know that? I'm guessing that, because none of my mates come in here guns blazing after that shot went off, they're all down for the count too?"

I shrugged my shoulders at his accusation.

"I don't know how you did it, but I am very impressed," Ben said with actual sincerity.

"I have learnt a few things since last time we met," I said with growing confidence. This guy liked to talk once you got him started.

"Talking about that night, I lost my best friend that night," Mr Shaved Head said, pushing the gun down harder on my father's skull, making his chin hit his chest. "As you can imagine I wasn't too happy when I came to, finding my friend with a big hole in his neck." Mr Shaved Head paused for a second, reliving the experience before continuing, "So who was that guy anyway? I wouldn't mind having a friendly chat with him too."

David had already told me they knew his name. Mr Shaved Head was just fishing and I wasn't going to take the bait.

"That was my guardian angel," I replied.

"Your guardian angel, you say," he said, looking around the room dramatically. "Well I don't see any white-winged creatures here to save you now. I guess he left you to get yourself out of this predicament. That night must have been a one time deal."

The gun left the back of my father's head. Ben swung it up towards me, slowly for dramatic effect, to gauge my response, to watch the fear grow. Before the gun was trained on me, before I was in the line of fire, out of nowhere, and so fast I could barely trace the movement, David's batten came crushing down on Ben's arm.

The blow had bone-snapping force. His arm was now bent at an impossible angle. The gun went off, lighting up the room as if a flash grenade exploded. The bullet put a hole in the floorboards at his feet.

Then unseeable to the naked eye, as fast as an eye blink, David brought the batten down again. This time on Ben's knee, making the knee crumble in backwards. The bone shattered, piercing through the skin, like a pin being pushed through a sheet of cloth. This all happened so quickly, if you'd sneezed, you would have missed it. Ben now lay on the ground writhing in agony. It was a pleasing sight, to the dark side of my yin-yang.

I choked my blood lust down. Mr Shaved Head lay with one hand on his knee that was now bent backward. His broken arm lay motionless beside him. This man didn't deserve to be breathing after what he had done, and who knew what other horrific things he had done to other virtuous people. He deserved to be put down like an animal with rabies, after it went wild and ravaged an innocent person.

I pulled out the gun I had hidden in my pants. I was going to get rid of this man from my nightmares. I was going to protect the world by eliminating such an evil man. The world would be a much safer place with him buried under six feet of dirt. I had never fired a gun before, but I reckoned it couldn't be too hard to figure out. I looked over the gun turning it in my hands, searching for the safety switch. I found it on the side of the gun with a red dot next to it. The safety was already off. All I had to do now was point and shoot, and as long as the gun didn't jam up, there would be one less homicidal bikie in the world to cause havoc. My hands were shaking as I lifted the gun, not from terror, but excitement. The sights lining up on the middle of Ben's shaved head, my finger on the trigger ready to squeeze. My beast roared in delight, it was about to feed.

A steady hand landed on my shaky one. It was David's. It was hot and controlled, but not forceful. He was not trying to move mine; he was leaving the decision to shoot Mr Shaved Head up to me.

"You can't fix evil, by doing evil, Sarah," David uttered. I spun round to face him.

"Look what you just did, you basically snapped his leg in half, and besides look what he did to my mum," I said with my voice wavering. David's stance didn't falter.

"You're not me Sarah, and I didn't kill him. I just incapacitated him from killing you. What you are about to do is cold blooded murder." I faltered, not knowing how to proceed. The dark side was telling me to shoot, the white side telling me not to. What side was I drawn to more?

David went on, "I have done terrible things in my past, and I don't deny that. But I didn't have someone there to pull me back from the darkness. You do." I looked into his eyes. The worry for my untainted soul dominated his features. Only a man that had tasted the darkness knew its flavour and David knew.

"You will always have me to pull you back," he said in earnest. I wavered, my inner light dissolving the darkness.

"Just look at him, is he really worth it?" he said wanted me to look past my wanting wrath.

I looked at him, and I mean really looked at him. He was pathetic, once fierce and deadly, now a little schoolgirl could finish him off. I looked down at the man who had walked in my nightmares. He was helpless and crying like a baby. I mean actual tears were running down his face. He was deplorable, not worth wasting any more of my time. I saw now with a level head what David was saving me from. If I killed this man, it would torture my soul. It would put a black mark on my heart. I would live the rest of my life in the black side of the yin-yang with only a little bit of white. Killing him would be like contracting cancer, it would eat away at me until it consumed me, until there would be no little white dot left and I would become the thing I despise.

I locked my beast away letting it scream without the taste of blood in its mouth. I lowered the gun, throwing it to the side. I pulled out the pocket-knife David had given me earlier, and then cut Dad's bonds. I didn't check to see if he was ok. He was alive, that was all I needed from him at the moment.

My mother, on the other hand, was not so alive. She was on the forefront of my mind the whole time. She wasn't dead but she must be close. There was just so much blood. I could see that she was still breathing from the movement of her rib cage, but was she conscious. I knelt beside her, my pants soaking up the warm sticky blood. I put a hand on her shoulder; she flinched in reaction.

"It's okay mum, it's over now. Just hang on till we can get you to a hospital," I said quickly.

She just smiled, her eyes locking on mine. Such love escaped her gaze it was terrifying. It was like she was saying I love you with a look. A look that would say I love you for all the years to come, for all the years she would miss.

"You're father, is he...?" she said weakly.

"He's okay mum. He's alive," I replied.

A hand rested on my shoulder tenderly. I didn't need to look around to know Dad was kneeling beside me in the same pool of my mother's life force, the life force that was draining away. She looked up at Dad with the same look that she had given me. Not many marriages went for over thirty years, and their love was still as strong as it had always been. That was my parents, soul mates for life.

My mother's skin under my hand was cold and void of colour. All the blood was leaving her body. I lifted my head to search for David, he hadn't moved, he was still where I left him. It was like this scene of us as a family in grief was affecting him as much as it was affecting us. He look stunned, as if he was in a trance. David was fighting his own demons at the moment.

"David," I screamed. David didn't move, didn't even seem to notice that I just yelled his name.

"David," I screamed again. This time he woke up from wherever he was inside his own head.

"Call an ambulance," I screamed, unable to speak civilly.

David went to argue but I snapped out, "I don't care if it will bring more people that want to kill us, my mother needs a doctor."

I didn't look to see if David made the call. I just looked back down at my mother, tears starting to well up in my eyes as I saw the despair in her situation. Seeing the lost cause for what it was.

She was able to raise a hand to my cheek touching it ever so lightly, her gaze switching between me and my father. The words came out soft and low like someone trying to talk right before falling asleep, "I love you both so..." the words trailed off, her eyes closed, her breathing became more and more shallow, as her rib cage stopped rising and falling.

My mother passed away in my arms.

I had no delusions. I wasn't going to pound on her chest and cry out, don't go Mum, don't leave me, come back. My mother was dead and there was nothing I could do to change that. At least in the end she had love in her heart, not fear or anguish. She got to say I love you one last time. Not that that was any consolation prize.

I turned to give Dad a hug, needing the support. I needed someone to help me through this. I needed someone to share the loss with, to share the pain with, and to share the rage that was starting to flow through me again, my beast trying to break down the door. I may not have pulled the trigger to end Mr Shaved Head's life, but that didn't mean I still wouldn't want to pistol whip his ball sack until his balls shot through his nostrils and his head exploded. I needed my father to lean on, but when I turned, my father had moved away from me. He walked over to where I threw the gun. He picked it up, and then pointed it at the man wallowing in pain from a broken arm and a shattered leg.

"Dad don't, it's not worth it," I said, trying to extend my understanding of what would have plagued me if I had pulled that trigger.

Bang.

The bullet struck him square in the head. Blood, brain matter, skull fragments splattered all over the floor. The room went silent, my ears ringing from the gunshot.

Dad walked right up close to the now dead man, his toes almost touching the lifeless flesh, and then he emptied the guns clip into Mr Shaved Head's absent beating heart.

CHAPTER 23

*W*hat happened next was a blur. David must have called the ambulance because I remember seeing red and blue flashing lights. I remember sirens filling my eardrums with squeals, and the noise slowly becoming vague and distant. I remember being almost dragged out of the house. I didn't want to leave. I didn't want to leave my mother. My father was beside me, I think. I didn't know if David had dragged him out as well or he came freely, but he was there in the car as I was almost tossed on his lap in the two-seater cab of David's ute.

Then I remembered nothing but the vision of my mother's eyes closing for the last time. That haunted loving expression on her face as she died in my arms will stay with me until the day I die.

When I realised that I was still alive, and hadn't perished along with my mother I grew sadder still. I know she would want me to go on living my life to the fullest, cherish her memory and not be consumed by it. Through me her memory lived on, through my beating heart I would always carry her with me. All I had ever wanted to do for my parents was make them proud of me, and all I would have to do to achieve that was live a happy fulfilled life.

But at the moment all I wanted to do was feel her warm hugs, feel her fingers running through my hair, stare at her smile that was so infectious that it always made me smile back. And if I couldn't do that in this life, I knew I could do it in the next. I had never been a patient woman. I would never do anything to speed up our next encounter, but in my current predicament I didn't think I would have to wait very long.

I wasn't a religious woman; my parents neither. I had always believed in something more though, something beyond our world, beyond our understanding, something hidden, something secret.

That's why I believed my mother was in a better place. If anyone deserved a place in heaven it was her.

I would never leave my father if I could help it. He needed me now more than ever; even though he wouldn't speak to me at the moment.

When the world around me made sense again I noticed we were held up in some log walled shack, I could literally see through the walls. The place was small, about the size of our living room, with no walls just a few lines of cloth making dividers. It had an old brick fireplace, a table with two chairs, which all looked like they were about to fall apart and give someone tetanus.

My father sat in the corner being non-responsive. He wasn't weeping, or crying, his eyes dry. He was just staring blankly into no man's land. I wanted to go over to console him, bring him back to me. But I didn't know what to say, or even where to start. How did you say, sorry I lied to you? Sorry that lie got your wife murdered? Sorry that those men weren't after you, they were after me? I couldn't find my voice, so I said nothing. I thought I would probably just make things worse at this point.

Thinking of my poor decision making, not filling them in about what happened, making up the lie about the car crash. It all made the guilt set in deeper, roots digging in and holding on strong. It was my fault my mother was dead. There was no way to make up for the lie I told her, no way to make things right, no way to bring her back. Then I thought about my last line of thought. Maybe I was wrong about making things right. I could get justice; punish those who took her away from me. I could bring down the entire Creatures of Chaos bikie ring. I could take them down one deadbeat loser at a time, even if it took me the rest of my life. Perhaps if I did that it would save the next innocent family from the same fate we experienced.

I got up off the ground, which was just hard dried cracked compacted dirt. I was going to stop feeling sorry for myself, and start doing something proactive. I was going to do something that would make my mother proud. I dragged David outside.

I didn't notice it before on the drive in, I was too lost in mourning my mother, too lost in my sorrowing state that I missed where we were. We were on a mountain top, gum trees stood tall all around us. The terrain was rocky. The dirt was rich and red and broken up with dried green-looking shrubs. It was gorgeous.

Before I could get a word out David said, "I'm sorry."

"Sorry for what?" I questioned confused.

"I told you I would get you all out of there. I failed," David said shamefully. He turned to the side, away from me. Failure was not something that happened to him often, I surmised.

There was a part of me that wanted to blame David for what had happened. I wanted to blame him for asking me to make up that lie. I could have told my parents the truth, we could have fled, and my mother would still be alive. But it wasn't his fault. I didn't have to go along with it. I didn't even truly believe they would find me. If we had told my parents the truth maybe things would have turned out differently. Then again, it could have turned out a lot worse too. If I had told my parents the truth, they would have most likely gone to the cops, and if the cops were in league with the bikies, then it was possible we all would be worm food right now.

If you really wanted to get down to it, if I hadn't run away from Sam and Tara screwing that night, and had the courage to stand up for myself, and thrown my shoes at them like I wanted, I would never have run into those bikies in the first place, so the blame falls on me once again.

"It's not your fault, David, you didn't pull the trigger, and if it weren't for you I would be parentless and dead three times over," I expressed sincerely. "Where are we anyway?" I asked, changing the subject, done with wasting my time pondering whose fault it was. I knew whose fault it was, who was responsible for all of it, the people that pulled the trigger, the Creatures of Chaos gang.

"Somewhere, where no one will find us." I looked at him wanting more detail, and he knew it. "We're about three hours north of the city.

This was my uncle's land. He left it to me when he died," David said. Then getting down to business he asked, "Why did you drag me out here? I'm guessing it wasn't to ask me where we are."

"I'm going to take them all down. The entire Creatures of Chaos bikie club," I voiced with such conviction that David almost had to take a step back. I went on, "I know you know people that can get us information. How else did you know they found out where I live?" David stood silent, so I kept going, "And I don't know how you do what you do, but you promised to teach me, so enough playing around, stop teaching me this timid bullshit, and teach me how to protect the ones I care about."

I stood panting, out of breath, full of emotion, full of conviction. All my goals, all my ambitions could only come to fruition if David decided to help me. The only way I would have a chance to crumble the club into the dirt would be with David's skillsets, in which I still hadn't fully found an end to yet.

"You want to bring down the Creatures of Chaos?" David said, stating the obvious.

I nodded before confirming, "That's what I said."

"Do you even know how big of a club they are? Do you know what resources they have at their disposal? How much money they have to bribe cops, judges, politicians with?" David asked.

"No. But that's why I need you."

"Ok. For starters the Creatures of Chaos are basically spread over every continent from here in Australia, to the UK, to the USA, they are even in Japan. You would never be able to take them all down."

I sighed. I wasn't going to give up. I wasn't going to get disheartened by the size of the club. Nothing was impossible. If I hit the right spot there was a chance I could cause an avalanche of sorts. Perchance I could knock over one standing domino at the front of the line, and watch as it took down the rest of its fellow tiles.

"Well you have to start somewhere. If I can't take down the entire club then at least put a hole in their network, cut off a finger from the main body. I'll start with the members in our city, the bikies that want us dead," I said defiantly. "So are you going to help me or not?" I asked, starting to wonder. "They're after you as well, don't forget."

I know I was the dreamer and he was the realist, but the world needs both to improve. David just stood there watching me like I was his favourite TV show. It seemed like he stood there staring at me for the entire length of *The Simpsons* series marathon. Then he did something unexpected, he just sat down in the dry dirt and crossed his legs.

"What are you doing?" I questioned.

"Meditating."

"Why?" I asked confused. This wasn't the time to daydream.

"I need to think about how to answer you."

This was stupid I thought. What a crock of cow dung. David was wasting my time. I needed to start doing something. I needed to punch something, kick a tree or something. I needed to vent my anger, let this frustration go, channel it towards an objective.

After a moment David said, reading my aura, "You are blind with frustration, your anger clouds your judgment and I can't seem to concentrate with you hovering over me."

"Well, sorry for breathing in your vicinity," I said childishly.

I expected David to react but he didn't. He just stayed calm, which was even more infuriating, before replying, "That's okay I forgive you."

A wry smile showed up on his lips after that. Before I had a chance to respond he added, "You should join me. I was going to teach you how to meditate anyway."

"Oh, really?"

"Yes. In a way you have already started."

"I think you dreamt that one."

"You ever wondered why I always told you to concentrate on the muscle group you were exercising?" He quizzed.

"Yer, what of it?" I shot back, seeing all that as pointless activities.

"I got you to do that to narrow your concentration on a singular aspect, to drive all other thoughts away, making you focus your mind. It is the first step in freeing one's mind," he said.

"Oh, I didn't know there was more to it," I reluctantly admitted.

"Do you know of the samurai?" David asked.

"Is it a pizza?" I said, guessing. David chuckled to himself for a second before he regained face.

"The samurai were ancient Japanese warriors. Before they went into battle they would meditate. They would clear their minds until their full focus was on the mission ahead."

That did sound pretty cool though, but I was meant to be angry. I wasn't just going to bend a knee, even if I was willing to let him teach me. My father's stubbornness, I suppose.

"I started taking meditating more seriously a few years ago," David began, filling my stubborn silence with words, "I had my own anger issues, very much like you. I haven't mastered inner peace or anything. I still battle with emotions like everyone else. At this very moment I am dealing with all the emotions failure brings. The most crippling is the guilt I feel for failing you and your mother. But I will not let it control me. I will not let it drive me to do something I will regret. That is why I must clear my own mind before I answer you. At the moment I want to hurt every last one of those bikies, but that might not be the right call."

I didn't know David battled with such compounding emotions. He always seemed so focused and in control. This stuff might really work. David didn't stop there.

"I'm not there yet, but I am on the path of mastering my demons. They still slip through sometimes but, in a way, meditation saved my life, it saved me from myself. In my experience and what I have seen, once you have grasped the first few steps, once you can distinguish between your mind, body and soul, you can achieve amazing things. For example, you can achieve a clear calm mind in a stressful situation just as the samurai did in battle. You can even learn to separate your mind from your body to block out pain." That would be a neat trick I thought with my defences starting to crumble. I continued to pace back and forward. David continued talking.

"With all that you have been through: your mother's passing, your break up with your boyfriend, your panic attacks, your violent interactions, and your craving for violence. You need a way to calm your mind, to find a way to relax, let go of your anger, and let in peace and tranquillity."

He was not looking a bit embarrassed about what he just said. I always thought this was for all those spiritual nut jobs out there, but it seemed to have worked for David. I had even seen the results I realised. The way he stayed so calm while Mr Big Bikie attacked him with a knife, the way he stayed so level-headed as he took down five men with guns at my house. After a little more pacing, a few stomps of my foot, I thought why not, what do I have to lose? I sat down in the dirt facing David.

"How do I do this then? Clear my mind or something. Because I have tried that and it doesn't work," I said. David reached into his pocket, and pulled out a red lighter.

"What you need to do is concentrate on a singular thing. It could be anything from a person, to an item, to an object, or like the Samurai, a task they must perform in the future." That made more sense I thought. Your brain never stopped thinking; even in sleep, you dream.

"What I want you to do is focus on this flame," he said.

"Why fire? Fire is destructive. Fire is rage," I asked.

"Because you have a fire inside you that is just starting to burn out of control, it's a fire you just learnt you have, and you need to be able to harness that inner flame, let it out in controlled bursts," David said knowingly, like he was talking from experience. David sparked the lighter, the flame burst into existence.

"Focus on the flame until that is all you see."

I focused on the flame, just as David said. I started by trying to cancel out all my surroundings. There were things I didn't even realise were there until I was trying to get rid of them. The wind in my hair, the sound it made as it passed through the trees, the sounds of birds singing their songs to one another, the feeling of the hard rocky earth under my feet, the heat from the sun against my face. All those things started to disappear one by one as if once I knew they were there I could delete them from my consciousness. I did this until there was only me and the flame left.

I closed my eyes still seeing the flame but it wasn't burning from the lighter anymore, it was burning from a long white candle. There was nothing but black behind it, nothing to be illuminated from its light, it was just me and the candle of flame. There was no wind, so the flame didn't dance to any rhythm, just stayed constant, not moving, just eating away at the wax in the wick. Then the candle started to melt faster and faster, until there was no more. I thought the flame was going to go out, but it erupted in an inferno, my whole world was alight.

I pushed back, centring myself. I tried to feel my inner strength, tensing it like you would a muscle. I was strong; I was the master of this domain. The inferno started to shrink, growing smaller by the second until it was just a single flame once again. Now the flame burnt from nothing, just a flame in its own right, like now it was alive and had a mind of its own. Now it was under my control, and would do as I instructed. I was queen and it was my knight, my sword.

I opened my eyes now centred, relaxed, calm, all my worries gone with the flame. Sorry, the flame wasn't gone it was controlled. David was staring at me with a strange understanding, it was radiating from him like he had just been inside my head with me.

"I will help you," David announced.

CHAPTER 24

"What's the plan then, David?" I asked.

"Now you have taken the first step in controlling your mind, the next step is to master your body along with it. So, before we go any further with Operation Bikie Takedown, I'm going to teach you some basic self-defence moves," David said, with his personal-trainer voice.

I stood facing him, the tall gum trees shrouding us in its shade, the sunlight only breaking through the gaps between the leaves. My heart skipped a beat with excitement. I had been waiting for this. Be cool I thought, be cool.

"I'm ready," I said, not sure I really was free from my inner beast's control. I had a leash on it at the moment, but the dark creature of my psyche was still there trying to dig its claws into someone's flesh and taste the sweet blood. It was unsettling how easy I fell into the rhythm of training with David. Everything seemed to fade away. The things that threw my insides around stopped. I was able to let everything go, like the bikies coming to kill me, Sam and Tara's betrayal, my mother's death, and purely focus on my training. When I trained, my whole world was just David and me.

"Okay, Sarah, if I was going to attack you what would be the easiest way to take me down or immobilize me?" he asked.

"Punch you in the face," I suggested, just guessing. It worked on Sam.

"It will slow me down, but it wouldn't stop me, try again."

"I would kick you in the nuts then," I said, thinking of the second move I made on Sam.

"That's better," he praised, "That would almost always work in stopping your assailant. There are a few exceptions, however; for one, your attacker could be a woman, and I don't think kicking a woman between the legs would give you the same outcome as if you kicked a man there. Two, your attacker could be on drugs, and a drugged-up guy will keep coming no matter how many times you kicked him in the crown jewels."

I noticed David placed a hand over his groin in an instinctive reflex when he mentioned *kick him in the crown jewels*. The movement made me follow his hand until it dropped down between his legs. I wasn't sure if my eyes lingered too long, but when I lifted my sight back up to meet his, I could feel my face start to flush.

"The best way to stop a man's attack is, as you pointed out, a quick kick to the nuts, but if that doesn't work I'll give you some other options," David offered. "Let's say, for example, that your attacker was out of his mind on drugs, another very effective way to immobilise your opponent is to blind them. Stick your finger straight in their eyes. If they can't see you, then they can't attack you," David pointed out. Gross, I thought, but I could see how it would be effective.

"Another good move is to hit both their ears with the palms of your hands at the same time. This will rupture their eardrums and cause great pain," David added while doing the action on himself. David was on a roll so I didn't want to say anything to stop the wheels turning.

"Another good striking area is to hit your attacker hard in the throat; if they can't breathe a person tends to panic. At least, until they're able to breathe again, which should give you plenty of time to run away." Then David went on to say "You're only a small girl, not overly strong."

"Well, thanks, that's a great confidence builder," I said, acting hurt.

"What I meant to say was, that you will need to know where to hit a person to get the most out of your attacks," David quickly added.

"Nice cover up," I said.

"Thanks," he replied, "For example, if you want to land a knockout blow, then the best spot to aim for would be the jaw or the side of the head at the temples. If you wanted to hit the body, aim for the base of the sternum," David said, pointing to the middle of his chest as he kept talking, "it will most likely knock the wind out of your opponent or you could fracture their sternum which is quite painful, also." That little bit of information could come in handy in a tight situation I thought. "But to hit someone in those locations you must know how to punch first," David added.

"Well, yer," I said, sarcastically.

"Normally I would teach defence first, how to block, counter and evade, but I don't think we are going to have a lot of time and I'm fairly positive you're more interested in the offence side of things first, am I right?" David said, knowing that he was.

"Y...e...ep," I said dragging out the word for a maximum yes. I didn't know if it was the guilt over my mother's death or the fact he actually thought I was ready, but either way my patience had paid off. I was finally going to learn how to fight.

"Alrighty then," David said, "Start doing the warm up stretches I taught you."

A moment later he left me doing my stretches and took off towards the car. When David got back he was carrying a pair of boxing gloves and two gloved pads. He handed me the boxing gloves as he put on the pads. The gloves smelt a bit used, like dried sweat, but I wasn't going to let that stop me. Stinky hands were a small price to pay.

"Now I'm going to show you just a few moves to begin with. It was Bruce Lee that said 'I fear not the man who has practised 10,000 kicks once, but I fear the man who has practised one kick 10,000 times,'" David quoted.

"Who is Bruce Lee?" I asked, with no friggin idea. David just shook his head sadly.

"Only one of the greats of the martial arts cinema," he said, changing what he was about to say mid-sentence. "If we get through this alive we will have to watch one of his movies together."

"It's a date," I put forth, without thinking. Then, when I realised what I just said, I could feel my face go a deeper shade of red. First I'd looked at his crotch for too long, and then I go and finalise a date. I was grateful when David didn't add any embarrassing comments to make my red face stain permanently. I did see his eyebrows lift with amusement, however.

At first, when David and I began our sessions together, the tension was a bit high, especially after what we went through together. But, as time passed and we became more comfortable around each other, David and I always seemed to get locked into a verbal kissing match when we hung out. Our relationship had always stayed platonic, however. It was nothing more than light-hearted flirting. It was then though I remembered the kiss, the kiss that changed things. The one he planted on me before my mother was shot. I am sure he was considering the outcome of never getting another chance to kiss me. That the bullet that claimed my mother's life could have been signed in my blood. I thought about asking him why he kissed me but, before I could put thoughts to words, David started up again.

"Okay then, Sarah, show me your best punch," David said lifting his padded hands up for me to hit. I didn't really know how to punch too well. When I punched Sam outside my house, I was just reacting. I didn't think about it, I just did it. Not really knowing what to do, I stood there and gave it my best shot. I punched the pad on David's left hand. As it impacted I had to take a step back or I would have fallen over.

"Did you see what you did wrong?" David asked, cocking his head.

"I nearly fell over, that's what I did wrong," I said, annoyed at myself.

"First you have to position your feet correctly. Once you know how, it will come as second nature to you," David pointed out. He placed one leg forward and the other behind, as if taking a step forward and then pausing. His body was slightly angled, but he was still facing forward. I should have known that. The Tae-Bo classes I took with Tara always started with positioning of your feet for balance. I realised I had seen the Tae-Bo classes as more of an aerobic thing, rather than a martial arts thing. I should have been taking some of the martial arts aspects out of the aerobic workout. I guess my sub-conscious did though, seeing how well I decked Sam.

"You're right-handed, so lead with your left leg. Copy me," David instructed. I copied David's stance.

"The first time you had your feet parallel. If you stand like that I could push you over easily," David said, then walked over to me and pushed my shoulders. I resisted not taking a step back. "See," David uttered, "much more stable." I just smiled. This was the kind of stuff I was waiting to learn. Patience was a virtue after all.

"Now throw another punch," David said, smiling back at me. So I did. This time when glove hit pad the recoil didn't make me lose my balance.

"Good, Sarah. Now I want you to twist your hips a bit more when you punch. Most of your power is generated from the hips," David said, then threw a punch into the air giving me an example. As I watched I noticed his hips moved first. They almost seemed to catapult his strike.

David held up his hand for me to hit once again. I positioned my feet again, left foot forward, right foot back, and then struck the pad twisting as I did. I could feel the power difference. I even heard the difference. The slap of the glove hitting the pad was much louder, denser.

"Good, good. You learn quickly," David praised, while shaking his hand.

"Thought you would have picked up on that by now," I said, feeling very smart. Then adding, "I may have lived in a bit of a bubble gum bubble, but all this," I said circling my face with my gloved hand, "Isn't just for looks."

"Oh, believe me. I know you're smarter than you look," he responded with a knowing grin. Now I knew how Joe felt.

"Was that a compliment or a poke?" I queried, crunching my eyebrows together. David just kept that half-cocked grin. I followed on, "Your last tip then." I raised my fists in readiness.

"When you hit the pad aim about six inches behind your target, but never over throw your punch. If you do you will lose your centre of balance making you unsteady on your feet." David pointed out. Then I remembered Mr Big Bikie lunging at David with the knife, and how David had countered that lunge by pulling him forward making him lose his balance then redirecting the knife back upon him. I was about to say my thoughts out loud, then thought better of it. That couldn't be a happy memory for him so I left it lie.

We must have been practising for an hour the same one-two punch. Left jab, followed by a right-handed power shot. The only other move David taught me was a straight up-front kick, good for kicking someone in the nuts, or if I could reach the height with my foot, under the jaw. We were both so caught up in the training that when a booming voice echoed through the valley it caught us both off guard, making David go rigid and ready to attack, and me jump a foot backwards.

The powerful voice said, "Stop that this instant."

# CHAPTER 25

$\mathcal{T}$he commanding voice rang through the valley. If there was someone anywhere in a five-mile radius they would have heard my father's voice as clear as if they were standing next to him.

"What do you think you are doing?" My father said, standing at the doorway of the cabin, eyeing off David like he was the devil himself teaching me the dark arts.

"I was teaching Sarah how to protect herself against an attack," David responded, unintimidated.

Dad was walking over to us almost stomping with each step, anger boiling over in his voice as he said to David, "Hasn't my daughter been around enough violence for you? Why are you encouraging her to get involved in more?

"I asked him to teach me," I said, cutting in, trying to calm the situation, hoping my father would see me and not be blinded by the rage that burned in his eyes. My father whirled on me, nearly unrecognisable. I wondered, was that what I looked like when I lost it with Sam. There was such animosity in his face. His expression said his humanity was hanging on by a thread. One more little annoyance would push him to breaking point.

"I'll deal with you in a minute, young lady," Dad huffed, and then spun back to David.

"If you don't want me teaching Sarah self-defence that's your right as her father to have that opinion, but Sarah is not a little girl anymore. She can make her own decisions," David said, with such calm I was amazed. To be confronted with such hysterics and keep so composed was a battle in itself. My father had a natural dominance about him, and he was in no way not looking for an excuse to start a fight.

I shot David a warning glance, trying to tell him with my facial expression to be careful. I didn't think he noticed though. David's full attention never left my father. I guess when a bull is charging at you, you don't take your focus off the pointy horns coming your way.

"You better learn your place, boy, before I put you in it," Dad said, threatening David to challenge him, and David did.

"You say you don't want any more violence, and here you are provoking it, wanting it," David said, wanting a rise from the older man.

"Violence is warranted when words have lost all meaning," my father countered.

"Words only have no meaning when people don't listen," David volleyed straight back.

Then out of nowhere an arm came flying up, and a fist headed straight for David's nose. What astonished me most of all was not that my father acted in such an outlandish way. I saw that one coming. No, what surprised me was that my old man knew how to hit. Everything David just taught me, Dad mimicked perfectly, his stance, technique, was all executed flawlessly; from my newly trained eye anyway.

My father had always seemed such a peaceful happy man. I had never even seen him get angry before, or more accurately out of control angry like now. This was a side of him I had never seen before. Then again I had never seen him go through so much suffering before either. Getting tied up and beaten, watching the love of his life being shot and then dying right in front of him, and worst of all he was totally powerless to prevent the bullet from falling. Then on top of that to dish out his own brand of punishment by putting a full clip of bullets into a man's chest, turning his black heart into meat mush inside his own ribcage.

The punch landed with such a thud that it echoed through the valley. David's padded hand went up just in time to catch the strike. I thought that punch would be it, but Dad kept going, throwing one punch after another. My dad was good, but he couldn't match David's speed, no one could it seemed. David was just too fast, catching each punch perfectly on the pads, whether it was a high-head shot, or a low shot aimed at his torso, they all landed dead centre on the pads.

David with a controlled calm non-puffed voice and with a raging bull of a man trying to punch his lights out was still able to say to me calmly, "Sarah, could you please go back in the cabin. You're father and I need to have a word." Reluctantly I agreed.

Walking back to the cabin all I could hear was the slap of fists hitting pads, and my father's heavy breathing.

CHAPTER 26

I must have been waiting inside that cabin bored out of my skull for hours. The sound of fists slapping leather only went on for about fifteen minutes, not that I could accurately say without a watch or a clock to go by. I could say without any word of a lie that I couldn't tell the time by the movement of the sun.

David walked through the door first. I was waiting for my father to follow in close behind. When he didn't, alarm bells started sounding in my mind. I always seemed to automatically go straight to the worst-case scenario.

"Is my father okay? Did you hurt him?" I blurted out in a panic. I know David wouldn't have hurt him unless he was forced to, Dad wasn't quite in his right mind, anything could have happened.

David just smiled a tired smile. He looked so run down. I guessed a full night without sleep would do that to the best of us. I never knew he could get tired, I always thought of him like an Energizer battery, they just kept going and going and going – so the ad said anyway.

"No, I didn't have to subdue him or anything. He just needed to blow off some steam is all," David said wearily and quite forgivingly too. David sat down in one of those rickety chairs, or you could say collapsed in one of those occupational health and safety high-risk chairs.

"Your father is outside waiting for you," David said, lowering his head on to his forearms, looking like his head was made of lead and he didn't have the strength to lift it back up.

"Why?" I asked.

"He wants to talk to you," David responded, sounding exhausted and already half asleep. I was about to ask talk about what, but then I could hear David's breathing steady into a rhythm, and the slightest snore at the end of each inhale. The man was already asleep.

"Have a good sleep, David," I whispered as I walked out the door, eyes scanning for my father. He was sitting on a rock about fifty metres from the cabin, staring into the gorge of rock and trees. I sat down next to him slightly apprehensive.

"Have you calmed down now?"

"I'm sorry about that, Sarah. I didn't mean to lose it at David like that," he said with genuine sorrow. I put a hand on his shoulder, letting him know I understood the wrath when it takes over.

"You wanted to talk to me?" I asked in my mousiest voice.

"That David is one hell of a guy, isn't he?" Dad uttered looking into space, still lost in his own mind.

"Yer, he is," I agreed. Dad ran a hand through his hair pushing the hair follicles back. It was the nervous twitch he did before getting into something deep.

"What happened to you no woman should ever have to live through," he said. His eyes began to go glassy with the pain and knowledge of what tragedies his daughter had gone through. The way he looked at me; he couldn't have just been talking about last night, his gaze was much more penetrating, more knowing. I was about to ask what do you think I have been through, but all I get out was "Wha...," before my throat closed up.

"David filled me in about what really happened that night after you came home all battered and bruised, and why he told you to lie to your mum and me," Dad said softly with no anger, but understanding.

"What else did David say?" I asked, now wishing I had been the one to tell him the truth. I felt a little robbed.

"What else is there to say?".

"He told you he killed one of them?" I said, starting off.

"Yes," Dad said, awaiting more bad news.

"He told you that they bashed me?"

"Yes," he said, slower this time.

"Did he tell you they were only millimetres away from raping me?" I said, barely able to get the words out.

"No," he said under his breath. He balled his hands into fists. He closed his eyes and took in some deep breaths trying to calm himself. He started to tremble too; his rage was chewing through his body. At least now I knew where my beast comes from.

"I'm sorry that happened to you. I can't imagine it was an easy thing to deal with all by yourself?" he whispered, his voice wavering slightly fighting to stay controlled.

"David helped me a lot," I pointed out.

"I could believe that. He seems to manage hardship very well, doesn't he?"

"Maybe too well," I agree, knowing David had had some practice with dealing with turmoil, he had admitted as much. I just didn't know what incited that practice. Dad gave me a knowing glance before he inquired, "Is there anything else I need to know?"

"I don't think so," I murmured under my breath, so quietly I wasn't sure if he heard. Then, I thought about it properly; there was more he needed to know. There was no going back for him as there was no going back for me. There would be no more holding anything back from him. He knew the events of the past that led us here, but he didn't know what I had planned for the future. So I spilled my guts.

"I am going to try and put all those motorcycle hooligans either in jail or in a wooden box," I said, not able to meet his eyes in fear of his disapproval. I couldn't take that right now.

I was waiting for a 'hell, no!' or an, 'that is way too dangerous,' or even a, 'don't be ridiculous,' but it never came.

What came instead was, "I don't think we have much of a choice do we?" he said. He kept going by adding, "Going off what David said, and I have come to trust the guy after our little talk."

Our eyes met then, the hardness in his features vanished and, seeing I needed the support, he leaned over and put an arm around my shoulders. Then he went on to say, "He tells me that they have the law-makers and the law-enforcers in their pockets, so that only leaves us with a couple of options. Running, and living in fear for the rest of our lives, or take matters in our own hands and stop these killers before they kill us."

My head went up in shock. I was not expecting that to come out of his mouth. He had a point to his logic. He quite elegantly took the bad part of our situation and put it into a simple objective.

"So you're going to help us then?"

My father didn't answer my question. I suppose he didn't need to. What he said next was a bit out of the blue. It wasn't what I was expecting at all.

"I have never looked at you in this way before."

"What way?" I had to ask.

"As a woman," he said, "You've always been my little girl, I must have missed it when you transformed into a woman." He stopped to take a breath then placed a loving fatherly hand upon mine.

"I see now you're old enough to make your own decisions. All I can do is help guide you. The time for telling you what to do has past. If you have made up your mind to nail those sons of bitches to the cross, then I'll hand you the hammer."

A smile grew on my face. It was good to have Dad back in my corner. To have him notice how much I had grown, to be seen as a woman, and no longer being seen as a little girl in his eyes. The feeling was uplifting. The truth was that I had only felt like a woman since *that* night. I was so naïve that all I saw before then was sunshine and rainbows. I never noticed the darkness of night that followed. But it was David who made me see that, even though there was evil and hatred in the world, there was still more beauty and love in it. Through him I realised the power of love would always triumph over hatred.

Keeping the truth from my father was to distance myself from him, and every woman needs her father. Besides, not to correct him, in some ways I will always be his little girl.

"You're not going to kick me out of the house now are you?" I asked bringing a smile to his face.

"Not just yet," he responded jokingly, leaving the door open for the possibility. At least I hoped it was in jest, not that we have a home to go back to now, anyway. After the humour faded away down into the gorge Dad went on to say, "You know you can talk to me about anything? And whatever you say, or whatever you have done, I will always love you." Dad told me this with all the love that a father can give, and then some.

"Yer, I know," I stated, with my heart swelling. I had to say something and I was terrified to say it. I couldn't take the blow if he blamed me, but I had to know.

"I'm sorry about Mum" I whispered, ashamed of myself. "I didn't mean for all this to happen," I continued, battling the lump in my throat. Scared of what he might say.

"It's not your fault, hun. None of this is your fault," my father came out with. "All the blame and I mean all of the blame falls on those bikie bastards." His grip tightened across my shoulders as he continued, "Don't you ever forget that. Alright?" I nodded, unable to do anything else. "We are all the family we have left, pumpkin," Dad said, as a tear rolled down his cheek. He was thinking of happy thoughts of my mother, happier times that we will never get to recreate.

"As for what happened last night," he paused, settling himself, "You were right."

"Right about what?"

"About taking that man's life, about firing that bullet into his cranium. It is one thing to kill a man in self-defence protecting yourself or loved ones, or even in the service of your country. But what I did was cold and vengeful and it made me as bad as him." He looked out over the horizon seeking the forgiveness from the gods that will never come. "If I was put back into that situation, I couldn't say I wouldn't do it all over again, but what I can say with certainty is that I'm proud of you for having the strength I didn't."

Tears were streaming down my face now. I wrapped my arms around my old man and we cried together. We cried for the loss of my mother, his wife, and being thankful that we still at least had each other.

Through a tear-stricken face and uncontrolled breath I was able to get out just one more sentence, "We will get through this together."

# CHAPTER 27

*O*ur first foot forward so to speak on operation Take-down the Creatures of Chaos, started with a visit to that mysterious man David had gone off with at his charity event. We were going to see the man who was wearing that old Driza-Bone jacket, and cowboy hat. David still wouldn't tell us his name.

"Just the three of us going to his place unannounced, might make the man slam the door in our faces," he said, so I didn't push the matter.

The ride there was not the most comfortable. David's car was a high price horse on wheels. I'm guessing it would make a lot of girls' panties drop just as they sat down in the front seat. But the car was only built for two; three was definitely a crowd in this car.

David insisted that we give Mr Cowboy hat a visit because we needed answers, and he was the best and safest way to obtain them. David also said that Mr Cowboy hat might not be able to get us all the answers we were seeking, but he would give us a place to start, and that was all we needed to get the ball rolling.

Mr Cowboy hat lived in the same rundown part of town as the homeless recreational centre David used for his soup kitchen. We pulled up next to this old apartment block that was three storeys high, all red brick and tinted windows. David, my father and I stood outside the entrance to the building. An old metal, paint flaking, very strong looking security door blocked our path into the complex.

The thought I had as we drew closer to the building was that looks can be deceiving. The door, while taking on the appearance of being decrepit, had been strongly reinforced. The welding looked DIY standard, burn marks still stained the door from the welder. I was guessing an elephant would have trouble ripping the door off its hinges.

David pressed the buzzer to Mr Cowboy hat's flat. The buzzer sounded like a dying car horn. It had the desired effect though, because only a second later a loud croaky voice boomed through the crackly speaker yelling, "Go away."

David looked a bit taken aback, he pressed the intercom then said, "You don't even know who it is you are telling to go away." I noticed Dad scanning the building, looking at it so intensely that it seemed like he was combing the bricks for ants.

"Yes, I do know who I am telling to piss off, David, take a hint and leave," the croaky voice said. David took a deep breath then pressed the intercom once again, "We had a deal. You said you would help me with my problem."

"And I did help you. Our arrangement has concluded. So take your guests and go away," the croaky voice insisted.

My dad leaned over and tapped David on the shoulder, then pointed his finger to a spot just above the door frame between two bricks where the mortar had been drilled out, and now a tiny round lens the size of a five cent piece now resided.

"Camera," David said after taking a second to spot it. "Does it have audio?"

"I don't think so, but I can't be sure," my father replied.

"Yes, it does," Mr Cowboy hat said, "so get off the front of my building. Jump back into that insanely conspicuous car of yours and bugger off out of my life."

David sighed, visibly getting frustrated. It must be those emotions leaking though his defences he'd told me about. It was odd to see him get so flustered over something like this when he could stay so calm and collected while facing down bullets. It was always the small things that get you I supposed. It was a surprise to see his humanity bubble outwards. I guessed it just showed that he was human with ever-pulling emotions just like the rest of us, and even David could get swept up by their forceful current despite the meditation and all.

"Okay, Frank," David said with an edge to his voice, not caring that he just told us Mr Cowboy hat's name, "You know we don't have anywhere else to go, we can't go to the cops, and we can't go home."

"Not my problem, now bugger off," the speaker crackled, sounded like it was about to fizzle out and die.

"Let me put it this way for you, Frank. We are not going anywhere until we have a proper chat. I will break down this door, and make my own way up there if you don't open up," David replied, growing ever more impatient. An elephant might have trouble with the door but not David, it seemed.

"I'll give you ten seconds then I'm calling the cops," Mr Cowboy hat, or Frank, which ever you prefer, said. David took a step back getting ready to test, undoubtedly, Frank's handy-work on the door. But before he had a chance to try and kick the door off its hinges, I cut in front of him, straight in line of the camera.

"Please help us, we really don't have anyone else to turn to for the answers we need. So, even if you call the cops, we have nothing to lose. This is the end of the road for us." It was a little more dramatic than it needed to be, I thought as I said it, but it just came out. "And, besides, you don't sound like the type that wants cops knocking on your front door. Plus we could just tell them you helped us, which you did, so you may as well just work with us rather than against us," I said, sounding as sweet as possible, while lightly threatening him.

"It's not my fight" the voice said, much quieter and less menacing than before.

"They killed my mother. Please let me try and get justice for her death. Please don't rob me of that," I didn't stop the tears falling, as I pleaded with him to help us.

The speaker made a, "Grrrr," sound, followed by the man's croaky voice saying, "There is nothing worse than someone with nothing to lose. Why did you let Sarah speak? Damn you, David." The speaker went silent, and with that silence my hopes went down the toilet too, flushed away. It wasn't worth breaking down the door if he wasn't going to help us. I turned to David and my father wiping the tears from my eyes, and just when I thought Frank was a selfish douche bag he did a wonderful thing, he buzzed the door open.

We climbed the stairs to Frank's apartment, where an open door awaited us. We all walked through with Dad at the rear. Frank closed the door behind us, locking all seven deadbolts. It was a bit of overkill if you'd asked me, but whatever made him feel safe at night. As he locked the door I got my first good look at the man without the Driza-Bone and cowboy hat.

Frank was a short rounded man. He looked like he must be in his late fifties, or early sixties. The skin on his face was weathered. He had white-silver hair that appeared not to have been brushed or washed in the past six years. He had massive thick-framed glasses that magnified his eyes tenfold. The spectacles sat on a straight little button nose that his cheeks nearly swallowed up, and he had thin tiny lips that finished off his round chubby face.

David went and sat on the couch then closed his eyes; I guessed he was doing his meditation thing to calm down before he snapped that little chubby guys neck.

My father walked over to Frank, hand outstretched in greeting, "My name is Conner, and this is my daughter, Sarah."

"I know all about you and your daughter, Conner," Frank spat out, ignoring my Father's handshake offer. He really was quite rude, I thought. I wasn't even going to bother trying to say hello if that was the way he was going to act. Besides he obviously knew all about me already, which I felt a little disturbing and, at the same time, impressed. For, if this stranger knew all about me, he was indeed the man we needed to talk to, even if he was rude.

"Thank you," I said, opting out of a salutation, hoping to bypass his rudeness. He mumbled something inaudible as he walked past me to his computer desk, he didn't even look at me. What was up with this guy I wondered, too much socializing through a microphone, and not enough face-to-face interaction, I bet?

Then Dad whispered in my ear, "I think he is shy around women. Maybe let me and David do the talking, hey pumpkin." That did make a piece of the puzzle fit. I lifted my chin in understanding.

My father walked over to Frank's workstation, on which sat five computer screens. The first screen I focused on showed the view of the security cameras. The camera above the front door of the building was only one of a dozen cameras he had set up. Another screen was playing the Channel Seven news; some make-up-covered woman saying something about something. She was quite pretty though, if only she would take off half that paint she had smeared on her face. The other two screens had rows and columns of numbers and letters; all it looked like to me was useless data. The last screen to the far left of the long desk had a picture of some sort of Orc monster thing standing in some fantasy world.

"What do you think you know about us then, Frank?" My father asked, testing, auditioning.

"Everything," Frank said with a smile. "You are Conner James Smith, born in Melbourne. You grew up on the south-east side of town. Finished your high school with a straight A average. From school, you went straight into the military for seven years working in intelligence; then left right before marrying your now deceased wife Jodie Sylvia Smith. You had a daughter Sarah May Smith, who is standing behind you. You now work as a transportation manager for your local council."

He finished speaking looking all smug rotating from side to side on his chair. When no one said anything, Frank added, "I can keep going if you want? I can tell you your driver's licence number, bank details, computer passwords, but I will have to pull up your file again. There is only so much I can remember off the top of my head," he said looking up at Dad as he continued to swivel in his chair.

"I get the point. You're good, but why do you know all that off the top of your head in the first place?" Dad asked.

"David paid me to look into your daughter after that night, in case they found you," he said. I felt my privacy violated at his words, but I was thankful David hired him. My Dad wouldn't be standing here right now if he hadn't. I assumed he hired Frank more so for his own family than me. I was just part of the bigger picture.

"So obviously you came up, Conner, being Sarah's father and all.

I am very thorough, when I look into someone," Frank continued, eyebrows lifted wrinkling his forehead. He was full of pride over his ability to find out anything with only a few finger taps on a keyboard. Frank had found out something I didn't even know. I had no idea my father was in the army.

"I didn't know you were in the army." I had to say. Frank sunk back down in his chair as I spoke. I think Dad was right about his shyness around woman.

"It was before you were born, sweetie," Dad stated, "I don't like talking about it much, and I left the service because your mum and I wanted to start a family. And I didn't want to be moving all over the countryside with a family." I still think I should have been told, but this was no time to hold a grudge after the secret I'd kept from him.

"In the army they repost you somewhere new every few years. You would have had to change schools each time and we didn't want that unstable lifestyle for you, so we decided to settle down and give you a normal childhood. If you have any more questions we'll talk later, alright?"

"Okay," I replied. Knowing we had a more important matter to deal with at the moment. Dad turned his focus back to Frank.

"What do you know about what happened to my wife?"

"Not much, just what I have seen on the news," Frank said.

"What are they saying happened?" my father asked.

"That you went all nutty. Tied up your wife then shot and killed her. Then you kidnapped your daughter and now you're on the run," he said with sympathy in his tone. I noticed that he didn't mention Mr Shaved Head's, head blown apart on our living room floor. The other bikies must have awakened from whatever David did to them, and cleared out, dead body in tow. Either that or the cops cleaned up the mess.

"What do you think happened?" Dad asked.

"I'm guessing it was the Chaos brothers. They needed to frame you so it gives them and the police a good excuse to release photos of you both. Making it easier to find you with the public's help," Frank said straight away, too fast to be lying, too fast to be making it up to tell my father just what he wanted to hear. Dad could command authority when he wanted it, must be from his old army days. A lot of things clicked into place with that bit of knowledge.

"Alright, Frank, now for what we came here for. What do you know about Melbourne's Creatures of Chaos motorcycle club, the guys that killed my wife?" my father grilled.

Before Frank had a chance to answer I felt the presence of David standing just behind me. He was so close I could feel his body heat. It made a nervous shiver run down my spine. It seemed David always had that effect on me now. It was quite off-putting and knee-buckling at the same time. A guy had never made me feel so vulnerable before, not even Sam. I tried to push all my feelings away. It wasn't a good time to be vulnerable.

"Not a great deal that would be useful. They are a criminal organisation after all, they do like to be very secretive," Frank said.

"Tell me what you do know, and we'll start from there," Dad put plainly.

"Wow, wow, wow, before I do anything, Mr Conner Smith, I haven't agreed to help you, and even if I did my time isn't free. If you want my help you have to pay for it," Frank said.

"How much do you want?" my father asked.

"Fifty big ones and I'm all yours," he said with a negotiation look on his face. "I know you're good for it," he added.

"Done," my father said without flinching. What was money worth when you've got a death warrant out on your head? Who knew if you'd be alive long enough to use any of your hard-earned cash, anyway.

"Damn," Frank said, turning back to his desk full of screens. "I should have asked for a hundred grand."

"Back to my question," Dad said. Frank sighed, believing he had just undercut himself.

"I can tell you who is in the club. Where their members live. Where their clubhouse is located. What they say they do for money; which I can tell you is partly all bullshit, and not much more worth mentioning. They have someone covering up their tracks electronically," Frank said, peering at his screens.

"Who tipped them off about the hospital records?" David said from behind me.

"It must be the same person cleaning up after them online, someone like me. Not as good as me of course, but good enough all the same," Frank said, sounding superior.

"Alright let's start with that then," my father said, placing a hand on the desk leaning in close to get a better look at the senseless data that filled the computer screen.

"Start with what?" Frank asked.

"We'll start with this guy that is cleaning up all the stuff online for the Creatures of Chaos," my father answered.

"Okay boss," Frank said, then he started banging on the keyboard with his thick fingers like a pianist banging on his piano. David then pulled me to the side.

"They will be there for a while, and there is nothing we can really contribute at the moment. We may as well relax for a bit." As David led me away I noticed my father pulling up a chair next to Frank. There was nothing I could contribute, but apparently that wasn't the case for Dad.

I sat next to David on the couch. The couch was surprisingly comfortable even though it looked very worn in, like very, very worn in. I became aware of how close I was to David. We were sitting close enough that I could feel the slope of the cushion under his weight, I had to lean to the opposing side or else I would fall on top of him. There was one thing that had been bugging me ever since Joe had let it slip out of his big mouth. I never knew the right time to bring it up, not that we've had a lot of time in between everything that had happened since.

There had been so much going on that I was nearly going to let it go. I thought about ignoring it. But I wanted to know, I had to know, and to find out was only a question away. Now was as good a time as any.

I thought I would have been more apprehensive at this point. I usually got jittery just thinking about asking him, but not this time. That's how I knew it was the right time to ask, so I just blurted it out.

"Joe told me that I reminded him of your wife." I paused gripping the couch in anticipation of a reaction. Then when it didn't come straight away I continued with, "Is that why you kissed me?"

David didn't say anything for a long time. All my insecurities leapt to the surface. I must be a bad kisser and now he was trying to figure out a way to let me down easy. Maybe Joe was wrong and I just opened up some old wound. My mind raced in all directions but I kept patient on the outside, just fidgeting with the loose thread that frayed from the couch. On the inside I was screaming at him, demanding he say something. But I was determined to wait it out, and I could see he was considering how to answer. When David finally turned to me, I couldn't help but lose myself in his eyes, everything that churned in my head fell flat, replaced with David's deep voice.

"My wife's name was Isabella. We were high school sweethearts, like you and Sam. I loved her with my whole being, she was my everything."

The sound of Sam's name made me cringe, but I didn't let it show. I thought I had loved Sam like that. It felt so long ago now, like it was a different life, like I was a completely different person when I was with Sam. I bottled all that up. I didn't want to stop David from talking. I had only just gotten him to open up. Besides Sam was a pig, and I found it easy now to push his memory to the back of my mind, and that was precisely what I did.

"We got married just a few years out of school. We had a baby boy," I could see he was struggling, but he went on, "We named him Ian after Isabel's Grandfather." David's eyes had gone glassy, and his voice choked up. He took a moment to regain his composure.

"Back then I used to box for a living. I had a few sponsors that kept the food on the table so I could box full time. I was pretty good too, undefeated in thirty-eight amateur bouts. I only had four pro fights. I won all four by way of TKO. But before my fourth fight one of the Creatures of Chaos boys, John Black, told me to lose or else there would be consequences. And me, being young, dumb and thinking I was invincible, told him to shove it," David stopped after that, a flash of hatred appeared on his face then disappeared just as quick. I could see he didn't really want to go on, but he went on anyway.

"The same guy that threatened me followed through with his threat. He didn't go after me, he went after my family." David took in a deep breath. I thought I saw his hand start to shake, but he clenched his hands into fists. I knew what he was going to say before he said it, that sinking feeling you get in the pit of your stomach. That feeling that comes from losing a loved one.

"I was out training at the time," he said. I saw a teardrop land on his jeans, darkening the fabric. "I wasn't there when they needed me, I failed them." He turned to me then, unable to hide his emotional pain from breaking through, "Just as I failed you. I didn't get there in time to stop them from hurting you that night, and I wasn't able to save your mother after I promised I would." He looked away, disgusted with himself. That was why he couldn't leave me to those bikies. That was why he has been so caring. He felt responsible for me. He was making up for not being there for his family.

I wanted to tell him that he didn't fail me, but that, in fact, he saved me. Both my mother and father would be dead now if it wasn't for him. But I had to let him finish his story.

"The cops ruled it a burglary gone wrong. The cops had all the evidence to catch the guy and put him away but, right before trial, all of it went missing. They must have been paid off, or maybe the club had something incriminating on them. Who knows what it was, but I knew who did it. I knew who to blame. I knew who to go after," David said, his face growing hard. Hard like a face that conveyed hatred, his face had transformed, looking menacing and fierce. "When I learnt of his whereabouts, I couldn't stand aside and let him get away with murdering my family. The guy had two mates over at the time. They were all laughing and carrying on with not a worry in the world. Like murdering an innocent woman and child was no more of a burden on their souls as squashing a few ants. I was enraged, but somehow I controlled it, I used it. I didn't go in there like a loose cannon, I went in strategically." The hatred seemed to hit meltdown mode on David's expression. I could see how he knew my craving for violence, he knew the taste himself.

"I destroyed all of them, leaving the guy that did the deed for last.

John Black, the guy that suffocated my son with a pillow. John Black, the man that raped and murdered my wife. John Black, the man I killed." David stopped. I thought he was finished after admitting to killing the man, but he continued, "In the end he confessed what he did, and when I heard the words, and his absence of empathy, I lost all control. I barely remember doing it, like I was a bystander to my own body. I beat him to death with my bare hands. I just kept on hitting him until there was nothing left of his face to hit. I broke three knuckles I was hitting him so hard."

He paused and then he looked down at his knuckles, remembering the pain, remembering the blood. That was why he looked at his hands that way in his kitchen when we first had that talk. He wasn't seeing Jordan Coles' blood; he was seeing his family's. He opened and closed his hands testing for lingering effects. "Then I got out of there. The cops never came after me. The club never came after me. The other guys I left alive didn't see my face to ID me, so I'm guessing they never found out it was me. The cops ended up putting it down as gang-related."

What do you say to that? Your wife and child were murdered, and then you go kill the guy that did it because the justice system wouldn't. I never knew David could lose control like that, and stay so focused. To kill that man so premeditatedly in his grief. To go to those lengths to get revenge for his family; it was terrifying, and in a much scarier way, romantically beautiful. I couldn't help but feel so sad for him, losing a wife and child would sting the soul with a deadly poison that would envelop you. You would think a man confessing to murder would be repelling, but before I could think to stop myself, I leaned over wrapping my arms around him. I held him in a close embrace, not frightened of this man, but enthralled by him.

I can see what he did eats away at him, but I don't think he would take it back if he could. Just like my father said he probably wouldn't. It was quite the dilemma, to feel bad for killing a man, and that man being the guy you hate.

"You don't remind me of Isabella, but I do see her strength in you, her fighting spirit. That was the part of her I loved the most. You have her moxie," he said with a smile, with the look of remembrance of better days. "The reason I kissed you was not that you reminded me of her, but because you made me feel something again, you made me know how it feels to love again when I never thought I would, or even could love again," he pulled away from me so I could peer into his mesmerising eyes. He wanted me to see the sincerity in his words.

"I love you, Sarah."

CHAPTER 28

*W*hen someone told me that they loved me, I always felt that I had to say it back, even if I didn't mean it, even if, for no other reason it was to spare their feelings. It felt that way when I said it back to Sam for the first time. But this time when David said those words I resisted that urge because it wouldn't have been true to me or to him.

The other thing I did when Sam told me he loved me was weigh-up whether or not I did in fact actually love him. At the time I didn't think I did, but the more I told him I loved him the truer it became. I wasn't going to do that with David. If I was going to say those words to him I was going to mean them. I didn't know if that was what he expected, but his eyes looked hopeful, like he was waiting for me to say it back, and when I didn't, I expected his look to change, but it didn't.

"I'm not sure how I feel towards you," I admitted. "There is something between us, I won't deny that. But with everything that is going on at the moment, with what we have just been through and what you just told me about your past, my head is spinning," I said, looking dead into his eyes, my gaze not shifting. I didn't feel shy or uncomfortable around him; he had always made me feel at ease that way. Speaking the truth to David was as easy as talking to myself in the mirror. Well, I felt that way around David when I knew he wasn't going to kill me.

I knew I couldn't say I love you to him if I didn't know myself if I truly loved him. This was something more than just mere puppy love. This was life changing for him and for me for that matter.

"I wasn't expecting anything, Sarah," he spoke as he reached for my hands, lifting them off my lap and holding them delicately with his strong broad rough hands.

"I just wanted you to know how I felt. I know my past is not an easy obstacle to jump over, but one thing I have learnt is, life is too short for you to go on living with what ifs. You brought love back into my life. You have already given me a gift that I thought was impossible," David said, with a glow about him. "The least I can do is to be honest with you, and live with the hope that one day you might feel the same towards me. And if that day never comes then, at least you know the truth about how I feel. You would also know that you have enriched my life just by being part of it." He lifted my hands to his mouth then kissed my fingers.

"I'll give you some space to process everything," David said releasing my hands as he got to his feet. "I should move my car down the block before Frank gets too upset anyway."

I had never noticed it before, but there was such love in his eyes towards me, and now I realized that it wasn't the first time I had seen it.

David left the apartment giving me the space I didn't even know I wanted until I had it. I wished for my mother. She was always the one I went to with this sort of thing. The person I went to for advice on these matters. My heart ached for her. I would never get to have her wisdom showered upon me again. I missed her so much already.

I had an idea about what Mum might have said, "Follow your heart, darling, for it knows what the brain doesn't." I thought I followed my heart with Sam and look how that turned out, or come to think of it, was it my brain I followed? I had barely known him before he asked me to be his girlfriend, we weren't even friends at that stage. I thought he was hot, so I said yes. It was just the way things went at school. It wasn't until later that I grew to love him, and even that might have only been because of the implications that a relationship brings. Being someone's girlfriend means you were supposed to love them right? Like a wife loving her husband after an arranged marriage.

If I had never said yes to Sam all those years ago, I never would have caught him cheating on me. I never would have run into trouble that night, and I never would have been rescued by David. My mother would still be alive, I wouldn't be on the run now, my life wouldn't be in danger and ultimately I wouldn't be sitting here discussing with myself if I love my rescuer or not. The world works in mysterious ways.

I wondered if this day would have ever come if my mother was still alive, the day I would have to rely on my own judgement. It was a little unnerving. I could ask for my father's advice, but he had never been good with girl talk. I knew he would try and give me his opinion, but this was a mother-daughter thing, not a daddy-daughter thing. And it kind of scares me to think what he would say about getting into a relationship with such a rough character, better to leave that one alone.

I asked myself was David really a man I wanted to be with? He was a revengeful, heroic killer. Killing for the right reasons is still killing. I was standing in his shoes not too long ago. I held a gun to the man's head that had murdered my mother, but he talked me down. He had no one to hold his hand back. He saved me from the darkness that surrounded him. I mean I was still learning new things about him every day. When he got frustrated at the front door of this building was just one more new side of him I had never seen.

David's past was so ferocious. What he did was something I was not totally sure whether or not he should go to prison for. I knew if it was up to the court he would be found guilty. If David should go to prison for what he did to his family's killer, then Dad should be in prison too. We lived in a society that every second movie was about revenge. I saw the comic book turned movie *The Punisher*. The whole movie was about a guy seeking revenge for the killing of his entire family, and in the movie he dished out his own brand of punishment, killing all of them in return. Are David and my father any different than this beloved comic book vigilante?

I thought the softly softly approach didn't always work when it came to criminals. I had lost count the amount of times I had heard of people being out on parole then committing murders or rapes. If our legal system did their jobs properly that wouldn't happen and, as I have personally found out, the world is corrupt and misinformed. So I couldn't find it in my heart to condemn them for their actions, I concluded. It may be a tough stance, but what they did was punishment, they played judge and executioners where they shouldn't have had to, if the system wasn't broken. My father and David killed killers; they were walking the steps of the fictional Dexter Morgan. They didn't hurt the innocent; they just carried out the punishment that the law had failed to deliver. If David's family legal situation was anything to go off, if my father didn't put a bullet in Mr Shaved Head with his connections he would have most likely walked free by bribing, or threatening the people there to sentence him. The man that killed David's family had already avoided jail, so if the powers that be won't keep us safe then it fell to us to protect ourselves.

If the guy that killed David's family over a petty bet could murder a woman and child and days later laugh and carry on like nothing ever happened, then the odds of him doing something like that again would be pretty high. And Mr Shaved Head pulled the trigger on my mother like it wasn't his first time. If he was let loose on the world I doubt his hands would have stayed clean from blood.

What my Father and David did to those men was no different than what a government would have done if they had been tried, judged, and then sentenced to death for their crimes. I know we here in Australia don't have the death penalty anymore, but a lot of the world still does, including America, China, Pakistan just to name a few. I asked myself was killing a killer murder? Or was it justice? I really didn't know. All I knew was that I would feel safer in a world without them in it. That was all I knew to be true.

To take a life was not an easy thing to live with if you had a conscience, even if that person was a murderer. I saw both David and my Dad struggle with it. Taking the law into your own hands was not how things should be done. If those laws were wrong or unjust and stopped protecting the same people that abided by them, then the world had a way of correcting itself. Like a paedophile rapist that has been sent to jail, and then gets a garden hose wrapped in barbed wire shoved up his ass by other inmates. That's Karma.

I won't hold what my father and David did against them, I know it wasn't just under the laws of the country, but I thought it was just on the moral rights of humanity. Agree with me or not, that was what I believed and felt.

I understand now the craving of rage and revenge after a traumatic experience, the way it forced its way to the surface calling for blood. I still wrestled with that emotion now. I know you're not in your right mind at the time; it is our primal urges overpowering us. That was what happened to my father and David, it was an overpowering need for revenge that I myself only just pulled back from. It was different to the enjoyment of killing, like Mr Shaved Head had. Killing, hurting people turned him on. He wanted to savour the taste of it. He was what I was scared of becoming.

I knew now I could never become like Mr Shaved Head, I could never hurt the innocent. I could hurt the wicked and sinful, yes; but never the innocent. I also couldn't condemn them because I just couldn't see the fairness in a world where murderers and rapists can go free while victims are traumatised for the rest of their lives and others didn't even get to live at all.

After much thought, some deep soul searching, I reached down to learn my true feelings about David. I did not fear him. I could not fear him for what he did. David had the heart of a protector; he saved me, he even saved the hungry at his soup kitchen. The one underlining thing my heart was saying was I don't want to live in a world without him in it.

That was love, was it not? To not want to live without someone, to look forward to seeing that person every time you were apart, to be counting down the seconds until you reconnected. For that was how I felt about David. But to jump into another relationship now would be wrong. I couldn't have my judgement clouded. I would wait until this was all over before I committed to anything. That was what I would tell David.

I love you too, but we will have to wait.

CHAPTER 29

*I*fell asleep not long after I finished that psychotic talk with myself. I just rested my eyes for what seemed like a second, and then I awoke to Frank yelling in glee. Somehow, without realizing it, I was lying down on the couch with a blanket covering me that smelt of dust and mothballs. It felt like I was only asleep for two minutes, but I must have been out for much longer.

I looked over to see Frank punching the air with his chubby fists yelling, "I got you punk. I am the king, and you are my Jester."

"What's up guys?" I said a bit groggily, still trying to wake up.

Frank's screams of dominance over his cybernetic foe ceased when my voice rang through the room. Frank quickly swivelled round in his chair focusing back on his computer screens. Dad and David turned to me, but it was Dad who answered.

We tracked down the computer wizard who's been helping the bikies." Frank spun to face my father. I couldn't see his face, but then my father added, "He is only an apprentice to your mastery, Sir Frank." Frank seemed pleased with my father's response, turning back to his computers once again, but this time with his head held a bit higher, and a mumble that sounded like, "You're damn straight."

My eyes then locked on to David's. Remembering my realisation that I had right before I fell asleep, I quickly looked away. Then I saw Dad looking between us. My father wasn't a stupid man, that look between David and me might have just told him all he needed to know about my intimate desires towards David.

Fifteen minutes later we were all piling into a white Toyota Corolla. Frank's car obviously; easily distinguishable by the smell of old stale takeaway food, and the left over packaging that littered the car seats and floor. I think he must take turns going to each fast food chain, because I saw the remnants of McDonalds, KFC, Red Rooster and Hungry Jacks. I didn't think I missed one unless you included pizza as fast food, and I wasn't game enough to start digging through to find any more. After shifting all the fast food rubbish to one side, I slid into the back seat. Dad jumped into the driver's seat, while David sat in the passenger's.

The drive to Mr Jester's house was in total silence. There was an awkward aroma in the air. I wasn't able to talk to David in such close proximity to my father. The conversation we needed to have was a private one. I think Dad knew that; that was why awkwardness was steaming out of him too. We should have had this talk back at Frank's, rather than rush away into an upcoming dangerous situation with our thoughts and emotions twisted. That first look we shared after he told me he loved me might have said more than words could have anyway. But telling someone that you love them had to be told, not assumed, and at the moment love wasn't enough to start something that I knew would be serious. If I did let David all the way into my heart, I knew I would fall in deeper than I ever did with Sam. If that look I gave David was enough for my Dad to get suspicious, then David would have his own suspicions as well. He might have seen the love he had for me wasn't all one sided.

My Father pulled the car over in a suburban street, houses lined both sides. The engine groaned to a stop, and then everything went silent for a second, well more silent then it already was. It was like the silence intensified, if that was possible.

"I don't presume to know what is going on between you two," my father declared. David shifted in his seat and I sat up straight, the tension obvious in both of us. My father took a deep breath, getting ready to say what he really wanted to say.

"You are both grownups, so I won't tell you what to do, but," he put an emphasis on the but, "I will tell you what I think, which is, starting something now is a bad idea; at least while all this is going on. It might make both of you lose focus on what has to be done. We are putting ourselves in extremely risky circumstances, and if your heads aren't in the game there's a chance one or both of you will do something stupid, and get the other hurt. Just be smart about it. Alright?"

Dad reached for the car door handle then with one foot out the door turned back and said, "Sort your shit out, and let's do this."

The car went silent once again. My heart pumped that tiny bit faster with the upcoming conversation. Butterflies fluttered around in my stomach with impatience, but they were unable to tell me where to begin. David broke the deadlock, turning to me with a sincere look. His eyes were piercing through my thin armour that the butterflies were holding up.

"You know, I would never pressure you into anything, and I don't want you to worry about hurting my feelings. You know how I feel, so whatever you have to say I'll accept, and be happy just to have you in my life," David expressed with not a word of falsehood behind it.

How could that not strip away your armour, setting all the butterflies free, leaving you naked and helpless under his gaze? David always had an uncanny way of smoothing the tension out of the air, making it easier and harder to say what I had to say. Easier, because the nerves and tension were gone but harder, because at this very moment I wished we could just drive away until there was no one who knew us, and we could live happily ever after.

"I love you too, David," I said, without even thinking before I said it, letting my heart talk for me. David's smile grew into one of euphoria.

"But," I said, just like my Dad did a moment ago. I waited for David's smile to falter under the upcoming exception, but it didn't, so I continued, "I don't think this is the right time to start up something." David leant over, reaching for my hand. I left it there for him to take. I was scared that I might never be able to pull it away. David lifted my hand to his mouth, kissing it.

"I could wait two life times after hearing you say you love me."

"Only two life times," I joked shyly, trying to bring down the swell of emotion.

"The ball is on your side of the court, Sarah. When you're ready to throw the ball to me, I'll be there waiting to catch it." David let go of my hand, then turned back around in the front seat. Back to business it seemed.

"Your father is right. For now we must have our minds on the game." He turned back to me, "I would ask you to stay in the car, but I know how that would go."

I smiled, "You're right not to ask."

"What I am going to ask you to do is to stay behind me and your father. Do you think you can do that?" David spoke with solid sternness, not leaving me much room to say no.

"If I have to," I remarked, going for the car door. David watched me get out of the car before getting out himself.

Earlier, before we parked, we drove past the house where Mr Jester lived. The dwelling looked quiet, and there were no rows of motorcycles in the front yard, or bodyguards standing at the front door. Frank told us that the house was owned by someone named Mark Johnson. An alias he assumed. That's why I was sticking with the name Mr Jester until we found out his real name or I got too used to Mr Jester to change it.

On paper Mr Jester was fifty-four years old, worked as a painter, owned the house we were now going to and had an old Ford sedan. That was all Frank could dig up on Mr Jester outside of his phony Mark Johnson paper trail. We guessed Mr Jester thought he was all high and mighty thinking no one could track him down or see through his façade, but he never met Frank.

The plan was to force our way into the premises, taking Mr Jester by surprise. Catch the guy, and then drill him for answers. Simple, but effective, hopefully. The plan should work as long as there weren't ten beefy guys in there with guns. If Frank was right about the fake paperwork then all the signs pointed to a geeky guy that lived all alone. Not unlike Frank. Not that I was calling Frank a geek, he was the king of his domain. It was just most people in his domain were usually a little geeky, not that I thought there was anything wrong with that. Geeks were useful; we wouldn't have gotten this far without one.

As we got close we noticed that the house looked like no one had done the gardening for months. The lawns were about a foot high, all the garden beds were full of weeds. The house stood out like a sore thumb. The rest of the street had vibrant green lawns that were finely cut, gardens that were immaculate with not a twig out of place, and then there was Mr Jester's house.

David took the lead, heading straight for the front door. Dad was close behind with me at the rear. At the front door, not slowing but using his momentum, David put his boot through it. The door exploded open, splinters of wood and plaster shattering everywhere. Even the architrave around the doorframe came flying off.

There was no gunfire as we stormed the house. That was a good sign, I thought. I was waiting for something to happen, someone to jump out of the woodwork and attack us, but the onslaught never came. Instead, David stood motionless in the entrance, just listening. Well that was what I thought he was doing. Because it wasn't until a noise like a door slamming rang through the house that David took off running. David was too fast on his feet for me to keep up with. He vanished around the corner like a cat after a mouse. Dad and I had to follow by the sound of his footsteps as sight was no long an option. I was still behind Dad so by the time I turned the corner to a long hallway I only caught sight of David's heel as he passed through a doorway.

The next sound I heard wasn't David's footstep. The sound was like an electric current getting injected into my head. It was fast and painful. The sudden shock made me stand straight and go rigid. David's scream of pain was horrifying to my ears. I sidestepped Dad then shot past him. I stopped under the archway of the door frame to a bedroom. What I saw next was kind of a comedic relief.

David was holding a pair of legs that were kicking frantically to get free. The man was half out the window dangling like an old cobweb. The guy's top half was hidden below the window frame.

With one backward heave by David, the man was flung back through the window and dumped on the floor. I heard a loud crack as the man was pulled back inside. I think the impact came from his elbow hitting the windowsill but I couldn't be sure, I hoped it was his head. The man hit the ground running. Besides favouring one arm, he was up on his feet in a flash and running straight for me, the person who was blocking his only other means of escape.

What happened next all seemed to happen in slow motion, but I was pretty sure it actually happened super quickly. First, I spotted the Stanley knife in the man's hand. The blade was out at half-length. Then I was yanked backwards by my father. I was spun around by the yanking motion and I hit the opposite wall of the hall with a thud. I looked back to see my father throw up an arm catching the man across the shoulders and neck. The impact was so hard that the man did a complete backflip, landing face first on the wooden floorboards. It was the perfect coathanger.

The man seemed dazed, probably wondering what just happened, and landing on his head wouldn't have helped. The knife was knocked out of his hand in the backflip, sliding under a set of drawers for safe keeping. Dad then pounced on the man's back, pulling his hands around until they rested on the small of his back just above his ass. That was when everything went back to normal play mode. Dad turned to David.

"Get me something to bind his hands."

A second later David came over with an electrical extension cord. It was maybe five metres in length. David handed the cord to my Father with one hand, while his other was tucked into his side. The arm didn't swing as he walked. It looked odd; it looked injured. A normal person moves both arms when they walk, like when you watch the one-hundred-metre sprint at the Olympics, the runners swing their arms crazily hoping for more speed. Walking was the same but just less dramatic. Then the cry of pain echoed in my ears.

Then I noticed the arm that was tucked away was becoming red from the elbow down. Blood was beginning to soak through his shirt at a more rapid pace it seemed. I put two and two together, remembering the Stanley knife. The blades on those things were extra sharp. I cut myself with one once while I was unpacking boxes for Tara after she moved houses for the third time that year. The cut bled like a sieve, and the slice that I made on my finger wasn't even that big, so I could imagine how much a large gash would bleed. My mother told me that a straight cut from something like a knife or a piece of glass bled more than when the skin was ripped open like, for example, if I went for a jog and caught my skin on an overhanging tree branch. I ran to David's side.

"Are you alright?" I asked stupidly. Of course there was something wrong, there was blood everywhere.

"It's okay, it looks worse than it really is," David responded acting tough.

I went to examine the wound. David tensed up as I started to remove the sliced open shirt out of the laceration. I looked up into his eyes.

"I thought it wasn't that bad," I said.

"It's not bad," David protested, before I cut him off with a smile and a big baby comment. I focused on the cut after I pulled away the fabric.

"I think it will need stitches."

"I think you might be right," David replied. "Could you pass me that T-shirt please?" There was an old green T-shirt lying on the unmade bed. I picked it up and handed it to David.

"Hang on, Sarah," he said, as I went to hand him the shirt. "Could you tie it around my arm?"

"I can do that," I said, reassuring myself, more than him. I looked the shirt up and down, "I hope it's clean," I added.

I twisted the shirt until it was tight, like you would twist a tea towel before you flicked it at someone's butt. Then I wrapped it around the wound. David closed his eyes, and gritted his teeth as I pulled it tight.

"Is that alright?" I asked.

"Yer, should be," David replied, opening his eyes and hiding the pain very well.

David's eyes shifted to the man lying on the floor, arms bound behind his back. My father dragged him up to his feet. I got my first good look at the man then. Sorry, no. My mistake. He wasn't a man, he was a boy. He looked eighteen if he was lucky. I was expecting a big beer-gutted middle age tradie, not a kid fresh out of school. Frank was right about the intel; Mark Johnson was definitely an alias. The kid was already covered in tattoos, with a shaved head, and he was as skinny as a bean pole. He had a narrow face with thick bushy eyebrows, and just the start of some bum fluff on his chin.

"You assholes owe me a new door," Mr Jester said in his childlike voice. His voice was high even for someone his age, he sounded a bit like Mike Tyson. My father walked him over and then pushed Mr Jester down on the bed. The boy landed with a squeak of the springs underneath.

"David, could you keep an eye on the kid?" My father asked. "If he moves knock him out."

"Hah, I crippled that guy. He couldn't knock out a baby," Mr Jester smirked. David calmly walked over to the kid. The kid quickly went from arrogant to shit scared in a split second as David approached. David then slowly placed a hand on the boy's shoulder. The boy tried to dodge David's hand; tried being the standout word.

"Get your hand off me, you pervert," Mr Jester spat out.

David squeezed the boy's shoulder. Actually it looked more like a pinch than just a squeeze of the shoulder. The boy cried out in pain, he let out a string of "Oww, oww, oww."

David eased up on the pressure, "Speak only when spoken to."

Mr Jester just stared back non-responsively. I saw David's hand tense again then the boy squeaked, "Okay, okay, okay." He definitely liked to repeat his words.

"What did you do to him?" I asked curiously.

"Pressure point," David said, flat faced.

"You have to teach me that," I told him. David responded with a half-smile.

"Conner, what are you doing?" David inquired as my father slotted a USB device into a laptop that sat at a desk on the opposite side of the room.

"Our friend," meaning Frank, I assumed, "told me to upload something on the boy's computer. I'm guessing this kid is our guy,"

Dad said with a pointing glance over at the Jester. David turned to the kid.

"Do you know who we are?"

"Bonnie and Clyde, and that over there is your dear old daddy," Mr Jester said in a mocking tone.

David smiled before saying, "You're half right kid but, no, I'm not Clyde, I'm David Powers."

The boy straightened up, not expecting David to announce himself like that. I was even a little surprised. It wasn't a smart idea to tell the enemy your name if they didn't know it, but David must have seen something I missed and with Mr Jester's reaction I think David got his answer in full, "So you do know who I am?"

"Yer, I know who all of you are, and so does the rest of the club. I was the one that found out it was you that killed Jordan," Mr Jester declared, like it was obvious. All his brattiness had now vanished, going serious, "You know you're a dead man walking, don't you?" David's eyes narrowed, even my Dad turned in his seat to look at Mr Jester.

"You killed Louis's brother," he said, leering at each of us individually. "You know Louis won't stop until he puts all of you in the earth. He's not like John Black who you killed after he murdered your wife and kid. John Black was a pussy compared to Louis."

I looked over at Dad in response to Mr Jester mentioning David's family. Dad's eyes went wider and he leaned back in his chair blowing out a long breath. It was new news to him. I guess David didn't bring that story up in that little chat they had.

Taking the silence that followed as a window to speak Mr Jester added, "It sucks to be you guys," and began laughing. David moving faster than the eye could catch, picked the kid up from upon the bed, almost lifting him in the air with his one good arm, and then threw him into the closet, slamming the door on him.

"The kid has been doing his homework," David said, with a sour expression spread all over his face.

CHAPTER 30

My father jumped out of the car to open a metal farm gate that crossed a red dirt driveway. The gate must have been half a kilometre from the actual house. The house looked like any other house you would expect to see on a farm. It had a wooden deck that surrounded the entire dwelling, which definitely needed a new coat of varnish. It had a galvanised sheet roof, and had that old inviting style look about it. David's arm needed stitches, so who do we know that could sew a man's flesh back together? Joe.

Joe lived on about twenty acres. His place looked like a farmhouse, but it wasn't equipped with all the animals. Well, not totally without animals. David told us he had two horses that roam around the property. Joe's closest neighbour was a five-minute drive, so Joe's house was as private as you could get. You could even say Joe lived in the middle of nowhere, but David informed us that that was how he liked it.

Once we reached the house, an old brown coloured, greying around the muzzle, Labrador came barking up to the car. David forgot to mention the dog; I was looking out for horse's hooves, not a dog's pointy teeth. David got out of the car to greet the barking dog. As the dog rounded the car to attack and ready to bite, it saw who it was. It then went from attacking mode to excited young puppy mode. David patted the dog on its head.

"Max you old boy, how you been?" David's hand went to the dog's collar and then he scratched underneath it. Max's head went to one side, and then his foot started to twitch.

Dad and I got out next, "Where's your old man, hah Max," David asked the dog, just as he would ask a young child. On cue Joe walked out the flywire screened front door with a shotgun in his hands.

"What have you done to yourself, now?"

"Thought I would make an excuse to come see my old friend," David replied.

"So your best idea was to go injure yourself. Smart," Joe said with a grin. Joe then looked at me, his grin never wavering.

"How you doin' sexy legs? Want to give your old friend, Joe, a kiss."

"Hey, Joe," I replied, ignoring the kiss comment, and letting it dissolve away. My Dad was not so forthcoming on Joe's kiss invitation though. We told Dad about Joe on the drive over letting him know he was an acquired taste. We also filled Dad in about how Joe was the one that patched all my injuries up that night. You would think my Dad would be thankful on the good job he did, but no. I guess Joe's flavour just didn't go down well with my Dad.

Dad stepped up to Joe, who was still holding a shotgun I might add, and said, "Watch how you talk to Sarah or you and I will have a problem."

Joe looked nonchalant as he replied, "Who are you, her father?" Joe commented, finishing the last word with a little chuckle.

"In fact, Joe," Dad said, verbally dragged out his name, "I am Sarah's father, so you better mind your tongue around me. I won't warn you again."

As Dad finished speaking, he gave Joe his hard, you better do as I say, stare. I had been on the end of that stare countless times. It got me every time, too.

Joe then cleared his throat, stood up a little straighter and said, "Sir," and then leant the gun on his shoulder holding the butt of the gun in one hand then lifted his other hand for a formal greeting to my father. Dad shook Joe's hand, veins enlarging as he squeezed.

"Can I trust you will be polite to my daughter from now on?"

"Yes, sir," Joe answered, like an officer answering to a superior. I can't believe I never knew my Dad had been in the military.

A little face peeped out the door. Clare's face lit up when her eyes drifted to David. The little girl came dashing out of the door, down the steps, and yelled, "Uncle David," and then jumped into David's one free arm.

"Careful, little one," David said, hinting towards his other arm.

"That looks bad Uncle David, how did that happen?" Clare asked with concern in her tone.

"A bad man cut me with a knife," David told his niece. The little girl's face looked horrified.

"Don't worry Clare, he won't do it again," David assured her.

"Did you make the bad man say sorry?" Clare asked innocently.

"Yes, I made the man sorry," David responded, putting a little spin on the words.

We ended up just leaving Mr Jester in the closet. It would have been fun for him getting out of there with his hands bound behind his back. We had got what we wanted from Frank's computer foe, and it wouldn't matter if he ran back to the Creatures of Chaos club, they already knew who we were. The only thing Mr Jester could report was what he lost on his computer. I hope it was important. We would have to wait and see after Frank takes a peek.

Clare turned her eyes to me next, "You look a lot prettier when your face isn't all messed up."

"Hello to you too, Clare," I said, thinking how kids can be so direct and straight to the point about what they were thinking. Life would be so much simpler if everyone was that honest.

The door to the house opened again then wheezed shut. This time Georgia walked out looking very unpleased as she leant up against the timber weatherboard wall. David looked up.

"Hey Sis," he called out. Georgia looked pissed off again. I didn't know if that was just how she always looked or she was just pissed off when I was around, I was guessing the latter. Either way David got a head tilt as a response.

A hand landed gently on my shoulder, I turned to see my Dad.

"I have to go back to Frank's, and drop off his USB. Did you want to come back with me?" Dad asked.

I looked at David holding Clare, and then back to my father, "I think I'll stay here unless you need the company?"

"Will you be alright with them?" Dad asked, looking in Joe's direction.

Joe straightened up again under his gaze, "Sarah will be safe with us, sir. You have my word."

David had a huge smile on his face seeing his friend squirm. Dad looked at Joe, weighing up whether to believe him or not.

"I'll be alright, Dad," I said giving him a kiss on the cheek. "Joe is alright once you get to know him." I had only met Joe once while awake, but I already liked and trusted the crude man.

"I'll be the judge of that," Dad stated. "I trust the dog to look out for you." He leant over and kissed my forehead, "I'll be back tomorrow. Take care." Then Dad was back in the car leaving a dust cloud in his wake.

"Your dad is pretty intimidating," Joe said, holding his gun a bit tighter.

"You don't know the half of it," I replied, somewhat proud to call him Dad.

Max came over and sniffed my leg, "I think he likes you," Joe said looking down at the dog.

"What makes you say that?" I asked, not wanting to move in case the dog reacted aggressively. I had never had a dog, so I didn't really know how to act around one. I saw the movie *Cujo*, and that was enough for me to tread carefully around dogs.

"He didn't bite you did he? That means he likes you," Joe answered happily, the tension in his shoulder's relaxing the further my father drove away.

"Let's go inside and get you patched up," Joe said, turning to David and Clare. "Let Uncle Joe, prick you with his little needle."

CHAPTER 31

*D*avid's lacerations needed nine stitches. He also needed a new shirt. Not that I was complaining that he was topless as he received the needle and thread. It was just a fact that his shirt was ruined; torn and covered in blood. Yes, that was why I mentioned it, not because I liked looking at David's toned, muscular body. Yes, he just needed a new shirt; that was the reason. Muscles. What was I saying again? David was getting stitches; that's right.

Joe's house was a lot bigger than it looked from the outside. Joe gave me the tour after patching up David. The house had four bedrooms, two bathrooms, kitchen and family room.

"Everything a single man and his dog needs in a house, and then some," Joe had said. He ushered me to one of his spare rooms.

"This one is yours for tonight," Joe offered. At the door to the room I was waiting for some sexist witty comment like, my bed is your bed, wink, wink. But it never came. So I had to ask, "Why so formal all of a sudden, my Dad's not here now." Joe straightened up again at the mention of my father.

"Your Dad kind of scares me. So I thought I better be on my best behaviour."

"Oh," I sighed, "you just got a lot more boring," I said trying to goad him into changing his reformed ways.

"Don't worry, Lassie, my best behaviour isn't that great," Joe said with his cheeky grin returning.

The room I was to sleep in was in fact Max's room. The room did smell a bit like dog, but overall not too bad for a dog's bedroom. I think Max gets pretty well looked after. The dog had his own room after all. Besides I couldn't be picky, I was kicking Max out of his room for a night. Joe had told me, "Max can stay with me for the night." Max probably wouldn't mind, unless Joe farted all night long. If anyone could make a dog run away from a stinker, my money was on Joe.

Georgia and Clare shared a room, while David had a room across from mine. I had a look around the room, there wasn't very much. A double bed with blue cotton covers and a dog bed that sat in the corner. The dog's bed actually looked more comfortable than the human bed, with brown soft fluffy blankets. There was even a pillow for Max's head. Joe picked up Max's bed, and then lugged it to his room.

The thought of sleep really did appeal to me, but I didn't want to go to bed without taking a shower. I couldn't remember the last time I took a shower. It would be mortifying if I left a rotten odour in the bed. I raised my arm to smell my armpit, and I was rewarded with the strong stench of BO. A noise came from behind me like a throat cough. I turned around with my arm still reaching for the sky to see David leaning up against the doorframe. I dropped my arm in embarrassment. I felt my cheeks start to heat up. He was the last person I wanted smelling me right now. I tucked my elbow in close to my body, hopefully locking-in the horrible smell under my armpits.

"Do you want a shower?" David guessed, with a grin from ear to ear.

"That would be nice," I said politely, trying to regain some of my dignity, and acting as if I hadn't just got caught testing how much I reek.

"The shower is down the hall to the left," David gestured. I already knew that from the guided tour, but I wasn't about to look the gift horse in the mouth. I took two steps forwards before I realized I had no clean clothes to get changed into.

"Umm, I have nothing clean to change into." David's eyes lit up.

"Guess you will have to walk around naked then."

"In your dreams, mister," I replied.

"Yep," David responded. Knowing I knew that he wanted me to

know he dreamed of me naked. Then he went on to say before things got awkward, "I'll bring you some clean clothes, and I'll leave them on the bed for you. There are towels in the bathroom. You will find them in the cupboard. You can't miss them." I pushed past him in the doorway then I looked back over my shoulder.

"Now you will be picturing me wet and naked in the shower, won't you?"

David seemed to get something caught in his throat before he blurted out, "I will be now."

I flicked my hair back over my shoulder as I walked down the hall to the bathroom, feeling a lot better about getting caught sniffing my underarms. The shower was awesome. I swear it was the best shower I had ever had. The hot water felt like a warm massage. I must have washed myself four times to get all the old grit, dead skin and gunk off me. I found some shampoo and conditioner. It was a man's brand, but it still cleaned and detangled all the knots. Once I was dry and back in Max's room, I found a folded stack of clothes on the bed. I didn't know whose they were and I didn't care. They looked clean, they smelt clean, and they looked comfortable enough to sleep in. So that was good enough for me, because that bed was looking ever so inviting.

That shower washed away all my worries, all my negative thoughts, and put me in a numbing peace status. All my strength was gone, my eyes had trouble focusing, and I didn't have a care in the world. I thought I would make the most of my opportunity while it lasted. I threw on the grey T-shirt that sat on the bed then pushed aside the tracky pants to find a pair of what I hoped was clean panties. Then I flopped into bed and slid under the covers. Once my head hit the pillow I was out like a light.

I woke to notice I had left the light on in the room. I was that tired I had forgotten to turn it off. The brightness in the room was misleading. Outside was dark, it was indeed the middle of the night but it felt like morning. I had no idea how long I was asleep, but when I awoke my stomach was making some funny noises. I was guessing it had started to eat itself due to the lack of food. I hoped Joe wouldn't mind if I helped myself from his cupboards, because I was so hungry my stomach twisted in knots searching for food.

I walked blindly through the dark house until I found the kitchen. I stumbled around guessing where the light switch would be. I got lucky on the third wall. I flicked the switch, and gave birth to a light globe. The kitchen was alight giving me a direct line of sight to my target. The fridge was calling my name, and I just hoped that there was something edible inside.

As I went for the cold box handle a voice pierced through the newly born light and attacked me.

CHAPTER 32

$\mathcal{T}$he attack on my eardrums shocked me into response. It made me raise my fists in defence, just like David taught me. He was right, with enough practice your fighting stance did become second nature to you. It took me a moment to identify the voice that slammed into my back. It was Georgia.

"There is leftover lasagne in the oven," she said

I regained my composure lowering my fists and replied, "Thanks for the heads up."

Georgia was sitting by herself in the dark at the dining table with a bottle of Jack Daniels; creepy much? The bottle of Jack was half empty, and Georgia's glass was half full. Georgia's words came out a little slurred, but I could tell she hadn't lost all her wits to the booze.

The need for food outweighed my wariness of the woman, so I found a bowl and got the lasagne out of the oven. My plan was to eat back in my room. I was attentive enough of Georgia when she was sober, and with people around as witnesses. The idea of sitting down with her while I ate, and having a heart to heart chat didn't sound like a smart move on my part, especially while she was tanked. But, like always, things never seem to go as planned. As I started to walk past Georgia, she kicked out a chair from under the table to block my path.

"Sit," she ordered, "You're not going to be rude, and leave me here alone are you? Dining room tables were designed for people to eat on after all."

The expression on her face said, sit or I will chase you down and force you to sit, but her tone was scary polite. So with some reluctance I sat. I ate as fast as I could. I got half my bowl down before I had to get one thing cleared up.

"I'm not a hooker, you know."

Georgia smiled a drunken smile. She had the same crooked grin that David had; lifting only one corner of her mouth so her cheek displayed a dimple.

"I know you're not a hooker, but that isn't going to make me like you."

I thought it might have helped a little. I guess I was wrong. I ended up not responding, thinking I would just make things worse if I opened my mouth again. Georgia obviously had it in for me for some God only knows reason.

"Do you remember what I said to you when we first met?" Georgia asked.

"You called me a prostitute," I replied, making it sound like she was a mega bitch to me, which she was.

With a giggle she slurred, "Yer, I did, didn't I?" Georgia took another sip of Jack not trying in the slightest to hide the fact that she thought it was funny to call me a call girl.

"What else did I say?" Georgia added, after placing the glass back down on the table. I shrugged unsure where she was going with her line of questioning.

"I told you if my brother gets hurt, there would be no one on this earth that could protect you from me," she disclosed. Georgia's gaze on me was focused, calculating and patient. She was waiting to see what I would do, waiting for a reaction. Georgia was letting the statement sink in, letting me figure out that David did in fact get hurt. She wanted me to know that her threat had come to fruition with that Stanley knife slicing into his arm. The thing she wanted me to stew in a pot about was if she would keep true to her word, and I would be in for a fight.

If she was going to do what she threatened to do; if she was going to attack me, then she was getting ready to swing that bottle of Jack at my head. I tensed up. I was in that state when you were ready to react at anything and everything. I didn't move, I didn't react at all; I didn't know what I should do. I wasn't going to take the first swing if that was what she was waiting for. I stayed seated, and tried not to give away any emotional tells. I should have been terrified. Georgia appeared to be one girl you didn't want to pick a fight with. If she was anything like her brother, then she could probably knockout most of the blokes on the planet.

Strangely enough though, I wasn't frightened. There was something primal inside me that knew she wasn't going to physically hurt me. I had been around dangerous people that wanted to kill me, and in this instance I didn't have that feeling. Those alarms that went off in the presence of danger were not ringing. I stayed alert, however, still keeping my guard up, I knew something was coming it just wasn't going to be a fist. The way she continued to look at me was like a snake looking at a rabbit that was cornered down its own warren, and the rabbit got a lucky break because the snake wasn't hungry.

"Don't worry little rabbit," she said, making my analogy a reality. "I promised David I would be nice to you." I let out a breath I didn't know I was holding.

"He loves you, doesn't he," Georgia stated, not asked. "And you love him?"

I didn't reply straight away. I was taking my time considering my words, but in the end I didn't need to. Something gave me away. Something I did unwillingly gave Georgia a perfect view into my heart. Maybe my eyes widened slightly, or maybe it was the fact that I didn't answer straight away. Whatever it was I'd never know, but what I did know was that Georgia had the same gift for reading people as David did.

"That's even worse than I thought," Georgia slurred behind the glass of Jack, before taking another sip.

"Excuse me?" I asked, with my uneasiness starting to turn into annoyance. Georgia's stare grew hard, her face contorted into something unrecognisable. She sat with the now empty glass placed on the table in front of her.

"At first I thought you were just a pity case for him to help, like that charity work he does. But you sunk your talons in deep didn't you?" Georgia seemed to relax a little as she poured another glass of whisky.

"I didn't try and snare him if that is what you are implying," I said, my voice coming out more defensively forceful and argumentative than I meant it to be. Georgia's eyes narrowed.

"You didn't try and snare him, you say?" she repeated, as a question. "It doesn't look that way to me. You always seem to be the little damsel in distress," Georgia stated. "Is that on purpose, or are you just so unfortunately unlucky that you are always the little innocent girl needing help?" She didn't wait for a response and just followed on, "You always need saving, Sarah, and you know my brother needs someone to save."

With that comment her anger of what was really bothering her came out. Georgia slammed the bottle of Jack down on the table. Her half-full glass spilt some of its contents in the same fashion as if an earthquake had shaken the table. Before Georgia even realised the mess she just made she hissed, "Now you have dragged David, me and my daughter into your idiotic crusade against those bloody bikies, putting all our lives in danger." Georgia stared down at the alcohol spattered on the table. She sighed, her rage fading as fast as it arrived.

"What a waste," she said sorrowfully. She took a finger, dipping it in the liquid, and then lifted it to her mouth sucking it clean, "Even if you are innocent, and putting my family under the bus wasn't your intention. That is still what's happened. It is still all your fault my life has been uprooted." I had heard enough. I wasn't her verbal punching bag.

"It's not my fault your family is in danger, it's the Creatures of Chaos you should be blaming," I proclaimed.

All the guilt and doubt I had ever had was trying to burrow its way inside me just as Georgia wanted. But then it hit rock. I had done nothing wrong. I had been bashed, almost raped, my father had been beaten and my mother had been murdered, and she dared to insinuate that I am just an attention-seeker.

With the tide smashing the waves on shore that was my mind, Georgia said, "I do blame the bikies. I want them squashed like a bug under my heel just as much as you do. But we had avoided all their bullshit for the past three years. We were free to live our lives again in safety. That was right up until you walked into David's life and put a bullseye on all our backs. If you weren't out there that night, we would all be safe from the wrath you brought down upon us."

I glared at her, unable to answer. She was right. I had blamed myself with those same thoughts, but she was leaving out one major detail I came to realise. The one thing that got me through my own self-reprimand was the fact that I was the victim. Blaming me was like blaming every other person who has ever been a victim of a violent act, all because they were in the wrong place at the wrong time. Georgia could hold this entire situation against me all she liked, but I know I'm not to blame.

I wasn't about to try and change her mind, especially in this state of intoxication so I was just about to leave when she spoke up again.

"David has been through all this before, and I won't see him go down that same dark tunnel again. So don't get involved with my brother, it will only end badly for both of you."

The fire was still burning behind my eyes. That's why I was about to leave. I was only seconds away from throwing the rest of my lasagne in her face, not caring if I lost the fight between us. It would just feel great to release this built up aggression on her. But I needed to keep the peace. I was the sober one here. I tried to stay calm. As I spoke, I couldn't hide the flames that danced off my tongue.

"I told David we shouldn't start anything yet."

"Good, just keep it that way," Georgia snapped back. "You're not right for him and he's too good for you, and you're definitely not good enough to be my sister-in-law. So keep your feelings bottled up princess, throw them in the ocean and watch them sail away into the distance."

I felt the tears roll down my cheeks before I knew I was crying. She had struck the right chord with that note. The rage I felt was still there, reaching boiling point, but my other conflicting emotions like self-doubt, worry, guilt just to name a few all pushed against each other throwing me completely off kilter. I had to leave before I did something

I regretted. I got up too fast flipping my chair over, its crash to the floor echoed through the dark house.

I turned to storm off when I pulled myself back. Georgia had been pushing me around with her words since we first started speaking, and she had finally brought me to tears. I pulled myself back because crying in front of her wasn't weakness or cowardice. No, running would be, and after *that* night I swore I would never run away again.

With salty tears running into my mouth I said, "You can hate me and blame me all you want, but like it or not we are stuck in this mess together, and don't worry, I don't want to be here with someone like you either."

"I'm glad we understand each other. Just keep your hands off my brother and we can go on silently hating each other," Georgia slurred back.

I didn't try to disguise the heartache in my voice, I don't think I could have even if I tried when I retaliated a response, "Your brother is a big boy. He doesn't need his sister injecting herself into his love life. And if I do decide to be with David it will be because I truly love him, and it will be none of your business, so back off, sister."

I didn't wait for a response. I didn't even look back as I left. I had gotten in the last word, so that was good enough for me. Georgia already knew by the falling raindrops on my face that she had hurt me as she forced the crowbar between my heart and David's. That was by her design.

I guess she did keep to her word. The pain she inflicted just wasn't caused by a fist to the face. For her to tell me I was the cause of all this mess surrounding my life opened a closed wound that I only just got a Band-Aid on before it started bleeding. And for her to say I wasn't good enough for David was like being a fragile wine glass being crushed under someone's foot, being broken up into a million pieces. It utterly shattered me inside. David was the one beacon of hope in my life. The happy ending that can only be found in dreams, and Georgia had turned that hope into despair. I think I would have preferred a punch to the face, rather than being skull-fucked by her words like that. Georgia hurt me more with her words then she ever could have physically. I was guessing that was her plan all along. She would have been great at psychological warfare.

I walked back to my room sobbing uncontrollably now. I put my face in the pillow to muffle all my cries, and to catch my tears. I could understand if she blamed me for being the catalyst that put her daughter's life in danger, even though she was wrong. She would have had to know I never meant for any of this to unfold the way it did. She would know I would rather be at home with my mother, rather than be on the run, hiding from people that want me dead. She just wanted to hurt me, and she succeeded at that. What hurt me most was not that she blamed me for putting her family's lives in jeopardy, I had walled that one back up double bricked this time.

No, what hurt most was that she thought I wasn't good enough for David. What made me so unworthy? Would I really be this upset if I thought what she said wasn't true? Did I think she was right? Was I really not good enough for him? Why did he love me if I was beneath him? Why did he even love me? Was I Patrick Swayze in *Dirty Dancing* and David was Baby? My mind boggled with questions that needed answers, I had to know. I wouldn't be able to sleep until I knew. I couldn't go on living without knowing.

I stormed into David's room, slamming the door behind me. I turned on the light, trying and succeeding to wake him up. David shot straight up in bed, shock, fear and confusion was displayed in his sleepy demeanour. When his eyes found me and clarity filled his head, I could see the tension leave his body. I had a thousand questions I wanted to…, no, I *had* to ask, but when I saw him sitting up in bed topless, his bare skin shining like a beacon attracting me to him. All the questions I once had vanished, leaving only one.

"Why do you love me?" I blurted out. He didn't answer my question he just asked a question of his own, which he already knew the answer to.

"Have you been crying?"

I asked again more urgently, "Why do you love me?" His face softened.

"You ran into Georgia, didn't you?"

"Why do you love me, if I'm not good enough for you?" I demanded, tears welling up in my eyes again. I fought to keep them at bay.

"Come over here," he gestured to the end of the bed.

"No," I said, stomping a foot down like a little girl chucking a tantrum.

"I would get up, but I'm not wearing anything," he said.

"So what, you've seen me naked," I said in defiance.

I didn't think he was going to get out of bed when I said it, but he flicked the blankets off revealing all of his manhood. It put me off guard, I wasn't expecting it. I didn't know how long I was staring, but when the reality hit me I looked away.

David was perfectly proportioned everywhere, and I mean everywhere. If an artist needed the perfect man to paint, then David would be it. But no painting would ever be able to do him justice. The light shining down from the ceiling cast shadows that fell into all the ridges that his muscular body produced. David's body was fully mapped out under the light, his physique being immaculately marked out by black shadow. The next thing I knew David was next to me holding my hands, no shame or shyness while he stood in front of me all exposed, not that he needed to be because, damn, he was perfect.

"Do you always sleep naked?" I asked, unable to look at him, but unable to get his god-like naked figure out of my mind's eye.

"Always," he answered, "I find sleeping with clothes uncomfortable, and to answer your question about why I love you." He paused, I felt a hand on my chin guiding my eyes to his, "That night I saved you; what really happened was, you saved me. You gave me a reason for living, you made me feel again. You woke me up out of my numb state of existence. You are an angel here to rescue me; it wasn't the other way around."

I was trembling, either from all my emotions fading down to just one, or it could be the naked man standing in front of me. David was only the second man I had seen naked. I had only had sex with one other guy, too. My hands found their way to his chest; the skin was warm, smooth with hard muscle underneath. My hands slid down to the grooves of his six-pack not daring to go any lower. My hands were still shaking; I could feel all the nerve-endings on my entire body, I was very aware of his hands that now lay on my waist.

"We don't have to take this any further if you're not ready," he said, knowing where this was heading. I didn't reply but I didn't move away. My hands were still exploring his torso, and my eyes followed my hands. David leant down slowly and kissed me. Softly at first. When my arms wrapped around him, and then started to investigate the contours of his back and shoulders, his kissing intensified. His hands ran down my back, skimming over my butt then lifting me up. My legs tied themselves around his waist.

David gently laid me down on the bed, my legs untwining from around his midriff, his naked body still between my thighs. He loomed over me, taking the vision of me in, and then kissed me with an animal attraction. He kissed down the side of my neck, sliding down my body until his hands hooked on my pants. He kissed the line of my leg, following the extraction of my pants and panties.

I took my own top off exposing my breasts. David flung my pants to the floor. My legs were now resting on his shoulders. I was glad for all the flexibility training he had me do. Who knew it would be so beneficial? He started kissing down the inside of my leg until his head found its way between my legs.

My breathing started to grow deeper, then faster, with my body growing hotter. All my nervousness was gone, replaced with overwhelming pleasure that was building, and building, intensifying. My body was searching for a climax with every second that passed, until the pleasure from his kiss boiled over to an explosion of ecstasy. David lifted his head. A grin of accomplishment was on his face. All my strength went with the explosion. I just lay there panting, reliving that moment over and over again in my mind.

I couldn't even remember the last time Sam made me climax. It had been a long time since I had reached the finishing line, and it all went so fast. I wanted more. I opened my eyes after an unknowable moment to see David staring at me still in between my thighs.

"God help me. I am so profoundly in love with you," he said.

I gently pulled on his arms that were resting on my legs to indicate to come up. He moved slowly kissing his way up, stopping at my breasts. Tingles started to run through my body again, another moan escaped my lips. I tried to be quiet but I couldn't help it. I had never been touched like this before. His touch was so compassionate, it was mind blowing. It was so soft, but so powerful at the same time. He kissed the side of my neck; stopping as he entered me. My back arched, my head went back, and another moan forced its way out of me. It was like his body was made for mine. He hit all the right spots, he moved in all the right ways. My legs were fastened around him, my hands on the small of his back finishing on his ass, feeling the flex of his butt with every deep thrust.

I had given up on trying to be quiet, the moans sang out of me now, uncontrolled. My body going on instinct mode, the exhilaration of his body on mine, in mine, was starting to boil over again. My excitability was reaching its Mt Everest. I took flight once more, but not alone. This time he pulsed inside me until his head slumped down to rest on my shoulder. Our breathing in unison, the pounding of our hearts synced, it was like we were one, so close, so physically and emotionally intertwined, there was no separating us, we were as one.

CHAPTER 33

*L*ouis Cole was in his office sitting at his desk in his most prestigious and most profitable brothel named Paradise of Eden. This brothel was all up to code with all the right paperwork, and stocked with all the highest quality of pussy. He had other brothels, of course, but they were for people with selective tastes. Tastes that weren't quite legal. It would have been in one of those brothels that Neil would have put Sarah, if things had worked out differently. Sarah probably would have gone to one of his customers that liked to kill the girl while they had sex with them. It would have been the smart move after snatching her off the streets; better to get a good payday and get rid of the evidence. If only his brother had listened to Neil that night, he would still be alive, and they would have more cash in their wallets. That's why Louis was the smart one.

Louis sitting on his throne in his castle sometimes felt like Al Pacino in *Scarface*; without getting killed at the end, of course. Today, though, wasn't one of those days. Revenge still plagued his mind. He wanted it. He needed it. He could almost taste it. Once he got his hands on this David Powers, he wasn't going to just kill him. No, he was going to make him beg for death.

After breaking a few bones, removing some skin, he thought he might gut this Sarah Smith bitch right in front of him. That might make him want to end it all, but we would have to wait and see, everyone had different breaking points. The fun was in the journey, however, not planting the flag at the top of the hill. Louis had envisioned the scene in his head a hundred times. He would hang the bitch up from hooks through her feet, and then slit her throat showering her blood all over him. He would bring the apocalypse to David. He would make the heavens rain blood. Then once David had given up, and begged him to introduce him to his maker, then he'd just sit back and watch his masterpiece.

Louis's passion on such topics was to break more than just their bodies. He liked to break their spirits. Only when Louis got bored with David's begging would he end it. He'd make sure the last thing he saw was his smiling face.

Louis held a cigarette in one hand and was spinning a thin silver six-inch throwing dagger in the other. The laptop that sat on the desk in front of him displayed the profiles of the two his vengeance sought. The girl between his legs started to tremble. She was scared. She knew the stories of the woman that couldn't please Louis Cole. She knew the stories were true. She had seen the aftermath of the girls first hand.

Louis wanted the rumours floating around his working girls, so they knew never to upset him in any way, shape or form. But most importantly he wanted them to fear him. He wanted everyone to fear him. He loved the dominance of standing over a quivering woman, all naked and exposed. There was nothing more empowering – except killing somebody, of course.

Louis's hand found the red curly hair on top her head. He pulled her head back hard. The girl's eyes slid shut, and she let out a groan of pain. Louis waited until the girl opened her eyes, then he said, "You have been down there for twenty minutes and I'm still not even hard."

The redhead was gorgeous. She was fairly new, too. He hadn't had her yet; he always found time to taste the delights of all his girls. Louis could see why she was fast becoming his best money-maker. The girl said nothing. A tear rolled down her cheek. Louis thought the girl might piss herself, it would make a mess but it would be worth it. He knew how scared these girls could get, this wouldn't be the first time one of them had wet herself in front of him.

Daisy, the redhead, was in fact quite good, better than most at her craft. But not even Pamela Anderson in her red swimsuit from

226 | B. C. Goodwin

Baywatch could get him hard at the moment. It was blood he wanted, not pussy.

Louis turned Daisy's head to one side, he placed the silver blade on her flushed red cheek, "Maybe I should cut a hole in your cheek, and then fuck that because you mouth isn't doing the job," Louis told her in a low deep voice.

The girl whimpered but stayed still; she knew better than to resist. The girl was brave. Most of them would have screamed for the heavens by now, but not this one. She would need to be broken down a little more he thought.

Now he could feel his loins start to wake up. The more terrified Daisy got, the more aroused he got. Louis took the point of the blade, and then sunk just the tip of it into her cheek. Daisy squeaked as the point of the blade went into flesh. Louis marvelled at how easy human flesh could be sliced into with a sharp instrument. It took less than a pound of pressure to cut through human skin. Louis had tested that theory more than once. He pulled the knife away from Daisy's cheek; a single drop of blood rose up from the puncture point on her cheek. Louis wasn't really going to face fuck the girl's cheek, but she didn't need to know that. Daisy was worth a lot more beautiful, than a disfigured freak. The prick on the side of her face would only leave a mark like a pimple, if it showed up at all.

Louis was many things, but stupid wasn't one of them. There was a reason why Louis was the king of the castle. Brains were a lot more effective than muscle when you wanted to control other people. Fear, he'd learned, does wonders when running a club full of large bearded men, and if his own brothers-in-arms were scared of him, then the rest of the world would be easy to convince.

Louis was a big man, not as big as his younger brother, Jordan, but not far off. Louis had the smarts, his brother had the aggression. Louis knew how to use his brother's gung-ho nature to achieve his own bigger plans. Together the brothers rose to the top of the Creatures of Chaos bikie ring. They stole, cheated and murdered their way up. Rising through the ranks until the Cole brothers ran the club. Once the club was theirs, then came the city. Louis's next goal was to take over the country and then, by the end, the world. That was until he found out that David Powers had shown up for the second time; he was one slippery fuck.

Three years ago David had taken down three of his men, and killed one, John Black. The death was so gruesome that Louis, along with everybody else thought it had to be the Insurgents. None of them suspected that one man could have done so much damage. Now they knew better. David had killed his brother, Jordan, with his own knife. He had killed one of his best friends, Ben, by unloading a clip of bullets into his heart. He put four other club members in the hospital, and that could not be tolerated.

David was dead; he just didn't know it yet. Louis couldn't have connections with failure. If one guy and his bitch could do this to him, then his rivals might start getting ideas. Something had to be done, something so violently extreme that it would put everyone back in their place, under Louis's boot heel where they all belonged.

Louis would use all his resources, all his money to hunt down David Powers and his slut girlfriend, Sarah Smith, if it was the last thing he did. Louis lost his state of mind with the redhead, his mood turned sour again with the thought of his brother's killers. No blowjob would make him feel better now. Not even watching this stunning red head squirm beneath his grip would cheer him up. Louis wiped the droplet of blood from Daisy's cheek with a finger, and then painted his tongue red with the blood. Louis then stuck his tongue down Daisy's throat making her taste her own blood, gagging on the sudden assault. The girl's eyes were wide with dread, her anxiety was unmistakable now, just the way he usually liked it. Not today though, not until David was screaming in agony.

"Get out," Louis ordered, pulling back from her, now bored with torturing the girl. Besides he still needed her to work in the brothel tonight. Make him his money. Daisy was a good earner. Better not scare her beyond repair, he thought. He would have her again, once all this was done.

Daisy got up slowly, not knowing if it was a trick. Once it was clear that Louis just wanted to be left alone Daisy ran for the large double wooden doors. Louis watched her naked ass run out the door. He couldn't wait to have his blood lust quenched; nothing else would ease his foul mood.

A very fit looking Asian woman walked in right after Daisy's exit. Bo managed the girls that worked for Louis. Bo was in her late forties, and still an absolute stunner. Black hair with a red streak running through it, manicured nails that could scratch out cats' eyes, and a don't fuck with me attitude. Bo only answered to one person, and that was Louis. Bo started off as a working girl, but Louis saw her potential. The woman had other skills that made her more valuable than just having her legs in the air.

"Do you have to scare the wits out of the girls like that?" Bo huffed, "It's going to take me ages to get her ready for clients again." Louis shot Bo a warning glance. Bo knew when not to push it, and now was that time.

"What do you want, Bo?" Louis asked.

"There is a young gentleman named Aiden waiting to talk to you," Bo answered.

"What does he want?" Louis said, irritated.

"I don't know, he wouldn't say. But the kid looks as white as a come shot to the face."

"Send him in."

A moment later a skinny shaved-head kid walked through the doors. Aiden walked in slow, he looked as frightened as the bitch had been between his legs. Aiden the computer-wise kid, or also known on paper as Mark Johnson, was terrified about something. Aiden was only eighteen, but the kid was a master on the keyboard. Louis paid him a lot of money to keep things in check, and Aiden had never disappointed. But, from the lack of colour on his face, something had gone terribly wrong.

Aiden stood in front of the desk, his voice shaky as he said, "We have a problem." Louis lifted an eyebrow and pressed his lips together hard, making his mouth form a straight line. Louis leaned forward bringing up the dagger, spinning it where Aiden could see. The kid gulped before he spoke.

"David Powers dropped in for a visit."

Louis rammed the knife into the desk making Aiden jump back about a foot.

"Please tell me you have him unconscious behind those doors," Louis said, knowing that would not be the case. Knowing the kid wouldn't be this afraid if that was so.

"David broke into my house with five guys," Aiden exaggerated. "They tied me up, and hacked my computer."

Louis could feel the rage burning inside, but what separated him from his brother was that he controlled his aggression. He looking down at his hand, which held the dagger embedded in the desk and then asked, in a controlled tone, "Did they get anything I should be worried about?"

"They got everything I had," Aiden said, ducking his head into his shoulders, knowing he was in deep shit now.

Louis got up, not saying a word. Louis walked smoothly over to the shaking rattling kid. Then, when he stood towering over the boy, he moved. In a blink of an eye he had lifted Aiden up by the neck then performed the rock bottom manoeuver, slamming Aiden down hard on the ground. The impact knocked the wind right out of him. Aiden gasped for air unable to expand his lungs.

Louis waited a moment for Aiden to realise what was coming for him. The last time Aiden and Louis were together Louis had helped Aiden kill his first person; it was a magical experience. This time, however, Aiden would be on the other side of death. Louis's hand was raised, the glint of the dagger in it.

"Now you die, kid."

Right before Louis was about to bury the blade into the boy's chest, Aiden coughed up a sound.

"What?" Louis yelled, the dagger hovering over the boy like a guillotine about to release its blade.

Aiden coughed two more times, then managed to say, "I have a plan to catch them."

CHAPTER 34

The sun shone through the window's vertical blinds. The golden light displayed on the wall looked as if we were lying in a bed behind the gates of heaven. At this moment I thought I might actually be in heaven. Was it so wrong of me to feel so happy at this trying time? I figured I had to enjoy life while I was still around to enjoy it. I would make the most of the life I had. Life was short and who knows if we'd get another chance. Even if we did get another roll of the dice I would never meet another David.

I rolled over remembering what I did last night. A smile forced itself onto my lips. I was naked, next to a gorgeous naked man, physically and emotionally satisfied. I may as well have been in heaven I couldn't think of a better place. David was still sleeping; he was graceful, even in sleep. I swung an arm over him pulling myself close to his warm body, and so every part of me that could touch him was touching him.

It was then I knew I didn't regret what I did last night. It all felt right. It felt normal to be with him. It was like this wasn't the first time I had awoken up next to him. It felt like we were an old couple, and I was used to seeing the same person next to me every morning. David stirred, starting to wake up. I began to lightly run my finger over his skin. David's eyes flickered open.

"Hello you," he said, his voice sounding a bit dry.

"Hello you," I said back.

"Did you want to get up or did you want another round in the ring," I asked the ex-boxer. My thigh was over his mid-section, so I knew he was ready to go. We had gone two more rounds last night after the first, all finishing the same way. I had never had a simultaneous orgasm with anyone before – meaning with Sam. Come to think of it, I think I had more orgasms with David last night than I did in my entire relationship with Sam. To come four times in one night, three times ending simultaneously with David, the night was beyond memorable. The man was a machine, a very sexy well-oiled machine.

"I'm kind of hungry," he answered. "I haven't done that kind of exercise in a while."

I was only half wanting a morning quickie, but I wouldn't have said no if he was up for it. Then the idea of walking out there, and confronting Joe, Georgia and Clare sounded naughty to me, like I now had something to hide.

"How do you want to handle this?" I asked. "Do you want them to know we hooked up last night?"

David was fully awake now, his full attention on my question.

"I want to be with you and I don't care who knows it. That includes my sister," he answered. My heart melted. How could I not love this man?

"But if it will make you uncomfortable for them to know, then I can play the part, if you want me to," he added, no mocking included. He had only ever wanted the best for me. I really didn't know what I had done to make him love me so. I thought about it for a moment. Thinking it might be easier for us if Georgia and my Dad didn't know about us right now. Dealing with their judging eyes didn't sound like my cup of tea. But the moment would have to come at some point. There was no going back for me when it came to David, I was wholeheartedly in.

"No I don't care either. But maybe leave the PDA's for when we're not around your sister or my father," I suggested. "And what about last night?" I inquired next. I could see David's bewildered face. He didn't understand want I meant, so I went on to say, "Do you think they are going to know what happened?"

"Well," he said, rolling his eyes, and then taking a pause looking all suspect. Then he put forth, "I think you were so noisy last night that Joe's neighbours would know what we did last night."

My jaw dropped; surprise taking control. I knew I didn't hold back, but I didn't think I was that loud. I rolled off him and said, "Well it was all your fault, I was so loud," shifting my embarrassment back to him.

He pulled me back on top of him then kissed me softly on the lips. All of my thoughts about loud volume sex vanished with his kiss. I thought he might want to take me up on my offer of another round, but he sat up with me on top of him. David's core strength was remarkable. I could vouch for that three more times over. Then the thought of coffee sprang in to my head, and the pull was too strong. We got up reluctantly from our naked bliss, having to put on clothes. I couldn't help but keep sneaking peeks as he put on his clothes; still never getting enough of that glorious sight.

Since we didn't do much talking last night there was one more question that swam back and forth in my mind. I had some inkling of the answer, but I had to know what David thought.

"Why does your sister hate me?"

I could see that David knew this was coming sooner or later. He had guessed that it was Georgia that got me all hot and bothered last night, so I didn't have to wait too long for a response.

"There are two reasons I know of," David began, "My late wife, Isabella, was Georgia's best friend. Georgia loved Isabella nearly as much as I did, so she gets a bit territorial over me now. She thinks she is doing it for Isabella."

That's probably why she threw in that comment about not being good enough to be her sister-in-law. Georgia was comparing me to Isabella.

"So her dislike for me isn't so personal?" I asked. David screwed up his face a little.

"The second reason is personal," he admitted, "She thinks you are just using me to get back at the bikies for what they did to you." David started putting on his socks as he continued, "then she thinks once you have gotten all you want out of me you will just leave me and break my heart. She's afraid that I couldn't handle losing another woman I love."

"Oh," was all I could think to say. I was so good with words sometimes. David walked over to me pulling me close. Then he lifted my chin so I was staring into his eyes.

"But that's not what I think. Georgia doesn't see the beautiful person I see. But she will. Georgia is stubborn, not stupid. Her stubbornness makes her blind at the moment. I guarantee she will eventually see the courageous, gorgeous soul I do," David said just above a whisper. Then he kissed me like he added a full stop at the end of a sentence. Even though David didn't agree with Georgia's current assessment of me, I still had to say what I needed to say, for my sake, if nothing else.

"You really should know that I would never do anything like that," I told David.

"I know," he replied.

"I really do love you," I confirmed.

"I know," he said again. "Don't worry about Georgia. She'll come around."

I felt a bit better knowing why she disliked me, but deep down it still bugged me. I would prove to her that this was not a use-and-abuse scenario, but a love-dove-from-above scenario. I loved David in a way that was foreign to me. What I felt for him was nothing like what I felt for Sam. What I felt for David was much deeper. The connection we shared went beyond words and feeling. This sounds corny but it felt more like he was my soul-mate.

CHAPTER 35

*A*s David and I walked into the kitchen I was surprised to see Dad staring back at me. I didn't expect to see him until this afternoon. Then I took a look at the clock hanging on the wall over the kitchen bench. I was shocked to see that it was three twenty-four pm. We must have really needed our sleep after, well you know.

When my eyes met Joe's, a wink escaped his face, followed by a cheeky smile that said I know what you did last night. Through my shyness that was trying to poke its head out, I noticed Joe was very careful to keep that wink out of my father's viewing capabilities. I did my best not to blush, but I think I failed miserably, noticing heat going to my cheeks. Brooding on the fact that David might not have been exaggerating about how noisy I was last night wasn't going to help.

Before I got swallowed up by my shyness I peered over at Georgia. She didn't even raise her head as we entered. I guessed she felt a bit under the weather after that date with Jack last night.

From behind me I heard David say, "Hey kiddo." I looked around to see David pick up a little girl with his uninjured arm.

"Is Sarah your new girlfriend?" the innocent girl asked.

David looked at me asking through the telepathy in his stare, how do you want me to answer. I shrugged, grinned and then nodded. My way of saying yes, you are now my boyfriend, and it's up to you how you want to handle it. It might have looked like I was saying, whatever, I don't care. Either way David got the point.

234

"Yes, she is my girlfriend." Clare looked at me with a smile that pushed up her cheeks.

"That means I'm allowed to like you now," she said in my direction.

"That's good to know," I said. "Well, I like you too," I quickly added making Clare's smile grow.

"Mummy said, you were not very nice, but if Uncle David loves you then you must be a nice lady," Clare said holding on to her beloved uncle.

"I'm glad you came to that conclusion," I responded, actually happy to have Clare's approval.

When I turned back around everyone else was staring at us. Even Georgia lifted her head up to look at us through bloodshot eyes. To kick the elephant out of the room I acted.

"Yes, David and I are now together." I looked straight at Dad when I said it. Then turned to Georgia and said, "And, yes, I really do truly love him and I'm not going anywhere. Accept it."

Georgia then did something unexpected. She did a head tilt, nodding her approval of my boldness, and then she manifested a half smile. I think it was the first real time I saw her face without animosity. It was a nice change. Looking back at my father, his eyebrows were lifted, and he was leaning back in his chair.

"Okay then," was all he said.

"It's about time you two hooked up," Joe gabbed. He was about to say something else, but then remembered who else was in the room; a glance over at my father muted his voice box as quick as a click of a remote. David sat at the table with Clare sitting on his lap.

"Now that is settled," David said, looking not at all unsettled from the past conference topic of his love life.

"Joe, where is the food at?" David asked, peering at Joe.

"Do I look like your butler," Joe said back. "Get up and get it yourself, lazy bones."

After David made us some coffee, then some bacon and eggs that all went down like a bottle of milk for a baby's belly, David, my Father and I took Max for a walk. The sun was hot for a spring day. There wasn't a cloud in the sky, or a breath of wind to ruin this perfect day. To me it felt like the eye of the storm. We had all had to trudge through so much crap to get to the lush green field of grass. Then once we'd wiped all the shit off our boots the pasture ended, and the walking through poo continued. But in our case instead of crap we walked through a stream of blood.

Max ran past wagging his tail; barking his mouth off at some birds that were minding their own business. The birds flew from the ground to the nearby trees to escape the jaws of the not so subtle predator. I sometimes envied the simple life of a dog. Their only worry was when their next meal was coming. The smallest of things got the biggest spark of enjoyment, such as going for a walk and chasing some birds, fun, fun, fun. Dogs didn't have any worries like paying bills, getting a job. They were free to laze about, scratch their butt on the carpet and lick their own balls. How I envied the simple life.

"How did it go with Frank?" David asked when we were out of range of prying ears.

"We got more than expected, but not enough on its own to take them down for good," Dad said with a wry smile. "We didn't get all their illegal business dealings like we hoped. I didn't think they would be stupid enough to keep digital records of that stuff, anyway. But what we got was all their dirty little secrets on all their associates. Their arsenal of persuasion."

"That's all good and well, but hurting their clients will only injure them, not cripple them," David pointed out. Then voicing the conundrum he added, "How do we use that dirt to get the outcome we want?"

"The bikies are very well connected, we all know that," my father asserted. "But that's the thing; their power of persuasion just became ours. Now we know who they deal with. Who they actually have dirt on, and who they don't. That gives us the advantage of," Dad paused to take a moment on how to phase it, "let's say, we can be the opposing force to the bikies. The people that do dodgy dealing with the bikies, the people they call friends we will blackmail. The people that want to get free from the Creatures of Chaos tyranny, the people they threaten to get what they want out of them, we turn to our side."

"Unless somewhere on that USB explains who is getting blackmailed and who isn't how are we to know?" I asked.

"That is our dilemma. Frank hasn't found anything yet that will tell us if they are friend or foe. I am assuming they have dirt on all their friends too, just to keep them in line," Dad replied, folding his arms across his chest. "We just have to do our research, and make an educated guess."

"What kind of people are on that list?" David quizzed my father.

"There are a few people in some high places like cops, judges, politicians, actors, sports figures and lawyers. We have started looking into all the higher profile people first. I won't know more until I get back to Frank," Dad answered while picking up a stick to throw for Max. Max looked like he had lost ten years, and was now bouncing around like a pup. Max must have lost interest in the birds, wanting a more exciting game like chasing a stick, fun, fun, fun. Dad let loose the stick into a field of long grass.

"Before I left, Frank told me about a cop that the bikies have photos of having sex with a woman that we assume isn't his wife."

Dad looked pained and disgusted with the man's actions. I could tell he was thinking of Mum just now. Before he fell into that bottomless pit that was the death of my mother, he quickly went on to say, "There is a video of a judge buying large quantities of cocaine from who we suspect to be the Creatures of Chaos. You can only identify the judge in the video. They cover their own tracks very well."

"We could use that," David said thoughtfully.

"Yer, we could," Dad agreed, "If that video got out he would be disbarred and thrown in jail. We will have to look into him further to see whether he likes his drugs more then he values his job and freedom."

"What if we just take all the information to someone like the channel seven news, publicly slamming all of them?" I said.

"We could do that, but it wouldn't help us in the long run," my father said, seeing the flaw in my plan after only two seconds. "It would hurt all their contacts and operations, slowing them down, just like David said, it would injure not cripple. What we got doesn't tie the bikies to their illegal activities. Everything Frank has found so far to do with their business is legit under the law. Their brothels that pull in a lot of their cash are properly licenced and have all the right paperwork. All the incriminating evidence we got is all on their associates, not any of their members. We know they run a lot of drugs, and have murdered people. They may even have illegal brothels. We just have to find a way to prove that. There is nothing we've found so far that a jury would be able to convict them on. Everything we got is just conjecture." My father was on a roll, so David and I didn't interrupt, plus I didn't want to make another stupid suggestion.

"What we need to do is get some of these guys to roll over on the Creatures of Chaos. Get them to give us some undeniable evidence to convict. If we just blaze away with this, the club will go untouched. They will be free to continue to hunt us down."

"We have to connect all the dots," David announced, saying his thoughts out loud.

"Right," my father said enthusiastically. "We have to align all the pieces until we get checkmate." I was a little naïve sometimes, but I was a quick study. I saw the board now. I saw the pieces. I saw the white queen taking down the black king.

CHAPTER 36

$\mathcal{D}$avid, Frank, Dad and I spent three full days sorting through, analysing and contemplating who we would target from the stolen data files. David and I took a few breaks to keep up with my training, however. But instead of paying him with money, I paid him with kisses. Training was a lot more fun when you could get all handsy.

Sorry, I forgot to mention Joe; I got a little side-tracked while reminiscing about kissing David. As we were sleeping under Joe's roof, he insisted on knowing what we were up to. We were under constant harassment so we ended up yielding to his annoyance letting him come along. Georgia on the other hand wanted nothing to do with it all. She told David she knew how to use a shotgun so she would be fine. Plus they had Max's teeth. Anyway, after endless debate, we eventually came up with our list of targets.

We wanted to end this with one fell swoop. We hoped to line up all the dominos and watch them all fall down with only one little push. We had to arrange all the pieces, hence people, perfectly to get our desired effect. And our desired effect was a very long jail sentence for all the Creatures of Chaos bikies that were after our blood.

We also needed to do it by the book; follow the rule of law. We had to find a way to use this bent out of shape law system that any mug with enough money could corrupt and manipulate it to our will. We had to use the law to put away the people that had the power to corrupt it. Tricky business to come up with a plan; it was like trying to get through an ever-changing maze. The rules of the game stay the same; get to the end of the maze. However, getting through an ever-changing maze would be almost impossible.

So what do you do? One option would be to knock down the walls. Effective, but might get a bit messy. Option two, learn how to control the maze for yourself, and then change it to suit your own desired path through to the end. It was much harder than option one, but more elegant. The plan we had so far was sound up to a point. All our dominos were lined up, except... of course there had to be an except. There was one blank bone domino that could be anything and her name was Alice Simpkin. We needed a witness to corroborate all the bikies wrongdoings and testify against them. We had a few options, safer options, but we needed some major dirt and we think Alice had it.

Alice was an actress on some not very well known ABC fantasy series. She was five foot five, dark brown hair with matching big brown eyes. Full lips and a drop dead gorgeous everything. I was pretty sure she didn't get her start in the TV industry because of her acting prowess. Alice lived on the south east side of the city. She drove to and from work in a blue Hyundai Accent, licence plate QRH534. Alice also had a gym membership at Focus Fitness, a place she routinely frequented.

That was where David and I were waiting for her. In the car park three spaces to the left of her shiny Accent. That was where we were going to confront this brunette bombshell, and find out whether or not she could be turned away from the dark side of the force. Dad and Joe were off doing their own meet and greets at the moment. I think Dad would have preferred to go with Frank, but Frank didn't do field work. Besides, at least I knew Joe would be on his best behaviour with Dad around.

We planned to meet the actress here because she should be alone. This should be the perfect time and place to approach her. The car park being a public place, but mostly isolated from an unwanted audience, plus we'd be close to our car for a quick getaway.

The gym was only a ten-minute drive from her suburban home. We discussed doing it there, but we wanted this girl to help us. Pursuing Alice at her home might come across as an invasion of her privacy and, besides, David didn't really feel like kicking down another door if things went sideways. Alice didn't have a boyfriend that we knew of. The love of her life was her pet cat Jojo, who had had all her necessary shots, and had been de-sexed by the local vet. Frank always goes all out with his research.

The file we stole from Mr Jester on Alice, wasn't that detailed, but there were pictures of her buying and using cocaine. The thing that caught our attention, and made it worth taking the risk on the actress was a disturbing twenty-second video clip of her crying like a baby with what looked like blood all over her. Alice looked like what I would imagine someone would look like if they stood in front of a person that got shot with a shotgun.

We assumed she was the bystander to the blood splatter so, if she was indeed a witness to a murder by the Creatures of Chaos, then she was exactly the person we wanted on our side. Plus Alice must know something about their drug dealing too, which could be invaluable information also. On the other side of the coin Alice was a risk because we didn't know what took place, and whose blood it was that was spattered all over her. We had no idea what really happened in that video and what her involvement was. We could only make an educated guess and, we guessed she witnessed a murder.

Going off her profile that Frank made up for us, Alice seemed to be a nice Christian girl on paper. Addicted to coke obviously, but we hoped she had good morals, and a kind heart behind the veil of drugs. We were guessing she was just in the wrong place at the wrong time, and now the bikies were keeping her mouth shut by threatening to do the same thing to her. We even considered that the reason for all the drugs was to escape the memory of the brutal death.

To make sure that Alice's mouth stayed zipped up, the bikies were keeping those pictures and that video as collateral. Using it as leverage to either expose her as a drug addict, ruining her acting career, unless she was the next Charlie Sheen, or maybe they would just blame her for the murder of Jane Doe or John Doe. Well, that was our assumption anyway. There was only one way to find out for sure, and we were just three car spaces away from finding out. As we sat in the car listening to the radio, waiting for Alice to exit the gym, David turned to me.

"Have you ever realised that nine out of ten songs on the radio are about boy girl relationship drama." I was about to say something, my mouth was open and everything, and then I actually thought about the statement before I responded. I had never thought about it before. Now that I had I couldn't place a song that wasn't about a love drama.

"I think you're right. I can't think of a song that is about anything else," I replied, still running through a list of songs in my mind. Then it occurred to me, I had never talked about music with David before. He could enjoy classical music for all I know.

"What music are you into then?" I asked curiously.

"Rap," he declared.

I chuckled out a laugh. David almost looked annoyed with the reaction.

"What's so funny?" he demanded. He was so cute when he was flustered.

"You don't look the type," I said through a smile.

"Why? Because I don't have dark skin and wear clothing ten sizes too big," he retorted.

"Yer, probably," I agreed. He smiled then pushed me playfully.

"Then what are you into? Taylor Swift?" he jabbed.

"A little bit, yer," I confessed.

"Why rap then?" I asked.

"Because artists like Tupac, Biggie, and Ice Cube produced music to tell people about what really goes on in the world. Not just the bubble gum crap you hear on the radio," David said passionately, so passionately in fact that he was about to go on, but then he turned to stare out the window, his passion falling flat, and his game face taking over.

Alice walked out of the gym with two other very fit looking girls, all wearing tight bright-coloured spandex. Alice gave each of them a hug, and waved goodbye. She then headed in our direction, towards her car. We made our way out of the car to intercept her, as we did Alice faltered mid-stride. A flash of recognition appeared on her face.

Well, that was what I thought I saw, but what I thought I saw was gone as fast as it appeared, she might have just farted. Unless she's a fan of *Crime stoppers*, I can't see how she would know us. Frank did say they had released images of Dad and me to the public. I did still have to be careful about being recognised, but if she had spotted me from the news report that had said, 'I had been kidnapped by my own father after he murdered his wife,' she wouldn't have converted back to such a carefree persona. No, I'm thinking it was just a fart face.

"Alice Simpkin," David called out as she drew near.

"Oh, hello," Alice responded all smiles, "you guys must be fans. Hang on one moment." She pulled her purse around and dug her palm inside.

I could see David stiffen, ready to react to any sudden aggressive movement. Did he think she was going for a weapon – a can of pepper spray maybe?

Alice searched through the handbag, still wearing a glistening smile that was plastered on her face, her high cheek bones casting shadows in the afternoon sunlight. After rifling around for a long while in her silver Gucci handbag, a bag in which I really didn't want to know the price of, because it looked expensive. People are always trying to keep up with the Kardashians.

Her hand eventually emerged out of the depths with a black permanent marker.

"It's always at the bottom of the bag," she said as she waved the marker around. "Do you have a picture or some paper for me to sign? If not I could always sign that broad chest of yours," she said to David with raising eyebrows. My heckles rose at the way she was leering at David. I was about to tell her where she could stick that pen, but then she turned to me with that painted on smile and added, "I'm happy to write my autograph on your chest too, if you want?"

The surprise on my face must have been plain as day. I really didn't know how to respond. A second ago I wanted to punch her in her perfect face, and now she wanted to touch my boobs. It was hard to get a read on this girl.

"No thank you," I muttered, after finding my voice.

"I'm always glad to sign for any of my fans," Alice announced, very chipper. If it was possible, her smile seemed to grow even bigger. I was glad to see her flirtation had no effect on David, but I was a little freaked out about her trying to entice me. I had never been hit on by a woman before; I didn't know how to react. David did relax slightly when the marker appeared, but I could see he still kept his guard up.

"Sorry, no, we're not fans," David declared. The famous smile faded in to a grin.

"Oh, then how do you know me?" she said, still sounding upbeat. She didn't seem freaked out at all, which I thought was a bit weird. If two strangers came up to me knowing my name, I would be a little suspicious. I had heard all people in the show biz were a little crazy. Maybe the rumours were true.

"We need to talk about your involvement with the Creatures of Chaos bikie organization," David said, tone flat, no emotion behind it. That was how I imagined a lawyer would talk to a criminal they knew was guilty, but had to defend them anyway. Not that we thought Alice was guilty. Alice's fading grin turned into a frown before she spoke.

"I don't have anything to say to you. I have no idea what you are talking about." She dove back into her bag and pulled out her keys as she added, "I have to go." Alice strode off to her car brushing past David. I saw real fear on her face, and in her movements. Alice shook as she fumbled with her keys. I could see her unease, I could taste it in the air, and I could use it. I had to bring her down until her only option was up. I cut her off three paces from her driver's side door. Her eyes were wide and starting to glaze over with tears.

"Do you really want to be that scared little girl your whole life, running away when things get tough?" I began. Alice tried to push past; I stepped to cut her off.

"Do you want to be the girl crying in the corner after getting pissed on?" I continued. Alice tried to push past again. I stepped. "Do you really want to be a puppet with them holding the strings." Alice pushed again, I stepped again.

"Do you want to be the mouse or the lion? Do you want to just absorb the punches or do you want to throw some back?" She looked up. There was something inside her, some darkness emanating from her. I could see it because the same darkness lived in me.

"I want to be the one who survives." She croaked out.

Alice didn't try to push past this time; she patiently waited for me to step aside. So I did, but as I moved out of her way I added one last thing.

"I don't know whose blood was sprayed all over you, but I know that's why you're so frightened." Alice stiffened. A single tear rolled down her cheek.

"They murdered my mother," I told her. Alice's tears began to flow freely now. "And I will do anything to get justice for her death. That is the person I am." Staring dead into her eyes I asked, "What kind of person are you?"

Alice leant up against her car. I knew I was getting through to her now, breaking through that pop-star façade.

"We come to you now because we have the evidence that the bikies have against you. We know you are tangled up with them, and we know you were involved either as a witness or the assailant of a very blood-thirsty altercation," I said.

"I watched it all happen," she sobbed. "There was so much blood, it was everywhere." Alice launched at me, I was taken off guard. I only had enough time to take one step backwards before I was wrapped up in a clinging hug. Her head nestled upon my shoulder, which was now gathering tears from her uncontrollable sobs.

I didn't know what to do. The look on my face would have been priceless. Once the momentary shock subsided I just hugged her back. I wasn't sure what else to do besides taking option B, which was to fight my way out. I peered over her shoulder to see that David was now at arm's length, ready to peel her off me if need be.

I put my palms face up, gesturing for help; miming, what do I do now. David just shrugged, doing the same signal back with his hands out stretched. The expression on his face read, you got yourself into this mess, it's up to you to get yourself out of it.

Alice was definitely crying real tears, I could feel the wetness soaking through my shirt, but there was something off about her blubbering, something that gnawed at my psyche. Then I just decided I was being paranoid, this girl was scared half to death. She needed our help. Alice was another victim of the Creatures of Chaos's brutality.

"We want to help you get out from under their influence. We need evidence and an eye witness to testify against them," I said. I let that seep in before I asked, "Is there anything you are willing to do to help us help you?" Alice's head shot up, nearly collecting my chin.

"I won't testify, but I do have evidence that will tie them to a murder, and I can tell you everything I know about their drug operation."

Better than nothing I thought, at least this wasn't going to be a total waste of our time. Besides we couldn't force her to testify. I wouldn't stoop to their level.

"I just have one condition," Alice announced.

'What now?' swam through my mind, but I swallowed my tongue and just replied, "What's the condition?"

"Leave my name out of it, and don't tell anyone you got it from me. I have a career I want to keep intact, and a life I want to keep living," she pleaded.

"If that is what you want, then we won't include you any further, but we will need to take that evidence and any information you can give us," I said.

"What and where is this evidence?" David asked, with a little too much of a non-believing tone.

Alice turned to David, makeup smeared all over her face, making the attractive girl look more like a clown.

"I have it at my house. I'll have to take you there, if you want it now."

"And what is it?" I quizzed. Pointing out that she didn't answer the whole question.

"I have the gun they used to murder my ex-boyfriend," she replied, sounding sombre.

"Alright then, I will go with you to pick it up," David pledged. "I'll drive your car. In your upset state, I think it would be wise if I drove." Alice just nodded.

I knew why David wanted to drive. Kudos on the wise move, I thought. Alice got in her car, still sniffling and wiping her eyes.

David gently grabbed my arm, "I don't trust her, but I'll interrogate her more in the car and get whatever info she knows about the Creatures of Chaos out of her, and if she really does have something incriminating against them we have to check it out."

"Yer, I thought the same," I agreed. "Didn't you do that Jedi, lie detector thing on her, like you did with me?"

David did a half nod and peered over at Alice then back to me before whispering, "I couldn't tell if she was acting or telling the truth. Maybe she was doing a bit of both, I can't be sure. She had her back to me for half of what she said. I can say this about her though, if she was acting then she's a lot better than what her critics say about her."

Now I had to peer over at the actress cleaning up her ruined makeup, thinking I had made the same assumption, but I chose to believe she was telling us the truth. David spun me towards him.

"I still don't trust her, so I want you to follow behind us; park on the street in front of the house. Keep the engine running, and if there is any sign of danger I want you to drive away, leave me if you have to," David ordered.

"No, I'm not leaving without you," I said unyieldingly.

"I'll be okay, do you see that café across the road," David pointed out, ignoring what I had said.

"Yes, but I'm still not leaving without you," I reminded him, trying to drum it into his head.

"I'll meet you there if we get separated," his eyes willing me to obey. "It won't take me long to get here if I run, even if I have to scale some fences along the way."

"I don't know if I can just leave you if I know you're in trouble," I said speaking the truth. I really didn't know if I could, my first instinct would be to run to his aid.

Oh, how I had changed, I thought. It wasn't too long ago I would have turned and fled never looking back. But now my love for him would outweigh my sanity and David knew it.

"I need you to do this for me," he pleaded, knowing me all too well.

248 | B. C. Goodwin

I knew David was just looking out for me, but we were supposed to be a team. We were supposed to look out for each other. David did know what he was doing. Even if I didn't like it I had to trust his judgment. If there was trouble I might only get in the way; so I would follow this command like a good soldier, but not before I made a promise.

"If we do get separated, and you don't show up at that café, then you know I will scour this earth to find you."

David just pulled me in close. Close enough for me to feel his heart beating through his muscular chest. He kissed me gently, making my head spin for an instant, then he whispered, "I'll always come back to you Sarah."

$\mathcal{J}$ sat out the front of Alice's suburban home with the car idling as instructed. Just like any good getaway driver would do. I was feeling a bit left out; being I was the one that convinced Alice to turn on the bikies, and give us what evidence she had. I didn't like being parted from David, but what could happen? Alice was a tiny girl and David was this war machine. He would be fine.

I was just being silly worrying like this, but nothing I told myself would settle my nerves. I felt I needed to be by his side, watching his back. He would be alright, I was just being paranoid I told myself once more. There was no way the Creatures of Chaos could know we sought out Alice. I was pretty confident that nothing was going to go wrong, but better to be safe than sorry I suppose. Hope for the best, plan for the worst, my father always said.

I watched as David drove Alice's car through her remote controlled automatic garage door, and kept watching as it closed behind them. As the door closed, the sight made me a bit edgy. David was fully out of eyeshot now. I knew David could handle his business but a girl could still worry, and I would continue to worry until his hands were holding mine again. The time seemed to drag on; every second feeling like a minute, every minute feeling like an hour.

The only thing I had to distract me was the blasted radio. Now after David shone a light on the stations' broadcast choices, I found myself trying to interpret every song to see if it was boy girl relationship stuff, and you know what? Every song was about boy girl stuff. Damn him.

Every song was about a boy loves a girl, or girl loves a boy, or boy leaves girl, girl leaves boy etcetera, etcetera. I think David just ruined every pop song I had ever listened to. Damn him and his insight into noticing the unseen obvious of the world. A song came on about a girl with a broken heart, when I noticed a black tyre poking out from along the side the house.

My eyes bulged, and my heart nearly leaped up out of my mouth. I tried to calm myself. It was nothing, just an old car tyre. To make sure it was just an old car tyre I stuck the car in drive and nudged it forward.

My stomach dropped, and my hands tightened on the steering wheel. What were the chances that Alice rode a Harley Davidson? The stats weren't very high on my logical scale. The bike must have been there the whole time too, because I would have heard and seen the thing roll up. Harley's are not the most subtle of beasts. That meant there was a high probability that there was a man in the house.

Our research concluded Alice only had a driver's licence. She didn't have a motorbike licence that was on the VIC roads database. There was a chance that she was minding the bike for someone that was not connected to the Chaos brotherhood, but if it smelled like smoke, then there must be a fire.

I played the confrontation with Alice through my mind again. Then like a hammer coming down, I felt like a fool. I couldn't believe I fell for it. Alice was a much better actress then I gave her credit for, David was right not to trust her. All those tears that were still, to this second, gathered on my shirt. All that time looking for a pen at the bottom of that overpriced bag. I would put money on that she was texting on her phone, warning whoever was in that house right now.

It was all too late to bother thinking about where we went wrong. I had to warn David. I knew I shouldn't go running into the house because I would most likely just get in the way, or slow David down at the least. I needed to get a message to him without leaving my post.

How could I warn him?

I brought my hands down on the steering wheel in frustration. My hand throbbed with pain, and then I focused on the little symbol of a horn on the steering wheel; how self-evident. The car horn.

It would alert the entire street, but if it did the job then I didn't care, and alerting the neighbourhood might not be a bad idea. Witnesses would be a deterrent, not that they would rat out the Creatures of Chaos, but it might make them think twice about killing two people in the middle of the day, in the middle of the street.

I held my hand on the horn. The car screamed and I waited in anticipation for that front door to open. I hoped with everything that the sound would reach his ears. I prayed that the bike belonged to a friend of Alice and I was just overreacting. With the car howling its tune, I saw the front door open. I saw David exit in a rush. Then all my concerns were brought to life as I saw David's face twisted with pain. He collapsed just outside the front door, shaking violently. Two wires snaking out of his back. A Taser was shooting an electric current through his body over and over again; every thrashing cramped movement evidence of the onslaught.

Alice's betraying evil face peered at me from behind David's raging body, a black gun-like thing in her hand. She waved it at me like she was saying hello, like I was meeting her for the first time, seeing the person behind the performance. My blood boiled at the sight. I had chosen to trust that woman. I wanted there to be more good in the world than evil; how stupid I was. I should have listened to that nagging voice inside my head. I should have smashed her pretty little face in, after the way I saw her look at David.

The demon inside me stirred at the thought; I was going to skin that woman alive for doing that to David. It was then I knew I couldn't leave David there to a fate of imminent death. I knew in that moment I would rather die alongside him than live in this world without him. Then I was back in that doorway with that Mr Jester rushing towards me with that knife; slow motion taking hold of reality once more.

My driver's side window shattered. Glass rained down on me, coating me in sharp square shards of safety glass. I had been so transfixed on the events unfolding at the front door I had totally missed the big bulky man in leather smashing in my window. A hand reached for me through the now windowless door, and then some primal instinct took over, some deep and buried survival aptitude took hold and without even realising it I moved my foot off the brake and stomped down on the gas. The car lurched forward. The man's palm missed grabbing my arm by millimetres; I felt the displaced air as it missed me. The arm that missed wrenching me out the car window slammed into the doorframe as I took off. I hoped it hurt. If the loud crack as his arm hit, and the foul language that came from the guy's mouth was any indicator, then it hurt like a mother.

I left the bikie behind in my rear view mirror. I couldn't remember if I left the car in drive after creeping forward to see the bike or if I threw it down from park, but before I knew it I was flying around the corner. In that moment of time alteration, David's voice flashed to me in the form of a memory, "I want you to drive away, leave me if you have to." I didn't see the wisdom when he said it, but I saw it in that moment. I knew now why he wanted me to get away, the whole reason why he wanted me to escape and it wasn't just for me to survive.

I remembered watching a documentary about Genghis Khan the greatest warlord that had ever lived. In his earlier years before he took on the name Genghis Khan, before he ruled over all the Mongols, his wife was stolen in a raid. He failed to defend his wife and prevent her capture. He was faced with accepting defeat and escaping or staying to fight and dying. Genghis Khan fled saying this, "They had taken my wife. I knew what I had to do. Only a fool fights a battle he knows he cannot win."

And you know what happened after that? Genghis Khan went back in force, rescued his wife and got his revenge.

I was not about to abandon David; I was going to come back for him. Living in a world without him was unthinkable to me, but I had to give us a fighting chance. If that bikie had indeed grabbed me, it would have been over – checkmate. I would be no use to him if I got caught alongside him.

I would get him back. I made a promise I would scour this earth to find him if he didn't come back to me, and I wouldn't break my promise. I thought I would be bursting out with tears, but I wasn't. There was a strange eerie calm that I was now experiencing. It must be something similar to what a soldier went through in the heat of battle.

There was no point feeling sorry for the captured soldier or weighing yourself down with grief and self-doubt, there was only the striving to resolve the problem at hand. If I was now that soldier heading back into battle, my mission was to get David back by any means necessary; *any* means.

I only drove for ten minutes before I found a good spot to hide Frank's car. I didn't want to go too far away. I needed to be able to make my way back on foot to Alice's house. I was going back. I wasn't stupid in thinking David would still be there, but I was thinking Alice would be, and I was going to split her head in two getting the answers I needed from her.

CHAPTER 38

*B*y the time I got back to Alice's house the sun had gone down and the stars lit up the sky; it was perfect. I preferred the dark for what I had to do. The last time I was alone on the streets at night with bikies nearby I was bashed and almost raped. Let's hope this time the outcome favours the righteous. Then again, I didn't think what I was about to do could be classed as righteous, maybe more psychotic or unethical.

This time would be different however. This time there was no running away. This time I would be the one saving David. I took my time making my way back to Alice's residence. I made sure I wasn't seen by anyone. I wasn't going to risk running into one of the Creatures of Chaos party. If I wasn't hiding behind a tree, I was diving in someone's front yard behind a fence or a bush. I may have been a bit overly cautious but I couldn't take the chance. I could not fail at this; David's life depended on it. I needed to get answers, I need David back, and I need him to still be breathing when I did get him back. I had an outline of a plan. It wasn't that great, but it was the best I could do for on-the-spot planning.

I found an awesome hidey-hole opposite Alice's dwelling, behind some rather thick bushes. I could see out, but no one could see in, either from beyond the front garden on the footpath or from behind so the owner of the property wouldn't spot me.

The one thing I made sure I checked before dashing down my burrow was to see if that motorbike was still down the side of the house.

It was, as I expected. Now curled up in someone's front overgrown garden, with two quite large rocks in my possession, I waited until the time was right. The first person that walked by Alice's house was an older Indian man, hands clasped behind his back looking like this walk was his meditation, like this walk was how he relaxed. I couldn't involve him. The next person to walk by was a middle-aged woman looking like she was on her way home after a long day's work. I didn't want to embroil a woman. Who knows what would happen if things went south.

The next lot people who walked by were perfect. Three young men aged between eighteen and twenty-two walked straight past Alice's front door. They all looked fit, healthy, agile and quick. God, I prayed they were fast on their feet.

I waited until they were just past Alice's driveway, and their backs were towards me. Then, with butterflies fluttering around in my stomach and my heart pounding, it was that moment I knew there was no going back if I cast the first stone, figuratively and quite literally.

I bit down on my tongue then jumped out from my secret location and with all my might I flung the first rock towards Alice's house and then the second. I was back in my burrow before the first rock landed on the middle of the charcoal Color-Bond tin roof. Hopefully, it sounded like an asteroid landed on the roof. The second went straight through the front window, glass splintering everywhere. That was for showering me in glass you bastards, I thought in a cheer.

The three pedestrians stopped to suss out the noise. Then what happened next was what I hoped would happen. That same guy that turned my driver's side window back into the sand from whence it came, came out shirtless and holding a cricket bat. Oh, I hoped those kids could run. The bikie spotted the kids. Run I wanted to scream, but I couldn't. The bikie pointed the bat at the kids.

"Was that you?" he demanded, sounding very pissed off. A man that angers easily, good find Alice. They all put up their hands in a gesture of 'it wasn't us' back-pedalling as they did. Run you stupid kids, I pleaded to the gods.

"Come here," the bikie yelled while walking towards them

swinging the bat so it rested on his bare muscular shoulder. It was then the boys ran; thank the gods for listening.

I planned that the bikie bastard would head off in pursuit, I just hoped those kids could run like the wind. I felt bad for implicating them, and for the quite real possibility of them getting beaten up with a cricket bat. I just had to have faith that they would get away safely. There were three of them; it was better than I had hoped. It would at least give them a fighting chance if they were to get caught. They would survive this I knew, but David wouldn't if I failed here and now. I wished the three of them luck, if only for my own selfish conscience.

Alice poked her head out the door, watching what I suspected was her boyfriend running after the innocent third party. Alice shut the door thinking her man would take care of it. Things were going perfectly so far, but it was now time for the exciting bit, or the terrifying bit, whichever your opinion falls on.

I ran for Alice's front door hoping she left it unlocked for her boyfriend to get back in. I paused with my hand on the handle; then I tested it, seeing if it would turn. It turned. It was unlocked. Before I opened it though, I peered over at the broken window. Better than nothing I thought.

I peeled off my shirt exposing my black bra. I picked up the pointiest shard I could find, wrapped my shirt around it so I wouldn't cut my own hand. Now I was as ready as I would ever be. I burst through the door. I locked the door behind me; I wanted to slow down the return of the boyfriend. Alice called out as I closed the door.

"Did you get those little turds?"

I didn't respond for obvious reasons. I followed the trail of Alice's voice to find her in nothing but her undies, sprawled on the coach ready for something naughty I bet. After I turned the corner and her eyes landed on me and flickered to the blade of glass in my palm. The surprise and shock on her face was unmistakable. I could have sworn I saw her face draining entirely of colour, turning bone white.

Alice didn't move as I waved the makeshift weapon at her, exactly like she had waved the Taser at me. There was nothing but malice in her eyes then, and now those eyes belonged to me. Time was short; I needed to be quick while I had the element of surprise. I couldn't mess around, and I needed to act before she could think of anything besides, oh fuck there is a crazy bitch out for revenge that is going to cut me up with a piece of my own house.

What I had to do next was something I had hidden away, something David helped me put behind bars. I promised him I would never hurt anyone unless my life depended on it; well my life didn't depend on it but his did. I was making that a loophole for what I was about to do.

What I had to do now was to unleash the monster inside. That same monster that rose to the surface when I kicked the shit out of Sam; that same beast inside me that enjoyed inflicting pain. I had pushed it back when I put that gun down right before I would of blown my mother's killer's head off. I had locked that monster away with David's meditation, silencing its cravings.

But I needed that monster now. I needed that untamed flame that burned inside me. I just hoped I could put the monster back behind the bars from where I released it, once all was said and done.

"Where is David?" I questioned.

"I don't know," she answered shakily – lying. Without thought or contemplation I swung the glass, slicing her thigh open.

"You fucking bitch," she hollered out after clutching her leg. I think she said it more out of the shock of seeing her thigh slice apart, more than the actual pain.

"I would put firm pressure on that if I was you," I retorted calmly and a little creepily. "I'll ask again, where did you take him?" I said in the same fashion.

"Fuck you," she spat clinging to her leg, trying to force the tissue back together.

"Wrong answer," I said, before punching her with my free hand, exactly as David taught me. My fist landed with a bone-crunching crack squarely on her eye socket. Alice's head snapped back, her hands lifted off her leg going straight to protect her face from another impact. But, in removing her hand from her leg, she freed the blood flow from her thigh. Blood started to pour out everywhere.

"I am not fucking around, Alice," I said with such hatred, it would have made Satan's knees wobble. "Tell me now or you will no longer be useful to me, and I will end you right here, right now. And I will make sure your funeral will be a closed casket because there won't be any skin left on your face." I lifted the shard, making it look like I was readying for the kill strike.

"One last chance," I offered, because in that moment I was not sure I would be able to hold back. The dark side of me wanted to jam that piece of glass up through her nose and into her brain. Alice was crying for real now, out of one eye only because the other had a hand upon it. Her other hand was now back on her thigh stemming the river of blood down her leg.

"I'll tell you, just don't kill me," she cried, seeing my not so certain bluff.

"I'm waiting," I said sounding annoyed. Sounding like I was robbed of my intake of mayhem.

"A couple of the Chaos members came and picked him up. They would have taken him to their brothel," Alice said between sobs.

"What's the name of the brothel?"

"It's called, Paradise of Eden." I lowered my hand.

"Thank you," I responded like she had just given me a present. "I won't kill you just yet," I said, wanting to keep her level of anxiety at maximum.

Then I stomped down hard on her foot, feeling the bones crack under the sole of my shoe. Alice screamed out in pain, it was like music to my ears. That was for David, I thought, not giving her the satisfaction of knowing what the broken foot was for.

"Oh yer," I turned like I had forgotten something. "You know you just signed your death warrant by telling me where to find David, don't you?" Alice looked at me like I didn't know what I was talking about, so I went on, "If they find out somehow that you blabbed to me about their affairs. You know, somehow like if you were to warn them that I am coming to rescue David." Alice huffed at the suggestion, like you better do better than that to frighten me, so I did.

"See, if you do that then they will know you betrayed them to me and you don't know what I am capable of. I could have possibly teamed up with anyone from the police, to the Insurgent gang. And now I'm about to bring down a world of hurt on the club. Do you really think they will leave you alive after something like that?"

That made Alice pay more attention to what I was saying, after she realised she could have done a lot more damage than just telling a lonely girl where to find her boyfriend.

"You could say you had to tell me or else I was going to kill you, but they won't care about that. All they will care about is that you betrayed them. All they will know is that you can't be trusted anymore and that is a death sentence in their line of work," I hissed out, my feral beast coating the tone with its own intimidating flavour.

Alice seemed to be really weighing up my words now. I could see that the thought of telling them I was coming had already passed through her mind, but now, doubt clouded over the idea. I grinned at her, taking a moment to breath in the blood and fear, loving, no, thriving on the taste of it.

"On the off chance that they don't kill you for telling me where to find David, or if I find out that you have lied to me and David dies as a result of that lie, then I will personally track you down and gut you in your sleep," I said pointedly, so she knew I would stick true to my word. "So it is in your best interests to just shut the fuck up and let me get on with my business. Comprendez." Alice nodded her understanding, too afraid to use words.

"One thing I want to know before I leave; the pictures we have of you with blood staining your clothes, who was it? And did you kill them?" I questioned. Alice fell extra silent, her cries slowing to heavy breathing.

"Don't make me cut it out of you. You only have two hands and I don't think you can hold closed another couple of wounds," I urged.

No reply.

"I warned you." I said, sounding like a mother telling her kid not to pick up a bull-ant before he does it anyway and gets bitten.

No reply, so this time without warning I went to slice open her arm when Alice spat out in the nick of time.

"I did it. Okay? I took a gun and blew my boyfriend's brains out, and the Creatures of Chaos helped me cover it up." She looked up at me through her one uncovered eye, "Is that what you wanted to hear?"

Alice looked venomous. That scared innocent act she pulled off in the car park was gone. This woman was a killer. She had no remorse for what she did. I could see it in her demeanour, that hatred, that blood lust in her eyes. The way she leered at me was like she was wanted to eat out my heart with her bare teeth. I bet she confessed that to me because she saw that same lack of empathy towards violence, that same killer drive in me.

"I don't care either way, I just wanted to know," I told her, then added, "but it does make what I just did to you that much easier."

I turned on my heels, and went to leave out the back door when I noticed stacks of hundred dollar bills on the kitchen table. It must have been at least two hundred grand.

"They put a bounty on our heads, that's how you knew who we were?" I questioned, merely thinking out loud putting the puzzle together. I looked back at Alice and she nodded. They must have spread the word to all their associates connected with the information we stole. My rage flared, my beast roared. I wanted to slap her across the face, raking my nails though her flesh. I wanted to feel her pain through my fingertips. She sold us out for money. It made sense though. People will do just about anything if the price was right and now, seeing the real Alice, I reckoned she would have sold us out just to see us bleed. I just hoped Dad and Joe didn't get caught in the same web. Then I heard the pounding on the front door, and that same deep voice that yelled at those kids.

"Alice let me in."

The back door was in my sights, all I had to do was go through it and I would be home free, but the allure of violence was drumming through my veins. That man behind the front door was halfway responsible for taking David away from me. I peered down at the glass in my hand; it wouldn't help me much in a fight against a man with a cricket bat. Then I noticed that Taser next to the pile of cash. Then that monster's voice rose up inside me and I had to listen, I had to obey. It had taken me this far, so I had to feed it dessert.

I picked up the gun, swapping the shard of glass to my non-preferred hand then walked back to the living area where Alice was crying and clutching her wounds. I turned the volume up on the TV, and made my way over to Alice.

"Keep your mouth shut, or I will stick this piece of glass in your neck," I said holding the shard close to her face. "And remember with that leg and foot of yours it won't be hard for me to chase you down."

Alice whimpered something that I took for an understanding to keep her mouth closed. I saw her eyes flick to the Taser though. Alice knew what I was about to do and I revelled in it. The fact that she was about to know what it feels like when your loved one was getting hurt right in front of you, that same feeling I felt when I saw David spasming on the ground. Then again, I would be surprised to find out that Alice cared about anything besides herself. That was why I knew she wouldn't shout out a warning to her man.

The man was now howling Alice's name, slamming his fist upon the door. If he wanted to come in, then I would let him in. I unlocked the door, took three paces back, and then raised the Taser. The door flung open.

"What the bloody hell, Alice?" The angry bulky man announced before he saw me pointing the Taser at him.

"Hello," I said cheerfully, just as someone might say in greeting an old buddy.

"You," was all the guy got out before the two prongs lodged themselves into his bare chest. His face went from surprise, to understanding, and then stunned pain. It was great.

I took out my hair tie wrapped it around the trigger then just left the twitching man lying at the front door before thinking, now I can leave.

I did take note that the wooden bat, which now lay on the ground next to the bikie, didn't have any blood on it. That was a good sign that those guys got away. I didn't bother saying goodbye to Alice. A bit rude I know, but I think she had more concerning matters to address at the moment.

Before I left I thought I might take a few things with me. The money that was gathered on the table was for David and me, so I figured it belonged to us. I found a gym bag, emptied it, and then packed as much money as I could in it. Then I went for the back door again, but yet again something changed my mind before leaving, I spotted her car keys. Why walk when there was a perfectly good car metres away. I took the bag of money. I took the car and rolled out the driveway saying goodbye to Alice and her man through the rear vision mirror. I was about five streets away when I beheld those three young men walking hard down a side street. I turned to follow.

I pulled up next to them and yelled, "Oy."

All three jumped, they were about to start running when they realised that I was a woman, and not some mad man with a cricket bat chasing them.

"I'm sorry for that, guys," I said. The three of them looked at each other, confusion bouncing from one to another.

"I am glad you fellas got away alright, I hope you can forgive me," I expressed with sincerity, and then I chucked what I thought looked like about twenty grand at their feet. All six of their eyeballs followed the green dollar notes as they hit the sidewalk.

"Have a nice day, guys," I said before putting my foot on the gas and driving away with the beast inside me purring with delight.

CHAPTER 39

*A*iden's plan had worked; offering up $250,000 per head for the capture of David and his friends was money well spent. Well, to be clear, the bounty only half worked. Louis really wanted the matching pair, but he would get his hands on that Sarah Smith eventually. Perhaps this time one of his club brothers would catch Sarah, saving him 250 big ones. Louis almost felt bad for having Aiden killed – almost. But Aiden had served his purpose, and Louis didn't tolerate failure on that grand scale.

Louis now stared down at the man that killed his brother, vengeance in the palm of his hand. Louis didn't love his brother. Louis didn't love anyone, but his brother was his brother, and Louis didn't like when someone took something that belonged to him. Louis was surprised that there was no fear in the man's eyes; nearly everyone was afraid of him. But this man wasn't, even though he was at his mercy; Louis found that very odd.

The man looked like he had accepted his fate, or maybe he even wished for it. He just sat there with a bored expression, like he just wanted to get on with it, but a quick death wouldn't come for this man. No, Louis planned to drag his death out for as long as possible, and with as much pain as possible. Maybe the man thought he warranted this sort of outcome for what he had done in his past; some people were delusional like that. Or maybe he wanted to be reunited with his dead family.

Louis didn't know what his deal was and didn't care; he wouldn't let it interrupt his playtime. Louis just wished David's family was still alive only so he could kill them all over again. Seeing that John Black had already had that pleasure, Sarah Smith would have to do. Louis didn't know how much David cared for that slut, but he would find out. Louis knew everything about David, he especially liked that he had killed John for murdering his family. He gave him kudos for that one, but, in his book, taking his brother away from him was punishable by death.

"Louis Cole," David stated, with the audacity of a man in an opposing positions "Jordan Cole's big bad ugly brother has come here to teach me a lesson I suppose." Then David cocked his head to the side, "I should have just said, uglier brother because I think your brother was a bit bigger than you. I can tell, you see, from the way I had to pull him down to stick his own knife in his throat."

Louis just smiled. David liked to play games. Louis liked to play games too. David was trying very hard to piss him off, but trying to piss off a person that had no loving emotional ties to anyone was pretty hard. David really did want to die, Louis knew. Fast, if possible, Louis assumed, hence the trying to enrage him. But Louis wouldn't kill him fast, on the contrary he was planning for David to meet his maker very, very slowly and no amount of banter would change that.

Louis pulled up a chair within arm's reach of David. David was zip tied to a chair with one arm zip tied to a table with his palm facing up. Louis ran a finger down David's exposed arm until he hit David's clenched fist. David tensed up from the contact, testing the strength of the restraints.

"Don't touch me," David shouted, but Louis ignored him. There was nothing David could do about it, the zip ties held him down too well. Louis admired the holes that had been drilled into the table so the zip ties could wrap around and hold David's arm in place. His minions had done well. Louis would have to thank them later. There was no better way to make a man more productive than to praise him for his creative good work.

Louis stared at David, and David stared right back, never breaking eye contact for even a second. Bold, very bold, Louis thought. Louis liked this guy more and more. He had guts or just a death-wish, Louis would go out on a limb and say it was the latter.

"Do you like your accommodations?" Louis asked like a receptionist would ask a guest at an inn. David surveyed the room, a concrete walled prison. He speculated that it had to be a basement of some kind. Underground, sound-proofed and hard to stumble across. He could see piles of junk on free-standing shelves. He could make out rusty tools, boxes of discarded stuff that had been long forgotten. Everything was coated in at least a centimetre of dust. It looked like this space didn't get used for much else than storage and the occasional murder.

"It's a dusty rat infested shit hole," David said, then added, "No offence to the rats."

"I'm glad you like it," Louis smirked, "It's much nicer upstairs." Then, with a grin, he went on to say, "Not that you will ever get to see it."

"That's alright, I'm guessing the whole place stinks of you anyway," David jabbed, "But I'm interested to know why you don't have an audience? I thought you would need some bodyguards to watch your back." David lowered his head along with his voice and said, "I'm pretty dangerous you know."

Louis crossed his arms, flexing his toned weight lifting muscles and said, "Do I look like a defenceless little schoolgirl?" David didn't answer; the answer was being flexed right in front of him. "Besides, what we are about to share is too intimate for an audience. Killing someone is just like having sex, best done behind closed doors," Louis claimed.

"Can you just get on with whatever you are planning to do because I am starting to get hungry, and I would rather get this over and done with before I die of starvation," David sneered, looking tired.

"I can read people pretty well," Louis said, "so I can tell you're really not afraid of me."

David just shrugged, "What's there to be afraid of?" He let the question sit in the air for a moment before staring at Louis once more with those penetrating eyes. "You?" David murmured, before letting out an exaggerated laugh. "What a joke." Louis leaned back in his chair.

"You really are quite fascinating. I am going to have a lot of fun with you I think," Louis looked amused. He tapped his fingers together, much like Mr Burns from *The Simpsons*. "You are not scared of death, that is plain to see, but how will you go with large quantities of pain," Louis snickered, leaning back in his chair. His excitement was growing knowing the games he had in store for David. Just the thought of them was making him giddy.

"Wait here," Louis said, chuckling with glee. Getting up from the table Louis went over to the dusty shelves. "Did you know, David," Louis began, just as a professor might start if he was about to begin a lecture to his students, "that the hands and feet are some of the densest areas in the body for nerve endings. They literally have millions of them?" Louis turned back to David to see if he was paying attention. It didn't look like he was, but Louis knew that he had his undivided attention, so Louis continued, "Those nerve endings are designed to keep you out of danger, so if you touch something that could damage your body, like something too hot or something sharp or in your case rough, you can recognise it and pull away."

"Sounds about right," David replied with no smartass retort. Louis knew David was wondering about the rough comment, just as he wanted him to. David stared down at his bound arm and up facing hand. Louis could see David wiggle in his seat as a shiver ran down his spine. David took a deep breath, released it and then turned his focus back to Louis. Louis walked back over holding a hammer and five nails.

"I have always wanted to try this," Louis said.

David stared at the hammer and nails in Louis's hands. Louis put four of the nails in his mouth leaving one in his hand.

"You are going to have to do better than a hammer and a couple nails to turn me on," David said.

"Oh no, don't get too excited," Louis said, looking as gleeful as a kid in a candy store. He peered down at the hammer and the single nail left in his hand and said, with the other four nails bobbing up and down in his mouth, "This is just to hold your hand out flat. I hope you don't mind?"

"Do I actually have a choice?" David asked, already knowing the answer.

"No," Louis said quickly. It would have almost been funny if it wasn't so terrifyingly serious and just nodded his understanding. All David's smart-arsary disappeared for what was to come, for what he had to prepare himself for.

"Just get on with it," David said impatiently. Louis placed a nail on David's thumb.

"Okay, are you ready?" Louis asked, wanting David to wait, wanting to build the anticipation of the torture. The expectation of pain was a torture in itself. Louis's hobby was to watch people squirm in their own piss and shit; to make them pray to a god that would never come. However, David just lowered his head and looked away. Not showing any signs that he was about to start begging or pleading for him not to do what he was about to do.

So Louis just said cheerfully, "I'll take your nonresponse as a yes."

The hammer hit squarely on the head of the nail, driving the nail straight through David's thumb and into the table, pinning his thumb to the table. David didn't scream, didn't even move an inch. In fact David didn't react at all; not even a flicker of pain showed up on his face.

"Well, that was disappointing," Louis said. He thrived off the fear and horror he inflicted upon others. Louis wanted the screams of agony. He needed the crying pleas for him to stop the suffering. It made him feel like a god. The power to hold someone's life in your hands is as god-like as you can get. To be the one to determine whether or not to give the thumbs up or thumbs down turned him on more than any hooker with her legs spread ever could. The thrill of that god-like power was intoxicating. He could never get enough. He was addicted to it, like a moth to a flame, or like a sex addict to pussy.

Although it seemed that David was going to be a tough one to crack, everyone cracked in the end, everyone. Very well, Louis thought. He was up to the task. There had never been anyone he couldn't break.

Louis quickly drove the second nail through David's little pinkie finger and another through each of other fingertips, splaying his hand out flat. David didn't even flinch as the nails drove home.

"Well, that was just the entrée," Louis said while getting up from the table. "Are you ready for the main course? You did say you were getting hungry."

David didn't say a word. He just raised his head with a blank expression, almost looking like he didn't even know where he was anymore. He shook his head from side to side. Louis focused on him intently noticing when the lights in his eyes came back on.

"I'll be right back," Louis announced.

He returned with a black power-cord that had a little orange LED light shining at the end of it indicating that the power was flowing through it. In his other hand he held a belt sander that he dropped onto the table.

"This is what I have always wanted to try," Louis said, as he plugged the belt sander's lead into the power-cord. "I have always wondered how long it would take before the sandpaper ripped through all the layers of skin and started polishing the bones underneath."

Louis went to lower the sander to David's palm then paused, "Oh yes, I forgot to tell you that I have been told that there are twenty seven bones in the human hand. I was hoping to count them all for myself, just to make sure I got my facts straight."

"Aren't you full of fun-filled trivia? Wouldn't want to get your answers wrong on the big stage now would we?" David replied, trying to dull the situation down to a TV game show.

The sander roared to life in Louis's hands. "It still works," he said happily, "That could have been tragic." He went on to say, "This was my father's you see." Lifting the sander in front of David's face, "She is fairly old, but she still has some balls for an old girl. My father was a builder. Good with his hands, taught me a few things like how to use a belt sander. I have only ever used it on wood, but I have always wanted to try it on human flesh. So you should be grateful that you're the one I get to experiment on."

"Lucky me," David said, before sighing and then looking away again.

The machine burst out with the noise and energy it took to spin the rough sandpaper around on a continuous loop. Louis lowered the roaring sander onto David's open, nailed-to-the-table hand, and started sanding his skin away one layer at time. It didn't take long before there was blood and shredded skin everywhere, all flung back by the sander.

Louis shifted his blood encrusted gaze from the spinning sander spraying blood to peer at David. David didn't move. He still didn't react even now with only half a hand left. David's absence of anything remotely humanly dramatic was starting to piss him off. David was ruining his fun with his silence. He needed him to be screaming, crying out in torment.

"What is wrong with you?" Louis yelled.

David didn't answer. He was in some sort of meditational state, Louis guessed. He was able to block out the pain somehow. His body was here but his mind wasn't. Louis raged in the knowing that there was no amount of physical agony he could inflict upon this man that would get his desired outcome. That feeling of being a god was elusive and the frustration was overwhelming him to his core. This had never happen before. There had never been anyone he couldn't break down, anyone he couldn't bend to his will.

Louis put down the now red stained sander, and walked around to stand in front of David.

"Look at me," he shouted. David didn't look up, keeping his head lowered to the floor.

"Look at me," Louis repeated throwing a slamming back-hand to the side of David's face. David's head rocked to the side then ricocheted back into place like that back-hand blow never happened.

Louis thought for a moment that David had passed out; that that was the reason for his lack of reaction, but Louis could see David's eyes were still open and concentration spread on his face.

Louis screamed in frustration, "I bet that bitch of yours, Sarah will scream when I do the same thing to her."

David's head snapped up as soon as Louis mentioned Sarah's name. His eyes then went wide with terror from the regretful reaction to Sarah's name.

Louis just smiled, "Now I know how to hurt you."

CHAPTER 40

I drove straight to Frank's apartment; parking around the corner, of course. I didn't want to explode his head with over-paranoia. Banging on the door with a woman's overwhelming haste, not even bothering with the intercom knowing he most likely saw me walk up the footpath with his little spycam.

I was still trying to lock that monster back up in its cage, working on getting a level bearing on the reality once more. But what I was about to do, or planning to do, meant I would still need that monster inside. I had to lock it away but keep hold of the key, ready to twist the lock and let it back out.

Our original plan to bring down the Chaos brothers can still be accomplished with a few tweaks to positioning and a move forward of our timetable, and I was confident it could still be done. If I was alive to see it was another story altogether, though.

I only ran away when David got captured in the hopes of getting him back, if I was too late in my endeavours, then life would have no more meaning for me. I would be with him in this life or the next. If it so happened it was the latter then I would meet him and my mother at the gates of the afterlife. However, I would not go down in the dirt without taking them down with me. That was why I was at Frank's home now.

I needed to get our plan back on track. I needed to know where this brothel was, and to learn as much as I could about it. I needed to know the layout so I could make an educated guess as to where they would be holding David. I needed to know what security they had in place, and anything else I couldn't think of yet.

I only banged on the steel security door once before the door buzzed open. Inside the apartment Frank was as awkward as ever. Even more so than last time; it must have been because we were alone. I didn't have time for this. I needed to get in and out of here as quick as possible. Every second I wasted trying to talk to Frank could be David's last heartbeat. I wished I knew why he was the way he was around girls, or if he was just weird around me.

I had to try and calm down; getting all worked up wouldn't help matters. This was going to take a lot longer to get everything ready if I was unable to communicate with him, so I had to ask, "Is there a way to make you feel more relaxed around me, so we can talk?" Frank eye's opened just a little wider and he started fidgeting with something in his hands.

"Do you need a beer or something like that guy from *Big Bang Theory*?" I suggested. Frank's only response was a poor attempt at a smile.

Well that's great, I thought. David could be dead or dying and I was getting slowed down by a man who couldn't talk to girls.

Frank walked off to his computer room. This just kept getting better and better I thought: now he couldn't even be in the same room as me. This was going to make things go very smoothly I muttered sarcastically, trying to rein in my frustration with poor humour.

Then a computer-animated voice came from the computer room. I would have thought it a movie or video game but it said, "I apologise for my rudeness, I am not very confident talking to pretty girls. I always say the wrong thing, so I say nothing at all."

I walked in slowly. Saying something stupid was normally in my repertoire and I confirmed that by saying, "Was that you, Frank?"

"Yes, that was me, Frank" the voice said.

Well at least we can talk now.

"Frank, the confrontation with Alice didn't go as planned. She is not going to help us and now they have David," I said, my voice cracking as I pronounced David's name.

"That's not good. Have you told your father?" the voice asked.

"No, and I want to keep it that way until the time is right. I need him to finish what he is doing. The plan is relying on it and, besides, if he knew what I am about to do then he would try and stop me," I admitted.

"What are you about to do? And what do you need from me?" Frank asked through the computer.

"I am about to walk into the mouth of the beast, and try to pull out last night's dinner," I replied a little sourly. "You can't tell my father either until his turned his objectives to our cause," I pleaded. "You have to promise me."

"Your father will kill me if I don't tell him," Frank retorted.

"They have David, Frank," I said, up so close I could smell chicken flavoured potato chips on him. I knew I would make him feel uncomfortable being so close, but that was the point. "I love him, and I need to get him back, and I need your help to do it." Frank's gaze was locked on his computer screen too afraid to turn and see any part of me.

"Who am I to stand in the way of love? I promise I won't tell Conner until you tell me to," Frank typed out. I kissed him on the cheek making his face go bright red, and then said, "This is what I need you to do."

The first thing I got Frank to do was warn Dad and Joe about the price tag on our heads. I didn't want what happened to us to happen to them. I then ran Frank through my ideas to the changes in the plan. Frank agreed it should still work. Then I asked him to dig up everything that he could on the Paradise of Eden brothel.

"What are you planning to do?" Frank asked me.

"The less you know the better. You're a smart guy. I think you'll be able to figure it out. As to the details you will find out soon enough. Showing is more surprising then telling." Then, giving him a hint, I added, "You know my father is going to be royally pissed off when he finds out, and that's what I'm counting on."

I knew what I was about to do was just as much heroic as it was selfish and stupid. Dad was one tough man, but losing me could push him over the edge. I realised that, but I had to believe that he would get through this, and finish what we started if I didn't make it out of this alive.

David and my father were the only people left on this earth that I cared about more than life itself. I would do anything for either of them. Risking my life for them was just a part of what makes love so mysteriously, breath-takingly, and life threateningly beautiful. I had lost too much already. I wouldn't lose anyone else I love to the hand of death.

CHAPTER 41

$\mathcal{W}$hat was left of the plan was taken care of from a foreseeable standpoint. My Father and Joe had done what they set out to do without that bounty falling down on their heads. Their side of things was a box ticked off. The timing side of my plan should pan out if Frank fills them in as promised.

Now only a witness was needed. We needed somebody that had seen the Creatures of Chaos's worst atrocities. Who would be a better witness than me? Proof was what we needed, and proof was what we lacked. For my part I needed to get evidence that would tie them to something worth investigating, or at least get enough to warrant an inquiry and search warrant into their affairs from a reliable source; and if it was my death that brought them down, then I would be fine with that outcome as long as I could get David out alive. If he was even alive now.

While Frank got all the specs and info I needed, I prepared myself. A better description would be transform myself. I found a pair of scissors to hack all my gorgeous long hair off, every falling hair follicle was matched by a falling part of my former self. I cut it so short my hair looked like a guy's spiked haircut. The scissors were old and used, they pulled as much as they cut, but eventually I got through it all until I looked as much like a dude as I could get.

Then I went to Frank's wardrobe searching for an outfit. Frank was only a little taller than me. A lot rounder, but only a bit taller which suited my needs perfectly. I found a plain navy blue T-shirt and a pair of denim knee length shorts. I found a belt to hold up the shorts, then a gauze bandage in a discarded first-aid kit to flatten out my breasts.

Once I was finished dressing I stood in front of the mirror gawking at myself. I could barely comprehend that it was me that I was looking at. I figured if I couldn't recognise myself, then hopefully no one else could either. As I peered at my reflection, my first thought was that I looked like every cliché butch lesbian chick in the world. Perfect I thought.

Thank my lucky stars for lesbians in the world. My plan revolved around pretending to be one. It was Alice that gave me this idea when she flirted with me back in the car park. That was my first sexual encounter with the same sex, not much of one I know, but the closest I had come to getting hit on by a woman. It was all an act by Alice, but so will mine be. I just had to get used to the idea to sell the performance.

When I walked back into Frank's computer room, Frank did a double take to be sure it was me. After the dumbfounded look wiped off Frank's face his computer spat out, "You look different." I thought maybe Frank could talk to me now I looked like a man, but I guessed he still knew what was under the disguise. No matter.

"You like?" I said, far too girly for my appearance.

"No," Frank typed out.

"You really know how to flatter a girl, don't you Frank?" I responded with a joking grin.

"Are they my clothes?" Frank asked next.

"Indeed they are, my computer-genius friend. I hope you don't mind?" I said, and then quickly added, "Do you think they look better on me?" I finished with a twirl like a ballerina, showing him both sides of the outfit, or costume whichever you prefer.

Frank just sighed back down at his keyboard as he said, "Yes, they look better on you, but they are my favourite shorts."

I walked up to the desk so I stood right beside him, "If I get out of this alive I will buy you ten pairs of shorts in interest," I said, with a much more serious tone. Frank went to reply on the keyboard, but I cut in first, "Do you have the final touch for the outfit?"

"It's all ready for you. I hooked it up to a live feed through an app through this phone," Frank's computer said. He placed an iPhone5 in front of me, "As long as the phone is turned on and in close proximity I will see what you see." Frank then placed a pair of spectacle next to the phone.

I picked up the phone and put it in my pocket. I then lifted up the black, thick-rimmed glasses. The camera was somewhere in the frame. I studied the spectacles searching for it, and I was glad to find that I couldn't see it. I bet my father could though, Mr Ex-army man Dad.

I put the glasses on my face to find the lenses were only glass. I didn't know why I was prepared for a prescription set of glasses, but they were plain old ordinary mini glass windows to peer through.

I was set. I had the camera in place on my face for whatever proof I could find while searching for David. I looked like a girl trying to be a guy, and I had the information I needed on the brothel. I was ready to go. I took in a deep breath, preparing myself for what was to come. I turned my head to Frank.

"Thank you Frank for all your help," I had to pause for a moment before I continued, "Please tell my Dad that I love him very much, and if there was any other way." I broke off, feeling my throat choke up. I was just able to add, "Tell him to finish this for me if I can't."

I turned to leave thinking I couldn't say any more, but surprised myself when I turned back and said, "Tell him I just couldn't leave David behind knowing there was a chance I could save him."

My hand reached for the door when I heard an unfamiliar voice, one that was not computer animated that said, "Good luck, and be careful Sarah." I smiled at the sound of his light almost feminine voice. Then Frank went on to say, "I want those pairs of shorts you promised me."

I just nodded back at him with a half grin, and then I walked out the door knowing that Frank may never get those shorts.

CHAPTER 42

It wasn't until I got close to my destination on the GPS device I was following that I noticed I knew where I was. With the awareness of my whereabouts came a shivering cold chill down my spine making me squirm in my seat as that night resurfaced in my mind. I was back to where it all started, where I first laid eyes on David. It was ironic to think it could be the last time I got to see him too. Fate can play a cruel game sometimes.

I first noticed where I was when I was coming up to Sam's window factory. I had been following the GPS so closely that I didn't take in my surroundings. The brothel was in the same industrial area. At least now I knew how I ended up being in the wrong place at the wrong time. I was basically knocking on their front door. You would think I would get anxious returning to the place of my nightmares, back to where my life got a reboot. Back to where I was awakened from my naive bubble of paradise, and then shoved into a world with violence, disloyalty, cruelty and mayhem. My eyes were opened to the larger picture of the world, but all was not lost. I also found fortitude, bravery, compassion and love. Amazingly at a most unexpected time and when I needed it the most.

No. Fear and anxiety was not my reaction at all. Being back here made me even more determined. It made what could be my final act all the more meaningful. This was where I would get my justice for the crimes that were done to me and mine. This was where I would get my revenge.

As I thought the word, revenge, I got the taste of blood in my mouth. The demon rose inside me. I pushed back on the gates that housed the creature. Settle petal, your time will come, I told the dark side of myself, it was time for deception, not wrath at the moment.

I sat parked on the side of the road, one street down from the Paradise of Eden. I had to play this safe. I couldn't take the chance that someone might recognise Alice's car. I had no idea how well she was connected with the gang. I knew it was quite possible, even with all my threats, that Alice would still tell them I was coming, and now I was walking into a trap, but the risk was worth the reward. I just hoped my disguise would fool the lot of them if that was the case.

The street was still dark, the only light coming from the overhanging street lamps and the iPhone screen in my hand. Frank uploaded to the iPhone all the information he was able to dig up. He wasn't able to find much, well much for his standards, but what he did find was very helpful.

Frank had been able to find the Council's blueprints to the brothel. The blueprints showed a four-level complex with a large foyer at ground level, and fifteen bedrooms, all with their own bathroom, on the upper three levels.

The ground level was mainly taken up by the foyer with the exception of four tiny waiting rooms – or introduction to the ladies rooms – a kitchen out the back, and an office space to the rear corner of the building. The next three levels were just the bedrooms where the business goes down, or up depending on the guy. Bad time for jokes, but it kept me sane, so deal with it.

The interesting thing I noticed on the plan was that it showed an underground car park, but as I made my sweep past I couldn't find a driveway leading to anywhere but an above ground car park. So either the club amended the plan after they first got permission to build from the Council, or the Council hadn't updated their logs after the changes were made. The club could have had to scrap the underground car park due to a lack of money, but I doubted it. It was more likely they built the space and then deliberately didn't put in a noticeable drivable entrance to cover up the fact that they have a whole underground car park to hide stuff. If they had a hidden car park, there still had to be an entrance somewhere. Perhaps it was at the back of the building or somewhere inside. Whatever the case the non-existent underground car park would be my first bet to where David was being kept.

My second bet now would be the attic. Because of the massive size of the building and the interior having to be done up to look like bedrooms, the whole third level ceiling was square set. That left a space from the ceiling of the third level to the pitched steel roof of the outer building giving them a lot of space for whatever they needed to store. The building actually looked more like a factory than a house. From the view outside the appearance was not far from Sam's window factory.

If the first two bets were called off that only left the fifteen love-making rooms. All the rooms were sound-proofed, so as not to hear the moans of pleasure coming from the room next door, I suppose. With fifteen rooms to choose from it would be safe to say that taking one room out of rotation for a while wouldn't hurt their profit margins. I am hoping to God that I didn't have to go door to door walking in on people doing God knows what, in positions God only knows how.

The only other thing Frank found that was worth writing down was their security system that had been installed by an outside contractor. The Paradise of Eden building stood apart from the surrounding warehouses. The closest building was fifty metres away. The Paradise of Eden structure was encased by a wire fence and had cameras everywhere. There was no way in without being spotted. The alarm system was directly linked to the local police station. Weird, I thought at first, but then again when you thought about it a bit harder it was not so weird if the cops were on the payroll.

As far as we knew there were no security guards patrolling the grounds, but I wouldn't know that for sure until I took a look for myself. Even if there were no guards I would put money on the likelihood that there would be someone trying to chase us down as we exited, but if things went to plan, hopefully I wouldn't have to flee at all.

Frank also found out that some of the working girls service men *and* woman. So that made my walking straight through the front door all the more spectacularly, deceptively impressive. Oh yes, and thanks to my good friend Alice I had money to burn on tits and ass too.

Hypothetically walking through the front doors was a lot easier than actually walking through the front doors. I was full of confidence right up until I rang the doorbell and a voice came through the intercom, "Hello, can I help you?"

I swear you could hear my heart beat for miles, but by some miracle the sound of my nervousness didn't transmit through the intercom when I replied, "I was hoping to meet some nice lovely ladies."

The person behind the intercom sounded amused as she countered with a slight Asian accent that I only picked up on second time around, "You won't find any nice lovely ladies here, only naughty ones."

My thundering heart seemed to stop at that. It was amazing how many thoughts you could have in a split second. Among the jumble of lines of thought was: Did that mean she was telling me to piss off? Was she testing me?

I had to get inside to find David, his life depended on it. What do I say? Play it cool. I had to convince her to let me in. Damn, she knew. Quick, say something.

"The naughtier the better," I finally replied, releasing a breath.

"Then this is the place for you," the sweet voice retorted.

The door buzzed open exposing a marble palace with a crystal chandelier hanging from the ceiling that was emphasised by designer mirrors on the walls. The place was as extravagant as what I would expect a billionaire's home would be like. Even the staircase to the second level was fancy. This was not what I had been expecting at all.

I slowly walked the distance from the front door to the front desk taking in the sights when I heard a familiar voice. A voice I had heard my entire life right up until a few months ago. A tall young blonde walked past the front desk with a middle-aged man on her arm making my suspicions a reality. The tall young blonde was Tara.

CHAPTER 43

$\mathcal{L}$uckily Tara didn't turn towards me as I stopped dead in my tracks staring straight at my former friend. If she would have turned and seen through my mask this whole charade would have been over. Instead, Tara walked right past me with the man in tow, leading him up the elegant staircase and not bothering to turn around to see a wide-eyed ex-best friend.

I was left mute and stunned in place. My nervousness tripling as I spotted Tara. She had a way of surprising me in the most unlikely places. Firstly being balls deep in my boyfriend and now working at a brothel. I really didn't know my best friend at all, did I?

Tara never actually told me what she did for work, and she never let me visit her to find out. I could see why now. I knew she worked nights and weekends. The same hours a bar girl might work. I hinted at a gothic bar seeing that was why she wanted to keep me away, she would know that a gothic club would be one place I wouldn't want to visit. She never corrected me on my guess, so I thought I was pretty close on my assumption. How wrong I was.

I was following Tara's long legs up the stairs when a voice broke me out of my trance, "That's Buffy. She is gorgeous isn't she?" the voice said, taking my shock as lingering attraction. She went by the name Buffy here. Tara did always love that *Buffy the vampire slayer* show.

"What?" I replied dumbly. Then the words actually registered in my brain, so I tried to cover up my misstep by adding, "Yes, she is."

"Too bad for you she only likes men," the voice declared. It was after those words I looked for the source of the sound. Behind the front desk was an older, maybe in her late forties, Asian woman. Past her prime, but still drop dead gorgeous for her age.

"That's alright, I'm sure you have other pretty girls somewhere," I suggested. The surprise of seeing Tara threw me off balance, but I couldn't let it slow me down. I had much more pressing concerns like saving David from being torn apart by crazy, angry, mad men. I would just have to keep from bumping into her, and if I did I might just have to unleash my beast on her, former best friend or not.

Behind the desk a smile was spread across the woman's face, which implied that I hadn't imagined her amusement through the intercom. It was confirmed when she said, "We don't get a lot of lesbian's come through our doors, but all are welcome. How can I help you?"

I was lucky I had spent the whole drive over running through scenarios in my head, so I had this one covered.

"I'm just after the company of one of your naughty girls for a few hours," I answered, emphasising the naughty.

"A few hours. Someone has some stamina," the lady said cocking her head to the side. "Well, we only have three girls on tonight that do girl on girl, and the price is more expensive. So it's going to cost you a pretty penny."

At that I slammed ten grand down on the desk, "Will this cover it?" I inquired, knowing money solves all problems and opens up many doors. The Creatures of Chaos bikie gang was proof of that with all the crimes they had gotten away with. The stunning mature lady's eyes lit up with dollar signs printed on them when she saw the money.

"For that much money babe, you can have me," she said looking me up and down with an all new appreciation.

"Don't tempt me," I retorted, playing along.

"I suppose I should introduce you to the girls first before you make your decision," she said, feigning disappointment.

"What do these ladies look like?" I questioned trying to keep up appearances.

"I wouldn't want to ruin the surprise for you," the lady said, getting up from the desk, never taking her gaze off the money until I picked it back up.

"Follow me, please," she gestured with a wave of her hand. She opened the door to one of the waiting rooms. I slid past her as I entered the room. I could smell her perfume as I passed, it smelt of Jasmine. The room had a two-seater couch along one wall, a small TV that sat opposite the couch playing, ironically, lesbian porn. I guess lesbian porn accommodates all sorts. I sat down on the couch then looked back up at the Madame of Eden's garden.

"One of the ladies is currently being entertained for the next half an hour. The other two will be with you shortly. My name is Bo, so if you need any assistance let me know." Bo's tone was all business now, but the wink she gave me as she left was confusingly inviting.

I was inside. I was past the first hurdle, or second, if you include Tara. I needed to start roaming around, but I thought the best approach would be first, to get one of the girls up to the room so I would have a few hours to search for David. If I left now the girl on her way to meet me would enter an empty room, and Bo would be on me in no time at all calling for all the backup she needed. So I'd play along for now. On the bright side, my disguise seemed to be working.

When Bo was obviously joking around with me, I was nearly going to try and accept her offer, but the woman looked super fit. Her arms were toned up to the max. I wouldn't want to fight that one I decided.

A few minutes after Bo left, a lovely petite dark hair, olive skin woman walked in wearing only underwear under a see-through dress. The woman looked mid-twenties, with Spanish origins and an accent to match the face when she spoke, "My name is Leia" as she entered the room.

"Like princess Leia from *Star Wars*?" I asked.

"Just like," she admitted.

Leia came over and shook my hand attentively. She seemed as delicate as a china doll. Leia stood about four inches shorter than me, and maybe ten kilos lighter, but what she lacked in size she gained in curvaceousness; big tits and a well-rounded ass. Leia was as beautiful as any model. This girl should be a supermodel not a prostitute, I thought. Then again, Tara was just as gorgeous as well and she worked here.

Leia spoke softly as she began our short small talk session that started with "What brings you here tonight?" and ended with a, "Cya soon, I hope."

Then an older blonde Anglo-Saxon woman walked in wearing just as little as Leia. I could tell the woman had had a lot of work done to her face trying to keep the look of youth, but in doing so she made herself look like a wax puppet. It was hard to tell her age due to the work done to her face, but my guess would be around fifty. Where Bo on the other hand was growing old gracefully and using fitness to keep things tight and toned, this woman used needles, knives and Botox. The woman was big too, towering over me at maybe six foot, and she wasn't fat so much as solid. Her voice was deeper than the average woman's too.

"I'm Money Penny, but you can just call me Penny," she launched out.

Are all the woman here named after movie characters I wondered before asking, "James Bond 007?"

"Sorry, I don't understand," she replied looking confused.

I didn't understand myself how anyone could not have seen a James Bond film in their life; so I decided to sidestep and responded, "Never mind."

Money Penny smiled a cheeky smile, "I'm just tickling your funny bone, honey. Of course I know James Bond, he was in last week," that made a real smile appear on my face.

I must have been looking a bit tense, which was no surprise seeing what I had planned. I only said this because Penny's smile and jokes were disarming. Penny came over and sat right next to me, her bare legs brushed mine, her hand landed on my thigh. The touch was unexpected and I almost flinched – almost.

I was able to keep myself steady, I was meant to act as if I wanted this woman. I was meant to want her like I wanted David, but some things are hard to fake. I could feel myself go as stiff as a board. I didn't know how to act under a woman's touch. I couldn't blow my cover, I needed to convince her, keep playing along until the time was right. I didn't know Penny from a bar of soap, she would most definitely rat me out if she realised I was straight. Then words of wisdom struck or words of deviance; they say the best lie was the one closest to the truth.

"I'm sorry, Penny, I have never been to a place like this before. I didn't know what to expect or even how this all works," I said honestly.

"I can tell, honey. You wouldn't be my first virgin," without thinking my eyes went to hers, wide with shock. Penny must have taken my stiffness as confirmation that I was a virgin, better than thinking I was straight and lying my fake lesbian ass off.

"You know, honey, I can be very gentle if I want to be," Penny assured me. I looked away still stiff as a rod, still looking like an awkward virgin.

"I don't think you are my type," I said knowing Leia would be a lot easier to subdue then Miss Money Penny. I had already made up my mind, already knowing Leia was the one I was going to pick.

Penny's hand started moving lightly up and down my thigh, moving ever closer to my inner womanly area. As Penny stroked my leg her other hand was now massaging my neck. If I wasn't so scared of this woman wanting to have sex with me, and if it was David touching me like that I would be putty in her palm. Her touch was that of an expert of pleasure. This woman knew what she was doing. If I was in fact a lesbian Penny would be my choice hands down, but in actual fact I wasn't gay and I was here for a totally different purpose than to get laid.

"What a shame. I would have had fun watching your hip rise to climax in my mouth," Penny teased as she leaned in to whisper in my ear, "If you change your mind I am only one lick away." Penny released me from her erotic touch then got up to leave, "If you choose Leia she will look after you, but she doesn't have my experience." Ever the sales lady this one I thought, "If you want to add a third party, remember how far away I am."

As the door closed behind Money Penny, I flopped back on the couch releasing all the tension in my body. That was as intense as it could get I thought.

Bo came in two minutes later, "Did any of my girls take your fancy? Or did you want to wait for Nikita? She will be ready to go in about ten minutes."

I smiled a fake smile, "Leia would be perfect," I said sincerely. She would be perfect to eliminate as an obstacle so I can explore this place in search of David, but Bo didn't need to know that.

"Well that's great, I'm a little shattered you didn't choose me," Bo dropped her lip in an act of sourness. "But Leia will be more than adequate to meet all your needs and on the slim chance she's not up to the challenge then I'll be here all night." Bo winked at me again, teasingly implying that I could go there if I wanted to. Was I just some same sex magnet or something? I wasn't sure and I really didn't want to find out.

"Now, down to business," Bo said with that professional demeanour returning. "It looks like you have enough to spend the whole night with Leia. How long did you want Leia's company for?"

"I'm not sure," I uttered, still playing the virgin to a tee. "Can I start at two hours and go from there?" knowing two hours would be more than enough time to search this place.

"Anything you want, honey buns," Bo said fluttering her eye lashes at me, which were unnaturally long, but I suspected they were as natural as the rest of her.

"How much do I owe you for two hours, then?" I asked.

Bo seemed to consider the price for a second before saying: "Because you're so damn cute I'll give our discounted price of $500 an hour, so that makes it $1,000."

The price seemed steep, but what did I know? Perhaps it was the discounted price. But flashing that wad of cash probably didn't do me any favours in lowering the price. Not that I cared how much it cost me, I stole the money from Alice who got it from the Creatures of Chaos anyway.

Bo then explained. "If you want to stay longer you can give the money to Leia." I handed over the cash. Bo smiled at the money like it was an old friend.

"Leia will be with you in a moment to take you to her room," Bo said, counting the money as she left, making sure I didn't stooge her.

A moment later, as promised, Leia walked in looking as scandalous as ever. She held out a delicate hand not in greeting but in accompaniment. I took her hand and followed her all the way up to the third level. I was hoping to check the basement first, but starting from the top and working my way down would have to be my revised plan.

Leia opened the door and I walked inside not expecting to see what I was seeing. The room was luxurious, a big king-size bed, at least six fancy coloured pillows laid out perfectly on the bed, and satin sheets everywhere. Before this I used to think of a brothel as gross and dirty, semen stains everywhere, but in reality this place was cleaner than most motels and twice as alluring. I walked in amazed at how beautiful the room was before Leia spoke.

"Penny told me this was your first time. You don't have to be nervous I'll take special care of you." I took my attention away from the room's décor to turn back to Leia.

"I think she really wanted you," Leia went on to say.

"I think you might be right," I agreed.

"Seeing this is your first time and all, I'll run you through how things work," Leia said, gaining my full attention.

I think she knew that I had my serious face on because she went on to say, "Don't worry it's not rocket science, we make this as easy as pie. Just go have a shower and I will run you through the rest when I get back."

"You're leaving me here alone," I questioned, not for the reasons she would assume but for the reason to know whether or not I could slip out of this room and start my exploration.

"Don't worry. I'll be back in five. Just go have a shower and then I'll make all your dreams come true," Leia said with such a cute innocent voice I would have thought she was the virgin.

By the time Leia got back I had had a shower, and made sure I left my spy glasses in the bathroom under a towel, I didn't want Frank over-stimulating his shy mind. When Leia walked back in I was sitting on the bed with only a towel on. I had thought about doing a runner on Leia, but I needed more than five minutes. I had to play the part if I want to act the act.

"So what are these other rules you mentioned before?" I inquired.

"Every girl has her own rules. Myself, I only have two rules, no kissing on the lips," Leia said, touching a finger to her mouth. Then she put a hand down her panties the only thing she had on now and sexually sighed as she touched herself, "These lips are fine to kiss, though."

"Rule number two?" I queried.

"No anal," she answered.

"Sounds easy enough follow," I retorted, "but no kissing on the mouth might be a bit difficult at times," I teased, acting the act.

"Who knows? I might change my mind. A girl is allowed to change her mind ain't she?" Leia said playfully.

"I suppose a girl is allowed to change her mind," I relented.

Leia went to the side of the bed and dropped the bag she was carrying on a cushioned chair, "I brought a few toys for later," she said, indicating to the bag.

"Oh," was all I got out, playing the virgin perfectly. Even if playing a virgin was the same as playing a frightened straight woman searching for her possible dead boyfriend.

"Is bondage on your list of don'ts?" I asked sweetly. Leia looked up impressed.

"You're a bit of a wild cat when you open up, ain't you?"

I just raised an eyebrow in acknowledgment, gesturing, you have no idea.

"Well that depends, do you want me to tie you up, or do you want to tie me up?" Leia asked.

"I was hoping to explore your body unrestricted," I pleaded. I could see that she was considering it so I sweetened the pot. "I'll give you an extra thousand bucks," I offered pulling out the cash and handing it to her. It didn't take long before Leia accepted.

"How can I say no to that?" taking the money with a glowing smile.

Leia lay down on the bed naked as the day God made her; arms and feet outstretched, and I started to tie her left hand to the bedpost. This was the first time I had seen another woman so naked up close. It was a bit offbeat having a woman so vulnerable, exposed and willing, right in front of me, but if it took climbing on top of a gorgeous girl to achieve my mission then that was what I was about to do.

"Just remember my two rules," Leia said, "I don't want to have to get you kicked out."

"I remember. No anal and no kissing on the lips," I recited.

"Right," Leia said, relaxing her arm so I could tie it.

"You did mean the lips on you face, right," I said double checking, with a wink and waiting for her to reply before fastening the straps.

"The lips between my legs are all yours for the next two hours," Leia offered.

Once I had all four straps done up tight, and was positive Leia wasn't going anywhere I jumped on top of her smoothly and in full control now with an extra length of satin in my hand.

A sickening thought was brought forth from the darkest depths of the demon I dared to open the cage for. It showed me how easy it would be to strangle the life out of this woman. The image of the thrill and excitement, and the overall powerfulness that would come from the act was pushed into my mind's eye. I gagged at the thought; feeling revolted at myself for even being able to think up something so vile. This girl was working for bad people, but that didn't make her a bad person. This girl hadn't done anything to me. She was probably just trying to make a living, and I don't think all her clients would be all toy-boys and supermodels.

I lowered my face to her ear; so close my breath would have sounded like a whirlwind, "Keep the money, and I'm sorry for this."

Before Leia could react I wrapped the cloth over her mouth and around her head. I jumped off Leia's now thrashing body. She was trying desperately to break free with no success.

"I really am sorry for this, but your employer has kidnapped my boyfriend and I think they have him locked away somewhere here," I told her unafraid of what she could do with that bit of information if she was to get free.

Leia stopped struggling against her bonds. She just stared at me with horror-filled eyes.

From that reaction she just gave me, I concluded that she had no idea what the people she worked for were fully capable of. I picked up a blanket and laid it over her nakedness, not able to leave her so undignified.

With that, I got dressed, gathered up my things and left the room, locking the door as I left in search of David.

$\mathcal{T}$he attic was a bust. Mothballs, spider webs and dust were the extent of it. Now I was stuck with the dilemma on how to proceed. Going straight down to the basement had the highest likelihood of where I would find David. To get there I would have to find the entrance that wasn't on the blueprints. I would have to go down four flights of stairs, past the reception desk, past Bo, past ladies and their potential customers, and all the while being inconspicuous. Or I could take the even longer road going from door to door to find David, and still going unnoticed by the inhabitants. Let's not forget Tara was in one of these rooms too.

I would be most certainly wasting precious time checking every room, but if David wasn't in the basement then I would have to make my way back up four flights of stairs, unseen by everybody and then go door to door anyway. I chose the slow road, not willing to take the gamble that David wasn't in one of these fifteen rooms of seduction.

Even though I knew I had to, I still really didn't want to open up every door. The possibility of walking in on two or more naked people doing the horizontal folk dance was kind of high, and kind of gross. Another reason was the risk factor. If one of the working girls saw me they might think I was some kind of pervert, and dob me in to Bo or, worse, a big scary guy wearing leather.

I passed the first door knowing there was no one in there besides Leia strapped to the bed, and I walked on to the next door. I knew the bedrooms were sound-proofed but on the walk up I was able to hear some slight murmurs. So my conclusion was that the rooms are sound-proofed but the doors were just doors.

I put my ear to the door; the sounds of loud moans, cries of pleasure and grunts of physical activity reflected back at me. I thought wow; this guy must be some kind of stallion or that girl was faking her ass off. Either way it sounded quite impressive, and I was pretty sure that David wouldn't be getting that kind of treatment here.

The next door was silent. I would have preferred the sexual screams to an absence of sound. Now I had to open the door to find out if David was inside.

I checked the handle; it turned, the door was unlocked.

I opened the door slowly, praying the hinges didn't squeak, readying myself to close it again quickly if need be. I had a gut feeling that David wasn't inside but I had to check. I couldn't leave anything up to chance. I couldn't leave any stone unturned. Ready for anything the door opened just enough for me to sneak a peek.

The room was empty.

A sigh of relief escaped my mouth. A momentary easement washed over me to find the room empty. I hoped to find David in there, but something inside me knew that it was never going to be that easy. Plus it was good not to have walked in on someone having sex.

The next room was empty, and then the next one wasn't. I was just lucky that the way those two were doing it they weren't facing the door.

All I saw was a hairy ass and two feet in the air. I thought it could have been a lot worse. They could have seen me.

After getting over the shock of being a peeping Tom on someone's well paid good time. I made sure the coast was clear before I went down to the next level. I also remembered which rooms were empty, just in case I had to duck into one if someone came my way.

The next floor was pretty much the same, a few empty rooms, a few moans, and no more peeping Tom moments fortunately. I crept down the stairs hoping none of them squeaked, checking like I did with the last staircase that there were no oncoming people down the hall, but this time I was halted by a man leaving a room. The same man I'd seen with Tara.

The man was straightening his hair as he left down the stairs at the other end of the hall. Tara was in that room, friend or foe I didn't know. I had the urge to go in there and demand answers, tell her she owed me that much for what she did to me, but she had already betrayed me once. The stakes were far too high now to find out she was foe, and not friend. A man's life hangs in the balance, David's life. I knew I could get at least some of the answers I sought from her, even if I had to hurt her to get them.

I walked over to her door. I was drawn to it, like a freezing man drawn to a burning fire needing its warmth and protection from the local wild animals. I couldn't help but put a hand on the door like I was reaching out to her. Tara was a possible friend amongst a sea of enemies in this place. I still couldn't believe this was where she had been working. She was so smart and beautiful; I didn't understand why she would be working here. I would love to know the answer but I lost all trust for Tara when I found her with Sam. I wouldn't risk David's life on the chance that she would betray me again as soon as I left the room.

I was about to move on to the next door when the door in front of me opened and I was suddenly leering into the eyes of my childhood friend. Without thinking I instinctively reacted. My beast broke through its cage and took over pushing Tara hard in the chest making her fly back and landing on her ass. I quickly rushed through the door locking it behind me.

I turned back around ready for a fight, ready for Tara to come at me with fists raised but, instead, she was crawling towards the bathroom, trying to put another door between us. Tara wasn't about to engage in war with me, she was scared and running away. Violence wasn't on her mind, escape was.

"Hello Tara. Or should I call you Buffy?" I said in greeting.

Tara stopped crawling after she recognised my voice. She turned slowly back around towards me asking sheepishly, "Sarah is that you?"

"In the flesh, but as you can see I have changed a little since we last hung out," I replied, my tone still playfully threatening.

"Have you come here to get back at me?" she inquired, more fear in her face than I had ever seen on her beautiful features before, and I was the cause of it. My beast delighted in the sight.

"No Tara, I'm not here for you, but I am here for someone," I informed her. Tara seemed to relax a little, knowing I wasn't here to bash her. Even though I lacked her height I had always been able to get the upper hand when it came to physical activities.

Tara got to her feet slowly, her eyes not leaving me as she asked, "How did you know I worked here? I never told anyone where I worked."

"I didn't know you worked here, you just happened to be working for the same people that have taken my boyfriend," I stabbed back.

Tara frowned before saying, "Sam's not here."

That statement made me frown. How could she think Sam was still my boyfriend? I thought Sam would have run straight back to Tara after I kicked him in the nuts and told him it was over.

"I thought Sam was with *you* now," I responded sounding confused because I was.

"I haven't spoken to Sam since that night. He won't return any of my phone calls," Tara sprayed back.

"But I thought…," was all I got out before Tara cut me off.

"You thought what? You thought Sam actually wanted to be with me. Please Sarah, he is just like every other guy, he just wanted to fuck me. As soon as you found out about the affair, he ran straight back to you. He even had the nerve to blame me for the whole thing."

I could see Sam hurt her too. I could see she felt used as she finished by saying, "No, Sarah, Sam wants nothing to do with me now."

"That's all news to me," I declared. "I guess you don't know I broke his nose, kicked him in the balls and told him to piss off?" Tara's eyes lit up with amusement and a smile appeared on her face.

"No, I didn't know that. I would have loved to see it, though." I smiled back at her, my beast remembering the exhilaration of inflicting pain for the first time.

Tara went and sat on the bed looking defeated as she said, "I'm sorry about your Mum. I always loved your Mum." The mention of Mum made my beast recoil back inside its cage, not able to deal with the conflicting emotions.

"She always loved you, too," I admitted truthfully.

"Did your Dad really kill your mother and kidnap you, like the news said? I found it hard to believe. Your Dad always seemed so loving towards you and your Mum. I couldn't imagine him doing that," Tara said with real suffering in her tone, like the news deeply impacted her. It probably did I realised; she was like a sister to me. She basically lived at my place. My parents were almost family to her too.

"It was your employer that killed Mum," I said bluntly. "You have no idea what the Creatures of Chaos club are capable of, and what they have put me through, do you?" Tara looked at me wanting more, so I gave her more.

"That night I found you and Sam together I ran away, as you know, but what you don't know is that I ran straight into three members of the Creatures of Chaos gang."

Tara's eyes widened. She knew what was coming before I said it. She would have had to know what else happened that night in the same industrial area. It was all over the news and directly linked with her work.

"One of those members was Jordan Cole. He mistook me for a hooker working for the Insurgents club. They bashed me because I wouldn't have sex with them. They were going to kill me, but not before raping me. I was only seconds away from being violated when David showed up and saved me."

"So that was you that killed Louis's brother, Jordan?" Tara said needing to confirm my words.

"David killed Jordan in self-defence, saving me," I enlightened her. "I have basically been in hiding ever since, but they ended up finding me, anyway. That was why they came to my house, they were searching for me. I wasn't home at the time, but my parents were. So they decided to murder Mum and punch the crap out of Dad. They would have killed Dad, too, if David and I didn't save him."

Tara covered her mouth; tears began to fall. Tara was a lot of things, even more than I thought after finding out about this, but somewhere deep down she still cared for me and my family. Her tears were proof of that, and I knew she couldn't act like Alice. Tara uncovered her mouth. Something unfolded behind her eyes.

"Did you say you were looking for a man named David?"

Seeing the name meant something to Tara I quickly replied, "Is he here? Do you know where he is?"

"No, I don't know if he is here"

"Please, Tara, they are going to kill him if I don't help him," I shot back.

"I really don't know, I just heard Bo mention his name," Tara claimed.

"Goddamit," I yelled out, making Tara flinch back from the anger of my outburst.

Trying to calm me down Tara quickly added, "If he is here he will be in the basement." I looked over to Tara sitting on the bed, hope burning bright again.

"Do you know how to get down there?"

"There is a back entrance from outside, but it is always locked. The only other way down is through Louis's offices," she said. I looked at her a little suspicious all of a sudden, wondering if she was trying to walk me into a trap.

"How do you know that?" I quizzed.

Tara dropped her head, shame written on her face, "All the girls have been in that office with Louis at least once."

I understood what she meant, she didn't need to go into more detail, but she went on anyway, "I got off easy compared to some of the other girls. I even heard a story about one of the girls who went in and never came back out. We all know about the basement through Louis's office."

"Why are you helping me?" I asked, "You hate me remember."

"I never hated you, Sarah, I just envied you. Besides, if they killed your Mum then they can all rot in hell for all I care." Seeing the truth in her eyes I didn't push the issue any further.

"You know what the funny thing is? I always felt like I was walking in your shadow," I confessed.

"So we envied each other," Tara said dropping her shoulders and hanging her head in shame once again, as she added, "At least you didn't try and hurt me because of it." I didn't respond to that. She would just have to live with that guilt. She had to own that act of betrayal herself because I would never had done what she did to me, and she knew it.

"Why are you even here Tara? You could be doing anything. Why are you working in a brothel?"

Tara seemed to be waiting for this question, no doubt she had asked herself the same question a thousand times, "You know how I always end up with the bad boys?" I just nodded, wanting her to continue. "I went out with this hot Creatures of Chaos guy for a few weeks and he told me about their high class brothel, and how I could make at least five grand a week if I worked there." That was a lot of money I thought. I only make about hundred and fifty bucks a day working at Target. It would take me months to make that cash.

"It planted a seed. I only planned to do it a few times. Make some quick cash and get out, but I found it exciting and even fun sometimes. But to be totally honest, though, in the end it was the money that kept me coming back," Tara explained. "I couldn't make that kind of money anywhere else." I smiled a weak sad smile at her.

"You know I wouldn't have looked at you any different, if you had told me."

"Yer, right," Tara scoffed.

"I would have told you not to do it like I am going to now, but my love for you wouldn't have changed," I said, reinforcing my words. Tara looked at me, almost seeming to look deep into the honest part of my heart.

"I think I actually believe you, Sarah."

"Just don't sell yourself short, Tara, you're more capable than you think," I said heading for the door. "I have to go check that basement for David now."

"I'll go with you. I can show you where Louis's office is" Tara stood up.

"No Tara," I shot back, with so much authority Tara fell back down on the bed. Then softening my voice I said, "Don't worry I already know where the office is." I could see Tara's brain wondering how I would already know where the office was located, but she took my word for it and left it at that.

Having Tara come with me could get me out of a sticky situation if I ran into the wrong person. I even trusted her enough to not hand me over to be crucified. The main reason I didn't want her coming along was I thought she might get in the way. She might have tried to stop me from releasing my inner beast on one of her friends that I needed to get past. She would divide my focus and cause a split second of hesitation that could result in a life or death call. Not only that, after everything she had done to me, I would still worry about her if things got dangerous, and I couldn't have any distractions right now. I now knew how David felt with me. The difference was, though, I'm not Tara.

"You won't be able to get past Bo without me," Tara warned, still wanting to come along and help. I guess she was trying to make amends for her actions, trying to atone for her sins. It did make me realise one thing. Through all the envy and lies, Tara was a friend, and she really did care for me. That was the only reason for that guilt that had built up in her stomach; you only get guilt if you do something you regret. I mean, her guilt was so strong that she would follow me into a deadly situation. I was touched by her willingness to help, but I had to trust my own judgment, it was all I had and it had gotten me this far. Wrong or right I would go on alone.

"Well I won't go past her then, I'll go through her," I said with unwavering vigour.

"Even if you manage to get past Bo you won't be able to get past Louis. The guy is insanely scary," she insisted.

"Just watch me," I said defiantly. No one was going to stop me from getting to David, not even Louis. "Thank you for telling me how to get down to the basement, but I can take it from here."

I put my hand on the door, opening it just a crack, "I am going to lock you inside the room now. I need you to stay in here because all hell is going to break loose soon."

Giving up on the idea of tagging along, Tara said, "I would stay here, but even if you lock the door from the inside someone can still open the door with the key from the outside."

"That is why I took the handle off and removed the pin from inside handle," I said waving the inner workings of the door at her.

"Just like that time we locked ourselves in your room when the door handle came off," Tara recalled.

"Yep," I agreed. "If anyone comes looking for you just say the handle fell off and you can't get out."

Tara looked at the intercom on the wall next, "Bo will call for me if I don't come down soon. She might even come up here and find out what is taking me so long."

I walked over to the intercom and ripped it off the wall and said, "Well she won't be able speak to you now and, unless she kicked down the door she wouldn't be able to get in either. If nothing else it might make a good distraction for me to slip past."

I looked at Tara one last time before I locked her inside the room.

"Be careful," Tara said as her parting words to me. I didn't reply because there was no being careful for what I was about to do.

I had to keep moving, I had already wasted enough time. At least I didn't need to check the rest of these rooms and, if Tara was right about Bo, I didn't have long before she found her way up here.

I found out that Tara was right on the money because as I turned down the hall I saw a very fit, uptight-looking Asian woman standing at the top of the staircase down the end of the hall.

CHAPTER 45

I knew Bo saw me close Tara's bedroom door. There was no talking my way out of this one, I was busted. I had had enough of this charade anyway.

"Do you know who I am?" I asked casually, as if all the hairs on my body didn't just stand on end, from the sudden panic of being found out.

"I could take a guess," Bo responded doing a phony impression of looking thoughtful. I knew she had figured out who I was now, maybe she had her suspicions all along, hence the wink, wink.

"You are Sarah Smith, I suspect. Good disguise, by the way. You look nothing like the photo I saw of you," Bo announced with that business-like persona.

"Thanks, I did put a lot of effort into it," I said, like I was at a fancy dress party. Getting back to business Bo said, "I'm guessing you have come to make a valiant effort to rescue your beloved?"

"You would be correct," I said in my most business-like voice, throwing my disguise to the wind, or more accurately I was placing my spycam glasses on the floor carefully so I didn't damage them with what I suspected was to come.

Surprisingly, I wasn't afraid, if anything I was a bit excited. This would be my first proper brawl. The other beatings I dished out were attacks of spontaneity and coercion. This one would be with both sides all in like mind. This would be an all-out war, only coming to an end when the other side stops moving. All that time running up a thousand stairs, all that exercise and training I did with David had led to this moment. My body was ready, but was my mind?

Now it was time to purposely unleash the caged beast inside me. I could feel the blood lust surge, but somehow, and for some reason things were different this time. I saw the darkest side of myself in that room upstairs with Leia, a side of me that wanted to strangle that innocent woman for my own amusement. Having that thought changed me. It tamed the creature inside. I knew then I could never be that person. I had more good than bad, more light than darkness, more love than hate.

At Alice's home I was wrath incarnate. This time my fury was more focused. It was like it surrendered itself to me, like it knew there were more important things to do than just inflict pain. I was never going to let it control me again. I was now in full control of the flame that ignited my violent desires. Now I would use my inner demon as a weapon, and not a crutch to lean on.

The raging tamed fire beast inside me awakened from my own fear. My instincts made all my senses more alert, dulling pain and fatigue, readying my muscles to be used at their full potential in speed and strength. My hands began to shake so I clenched them into fists. I wasn't shaking from frightened terror but from adrenaline.

I may have only been shown a few moves by David, not nearly enough to take down an experienced fighter like I assumed Bo was from the way she was standing and readying herself. But what I lacked in skill, experience and knowledge, I hoped I could counter with raw forceful determination.

"Are you going to take me to David? Or will I have to make you take me to him?" I threatened, acting confident in my ability to force her to do it.

"Oh, I'll take you down to the basement to reunite with your David," Bo replied with an unflinching command. Then she added, "I will have to drag your unconscious sack of bones down there, but you will be together soon."

I was only three paces away from Bo now. I stood, just like David showed me, ready to begin our dance at any moment.

"Before we start I just want to say thank you for confirming that David is in fact here and he's down in the basement," I said, thinking that would throw Bo off-guard when she realised her slip, but it didn't. She must be so confident that she would wipe the floor with me that she meant to give me that titbit. Maybe she wanted me to get my hopes up, only to bring them crashing down along with her fists. But I could use that over-boldness. Pride wasn't one of the seven deadly sins for nothing.

"You know, I really didn't know how I was going to sneak past you," I said, lifting my fists like a boxer, how David showed me. Bo smiled showing her perfect teeth.

"No one gets past me," she said boldly.

"So I'll be the first then. Cool. Get ready then to be knocked down from that high horse, lady of the house," I said fuelling my blood with a hot temper, ready to boil over on to Bo.

With a crack of her knuckles Bo rushed me.

CHAPTER 46

*B*o's fists were like a blur of hailstones; too many to count, too many to try and catch, and far too many to stop at least one from hitting me. I was able to block the first two attacks before knuckles slammed into the side of my face making my head snap to the side. I lost my focus temporarily as my brain went back online. I was able to raise my arms again just in the nick of time guarding my head from another haymaker.

Raising my guard high protecting my head exposed my torso to attack. A fist connected with my ribs. I cried out as all the air in my lungs got knocked out of me, making it hard to breathe. I took a step back, sick of getting pummeled. I needed to fight back. I needed to take a chance and hit back. I had a glimpse of Bo's face between my own blocking arms, and Bo's flurry of fists. I took a gamble, and I launched a straight right where I thought Bo's face was. I did exactly as David instructed. I had good footing, twisted my hips in the motion, and aimed six inches behind the target. I did however have my eyes closed. No one is perfect.

My fist hit something. I followed the line of my arm as I pulled it back to my body. Bo's nose instantly began gushing blood, running down her face and all over her shirt. She looked stunned, totally taken aback by the blow. I bet she didn't know I had it in me.

The punch was guided out of luck and desperation, its landing was a full fluke. The only thing that wasn't a fluke was the how, and the technique. I guess Bruce Lee was right, "Be more afraid of the man practising one punch a thousand times, than the man practising a thousand punches once." With Bo stunned and me getting over being stunned that I actually landed a hit, I didn't want to wait around for Bo to start up again, so I lunged. Bo was faster than me but I had the strength. All that training with David had paid off.

I grappled Bo to the ground. This time technique went out the window. Now it was just a street catfight. I grabbed hold of Bo's hair. I tried and managed to slam her head on the ground. I got two skull-cracking thuds in before I copped a karate chop to the throat.

I started gasping for oxygen. I thought I was choking to death. I was fully freaking out that my windpipe was crushed and that I may never be able to breathe again. In my state of panic, all I could think about was trying to take in that next breath and in doing so I let go of Bo's hair.

Losing my advantage, Bo was able to fling me off. I toppled over on to my side grasping my throat, trying desperately to suck air back into my lungs. Bo was now in my peripheral vision. I was unable to focus on the looming threat she posed, unable to concentrate on anything but trying to inhale oxygen.

Bo was back standing on her feet, circling me like a shark waiting for someone to fall out of the boat. Then she used one of those circling feet to kick me hard in the ribcage. What I thought was impossible happened. More air seemed to get pushed out of my lungs from the impact. The impact rocked me to my core. Bo's show of affection felt like she shattered all my ribs. It felt like they splintered into a million pointy pieces.

After that kick to the guts I thought that this was it, game over. I thought I would die with my face as blue as a Smurf's. It was then something unexpected happened. I don't know if it was the next kick to my gut, or if it was my throat fixing itself but following that next assault on my midriff I was able to suck down a gulp of air. It burnt my lungs, but I didn't care, any air was good air. Every breath hurt, but it was still a breath my body frantically needed. The force of the kick made me roll completely over. I rolled again using the momentum trying to put some more distance between us, trying to catch one more fleeting breath before Bo's attack continued.

Assuming I was safe for at least a second, I looked back up to see where Bo was. All I saw as I crouched on my hands and knees was another foot heading straight for me. Before I even had time to think of moving out of the way, or to try and block, or to do anything for that matter, my vision exploded into white from a savage blasting of pain that echoed through my head. I had experienced this kind of wallop before when Mr Shaved Head struck me. It was one step from all your lights going out. I felt that before too. I knew I couldn't take much more of this. Knowing and understanding my predicament my mind and body went into survival mode. I understood I had to stay awake not just for my own sake but for David's too.

David was depending on me, and I refused to fail him. I willed myself to stay awake. I had to get up and fight. I had to win. I had to rescue David. I was the only hope he had left in the world. I ordered myself to stay conscious, to stay vigilant. I would see David again, and I would not be in chains when I do. I had come too far to lose to this bitch. I wouldn't let her beat me, I demanded victory. I swayed a little making it look like I was about to collapse, acting like I could barely support my own weight.

"Night, night, Sarah," Bo taunted, seeing the end in sight.

The next kick to my face came as expected. It was her finishing knockout blow to put me down on the canvas. It would have done the job too – that was if it had connected. That's if I wasn't ready for it. I wanted her to go for that king hit. I moved forward into her kick rolling my shoulder into her knee joint making her leg hyperextend. I wanted her to think that I was too hurt, and unwilling to fight on. I needed her over-arrogance to shine through.

A cry of pain shot out down the hall of debauchery as Bo's limb bent the wrong way. The beast inside me showed its toothy smile. Before Bo's leg could even touch down on the ground I had it between my claws. Then with all the strength I had left to possess, I sprang myself up off the floor with Bo's leg clutched in my talons. Bo's foot went skyward, flipping the rest of her backwards. If I had known that the stairs were right behind her I might not have flipped her backwards. Who was I kidding? I would have still done it. The slut kicked me in the face. I would let the beast have that one.

Bo seemed to bounce down the steps, her body bending and twisting at all unnatural angles until she lay motionless at the bottom of the stairs all bent out of shape. I thought I had killed the bitch until I reached the last step and I saw her chest moving with shallow breaths. As much as I disliked the woman, I didn't want her death tinting my soul. To see her still breathing was a slight relief. I had won. I had crossed the troll-guarded bridge, knocking the troll over the edge into the depths of the cold water below. I was free to pass. Now there was no one left to stop me reaching David on the other side.

CHAPTER 47

$\mathscr{B}$efore moving down to the basement I went back to pick up the spycam glasses. As I put them back on my face I wondered what Frank would be thinking right about now? I bet he would have been on the edge of his seat nearly having multiple heart attacks watching me get my ass whooped. I was just glad it wasn't Joe watching from afar. I could see him with a bowl of popcorn screaming, "Finish her, finish her. Take off your shirts." I knew that no one would or could stop me now from reaching David, but walking through that door was one thing, walking out was another. I had to be prepared for anything or anyone in there with him. I would have loved a gun, but I was shit out of luck on that front.

Unless…

I made a beeline straight to the front desk searching for anything that I could use as a weapon. I was hoping for a gun, but instead I found a bat, a metal baseball bat, that is. The baseball bat would have to do. The only other things behind the desk were a laptop, printer, paper, a few pens, a stapler and an eftpos machine. I could try and paper cut any foe I come into contact with but I thought it might not cut it. Sorry, I had to put in the bad pun.

Drawing closer to Louis's office, closer to David in the basement, I thought it couldn't hurt to have a backup weapon, and I knew exactly where to find one. Turning around I headed straight for the kitchen.

Walking through the door I found four sets of wide eyeballs fall upon me. All four girls' mouths were as wide open as their eyes. They all had gaping expressions on their faces. What a sight I must have been. They all looked like they just stopped suddenly, mid-sentence becoming frozen like a statue.

I went straight for the knives and forks drawer, not bothering to give the sexy lingerie-wearing working girls any more notice than to find out whether they intended to try and stop me. None of them moved a muscle, but one had the gall to call out, "Who the hell are you?"

I needed to be left alone. To do that I needed them to fear me so much that they would stay away from me and leave me to my business. I inhaled rage, lifting the bat so it dangled vertical in my hand, then I exhaled wrath thudding the baseball bat down hard on its head. The bat vibrated so hard that the waves shot up the length of my arm. The sound spread through the room like a warning bell, and that was exactly what it was. I took in a deep breath of annoyance and made sure they were all witness to it.

"I'm the one who just laid out your Alpha bitch queen Bo at the bottom of the stairs," I said making sure that the annoyance followed through to my tone of voice. After that I just heard murmurs and whispers to each other, not one took a step towards me. They posed no danger; they reeked of non-threatening armour that was perfume to my objective.

I turned back to the drawers rummaging through until I found a large enough, sharp enough kitchen knife. I left the kitchen without even a glance towards the girls. Right before I reached the door, now armed with a bat in one hand and a kitchen knife in the other, one brave girl yelled out, "Stop."

I don't know why I stopped. I could have just kept on going but I did as instructed. I had no time to waste, but something nailed my foot to the floor. I needed to control the situation, or maybe it was just to make certain they wouldn't follow me down to the basement. I'd never fully understand the reason, but nonetheless, I stopped.

I stood staring blankly at the door, silence filling the room with a thick tension of a clouded uncertainty of violence. I could almost feel the women recoil. I turned and glared a, don't fuck with me stare, I had learnt from my father who most likely learnt it from his years in the army. Then I responded with a voice that was as cold as ice, which even gave me the creeps.

"If you try and stop me I will beat your heads into pulp with this bat." I raised the bat so it pointed straight at the women. "Then I will cut out your heart with this knife and stick it up your ass."

I lifted the knife so both the knife and the bat pointed directly at the gutsy blonde big-boobed woman who I thought had spoken. I twisted the knife so the light reflected off the blade for an extra effect. The daring woman was standing like she was thinking about making a move on me. That was until I finishing speaking, and then she seemed to fall back into her chair pushed by the insanity of my words, or it could have been the knife and bat directed at her. Whichever the case I didn't think they would be bothering me anymore. The giveaway telltale signs were evident from their mouths being as wide open as their legs while working, and then shutting closed like a bear trap on a guy's cock that had no money. Also their eyes diverted away from me unable to hold my stare from fear of getting their hearts cut out.

I must have been very believable in my acting. This time it was just an act, last time when I threatened Alice I didn't know whether or not I would follow through. This time was all a bluff, I couldn't cut out someone's heart, but I could bring out the demon in me just enough to make it look like I would. Step over Alice, I'm coming for your acting job next.

However, I really didn't want to think about how insane I must have looked to Frank, and to whomever else that would inevitably watch the video that was being recorded through the spycam. My face being black and blue coated in red war paint, blood, threatening to kill people in a most gruesome way, and throwing someone down a flight of stairs. I must be the epitome of a crazy bitch. I couldn't waste time surmising about that though. I had to focus on the task at hand. I had one goal. A goal I must achieve as if a life depended on it, because there was one.

I made my way to the basement with no more interruptions. No people getting in my way, no locked doors. I had made it. I stood in front of the door. This one I knew had David behind it. David was only one door away from me now. I could feel the truth of it down to my bones. Before I opened it, I whispered out loud so the recording would pick it up.

"Please forgive me, Dad. I love you."

Then I walked through the door.

$\mathcal{M}$y eyes took a moment to adjust from the half-lit staircase to the bright florescent lights in the basement. Once I walked through the door it was like a part of me already knew exactly where David was positioned in the room. My eyes locked on his, like a honeybee locks on to a flower. Before I walked through the door I had tried to prepare myself for anything. I prepared myself to walk in and see a body bag with David inside. I braced myself for an onslaught of bikie gorillas coming to rip me apart.

But when my eyes found David's, nothing else existed. I wasn't looking into the eyes of a dead man. I was looking into the eyes of the love of my life, and they were looking back. I could tell he saw straight through the disguise, looking straight into me, just as I looked into him. I couldn't explain it, but our bond goes beyond the physical, beyond words, into a meaning all of its own. Love was yet the beginning of what our relationship was. There were deeper levels yet to go.

I looked him up and down. David's face was badly bruised and swollen, but nothing serious that wouldn't heal. He was sitting in a chair, or more accurately tied down to a chair. Then my sight drifted to his mutilated hand. I didn't know how I failed to see the blood splatter first; it was everywhere. It was like someone had thrown a bucket full of blood into a fan and watched it spray outwards. I nearly gagged at the horrific scene. It was something out of a horror film. To think that that beautiful hand had caressed the curves of my entire body not a few days ago, and now it was barely a hand.

The fury rose inside me once more. How anyone could be so fucked up, and twisted inside to do something like that was beyond me. Even if I lost myself to the darkness, I still couldn't do something like that. You would have to be one seriously messed up guy to be able to do something like that I thought, choking back down some bile in my throat.

I looked away from David to survey the room. There was only one man standing alone ten feet away from David. The man was holding a mobile phone to his ear and had a very large smile that spread across his face.

The man I recognised as Louis Cole said into his mobile phone, "Never mind, she found me." Then Louis hung up the phone, never shifting his gaze from me. Louis had blood splattered all over him. Correction, Louis had David's blood splattered all over him. He was the one that ripped David's hand apart. It was he who orchestrated my mother's death and framed my father. Louis had to pay for his crimes. Louis had to die. There was no way out of this room unless his breath ceased to blow past his lips.

I had placed the knife along my waist, tucking it in under my belt. I figured that the knife was a weapon you needed to get up close and personal to use, whereas the bat had more reach – a much better option to start with. I saw that Louis wasn't carrying a gun, or any weapon for that matter. Louis was unarmed and about to get his head smashed in. I held the bat with both hands raising it up over my head like I had seen baseball players do on TV.

My goal was to save David, and to do that my last obstacle was Louis. There was no one else here to stop me but Louis. I was so driven by rage, so determined to kill Louis that David's voice was just a background noise, like a bird in a tree singing its songs while you walked past. I think he said something along the lines of, "Get out of here Sarah, he will kill you," but I couldn't be sure. Nothing was going to stop me from attacking this out of control, self-absorbed lunatic.

Once I was two steps within swinging my baseball bat at his head Louis said, "So you want to play?" Not slowing down I replied. "I want to play with this bat and use your face as the ball."

I swung the bat directly at his face as hard as I could. I thought it was odd that Louis didn't move. He just stood there waiting for me to swing the bat at his head. I was so blinded by anger I just thought, all the better to hit a non-moving target. The bat came down full force, stopping inches from his face. A large hand gripped the bat, stopping it dead in its tracks.

As if I was a child holding a lollypop, Louis ripped the bat out of my grip. Shocked with the sudden outcome of events I hesitated, and it cost me. I was so sure I was about to pulverise his face, then a split second later the bat was clattering along the ground and Louis had me in a headlock. I tried to wrestle free, but he was too strong. It was my futile efforts to get free that reminded me that I was also carrying a knife. The whole time in a corner of my consciousness I could hear David screaming something, but I wasn't paying it any attention. I was too focused on trying to destroy Louis.

Louis had one massive arm around my neck in a headlock and his other arm was wrapped around me just below my chest restricting my arms so I couldn't claw at his face. Louis had minimised my arm movement, but he hadn't fully immobilised them. I wiggled my arm loose enough to seize the handle of the knife at my hip and pulled it free. I then plunged it deep into his thigh.

The thundering scream that came out of Louis sounded more like annoyance than pain. The sound bombarded my ears deafening me momentarily.

The gratification that fed the beast inside was short lived because as fast as the knife went into Louis's leg, it was pulled back out again. Louis had taken his arm from around my middle, and pulled the knife out of his own leg. Then, in one fluid motion, he released me from the headlock, snatched up my hand forcing it down flat on the table not two feet away from David's. With my hand pressed down on the spray of David's flesh and blood, Louis drove the kitchen knife through the back of my hand burying it deep into the table, pinning me down, making me as helpless as a duck in a barrel. I pulled hard on the knife with my free hand trying to dislodge the blade from the table with what was left of my strength. With everything I had I couldn't even make it budge; all I could do was create more torment for myself.

It was in that moment with pain shooting up my hand to my brain that I realised my stupidity. I had entered a fight I could not win. The man was five times my size, weight and strength. I would have seemed like a kid in comparison. My madness of invincibility thought I could beat any foe that came my way, but sometimes you are just outmatched, even when you have the deck stacked in your favour; hence fighting an unarmed man with a bat and a knife and coming off second best. Then a thought occurred to me. I had lost the fight, but maybe not the war. I still wore my glasses.

"You fucking bitch," Louis yelled out, moving away from me, knowing I wasn't going anywhere after failing to dislodge the embedded knife. I tried to move my hand again and a fresh shot of pain ran through me. I really wasn't going anywhere in a hurry. I could only see one way out of my situation and it wouldn't be pretty. Unless I wanted to slice my hand in two, there was no other way out. I would have to make my hand look like a camel toe to get free. I was not talking about the camel toe between ladies' legs. I was talking about an actual camel's foot.

I looked over at a just as helpless David. The despair on his face was portrayed as concern for me. It was evident on his features. I was the cause of his suffering not the mutilated hand. The one thing that was getting him through this was the fact that I was going to be okay, and now I had crushed that hope. With me here, his blood-lacking white face was that of a defeated man. I could tell he couldn't see a way out of this mess, but he didn't know what I knew.

"I'm sorry I couldn't repay the favour by saving you," I said with a fake smile.

"You shouldn't have come, Sarah," David sighed. "You have no idea what he will do to you. He knows the only way to hurt me is to hurt you. He is going to cause you agony beyond belief and I can't stop him."

David's voice was enveloped with so much love for me but it was also entangled with as much sorrow for what he imagined would come. The powerlessness David must have felt would have been intoxicating. I couldn't imagine anything worse, for a man with such power, strength and skill to be tied down with extreme adversity staring him straight in the face.

Then there I was handing myself over to Louis on a platter, bringing David's worst nightmare to life. I imagined that that was what a wild lion would feel being caged in a zoo. Knowing if he was on the other side of the glass he'd be eating human innards within moments.

I looked down at his hand, "I think I can guess what he has planned for me," I said sourly, and then added in a whisper so only David could hear, "But he has no idea what is in store for him." A light sparked behind his eyes with that comment. The wheels started spinning once again. That defeated look turned to a glimmer of optimism. I winked at David, hinting to follow my lead. Louis shuffled back on one leg and then plopped down onto a chair at the end of the table that David and I were stuck to.

"Well, now you have us pinned like a rabbit down a hole and you are going to get your deluded idea of revenge, or justice, or whatever your twisted brain can come up with to justify what you are doing," I said, while watching him tie a belt around his leg where I had stabbed him.

Louis's eyes lifted to mine as I continued, "So the least you can do is give me some answers before you kill me." Louis smiled at me, and then looked back down to what he was doing.

"What do you want to know, Miss Stabalot?" Louis looked back up at me, finished what he was doing to his leg. He placed his hands on the table then let out a breath that was laced with a sigh, "I suppose I can grant you a last dying wish. Ask away, sugar tits."

"First, I want to know why you ordered the hit on my family?" I asked, with a tear forming in my eye from reliving the memory of my mother's death. The tear formed but didn't fall. I would not cry in front of this man.

"I thought that was obvious," he retorted, looking at me like I was a complete moron. Staring back at him blankly, making sure he was going to answer me. I only had to wait a few breaths before he continued, "I sent my boys to your house to kill whoever was inside and bring you back to me so I could kill you myself." I'd figured that already but I needed him to say it out loud. I got you, you son of a bitch. Louis leaned in; eyes narrowing to study me intently, not yet done with his answer.

"So, if you think about it, it's really your fault your Mum is lying dead on a cold slab in a mortuary."

I realised I hadn't thought twice about my mother's body. To me death was the end. She was never going to look back at me with blinking eyes. Then I felt ashamed. I could tell Louis poked me for that response. I didn't feel ashamed for the reason he thought, but he got his desired result anyway. I felt ashamed because I wasn't there to take care of my mother's body. To show her body the respect it deserved. I didn't get to organise a funeral, or cremate her body as per her wishes. I was too busy seeking my own revenge; selfishly thinking of my own wants, thinking that that would give me peace. I knew I couldn't have done any of those things for my mother anyway under the circumstances, but I should have at least thought about it. I just hoped it wasn't too late.

David's voice broke me out of my stupor.

"It was you that couldn't leave us well enough alone, and it was your boys that pulled the trigger, not Sarah," David spat out, fully fuming, the blood loss not damping his words.

"Semantics," Louis replied, shrugging off David's words, like they were dandruff flakes on his shoulder.

"One last question, Sarah, then its playtime," Louis said eagerly.

Before I could really think about asking a better question I asked, "Why are you doing this to us?"

Louis slammed his fist down making the whole table jump. In doing so made everything else move that was attached to it – like my hand with a knife through it. A fresh dose of blasting agony enveloped my mind making my knees nearly give out.

"You really are a stupid bitch," he growled, "Do you have any idea what you two fuck faces have done to me and mine?" Not wanting to rile him any more I stayed quiet, I was at his mercy after all.

"You two made me look weak in front of my enemies," he said, pointing a finger at David. "You knocked out one of my best bruisers with a single hit. You scared the crap out of my best drug runner making him run away like a cowardly headless chicken, and that's not even mentioning what you did three years ago." I was glad Louis didn't go into more detail about the John Black incident, not that it would matter if we were both dead. Louis got up from his chair, his face beginning to go red as he continued, "Then I had to spill Neil's guts all over my lounge room floor for his insolence. No one in my club runs away like a coward and lives to talk about." Louis actually looked taken aback a little from his last comment dropping his head slightly.

"And I hate killing my own," Louis added lowering his voice back to normal, but every word was still coated in poison. He was on his way over to me with violence in his gaze. Twenty questions were nearly over.

"And most importantly you took something that was mine," he said in a softer tone, like a snake licking his tongue, tasting the air before he struck.

"We didn't take anything from you," I pleaded, knowing suffering was in sight.

"You took my brother away from me," Louis countered.

"Your brother took himself away from you. I was only protecting myself. What I did was in self-defence. I gave him every option to let Sarah go and walk away," David said, slowing Louis down.

"Oh, I know it was in self-defence. My brother was always starting trouble, but that's beside the point. It was still your bloody hand that killed my brother, self-defence or not," Louis said, gesturing to David's disfigured hand. Louis then turned his attention back on me.

"And you were the catalyst, my darling," Louis said placing a hand on the back of my neck. His gargantuan hand rubbed my back softly like a lover would.

"Don't touch her. You animal," David yelled. I couldn't see what Louis was doing behind me. My sense of touch was my only indicator of his whereabouts. I squirmed under his fingers. His touch lifted, along with my shirt. Louis tore the back of my T-shirt in half. The shirt fell off my shoulder exposing my bare back. The shirt fell down my arms until I caught it with my free hand, covering my chest instinctively with the fragmented shirt.

"Time for questions is now over, my darling," Louis whispered in my ear getting so close I could feel his breath.

"I'm not your darling," I said in defiance.

Louis then moved towards the machine covered in blood. It was the machine that tore David's hand to shreds, and the machine that would do the same to my back.

"I was impressed that you got past Bo," Louis said appreciatively, "By the looks of it, she left her mark on you though. It must have been quite the catfight. I have seen Bo take down guys twice your size."

"Well, what can I say, I was the better woman on the day," I replied with dignity, knowing what I had to do, but being afraid to do it. However, the sander was a great motivator.

"I suppose you were the better woman," Louis said, "But now it is time I left my mark on you."

Louis put his hand on the sander lifting it up. He pulled the trigger letting it roar to life once more, but only for an instant, just for show, just to try and scare me.

"David deprived me of a good screaming," Louis said, glaring at David before focusing back on me. "This way I hurt the both of you at the same time. Two birds with the one stone, as it were."

David thrashed in his chair, but with all his strength and big muscles his bonds didn't relinquish. Giving up the thrashing, knowing it was a fruitless endeavour David said, "I was the one that killed your brother. I was the one that saw the surprise cross his face when he knew he was going to die. I started all this; make it end with me. Let her go, and get your jollies off torturing me."

"We tried that David, it didn't work," Louis said, looking like he was getting excited. I had one play left and it was going to be painful. Camel toe hand here I come.

If I was going to act, it had to be now, or else the skin on my back would become confetti. I would take a hand split in two over a skinless back any day of the week. I tried to prepare myself in the short time I had left. David had said you could block out pain with meditation. I wasn't going to use mediation, I was going to use hatred mixed with fury. I was going to fully unleash my inner demon one last time.

I waited until Louis was close enough, but just out of reach of sanding my back apart. I had to be fast. Think speed, I thought, speed. I forced my immobilised hand back as hard as I could. If the knife had been plunged in my hand any other way this trick wouldn't have worked, but the blade was perfectly positioned for the manoeuvre. In one fast swift motion the blade sliced straight up the length of my hand exiting between my middle and ring fingers. The pain would come I was sure of that, but at that moment it was overshadowed by what I had to do next.

I whirled on a very shocked and surprised Louis. I went for the kick to the nuts. I think it landed, I couldn't be sure. I could have just hit his inner thigh, but that wasn't my desired target.

Louis thrust the power sander towards my face, I side-stepped the oncoming blow, getting in close. Before his other hand could grab me I dug my good hand's thumb directly into his eye socket. I plunged my thumb in as deep as it would go. The feeling was pretty gross, but totally worth it.

Louis released the power sander, dropping it to the floor. Before Louis's sander-holding hand could repel my thumb from his eyeball, his other arm got to me first. Slamming into my now exposed chest, forcing me back so hard I skidded along the floor like a fallen bowling pin.

It was Louis's turn to cry out in pain. He howled out some very unkind words towards me. With a hand on his face covering his eye, or what was left of it anyway, he continued to convulse around like he was having a fit.

I was barely able to regain my own senses before that one venomous eye fixed on me. I shuffled backwards on my bum as Louis limped towards me. Louis was so transfixed on me he didn't see David's foot in front of him. Louis wobbled but caught himself. David spat out, "If you lay a finger on her..." but he was silenced with a haymaker punch to the face.

The trip gave me a few more seconds, but it was never going to be enough. There was nowhere to go, nowhere to run. I had lost the fight. I had failed David. This was the end for me, and Louis knew it just as well as I did. My bag of tricks was now empty.

Before I knew it Louis's hands were around my neck. All the scrambling, thrashing, scratches, punches and kicks were hopeless. It was like trying to fight off a bear once he already had you in his jaws.

"I wanted to finish you off nice and slow, and excruciatingly painfully," Louis said, with bits of saliva flicking on my face, "while making David watch every agonising moment appear on your face. But you have pissed me off to a point I just want to see your dead corpse twitching on the ground," Louis's hands continued to tighten. There was no escape this time. I was powerless to stop him. My knight in shining armour was tied up unable to rescue me, having to watch his beloved die.

"Bye, Sarah," Louis said.

I would have bet my life savings that this wasn't the first time he had ever choked the life from someone. I could tell he could feel my life slipping away. This was what he lived for. That masterful feeling that made him feel like a god. Just like every sick psycho I ever heard about. This wasn't like getting hit in the throat, and gasping for air to survive. This was the depletion of blood flow to the brain. The feeling of passing out came on much faster. I was dying.

I just hoped my father would forgive me for leaving him behind. I hoped I had given David enough time for our plan to come to fruition. At least I would give my father the evidence to clear his name and take down Louis with my own death being recorded on my spy specks that somehow managed to stay on my face.

In those last fleeting moment's I wasn't scared. I had foreseen this outcome. In these last moments I was grateful. I was grateful for the time I got to spend with David. I was grateful to have had two wonderful parents that loved me unconditionally. The last thought I had, the last thing I was grateful for, the silver lining to be dying at the hands of a mad man was: I will get to see my mother again. All pain was gone now. I was ready to pass on through the void, to pass onto the other side.

Then I saw my mother. She was there with me, trying to pry off Louis's deadly hands. It didn't seem possible. There was no way my mother could pull this hulk of a man off me, but somehow the hands around my neck let go and I fell to the floor. I couldn't take my eyes away from my mother's face. God, she was so beautiful.

I was struck dumb with how she was able to pull Louis off me, and then more importantly and more confusingly, how could she still be alive? It all didn't make any sense. Then a frightening thought crossed my mind, maybe I was dead.

CHAPTER 49

$\mathscr{L}$ouis's hands tightened around Sarah's neck. Sarah's face was beginning to change colour for the better. It wouldn't be long now he thought. Louis was an expert at this now. He had mastered the art of strangling someone a long time ago. It was his favourite way to kill. Using a gun was too easy, no challenge, any fool could pull a trigger. A knife was better, much slower, more up close and personal, but nothing beats using your bare hands to end someone's existence. Feeling a person's body go limp under your fingertips, and watching the light go out behind their eyes; there was nothing in this world that excited Louis more.

Sarah's eyes began to lose focus. There was nothing holding her up but the strength in Louis's arms. Almost there, Louis speculated. This bitch will be gone from his plane of existence, never to fuck up his shit again. Once she was dead David was next. Louis would start sandpapering his face and see if David could meditate his way out of that one.

A blast of noise sounded from behind Louis. The sound was of a door flying open. Louis turned to see who was interrupting his moment of victory.

It was Conner Smith, looking crazy menacing. Aiden had forwarded Louis a picture of the older man. Louis knew the man's face but seeing it all twisted up in earnest was a different sight altogether.

Louis looked behind Conner. He wasn't alone. Conner had brought back-up. He was accompanied by two other men, Daniel Spade and

Andrew Snow. Two cops on the take, two cops on his take. Those two pigs had turned on him. Louis's hands tightened even more around Sarah's throat at the sight, his fury adding to the pressure. If Louis was going to accomplish anything tonight it would be Sarah's death.

As soon as Conner spotted Louis he charged.

"Let her go, Louis," one of the pigs yelled from behind Conner's rushing shoulder. Louis wasn't sure which one of the pigs had spoken and he didn't care. How dare they betray him, did they not remember who they were fucking with? Once this was all over he would have to discipline them in the most painful way possible.

Conner and those pigs were not going to deprive him of this moment. Louis's fingers compacted even harder, tensing his whole hands as tight as they would go. He had to finish the job off quickly before they reached him.

Conner got to him first. He rammed his fist into Louis's skull. The blow made him see a couple of stars, but Louis had been hit a lot harder by people a lot bigger. It would take much more punching power for him to loosen his grip on Sarah's throat. He would not be denied his wrath on this bitch, not after taking his eye and putting a hole in his leg. He would not wait any longer to kill her; it had to be now.

Conner changed tactics, knowing punching Louis would not stop him squeezing. He went for Louis's hands around his daughter's neck next, trying to pry the fingers back. Conner was able to bend a single finger back. Louis felt the snap as his finger bend backwards. Conner was only able to remove one finger at a time. Louis knew Sarah would be dead before Conner got to the third she was so close now.

Then Daniel and Andrew launched themselves at Louis. One pulling at Louis's other arm and the other wrapping his arm around Louis's neck. Louis held fast against the three men putting every bit of strength into his hands. Sarah was almost there. She could quite possible already be walking on the other side of life. Louis peered down at Sarah through his one working eye not sure of the moment of death. Louis could always tell when the end came, but that was when he was killing unhindered through the process. He was too distracted at the moment to feel the pulse of blood stop under his finger. He was too obscured by the three men tackling him to feel the body's weight lighten just the slightest amount as her soul left her body.

Louis was a bull of a man, stronger than two men, but not three. Under the weight of three grown men he buckled, it took a moment but Louis was forced to let go of his prey. He screamed out in anger, yelling, "You fucking assholes. I am going to fucking kill all of you for this." Louis hollered, spat and thrashed on the ground while Conner, Daniel and Andrew handcuffed his hands behind his back, making him kiss the cement at Sarah's feet.

Knowing Louis was subdued, Conner sprang up and franticly made his way over to Sarah. Louis peered up following Conner's telemetry as he lay on his belly. He had failed to complete Sarah's transition to the other side. Five more seconds Louis guessed and the job would have been done. He roared out in rage, filling the concrete walled space with the sound of primal frustrationed anger.

"She's not dead," Louis howled, seeing her still breathing. "Let me go so I can finish what I started, and then I may not kill you pigs," he growled at the two men in blue holding him down. A hand pulled Louis's head up by his hair then smashed it down hard on the concrete floor.

"You're lucky she is still alive you barbarian," Andrew said, releasing Louis's hair. Louis took a second refocusing his one eye, seeing his blood dripping on the floor from the concrete's impact.

"What the fuck are you two doing? You work for me," Louis yelled out.

"Not any more," Daniel said from behind him. "Just be thankful we don't put a bullet in your cranium."

"You better put a bullet in me or else when I get out I'm going to put five in the each of you two," Louis threatened.

"You are never getting back out after this. Did you think those glasses on Sarah's face were just a disguise?" Daniel said lightly to Louis.

Louis looked up at Sarah. The black-framed glasses somehow managed to stay on her face. Louis saw them for what they were, a camera.

Louis laughed before saying, "Is that all you got? I'm sure I can bribe one of your colleagues to lose that evidence. You two should know how easy it is seeing you did it for me more than once."

"Not this time. Do you think that those glasses are the entirety of their plan? You should know we always pick the winning team," Daniel advised, "And you just lost big time."

Louis went silent after that with nothing left to say. He didn't close his trap from fear, but from contemplation, his mental cogs were turning in all directions. This wasn't over by a long shot, Louis swore to himself. Sarah and her group of nobodies had made him look weak, turned his assets against him, handcuffed his hands behinds his back and stopped him from his killing climax.

They had won this round by the flakes of skin on his shirt, but as long as he was alive the game would not be over. Louis always had a trick or two up his sleeve. I would come back from this, I had climbed up from the bottom before, and I'd do it again, and this time would be no different, Louis thought, prophesying his return back to being crime king.

The first thing Louis planned to do once he got released was to finish what he started with these two love-birds. He might even allow Conner to live knowing he couldn't protect his women. It would be a good sentiment for Conner to take David's place as lone family survivor, after David was dead and being eaten by worms.

Then he would deal with these two pigs and their families for betraying him. Once his vengeance had had its fill of gore, setting a new image that would terrify the Devil himself, and making sure nobody would take from him again. The whole way back to the pig station Louis started connecting the dots, putting all the pieces together. Their plan would crumble against his money and connection.

It was pretty obvious that Sarah and David's people, whoever they may be, took the information they got from Aiden and turned all his minion puppets against him. They most likely did it in the same fashion Louis himself pulled their strings. They were all going to die too. But Sarah and her people only got the information he shared with

Aiden. Louis had a lot more people in his little black book that owed him favours.

Louis began to make a mental note, or better put, a mental list of all the people he was going to kill. Louis wouldn't go to jail for long. He still had too many people that needed him. Too many higher ups that would help get him back on the streets. He would be out by tomorrow night.

Before Louis went to his cell at the piggy station they at least patched up his leg and eye. The leg would heal. It would be back to normal in no time at all, but the eye was suspect. The doctor gave him a ten percent chance of full recovery. He would have a ninety percent chance of being partly blinded in one eye for the rest of his life. That Sarah slut had made him look like a one-eyed pirate. Even now his head was half covered in bandages. Sarah was so going to die screaming out his name next time.

Louis lay down in his single-bed caged cell. His head was leaning up against the cold metal bars of the cell formulating ideas to burn down the entire fucking world. It was those happy thoughts that helped him get to sleep that night, and he slept like a baby knowing his revenge wouldn't have to wait very long at all.

CHAPTER 50

I thought I was dead, reunited with my mother. I thought Louis's hands had squeezed the life out of me. But then life dragged me back. My mother's face morphed through a haze of colour into my father's distressed one.

"Are you alright, Sarah?" I heard him say. I heard the words but didn't understand the meaning. The words could have been spoken in Japanese for all the good it did me.

"What?" I tried to say but only air was in its place.

"Are you OK?"

It was hard to speak, so I just nodded understanding this time, my brain starting to process words again. I raised my good hand to his face to make sure he was real. I felt the prickly rough stubble on his cheek; he was real.

"You made it," I painfully choked out.

Dad took my hand in his at his cheek and said, "An ambulance will be here in a minute just hold on, sweetie."

I looked past him and saw two men in blue uniforms, cop's uniform I came to realise. The men were restraining Louis on the ground. One of the cops smashed his face into the cement floor. It was a nice sight.

I then looked past them to see David still tied to the chair but breathing, staring back at me with shock that we survived, concern for my injuries, and love in his heart. A smile appeared on my face that I couldn't have held back even if I'd wanted to. I had done it. I had saved David. Hope and love filled my groggy body until I saw the look in my father's eyes turn towards Louis. It was the same look I saw in him when he put a bullet into Mr Shaved Head bikie's brain.

He started to get up leaving me again for vengeance, but this time I tightened my grip on his hand making him turn back to me. I only had enough energy for three words, "I saw Mum." My Father's facial features softened, the blood lust gone from his gaze, sorrow replacing it.

Then the last thing I remember from that night, before I passed out, was my father replying, "Your mother will always be with you."

CHAPTER 51

*W*hen I looked back at seeing my mother whilst knocking on heaven's door, it made me even more confused. The lack of blood to my brain must have given me delusions. The mirage of my mother was one fantasy I really didn't want to come back from. It was good to be alive, but bad to be apart from my mother once more. That night's events left me disorientated, not knowing if up was down, a second was a minute, or if my mother was actually there with me or not. Thinking like a sceptic; it had to be a delusion, right? There was no such thing as ghosts?

I guess the only way to answer those questions was to die and find out for ourselves. But I was not quite ready to find out the answers that had plagued mankind since the dawn of time. Not yet anyway. A part of me wanted it to be real. To be honest all of me wanted it to be real. To have my mother back would have been bliss. I would never know if she was in that room with me or not, but I would like to think that she was, and she watched over me still. Except for when I am alone with a naked David, and then she can go walkabout.

Oh yes, you probably want to know how it all went down.

The files we stole from the bikies' hacker kid had more information than we first thought. It just took Frank a bit longer to find it all. I didn't understand computers like Frank, but I was guessing hidden files within hidden files. I didn't know, but that was what Dad told me. All I knew was there was hidden information he found after I got my hand sliced in two.

Firstly we, air quotes, convinced a judge that was on our bikies' hit list to sanction an arrest warrant for Louis. Then, knowing the cops wouldn't touch Louis from either fear or loyalty without a little coercion, we told the selected few city protectors that we had all their secrets now and the Creatures of Chaos didn't, and if they didn't help us we would leek those secrets to all the right people and they would end up being prison mates with the leader of the Creatures of Chaos's Melbourne chapter. It had the desired effect.

In the end they all came around and chose the right option, our option. It was quite easy to convince people to do something for you if you had something they wanted or, more precisely, what they didn't want anymore.

All we had to offer them was the deletion of certain dirty little secrets. That was all the incentive they needed, plus not having their naughty mistakes flashed to the media and their families was good incentive too. Originally we only needed a couple of cops to turn on Louis and a star witness, Alice, to roll over, but as you all know things didn't go quite as planned on the Alice front.

In the end, the video I got of Louis torturing us, admitting to murder, admitting to sanction murder was good enough to put him away for a long time. Well, it would have been good enough anyway. With all our steps going terribly wrong, our schedule had to be sped up and, as you know, I became the star witness.

I had to give credit where credit was due though. I wouldn't be here if my father and Joe hadn't played their part exquisitely. Everything fell into place perfectly on their side. They were the ones convincing all the judges, cops and lawyers to do our honourable bidding. So the fall of the head of the Creatures of Chaos belonged to all of us, even Frank – even if he got paid to help.

It would have been nice not to have gone through all that torment but, without it, I never would have got Louis's confession. The video did have Louis confessing to the ordered hit on my mother and the self-defence claim of his brother's death against David.

Our plan didn't just stop there though. We had all the judges and lawyers in place to get a guilty verdict just in case Louis tried bribing or threatening his way out from behind bars.

That part of our plan was all ready to go when one of our newly acquired informants told us that after Louis's arrest, when a search warrant was carried out on all his properties, it uncovering illegal firearms and millions of dollars' worth of cash and drugs. The most disturbing thing they uncovered was drugged up sex slave workers in undisclosed brothels. After hearing that I realised I could have found myself in one of those brothels if Mr Druggy had gotten his way. The thought made me shiver with sorrow for every girl that went through that horrific ordeal.

They also followed up on Louis's comment about killing his club brother in his living room. They found traces of blood all over his lounge room floor, right where Louis had told us he'd gutted the man. Everything was ready to go, it was a done deal. Louis would rot in jail for the rest of his life. His own Chaos brothers wouldn't even have anything to do with him after finding out he murdered one of their own.

We had done it, our plan would have worked, but as always a spanner was thrown into the works. About twenty-four hours after the night that Louis was pulled off my almost lifeless body, he was found dead, hanging in his cell.

The report was suicide, but surrounded by crooked cops with careers to lose if Louis opened his mouth up wide, and a lot of people ousted out of a lot of money and drugs, it wasn't too far of a stretch to assume that Louis was helped with that noose. It was a bummer that our plan didn't come to fruition, but I wasn't losing any sleep at night knowing that that sick, mentally deranged man was dead.

With Louis dead, and my father and David cleared of all charges, we were not looking over our shoulders anymore. The Creatures of Chaos local chapter had been crushed, and their successors had no beef with us. If anything the new guys should be thanking us. I just pray the new bad guys are better than the old bad guys. When it comes to crime I had learnt that when you cut the head off the snake, that snake always found a way to grow another head back. Maybe one day, somebody would be able to kill the heart of the thing but that somebody ain't me, my job was done.

Camel toe, yes, I nearly forgot. After a few stiches and a few surgeries my hand was pretty much back to normal. I could still use it anyway. It was a bit numb in places and a bit harder to clench a fist, but all in all it wasn't too bad.

David had to have a few skin grafts on his hand that made it look like what you expect Freddy Krueger's hand would look like. The hand was disfigured but his attitude on life wasn't. The hand didn't slow him down any. If anything it was a fun way for David to scare Clare. Ever seen the movie *Liar Liar*? In that movie Jim Carey used his hand as a monster called the Claw; think of that but with an actual scary hand.

My father and I finally got to bury my mother. It was a sad day but at least I got to say a final goodbye and not a hello in the afterlife. That greeting can wait for another day. Dad was never the same after my mother's death, but he always put on a brave face for my sake. My father was a strong-willed man. With time the pain would ease. He would be okay, I was positive of that, and I would always be there for him as I knew he would always be there for me.

Frank got his fifty grand, so he was happy. I was pretty sure he tucked away a copy of all those captured bikie files too, not that he would admit it. He also got ten new pairs of his favourite shorts as promised. When I walked through the front door Frank was so happy to see me he hugged me, he actually hugged me. It was a bit like hugging Humpty Dumpty. After he realised what he had done, he went all red faced and retreated to his computer room without saying a word. I wasn't sure if the hug was for the shorts I owed him or for seeing me alive after witnessing me get beat up by the madam of Paradise of Eden, and almost being strangled to death by Louis Cole. Either way he was happy to see me.

Joe went back to his secluded home alone. Sorry, Joe went home to his best mate, Max, the old friendly guard dog. Just don't tell David Joe's best mate was Max, he might get jealous.

We still visit Joe from time to time, and he was still as crude as ever. Well, when my father wasn't around anyway. Georgia still doesn't like me all that much, but at least now she accepts me. She knows how much I love David. She knows what I went through to save him, and for that she wouldn't try and kill me; so, progress.

Clare, the little cutie, was still as honest as the day was long. She still thought David was the best guy in the world too; I had to agree with her on that one.

Then there was the person that started it all, the person I had once loved, the person that made my love turn to hate, the person I was now indifferent about; Sam. Good old Sam. I found out that Sam met another girl, and rushed in and tied the knot. I didn't go to the wedding, if you were wondering. We don't keep in touch, but I have heard the odd thing from time to time. I heard somewhere down the grapevine that Sam's new wife left him for the pool boy and took half his stuff. Karma can be a bitch.

The other girl wasn't Tara, by the way. She wasn't fibbing about Sam cutting her out of his life. Tara and I never became close friends again. I would say hello if I saw her in the street, but we would never get back that sisterly bond we once shared. I know she quit her job at the brothel, and started bar tending at a gothic club, of all places. I thought it was quite ironic. Maybe she just didn't want me showing up at her work again. Whatever the reason I was glad she got out of that life.

And David and I, not to sound too much like a fairy tale, but we lived happily ever after. I finally moved out of home to live with David. I still spend half my time at Dad's to keep him company though.

My beast had never resurfaced, thanks to a few more meditation sessions with David. It helped that no one was trying to kill me now. The darkness hadn't fully gone, I didn't think it ever would fully disappear after I had experienced its intoxicating lust, but it had been tamed, controlled and put back behind its cage.

So that is about it, this is where I say goodbye.

Before I sign out I need to clarify that this story was not about me taking down the Creatures of Chaos bikie club. No, this was my experience of tasting, spitting out then swallowing love. This was my physical and emotional love trial, the story where I found the love of my life, David.

This was the story of how we came to be and how we fell in love. How we conquered adversity and stayed alive long enough to fall so deeply in love that it had no edges. This was the beginning of our story together, and the way it worked out it wasn't the end. The rest of our story is for me to know and for you to know only as happily ever after.

EPILOGUE

The night Louis was dragged to the police station he fell asleep with dreams of the world bowing at his feet and calling him a god. It was the same night he was stuck in a cage after those pigs arrested him.

Louis didn't know it yet, but that night was the last night of his life. He would never get to see the way the moonlight dances over spilt blood ever again. The cells were quiet that night. Louis was the only prisoner encaged at the cop shop. Only two cops were on duty that night, only two cops who had to turn a blind eye as Sergeant Daniel Spade and Officer Andrew Snow lowered an outfitted noose made of bed sheets over Louis's head while he slept.

They had positioned the bed up against the bars for this exact reason, even making sure the pillow lay at that end, just to make sure Louis would lay his head up against the bars.

The two men pulled on the make shift sheet rope. The noose tightened around Louis's neck, lifting him up so his head touched the top rail, making his feet dangle eight inches off the floor.

Louis clung to the bed sheet around his neck, trying frantically to pull loose from the fabric snake curled around his neck, but in the end it was no use, he couldn't break free.

Even though Louis knew it was futile after the first ten seconds he still continued to kick and writhe as the weight of his own body pulled down on his neck. It was ironic that the way he loved to murder people would be pretty much the same way he would find his own demise.

As Louis slowed and his movements became more laboured, his kicks looking more like spasms than attempts to find footing, a voice broke through to his consciousness, "Sorry we had to do this to you old buddy. We did have a good run there for quite a while, but we couldn't let you tell anyone any of those secrets you know about us. We have families after all."

Louis could tell he was about to die, he knew death. Louis had been close to death his whole life. He had just always been on the other side of it. Louis's last thought that flickered through his brain before he died was of Sarah. The woman that did him in, the woman that had taken him down where so many other men and women had failed.

In the end Louis died with a smile on his face. In the end Louis had as much hatred for Sarah as he had admiration for her. The girl had more balls and more spirit than anyone he had ever met. Sarah was the only person to escape from his mighty hands of death, and now, unknowing or not, she had returned the gesture.

One year after the death of Louis Cole.

I lay wrapped up in a blanket of naked David skin, with my eyes fixed on the TV screen. A man with nunchucks was beating the crap out of a million people. I tried to use nunchucks once; cracked myself in the face. They are much harder to use than you would think. I was very impressed. I had never seen an actor move like that. Jackie Chan comes close but still the cigar goes to Bruce Lee. This wasn't like the newly made eastern Kung Fu films where they fly around bending gravity to their will. You could just tell this man dedicated his life to perfecting his art form. The speed of the guy was incredible too. I had to get David to rewind, pause and move through frame by frame just to make sense of a few of his moves.

I told David he would have to teach me some of his moves in our training, his reply was a kiss on the neck. I don't know how I went through my entire life without knowing who this guy was. When the *Enter the Dragon* movie had finished I looked up into David's eyes and asked, "Does he have any more movies?"

"Yer, but they're all Chinese-made and dubbed to English," David replied, then added, "Some of the films dubbed to English don't have the same meaning as if you watch them in Chinese."

"Do you have them here? And, if so, do you want to watch another?" I asked enthusiastically.

David formed a smile. He must really like his Bruce Lee films I thought, and now I think I do too. But instead of putting on the next movie he said, "There is plenty of time for another film later, right now I want to see you from a different perspective." Knowing the look in his eyes and where he was going with this, I asked tauntingly, "From what perspective might you mean, good sir?"

David rolled me over onto my back, following along with the motion himself so he lay on top of me.

"This perspective."

ACKNOWLEDGMENTS

It would be easy just to say, everyone knows who they are that I would like to thank. It would be the best way to cover all my bases, but I thought I better say a few more words.

First and most importantly I would like to thank my beautiful fiancé, Marilen. She was the only one I told about my interest in writing for a long time. I was a bit shy about my writing. I am good with words but bad with spelling, and as I am a perfectionist it is quite the contrast. Even now with this novel I reckon there are things I could do better or fix up. I was partly shy because I thought I could never make anything close to the classics. But if you never try you will never know. Anyway, Marilen was the one person there for me in my shy little bubble. She also helped me with the editing, she helped spell the words I couldn't, and even helped design the cover. She is my other half, my better half, and I couldn't have done this without her.

Next I would like to thank my old man, Simon. My bubble got that little bit bigger with him in it. He gave me the encouragement and support to believe in myself. He was the third person to read the novel; I will get to person number two in a second. Dad loved the book. I think he might have been a bit biased, but still it was encouraging.

Andrew Murphy, person number two. My only friend that likes to read novels. He was the first person to read the rough, rough draft of the book; beside Marilen of cause. After giving him all the A4 size paper filled with all my words the shy bubble popped, and getting a good review out of him lifted a fear off my shoulders.

If it wasn't for Simon and Andrew liking this story, this book might not be here. So thanks for the courage to take the next step forward with my hobby.

My kids Athena and Ashton; all I can say about them is, the book wouldn't have been the same without them annoying me all the time while trying to write. So thanks for shaping me into the man I am today.

Siri. It might be a bit weird thanking an Iphone program, but still I couldn't have done it without her helping me spell all the words I couldn't.

I have to say a thank you to my editors Richard, Graham and Margaret Murphy. The book would be a lot different if you two didn't help me straighten it out. You really helped me take it to the next level, so cheers.

To the rest of my friends, family you know who you are. Thank you for being part of my life, giving me the influences I needed to write this novel. I wouldn't be me without all of you.

Printed in the United States
By Bookmasters